The World's Great Detectives

*the text of this book is printed
on 100% recycled paper*

The World's Great Detectives

and Their Most Famous Cases

Bruce Henderson and Sam Summerlin

BARNES & NOBLE BOOKS

A DIVISION OF HARPER & ROW, PUBLISHERS

New York, Hagerstown, San Francisco, London

A hardcover edition of this book is published by Macmillan Publishing Co., Inc., under the title *The Super Sleuths*. It is here reprinted by arrangement.

THE WORLD'S GREAT DETECTIVES AND THEIR MOST FAMOUS CASES. Copyright © 1976 by Bruce Henderson and Sam Summerlin. All rights reserved. Printed in the United States of America. No part of this book may be used or reproduced in any manner without written permission except in the case of brief quotations embodied in critical articles and reviews. For information address Macmillan Publishing Co., Inc., 866 Third Avenue, New York, N.Y. 10022. Published simultaneously in Canada by Fitzhenry & Whiteside Limited, Toronto.

First BARNES & NOBLE BOOKS edition published 1978

ISBN: 0-06-464023-X

78 79 80 81 82 10 9 8 7 6 5 4 3 2 1

FOR CYNTHIA
who made it all possible

S. S.

FOR CHERI, LAURIE AND MARK
may your world,
and that of your loved ones,
forever be safe,
secure and civilized.

B. H.

Contents

Contents

Foreword

For more than a century, ever since Edgar Allan Poe wrote what is acknowledged to be the first published fictional detective story ("The Murders in the Rue Morgue"), readers the world over have been enthralled by the exploits of make-believe criminal investigators. Be the protagonist the Paris investigator C. Auguste Dupin, who solved the grisly "Rue Morgue" crimes, or the modern-day Martin Beck, millions have vicariously joined imaginary sleuths in pursuing the trails of evildoers.

Comparatively little, on the other hand, has been written about real-life detectives. Oddly, names of master criminals become well known, while the men who caught them are lost in the back pages of history. Why this is so has been suggested by one criminal attorney who wrote, "The public can send up outraged cries of esteem for its policemen when they fall in the line of duty; yet these same public servants receive little, save apathy, when they manage to do their jobs and live. We seem to say that the task of our police officers is to do those chores that we would prefer not to perform ourselves."

This irony would appear to be even more glaring today, given the rise in crime in recent years. To be sure, New York City detective Eddie Egan became a celebrity in *The French Connection* as did his colleague on the force, Frank Serpico, in the movie that bore his name. Yet their fame, along with that of a few other contemporary law officers, is a rare exception to the largely anonymous roster of other tireless and dedicated crime fighters who carry out their difficult—and often dangerous—work around the globe.

Our purpose in writing this book has been to seek out some of the most distinguished detectives of today, around the world, and to re-create how they solved their most famous cases. In our interviews with these investigators, we have also been interested in their opinions about the problem of crime, and what society can and should do to alleviate the current epidemic of law-breaking.

The officers we have picked out have either been suggested by their colleagues in the investigative community, or confirmed by them, as most deserving of recognition. Thus, by the word of their own police peers, the detectives cited in this book represent a roster of the world's most talented and effective criminal investigators. Their names—Read, Chenevier, Igii, Kuso, Noble, Hansen, Le Cocq, and others—amount to an international gallery and a multiplicity of styles. They are, above all, super sleuths.

It is indubitably true, as borne out by the research for this book, that in law enforcement, as in other areas of modern-day human endeavor, teamwork and technology have become increasingly important. Organized on a national and international scale more efficiently than ever before, armed with a formidable array of new scientific weaponry, ranging from voice prints to ultra-sophisticated lie detectors and listening devices, today's police forces might be likened to the contemporary business corporation in their impersonal efficiency. Nonetheless, old-fashioned individual determination and investigative genius still play a major role in cracking crime.

In researching this book the little-known but unique role that the criminal investigator plays in every country was brought home to us. If the criminal mind transcends national boundaries, it is equally true that the world's crime fighters make up an international fraternity. From New York to Nice, from Scotland Yard to the French Sûreté, from Tokyo to Tel Aviv, the dedicated detective is a breed apart, singlemindedly stalking his suspect to the near-exclusion of the political and social world beyond both.

Why do detectives do it? What attracts them to, and keeps them in, a nether world populated by society's misfits and scum—murderers, rapists, gangsters, armed robbers, burglars, muggers, pimps, prostitutes, psychopaths? What hardens them to viewing the macabre remains of victim after victim of the savage violence humans are capable of wreaking on each other? The reasons will be spelled out later, but we might quote here, as a succinct clue, a remark by one veteran policeman, stationed for years in New York's Bronx.

"To the majority of detectives," he said, "time means nothing. There are certain cases you take to heart, you get personally involved in. The victim could have been your mother or sister."

Moreover, the criminal investigator's role is, unfortunately, increasing in importance, if for no other reason than that crime virtually everywhere around the globe has been on the increase. Not only in the United States, but in such tradition-rooted societies as Great Britain, Japan, and Israel, to cite only three, there has been a diminution of respect for law and order. Not even the rigidly ruled Communist countries are immune; the Soviet Union has openly admitted to a rise in "hooliganism."

All of which would seem to make the task, and views, of professional detectives even more important to the world. It was this that prompted us to pose such questions as: Who are the most canny contemporary criminal investigators in the United States and abroad? What drives them? How do they—in common ways and different ways—go about solving their major crimes?

The answers to these and other questions form the substance of this book, which it is hoped will shed new light on a fascinating profession that is still insufficiently appreciated—both in terms of its intellectual demands and its contribution to society.

All cases and events described in this book are true. Certain names have been changed or omitted in order to protect the privacy of some witnesses and others who were arrested but not convicted of a crime.

The World's Great Detectives

1

Cracking the Cockney Mafia

THE DOOR TO the London East End apartment burst open, catching the two burly twin brothers asleep in bed—one with a young woman, the other with a young man. The diminutive detective at the head of the raid, uncustomarily armed with a .38-calibre Webley revolver, personally dragged one of the twins out of bed, announcing in a clipped British accent, "You know who I am. You are under arrest."

The still-groggy brothers were not long in waking up to what was happening to them, and they knew only too well who had so rudely interrupted their sleep—Superintendent Leonard ("Nipper") Read of Scotland Yard, renowned as Great Britain's most tenacious sleuth. The dawn raid climaxed one of the most suspenseful and painstaking criminal investigations in the history

3

of modern England—the jailing, and subsequent convictions, of the infamous Kray twins, a deadly duo who enjoyed the dubious distinction of commanding London's "cockney Mafia."

For years prior to that spring morning in 1968, when "Nipper" Read kicked in the door of their pad, the Kray twins, Ronnie and Reggie, had held London's East End in a reign of terror. The key to their power was intimidation. Coincidentally or otherwise, anyone who crossed them was apt to suffer terrible misfortunes. In the meantime, the Krays went about prospering from a variety of rackets, ranging from protection to white-collar fraud, and expanding their criminal influence nationally and even internationally.

In the often senseless violence they visited upon their victims, the Kray brothers, former boxers, were like something out of *A Clockwork Orange*. In the power and fear their organization wielded, along with its contacts in the worlds of politics, entertainment, and business, the Krays' criminal network paralleled that of the American Mafia to which, in fact, the Krays had ties.

A peculiarly British phenomenon, Ronnie and Reggie Kray were born in the Bethnal Green section of London's East End—a Dickensian poverty-ridden urban ghetto that had long been a breeding ground for criminals. Their father, a hard-drinking cockney, was an itinerant dealer in hand-me-down clothing and old gold who toured the provinces with a clothes bag and a pair of gold scales. The burden of rearing the Kray boys fell on their mother, who doted on them.

Inseparable from the start, the Kray twins soon became the toughest kids around in the unaccredited school of violence that is London's East End. They were only seventeen when they experienced their first serious run-in with the law. A youth who had been badly cut and beaten in a gang fight testified against them. But their trial at Old Bailey proved to be only a preview of many trials to come involving the Krays. Witnesses suffered sudden inexplicable lapses of memory, and the case was finally dismissed for lack of evidence.

Briefly embarking on a somewhat more respectable pursuit, the stocky, barrel-chested twins became professional boxers, but their careers were cut short by military service. Unsurprisingly, the discipline proved too much, so they deserted and spent the next two years either as fugitives or as inmates of military stockades. Behind bars, they met a number of aspiring young criminals and assertedly arrived at a conscious decision to earn their living by making crime pay. After both were dishonorably discharged in 1954, the twins returned to Bethnal Green to pursue their criminal goals with a passion. And for a time, crime for them paid very well.

The London *Daily Express*, not known for understatement, described the thick-featured, beetle-browed Kray twins as "the

The Kray Twins, Ronald (*far right*) and Reginald (*second from left*), are pictured attending a charity event at a London club. In spite of their underworld activities, the twins cast themselves · as humanitarian benefactors of worthy civic causes. (*Keystone*)

most violent and feared gangsters Britain has ever known." Their chief stocks in trade, according to Scotland Yard, were protection rackets, long firm frauds*, transatlantic trafficking in stolen securities, assault—and murder. Yet they also had a curious

Scotland Yard Super Sleuth Leonard (Nipper) Read (*front row center, light overcoat*), shown with the team of investigators who helped him to bring the Kray Twins to justice. The team was nicknamed "Nipper's army." Second from left in rear row is Detective Frank Cater, who assisted Read in the actual arrest of the twins. (*Keystone*)

---

* "Long firm frauds" are a uniquely British white-collar crime. Three individuals, or three small groups of individuals, set up "paper" companies— each with offices, desks, letterheads, and other trappings of an authentic enterprise. Each of the "businesses" is given credit references by the other two. (In British business transactions it is customary to give two credit references, hence the organizing of three phony companies.)

genius for publicity and public deception. Even as they ran their criminal empire, Ronnie and Reggie Kray managed to make themselves known as philanthropic East End businessmen solicitous about helping underprivileged youths. Frequently photographed in London's best restaurants and night clubs, the Krays made friends in high places and moved in celebrity circles. They used the friendship of peers and MPs to enhance their image, and fatuous questions were even asked on their behalf in Parliament.

Their most effective weapon, all the same, was their reputation for violence—not just the dispassionate, workmanlike brutality of the professional enforcer, but butchery for the added thrill of it. When the Krays sliced someone, they did it as much for the fun as for profit. Ronnie, who had been certified insane as early as 1958 while serving a three-year prison term for assault, was a paranoid schizophrenic with homicidal tendencies, and a homosexual who was jealous of his muscle power. Thus, after George Cornell, a member of another gang, was said to have called Ronnie "that fat poof," Ronnie shot him once through the forehead with a 9-mm Mauser in The Blind Beggar pub. "I never like hurting anybody unless I feel it personally," Ronnie was

---

The swindlers then go to one or more manufacturers and order some goods. The first order will be relatively small, say, £250 ($500) worth. The manufacturer not only has the references, but since the amount involved is small he does not investigate the company thoroughly, and so delivers the goods. The false companies pay promptly within the customary 30-day credit period. They then order again, this time perhaps £500 ($1000) worth of merchandise. Again they pay promptly. This routine is repeated several times, with ever-larger orders but with prompt payment for each purchase.

Ultimately, the phony firms place enormous orders, usually in the £150,000 to £200,000 range. Upon receiving this largest delivery of goods, the crooks sell them to not-too-reputable retailers at discount prices—and disappear without paying. The manufacturers are thus defrauded of the last consignments.

Normally the goods are quickly disposable consumer items such as watches and clocks, garden tools, household products, radios, and chocolates, and generally show up later in street markets to be sold as bargains.

The word "long" in "long firm frauds" refers not so much to the time required in the operation, as to the long-drawn-out process by which the final swindle is achieved.

once quoted as saying. And when Joe, a boxer, jokingly remarked in a bar on the fact that Ronnie had put on weight, Ronnie left, only to return a short time later in his chauffeured car and invited Joe into the washroom. There, using his favorite knife, Ronnie sliced Joe's face to ribbons, calmly washed up, and walked out. It required more than 70 stitches to sew Joe's face back together but at least Ronnie had conferred upon Joe a nickname; Joe was known thereafter as "Tramlines."

As for Reggie, the feat for which he was most notorious was the sadistic carving up of a hapless hood named Jack ("The Hat") McVitie. According to a witness, while Ronnie Kray

"Nipper" Read displays a tie clip in the shape of a pair of handcuffs presented to him by London's Marlborough Street Association. (*Keystone*)

locked Jack The Hat's arms behind him, Brother Reggie, wielding a carving knife, stabbed McVitie under one eye, in the stomach, and in the chest, finally leaving him impaled on the floor with the knife through his throat.

Scotland Yard was well aware of the Kray twins, the magnitude of their operations, and the scope and viciousness of their crimes. But for years it had been difficult if not impossible to compile hard evidence implicating the two brothers. In the East End's tightly insulated demimonde, potential witnesses were all too easily intimidated into silence or witness-box amnesia. All the while, the Krays were building their criminal empire into formidable proportions. At their height the Krays had the East End completely under their domain, selling "protection" to gaming clubs and betting shops, and a large part of London's West End too by arrangement with the Mafia.

British authorities finally decided that the Kray twins had to be brought to heel. Their violence and influence had gone too far. They were becoming a national menace. In September 1967, Scotland Yard Detective Leonard ("Nipper") Read was called in by his superiors and told, "Get the Krays."

A better man for the job could hardly have been selected. Since joining London's Metropolitan Police (the formal name for Scotland Yard) two decades earlier, "Nipper" Read had been instrumental in solving countless murders, frauds, and other acts of wrongdoing, and had built a reputation as one of the shrewdest investigators in the annals of the Yard.

Detectives seem to come out of middle-class backgrounds, and Read was no exception. He was born on March 31, 1925, in Nottingham, in the Midlands; his father worked in a local knitting factory. After receiving his elementary school certificate at age fourteen, young Read left school and went to work at a John Players Tobacco factory. At seventeen, he joined the Royal Navy. During World War II Read saw duty in the Far East attached to a combined operations unit, and spent much of his time repairing landing craft engines. Ironically, in view of his later defeat of the ex-pugilist Kray twins, while in the Navy Read took up amateur boxing.

Demobilized in 1946, Read joined London's Metropolitan

Police. His performance with Scotland Yard speaks for itself. An unabashed believer in the use of disguises, Read has at various times posed as a postman, railway porter, milkman, chauffeur, market researcher, newspaper reporter, and priest.

"It is my opinion," he says, "that one of the main essentials of the investigator is a chameleon-like quality; in other words an ability to change techniques as the situation demands and, therefore, flexibility is the keynote."

"As an example," Read adds, "one could interrogate a leading cashier from a large banking concern one minute and a Mafia-like professional criminal the next. The important thing is to be credible and acceptable to both." This is one reason why, as Read puts it, "I believe enormously in the use of disguises, but the less elaborate the better, in my view." Once, while preparing to pick up a man wanted for drug smuggling, Read waited at London Airport disguised as a chauffeur sporting a Hertz "Rent-a-Car" badge. Another time, assigned to arrest an escaped murderer, Read borrowed a "milk float" (a British term for a small pushcart or midget motor vehicle used by milkmen to make home deliveries), along with the white coat and cap of a milkman, to approach the door of the fugitive's hideout unnoticed and nab him. In still another case, while investigating a protection racket that had been putting the strong-arm on a bookmaker, Read posed as a betting clerk—complete with horn-rimmed spectacles and ticker tape round his neck—to eavesdrop on the conversation that would later convict the racketeer.

All the same, the use of disguises carries its risks, as Read makes clear in recalling two incidents.

"At one time I was keeping observations in a public house [pub] to obtain evidence of betting. The place was frequented by railway employees and I posed as a porter, wearing the regulation-style uniform and cap. Whilst in there drinking a beer I was approached by the foreman porter who demanded to know what I was doing. I told him that I was 'No. 1 Parcels'—the first thing that came into my head. At this he exploded and shouted, 'Your relief is not for two hours, get back to bloody work!'

"On another occasion I was acting as undercover man 'buying' a lorry load of Scotch whiskey from the thieves who had stolen it. The plan was that when they were all assembled in the warehouse, I would give the signal to my colleagues and then be allowed to dash to freedom when they burst in—in the hope that my identity would not have to be revealed.

"In order to ensure the success of the plan, a particular officer had been detailed to 'chase' me. Unfortunately, however, a new detective amongst the raiding party, seeing me take to my heels, followed by one of his elder companions, joined the chase. Needless to say he soon outstripped the 'plant' chaser and was gaining on me rapidly when I decided to capitulate. I therefore ran onto the lawn of a house, so as not to be observed 'surrendering' myself. I then tried to indicate to the onrushing officer that I was one of his own, but to no avail. He obviously fancied himself as a rugby player, because he hit me just above the knees, carried me about six yards across the lawn so that my body from the trunk up landed in an ornamental fishpond full of stagnant, evil-smelling water.

"Of course there was absolutely nothing I could do about it as, being new and full of zeal, the officer was sure he was making the capture of the operation. Faces were red all around."

In 1963 Read was seconded to Aylesbury, Buckinghamshire, to assist in the investigation of Britain's Great Train Robbery. In 1966 he was made responsible for ridding London's West End of pickpockets and con men during the World Cup soccer tournament. As Read recalls with characteristic matter-of-factness, "This squad made a number of excellent arrests, reduced crime in the West End of London by forty-five percent, and closed strip clubs in the area."

Nicknamed "Nipper" because of his bantam-rooster size—144 pounds, five feet eight inches—Read nevertheless managed, in addition to his investigative achievements, to become Scotland Yard's lightweight boxing champion.

Still another vital professional quality that the successful detective must possess, declares Read, is the ability to convince the underworld that he can be trusted. What this generally boils down to, in practice, is coming through with promises of immunity from prosecution or reduced charges in return for information or other forms of cooperation which the police can use to help them arrest more important criminals.

As Read points out, many if not most crooks think of police

as "natural enemies." When criminals find that they can trust a "copper" to keep his word, they can often be surprisingly truthful and helpful. "I have always been hard, but criminals have always been aware that I was ruthless in pursuit of the truth and yet they would never have cause to question my fairness or integrity."

It was this quality of Read's, more than any other, that led to his most brilliant accomplishment, one that earned him the status of a national anticrime hero: the bringing to justice in 1968 of the infamous Kray twins and the related breakup of London's major gangs, or "Cockney Mafia," in the East End.

Read had had his first run-in with the Krays three years earlier, and it had not proved a happy one for the detective. Newly arrived in the East End from a previous station in Paddington, Read became increasingly interested in getting a firsthand look at the twins. The name Kray had cropped up repeatedly among the criminals he knew in Paddington, and the more Read learned of crime in the East End the more important the Krays seemed to be.

Nevertheless, whenever Read inquired about the twins, East End informers tended to start talking about the weather or the horse races. Naturally this only whetted his curiosity.

In late 1964, the son of a wealthy baronet and owner of a club in Soho, the Hideaway, complained to Read that the Krays were asking for a half-share in his profits. Shortly afterward, a brawl broke out at the Hideaway, with pictures smashed and threats made. Read had the Kray twins and a friend arrested on charges of demanding money from the club owner with menaces.

The brothers were not to be underestimated. As part of their elaborate defense structure, they retained one of the sharpest private eyes in London. This latter worthy unearthed the fascinating fact that several years earlier that same club owner had appeared at Scotland Yard in various cases involving homosexuals, with something of the character of a habitual police informer. This was enough to discredit the owner as a witness and halt the Krays' trial. The twins and their friend gleefully walked out of jail free men, and "Nipper" Read went off to help crack the Great Train Robbery.

However, neither the Krays nor Read forgot each other, although neither side could have known how soon their paths would cross again.

In 1967 Read was named to Scotland Yard's famed "Murder Squad," made up of the Yard's twelve top-ranking detectives. It was soon after winning that honor that "Nipper" was ordered to go after the Krays once and for all.

To do so, Read, who with the assignment was promoted to the rank of superintendent in Scotland Yard's Criminal Investigation Division (CID), fell back on his fundamentals. Particularly crucial in this case was the need for the detective to be able to develop a sense of trust on the part of the underworld. As Read described his modus operandi to the authors:

"The Kray twins had built in this country a criminal empire which depended for much of its successes upon the dominance of the organization by fear. It was impossible to encourage the cooperation of the victims of the protection rackets, long firm frauds, or serious and grievous assaults. These people were so overwhelmed by the fear of reprisals from the Krays and their associates that they would deny emphatically any association or knowledge of the Krays whatsoever. It was important therefore to infiltrate into the inner circle of the hierarchy of the gang.

"This was only possible by generating and establishing a foundation of confidence between myself and the criminals I intended to use.

"Because of my reputation for fairness I was able to effect this with the result that certain of the higher echelon of the Kray hierarchy defected, and provided me with information which eventually resulted in the Krays' downfall."

Read started the Kray gang investigation with himself and two sergeants. It didn't take long for the East End criminal grapevine to spread the word that "Nipper" Read was after the Krays—or for Read to learn subsequently that a price had been put on his head. This made him understandably cautious. Among other things, he took to driving his red Volkswagen home each night by a different route. (Nevertheless, Read was slightly miffed when he learned, just before the Krays went on trial, that the standing offer to anyone who could kill him had dropped in price.)

All Read had going for him in the East End was a reputation for honesty and decency. His main task was to convince potential witnesses that the Kray twins were not invincible, and that the police would protect anyone who would give them information. Read even offered the witnesses a "safe home" in London and police guards both before and after the Kray trial.

The twins again fought back. Several victims of their violence, men who had been shot and wounded or beaten up, were brought to lawyers and ordered to swear affidavits exonerating the twins. Each member of the gang was made responsible for keeping an eye on two or three potential witnesses. When Read asked one man whom the twins had maimed why he would not cooperate in bringing them to justice, the victim replied, not without a certain logic, "I hate the sight of blood, particularly my own."

Read had a long session with police prosecutors, and won their reluctant assent to overlook serious crimes on the part of potential witnesses in return for their talking. Read wrote down a roster of names in a small black notebook which he called his "delightful index."

"This," he recounts, "was the basis upon which the operation was mounted. I had a list of thirty members of the Kray organization earmarked as possible sources of information. These were seen systematically, and whilst on a number of occasions the overture was rejected out of hand, others received me with mixed feelings and as the operation developed they were persuaded to help in certain fields.

"One had become completely disenchanted with the Krays because of a power struggle within the structure of the organization, and after a number of confidence-building meetings and with a guarantee of immunity from prosecution, he eventually agreed to give me the information I desired."

Read got this first break in the case within four weeks. The inspector and his two sergeants found the man who was willing to "make a statement." At that point, Read increased his staff of investigators to ten, which remained the total of what became known as "Nipper's army" until the day of the big roundup raid, when reinforcements were brought in.

The informant was one Peter Lane. He was approached as

part of Read's methodical plan to check all persons who had had contacts with the twins. Lane, who had been the target of a bungled attempt by the twins to have him assassinated, was ready to talk. The interrogation lasted three weeks. His statement ran to more than 200 pages and detailed everything he knew about the Krays. All "Nipper" needed now to win his war was supporting proof and witnesses.

Read's police task force was mobilized and began working on the case around the clock. Victims had to be interviewed before the Krays got to them. As a safeguard and inducement for witnesses, Read devised a clause attached to all of their statements which guaranteed them that the evidence would not be used until the Krays were safely under lock and key.

To the Krays, "Nipper's" war against them became a personal affair. Ronnie cursed Read as a "cunning little bastard." Ronnie himself, in his more rational moments, conceded that if anyone could ever put him behind bars for good it would be "Nipper" Read. To air his contempt for Read, Ronnie—knowing that his phone was tapped by the Yard—telephoned the pet department of Harrod's department store and ordered a snake. Harrod's dutifully delivered him a python, which Ronnie promptly named Read.

Insults aside, Ronnie was for killing Read, but Reggie Kray in this instance was cooler-headed. He had learned about the clause that Read had inserted in the witnesses' statements, and shrewdly counseled his volatile twin that if the gang, or the "firm" as they called it, lay low and did nothing to land them behind bars, Read would be stymied because he would be unable to use the statements. For a time, Ronnie went along. While Read and his "army," under increasing pressure to wrap up the case, labored eighteen-hour days striving to glean more evidence, the twins and their hangers-on shifted into a role of conspicuous leisure, partying and spending weekends in the country. All the while, however, the Krays tightened the screws on potential witnesses. Word was passed, "If we go, half of London will go with us."

Although the Krays' activities were many-sided, a main source of their income, and a central point of Read's investigation, was stolen negotiable bonds from the United States and Canada that were brought into Britain to the Krays, who disposed of them on the Continent. According to Read, this operation was basic to the twins' criminal empire.

Following up Peter Lane's charges, Read relates, "Investigations were then made into these allegations which concerned long firm frauds, the protection rackets in this country, and the traffic between Canada, the United States, England and the Continent of negotiable bonds stolen in the United States.

"At that time I took the view that as the Krays were still free and powerful in the criminal underworld, it was not prudent to investigate murders of which they were suspected as most certainly this would result in potential witnesses being eliminated."

However, not long after Lane talked, Read got the break that he needed. As he relates it, "We knew there was a predilection for violence in the Krays and their gang. We got a tip-off when a man was sent to Scotland to pick up some gelignite. The man—one of the Krays' boys—went to a crook to pick it up. I flew up and arrested the man. He cracked quickly and told us it was intended to be put in the car of a club owner in the West End. He said he had been sent on behalf of the Krays. That was the break. It was enough for us, eventually, to charge the Krays with conspiracy to murder."

Read adds that the informant also declared that the Krays wanted him to kill a man who was to be a witness at a trial in the Old Bailey, London's criminal court. The would-be killer was to use what Scotland Yard's chief pathologist later described as a "diabolical murder weapon"—a small suitcase fitted with a spring-action hypodermic needle containing cyanide. The plan was to come up behind the intended victim and "accidentally" brush against him with the suitcase, jabbing him with the protruding needle. The poison could kill a person in eight seconds, and it would be thought that he had died of a heart attack. The reaction and general "seizure" would have been the same, and only minute laboratory tests could have uncovered the poison.

This diabolical killing never came off, but there was little doubt of the seriousness with which it was plotted. Searching the arrested man's house, Read discovered the suitcase, the hypodermic needle, and a small bottle of cyanide.

Armed with Lane's allegations, the statement of the suspect in the conspiracy-to-murder case, and an impressive array of additional statements from witnesses against the Krays, the unrelenting "Nipper" Read decided that he had collected enough evidence to arrest the twins and their gang. It had been five months since Read received the case.

As Read puts it, "After five months of intensive inquiries, sufficient evidence was on hand upon which to arrest the Krays and twenty-four of their confederates on various charges of fraud, assault, blackmail, and attempted murder."

These were serious charges, strong enough certainly to ensure that the twins would be detained without bail. This would immediately unlock the safety clause holding back the use of Read's mass of statements. Once the Krays were in custody, such witnesses as the barmaid at The Blind Beggar pub, who had steadfastly refused to identify Ronnie as the murderer of George Cornell, might be persuaded to talk.

The decision was made: the Krays and their "firm" would be picked up.

On May 8, 1968, Read put all of the detectives in the Metropolitan Area's Crime Squads on standby alert. At 3:00 A.M. the following day, he ordered forty-four men from the Crime Squads to report to him at 4:00 A.M. at his office in Tintagel House on the south bank of the Thames.

At the appointed hour, the short-statured Read mounted a filing cabinet, unfolded his complex plan, and allocated duties among the assembled Scotland Yard sleuths. Coffee and sandwiches were served. Photographs and descriptions were distributed of the confederates of the Krays. The Crime Squad men were to swoop down on those twenty-four while Read and his assistant, Chief Inspector Frank Cater, arrested the twins themselves.

At 5:00 A.M. Read ended the session with a declaration that the twenty-four arrests would be made in exactly one hour—a dawn swoop throughout the East End at precisely 6:00 A.M. As the briefing session broke up, the Krays, who had been under continual surveillance, were reported leaving the Astor Club after a night on the town and heading home to their apartment.

Although ordinarily not armed (in conformance with British

police tradition), Read and Cater this time equipped themselves with Webley .38 revolvers. "We received information," recalls Read, "that the Krays were going to give us a real Chicago-style shootout."

Such was not the case. While their colleagues swept down on the Krays' underlings, Read and Cater kicked in the door of the apartment that the twins shared. Both were in bed sleeping like babies, Reggie (whose young wife had committed suicide) with a girl from Walthamstow, Ronnie (as was his bent) with a fair-haired young man. The twins were hardly awake before Read had clapped the handcuffs on them.

Referring to his own longhand notes in a dog-eared notebook that he carried at the time of the raid, Read reconstructed the scene for us.

He personally dragged Ronnie Kray out of bed, said to him, "You know who I am. You are under arrest. I'm going to take you to the West End Central Police Station."

Read then related to Ronnie the standard cautionary statement, required in Britain as well as in the United States, that anything Ronnie said could be used in evidence against him.

Ronnie Kray replied, "Yes. All right, Mr. Read, but I've got to have my pills, you know that.... You know what they are. Stematol [a tranquilizer]. I've got a letter from my psychiatrist what says I've got to take two a day. I'll have to have that as well. Could you bring that along please, Mr. Read? It's in that book, my address book."

A bit later, when Read informed Ronnie that he would be charged with conspiracy to murder, Ronnie replied, "All I can say is, that it is ridiculous. Murder. I don't know nothing about murder. Did you remember about my pills, Mr. Read? I shall have to have them."

Read points out that here was a sadistic, violence-prone criminal and murderer who was almost obsessively preoccupied with his tranquilizing pills. Read arranged for Ronnie to have them.

For his part, Reggie Kray, when advised by Read that the charge would be conspiracy to murder, snarled, "Yes, Mr. Read. We've met like this before. We've been expecting another frameup for a long time but this time we've got witnesses. There's plenty of people who will want to help us."

It remained for Ronnie Kray to utter what he obviously hoped would be the ultimate epithet to the twins' nemesis. When Ronnie was formally charged with conspiracy to murder Jack ("The Hat") McVitie, Ronnie announced contemptuously to Read, "Your sarcastic insinuations are far too obnoxious to be appreciated." Ronnie liked to use big words, and Read comments wryly that he is convinced this flight of hyperbole was carefully rehearsed by Ronnie beforehand.

With the Kray twins in detention, Read pressed on with his methodical drive to construct an airtight case against them. And again, the tireless officer went to great lengths to protect the sources who would help him. "Whilst interviewing members of the Kray organization who were in custody," Read recounts, "it was essential that no one other than the governor of the prison should be aware of my presence. I therefore disguised myself as a priest and held interviews in the prison chapel."

Scotland Yard had only a few weeks before the twins' scheduled preliminary hearings to clinch the case and persuade major witnesses to testify. The Krays' power had by no means been broken. Virtually holding court in Brixton jail, receiving a stream of visitors of both high and low station, the Krays easily sent word to the East End grapevine that a "reprisal force" would deal severely with anyone who proved disloyal to them. As "Nipper" Read realized only too well, this time he had to be able to guarantee that the Krays were finished. Otherwise, as one old cockney predicted, "If people talk to the police and the twins get off again, they'll have to send the plague carts into Bethnal Green and shout, 'Bring out your dead!'"

With so much at stake, Scotland Yard let it be known that it meant business. The police spread the word that they would tolerate no nonsense when it came to the Kray case. Then the Yard scored another important point. Harry, a young cousin of the Krays, and a man called "Scotch," who had been with Ronnie Kray when Cornell was murdered, were found and picked up after having escaped the original dragnet. Word around the East End had had it that Harry and Scotch headed the Kray "reprisal force"; now that they too were in custody, fears of retribution eased, and witnesses started edging over the line to the police side. It became increasingly clear that Ronnie and Reggie Kray were losing their last battle.

They were ultimately tried for double murder in the killings of George Cornell and Jack ("The Hat") McVitie. Reggie was accused as an accessory to the Cornell crime for knowingly helping Ronnie after his escape.

By the time their trial began, the twins had lost much of their bravado. Sitting in the front row of the dock, grim-faced and unsmiling, they heard themselves denounced repeatedly by old enemies and sometime friends. In a surrealistic parade out of the twins' past, orchestrated by Read, forgotten victims and former accomplices filed one after another into the witness box. There was the ex-lightweight boxer and bodyguard of Ronnie who testified how he used to run the Krays' long-firm frauds. The turning point was the surprise appearance of the frightened barmaid from The Blind Beggar. She testified that she had previously been intimidated in the George Cornell murder investigation but clearly recognized Ronnie and "Scotch" as the men who fired the shots.

It was the longest and most expensive criminal trial in British history. It was unique in another respect: as far as anyone knew, there had never before been such a criminal case involving twins as defendants. Last but not least, the trial was a resounding triumph for Read. The Krays were convicted of double murder and sentenced to life imprisonment, which the judge recommended should be not less than thirty years. The judge, when sentencing Ronnie Kray, said to him: "I'm not going to waste words on you. In my view society has earned a rest from your activities."

Nor was that all. By the time "Nipper" Read was through with the case, not only had Ronnie and Reggie Kray been put away, but also no fewer than seventy-five of their associates. In all, seventy-seven members of the Kray gang were arrested and, in the end, received prison sentences totaling 298 years. Of the seventy-seven defendants, eleven were charged with murder or conspiracy to murder and received a total of 159 years. The total sentences are believed to be a record in Great Britain for cases resulting from a single investigation.

The judge, summing up at the conclusion of the trial, declared to the court: "The debt the public owes to Superintendent Read and his officers is one that cannot be overstated and can never be discharged."

The following year, in October 1970, Read was promoted to the post of Assistant Chief Constable of Nottinghamshire, his home country. In April 1972 he was appointed National Coordinator of Regional Crime Squads, Britain's closest equivalent to the Federal Bureau of Investigation (FBI)*, and returned to London. In this position, Read presided over nine Regional Crime Squads in England and Wales embracing a total of 900 detectives, among them 50 women, operating from 60 branch offices.

In taking over as National Coordinator, Read made oblique, modest reference to the breaking of the Krays, England's last big criminal gang. He said, "Recent activities by the police have broken up organized gangs to a great extent and the job of the Crime Squads is to prevent the criminals from becoming organized again. There are a lot of professional, skillful criminals traveling about the country and it is on these that the squads will concentrate. Smaller groups are being formed, but it is not possible nowadays for them to become large organized groups as in the past."

Read's performance in the Kray case would seem to be a classic example of how to crack organized crime by undermining its structure. Read subsequently received Britain's highest recognition when he made the annual New Year Honours list. Read was awarded the Queen's Police Medal for distinguished service, presented to him by Queen Elizabeth II at Buckingham Palace.

As National Coordinator, "Nipper" Read operated out of a large

* Although their responsibilities are quite different. Great Britain has forty-seven autonomous provincial police forces, and superimposed upon them is the Crime Squad organization. The country is divided into nine regions, each of which has a squad of varying strength under the command of a detective chief superintendent. The squads concentrate on investigating more serious crimes and organized crime. It was Read's function to coordinate the efforts of the nine regions.

office on an upper floor of Tintagel House—one of the buildings housing Scotland Yard. Tintagel House is situated on the south bank of the Thames (the Albert Embankment) and is one-half mile upstream from Big Ben and the Houses of Parliament, which are clearly visible across the river from Read's office. His office, a corner room overlooking the Thames, was plainly furnished with a table desk, two reddish leather chairs, cabinets lining the walls, a large table, and a few additional chairs across the office from his desk.

Read himself, despite his small stature, is strongly built and still trim. Betraying a slight waistline bulge, he is not quite in his boxing trim but is still fit and sprightly.

Observing Leonard Read behind his desk, you might never guess that he is a super sleuth of Scotland Yard. From his pleasant, unassuming manner, he could be a moderately successful British businessman. Yet on closer inspection, you can sense that beneath that mild exterior is a core of steel.

Read is not pretentious and speaks with down-to-earth directness. In an interview for this book, Read was attired in conservative dress that matched his conservative manner; he wore a blue serge suit, black shoes, pale blue shirt, and dark blue tie that was plain except for a small design just below the knot.

Ruminating about crime and crime detection, "Nipper" Read allowed that he did not think much of the detective in the movie version of *The French Connection* who waited for hours across the street from a restaurant where his suspects were eating.

"He should not even have been on the street," said Read. "You must always be above—or even below—the street. We often go into houses and ask people to let us use a room. They are always willing to cooperate."

When all is said and done, Read contends, the detective, for the most part, has to rely on individuals for providing information. Since most respectable persons have no idea what criminals are up to, he argues, the detective must, perforce, associate with the underworld. This, in Read's view, involves not so much maintaining contact with the really serious criminal element— although that often must be done—as associating with those on the edge of crime, persons who live in a twilight zone, not accepted by respectable citizens but not accepted by the truly criminal world either. "Mixing with criminals is terribly important," says Read. "You must have contact with the underworld."

As for the broader social problem of crime and how to deal with it, Read concluded, "Like most unenlightened detectives, I am perhaps rather old-fashioned in my outlook towards crime generally. I speak, of course, about the eight percent or thereabouts of crime committed by the purely professional criminal, a man who, in my view, is not capable of rehabilitation. Too many people today are over-eager to excuse criminality on psychological grounds—you know the kind of thing. They will want to forgive a man a particularly nasty rape because he was in love with his rocking horse as a child.

"Well, I may be old-fashioned, but I firmly believe that a criminal is provoked by two senses—idleness and greed. I don't subscribe overmuch to causation being attributable to environment, broken homes, disfigurement, etcetera, as there are startling examples of people who have overcome these limitations and become successful. My view is that the *professional* criminal makes a conscious decision to opt out of recognized society to join the 'other' society of the criminal—and believe me this is as clearly defined as ours.

"Having taken this step, a criminal will enjoy all the benefits of the society he subscribes to, until either he becomes so successful that he can become legitimate and revert to recognized society, or he is too old to follow his profession, when he will sneak back to enjoy the comforts and benefits of the establishment.

"I am confident that the great majority of people in the world want a return to a stable, ordered society which demonstrates its responsibilities by punishing the wrongdoer when such punishment is distinctly to the advantage of the law-abiding. element. If, therefore, the law enforcement agent or the criminal investigator is successful in pursuing his quarry—the major criminal —and can indicate that his motivations were lust, greed or idleness, then, providing society takes heed, the detective is making some valuable, albeit small contribution to it."

This was more than proven on that dawn morning in 1968 when "Nipper" Read and his partner kicked in the door of the East End flat, to put the Kray twins and the rest of their cockney Mafia behind bars.

2

Rum Before the Guillotine

On the night of June 8, 1949, three men sat dining unobtrusively in an elegant restaurant on Paris' Avenue Bosquet. One was small and black-haired, with cold eyes. His unimposing appearance belied his notorious identity. He was Emile Buisson, gangster, fugitive, and France's Public Enemy No. 1. A second man present was a Corsican named Orsoni. The third man at the table was one Desiré Polledri, a member of Buisson's gang. Little did Polledri know that this was to be his last supper.

Polledri had been Buisson's friend, but to Emile that did not matter now. Buisson had become disenchanted with Polledri, whom Buisson accused of having murdered by mistake another member of their band, Maurice Yves, nicknamed "Yves the Fishmonger," and of talking imprudently. After deciding to eliminate

Polledri, Buisson had pondered for days how to go about doing so without risking suspicion. Buisson concluded that the best site would be the quiet Landrieu alley near the Avenue Bosquet. He ordered two of his henchmen to drive to the alley at 10:00 P.M. sharp on June 8.

That night, Buisson invited Polledri and Orsoni, a crony whom Buisson had not seen for some time, to have dinner. Who would suspect what Buisson had in mind?

Time passed. It was now 9:30 P.M.

"Let's have a last cognac," Buisson suggested.

When the waiter had filled the glasses, Buisson raised his, clicked it against Polledri's, and offered a Machiavellian toast, "To your long life."

Playing the part of the generous host, Emile paid the check, and the three emerged into the dark street.

"Come, we'll take a walk to stretch our legs," Buisson proposed.

With brisk steps, the trio strolled into the night. Polledri and Orsoni, suspecting nothing, accompanied Buisson into the Landrieu alley. Suddenly they heard a car approaching. Buisson whipped out his Colt pistol and pumped a deadly volley of shots into Polledri, who sank to the sidewalk while Orsoni fled.

The victim was breathing his death rattle; the car had stopped. Buisson started to get in but changed his mind momentarily. Returning to the dying Polledri, Buisson, in the darkness, searched for the mouth of the man who had been his friend, plunged the gun barrel between Polledri's lips, and fired the last bullet into his tongue.

"Like that, he won't talk anymore!" shouted Buisson as the car sped away.

The diabolical murder of Desiré Polledri was only one of the myriad crimes committed by Emile Buisson, who ranks in Gallic criminal history as the French Al Capone. During the years immediately following World War II, when bands of gangsters armed with guns left over from the war roamed France at will, Emile Buisson was the most-wanted outlaw of them all. Between 1947 and 1950, at the height of his criminal career, Buisson eluded the police of France virtually at will: An accomplished escape artist and expert at hiding, Buisson—whose nickname was *L'insaisissable* ("The Uncapturable One")—ran unfettered in the streets of Paris and in the French countryside, robbing, assaulting, murdering.

France's real-life "Inspector Maigret," French Detective Charles Chenevier, in his office on Paris' Left Bank. Now retired from France's Sûreté Nationale, the famed investigator continues active as a private eye. Mural on office wall depicts scene of medieval Paris. (*Bruce Henderson*)

There was nothing particularly special about Buisson's physical makeup—only two quick, cruel black eyes that were impossible to forget. Indeed, Buisson's commonplace mien, along with a certain theatrical flair, was a principal factor behind his slipperiness as a fugitive. Depending upon the needs of the moment, Buisson could assume the appearance of a French common worker, characteristically dressed in a threadbare suit and stocking cap, or just as easily assume the guise of a Parisian businessman, with snap-brim hat and umbrella. How to track the spoor of such an elusive and dangerous quarry?

The task fell to Commissaire Principal (Chief Superintendent) Charles Chenevier of the French Sûreté Nationale, one of France's most distinguished and canny detectives, who is known among his countrymen as the real-life "Inspector Maigret."

Thus, the pursuit of Emile Buisson represented an ironic convergence of the destinies of two men who were classic symbols of the hunted and the hunter—the one a wild animal, pillaging and killing with abandon; the other a stalker, pursuing his quarry with cool patience and endless determination. Ultimately the silent contest between Buisson and Chenevier, which unfolded for more than a decade, took on the aspect of an intractable struggle, what Chenevier recalls as "a veritable game of poker."

Emile Buisson's destiny was marked from childhood. He was born on August 19, 1902, in the small city of Paray-le-Monial. His parents had had ten children, five of whom died before they were twenty. His father, a chimney-builder, drifted into alcoholism and died during an attack of delirium tremens. Emile's mother, daughter of cemetery-keepers, died raving mad in an insane asylum.

The children had to steal to feed themselves. It was thus that little Emile, who never went to school, began his apprenticeship in life by pilfering from hen houses and gardens. He was first arrested at the age of nine when, in the company of a fifteen-year-old girl, he tried to make off with the till receipts from a hardware store. He was let off with a talking-to, but two years later was brought before a children's court for another misdeed; again he was released because of his youth. The Buisson family then moved from Paray-le-Monial to Lyons. In that large city, and in the company of a brother, Jean-Baptiste, Emile pursued his distorted education as a lawbreaker. On November 14, 1918, three days after the end of World War I and at the precocious age of sixteen, Emile won his first conviction, a suspended sentence for robbery.

From then on, his conviction record grew—Lyons, 1921, robbery; Lyons, 1922, robbery; Orléans, 1925, battery; Tournon, 1931, robbery.

In 1934, Emile helped his brother Jean-Baptiste escape from a hospital. (In the Neulhouse prison for robbery, Jean-Baptiste had managed to get transferred to the hospital by jumping off a parapet overlooking the prison courtyard and breaking a leg.) The two embarked for Shanghai where, operating out of a nightclub called the Fantasio, they engaged in gunrunning and other illicit activities. Two years later, squeezed by the international police, they returned to France.

In spite of his cold-blooded cruelty and his greed for ill-gotten gain, Buisson sometimes displayed an uncharacteristic generosity. He spent untold thousands of francs to have his sister Jeanne, who had become deaf after a bombardment, cared for. He liked little children, which may have resulted from a tragic personal experience.

In Marseilles, Emile lived with a prostitute, Odette Genvois, called "Little Hand" because of a malformation of her left hand. She bore Buisson a daughter. Later, during one of his many confinements in prison, he officially married his mistress and acknowledged his daughter. The child, who was fragile, was put into the care of a wet-nurse in Ris-Orangis, but died of meningitis at three. Odette Genvois, who was tubercular, soon followed her daughter to the grave.

Many times Buisson said during his interrogations, "If my daughter had lived, I would have straightened out. . . ."

Afterward, he transferred his love of children to animals. This bloody-handed bandit, who did not hesitate to kill a man, could not stand to see an animal suffer. Once, while walking in the country with some of his gang, Buisson heard the squealing of a hog, which a peasant was slaughtering in a pasture along the road.

"That butcher is an assassin!" screamed Emile pulling his Colt revolver out of his pocket and approaching the farmer.

The latter stepped back frightened, but he was not the target. Buisson dispatched the hog with one bullet in the head and, calmly replacing his pistol, said, "There's no excuse for killing so awkwardly."

That night he and his friends had to depart the area quickly, since the incident had started rumors in the countryside, and the local police had begun looking for the strange pig-killer with the revolver.

Still, Buisson's genius for fraud and deception could not be overestimated. One night, after losing at poker in a Montparnasse bar, he agreed to sell the Hotchkiss automobile he had parked out front to a fellow customer who was interested in buying it. The next day, showing up to close the deal, Buisson feigned a broken arm, accepted the 250,000 francs agreed upon, and asked the other fellow to sign his, Buisson's, name to the receipt. Later, when the car turned out to be stolen, the buyer was arrested. Hauled into court at the latter's behest, Buisson pleaded that he knew nothing about the case, and pointed to the fake signature on the receipt. The Hotchkiss admirer received a six-month suspended sentence, and Buisson got off free.

Not even World War II and the Nazi occupation halted Emile Buisson's criminal career. In 1943 a German court attached to the *Feldkommandatur* of Orléans sentenced him to one year for withholding arms. The same year a French tribunal at l'Aube condemned him to life in prison at forced labor, for armed robbery.

Transferred to Paris' Santé prison in 1945 to answer for an assault committed on the capital's rue de la Victoire, in which a man was killed, Buisson put on an Academy Award-winning performance simulating madness. As his trial went on, he paced to and fro in his cell all night and became insufferable to guards and fellow inmates alike. Put under observation in the infirmary, he succeeded in fooling all the doctors charged with examining him. Finally, upon the recommendation of psychiatrists, he was committed to the mental hospital of Villejuif—from which, on September 3, 1947, with the help of his brother, Jean-Baptiste, and three other accomplices, Emile hoisted himself by a rope ladder over a wall and escaped.

Emile Buisson's flight from the Villejuif asylum was his vault into the big time. For nearly three years afterward, he reigned as uncontested underworld boss on the streets of Paris, accumulating a career record of armed robberies, assaults, and murders carried out with the professional's composure. Miraculously, for thirty-three months he succeeded in eluding platoons of police trying to sniff out his trail, even though during most of this period he was either in Paris or in the surrounding countryside. The French judicial police officially pronounced Buisson to be France's Public Enemy No. 1.

For Commissaire Charles Chenevier, a laconic, black-haired sleuth with the Frenchman's delicious sarcasm, the assignment to track down Emile Buisson opened the last chapter in what had become a personal duel between the two. Chenevier had twice before run Buisson to earth, and had locked him behind bars, only to see him regain his freedom by one ruse or another. Thus, for both the detective and the desperado, Buisson's latest escape from custody and his criminal rampage represented a final showdown.

Of the same generation as the fugitive he was pursuing, Charles Chenevier was born on November 2, 1901, in Montelimar, the son of a career army officer. As a boy, Chenevier was enthralled by newspaper and magazine accounts of police adventures, and would hide such stories in his schoolbooks to keep them from parental surveillance. Especially etched in his memory as an example of the drama involved in law enforcement is an incident that occurred in Montelimar when he was a child—an ex-convict and an inspector of the judicial police of Lyons, who was trying to arrest the former, killed each other in a blazing gun battle.

After pursuing higher studies in Paris, Chenevier tried his hand at journalism, working as a writer and reporter for the *Revue de Paris* and *Quotidien*. As a journalist, he was attracted to the police beat. In 1925, he embarked on what was to be his permanent profession. At the beginning of that year, the French authorities decided to initiate a campaign against a wave of assaults and murders on trains. It was decided to create a special police corps charged with ensuring the safety of railroad passengers. Chenevier entered the competitive examinations, and was accepted into the Sûreté Nationale.

On March 1, 1925, he began his career in the special railway police. Chenevier's talents as a criminal investigator, his ability to mesh shrewd detective work with uncanny good luck, were evident from the start. His first post was in the Paris railroad station of Saint-Lazare, and he solved his first case in exactly two hours: at nine o'clock one night, an Englishman who had just arrived at the station from London reported that he had been robbed of a valuable coat. Two hours later, at 11:00 P.M., Chenevier was able to telephone the complainant at his luxurious hotel and advise him that the coat had been recovered. While visiting, one by one, all the cafes bordering the railroad station along the rue d'Amsterdam and the rue de Budapest in search of a lead, the young French detective had suddenly come upon the thief as the latter was trying to sell the coat to an intermediary.

The victim responded with what, for an Englishman, was the ultimate compliment. "I am very pleased," he told Chenevier. "You are much better than Scotland Yard."

After three years in the railway police, Chenevier was transferred to the frontier police and posted in the north, along France's border with Belgium and Germany, making passport checks and intercepting contraband. Not long afterward he was selected to join the judicial police, that branch of the Sûreté Nationale that specializes in the investigation of serious domestic crimes such as robbery and murder.

It was in that role that Chenevier had his first encounter with Emile Buisson. On April 6, 1938, Chenevier arrested the aspiring gangster on charges of having been one of several bandits who held up three cashiers of the Credit Lyonnais bank of Troyes four months earlier. The detective had tracked the fugitive through Buisson's mistress, Jeanne, for whom Buisson had purchased a cafe in Lille with his part of the bank loot. It was there that Chenevier arrested him. At first Buisson denied any participation in the robbery, adding that if Chenevier persisted in the idea, he would fail in court. Chenevier calmly responded, "Before going back to Paris, let's go see what we can find of interest in your room."

In the course of the search, Chenevier caught sight of a woman's umbrella in a corner. Opening the umbrella, he was inundated by a shower of 100-franc bills that wafted to the floor.

Buisson, incredulous, could only stare open-mouthed. Jeanne had hidden her savings, taken by stealth from time to time from the pockets of her lover, inside the umbrella. Unfortunately for Buisson, the serial numbers on some of the bills corresponded with those stolen in the bank heist. Chenevier recalls modestly, "I therefore really had the last word."

Imprisoned for the crime, Buisson soon escaped with some of his fellow inmates. In July 1941, Chenevier became interested in one "Charles Metadieu," who was hiding, Chenevier was told, in Orléans, and who was described as a "tough guy among the tough guys." It did not take Chenevier long to discover that "Metadieu" was in reality Emile Buisson. Chenevier materialized a second time in Buisson's life to put the French gangster behind bars.

It was in May 1943 that Buisson received his sentence of life imprisonment at forced labor. In November of the same year, Chenevier—who had belonged to the American-directed French Resistance unit "Jacques OSS"*—was arrested by the Gestapo and deported to a German prison camp. After the war, the cat-and-mouse game resumed. Following Buisson's 1947 escape from the Villejuif insane asylum, Chenevier was appointed to head a nationwide police offensive aimed at crushing the criminal gangs plaguing postwar France. Thus the paths of the detective and the desperado were destined to cross again.

In the wake of his flight from Villejuif, Buisson set about in earnest to make a lucrative business out of his life of crime. Establishing his underworld headquarters in Paris, he organized a gang numbering more than a score of persons, both men and women, that carried out armed robberies, assaults, and the disposition of stolen goods. Buisson was not only the mastermind of this clique of criminals, but most of the time was in the thick of the action himself—organizing assault teams based on the opportunities of the moment, acting quickly, and disappearing even more quickly.

Between 1947 and 1950 Buisson's gang carried out twenty-four armed robberies that reaped approximately sixty million francs,

* The World War II Office of Strategic Services (OSS) was the forerunner of the Central Intelligence Agency (CIA).

organized three prison escapes, and committed nearly a dozen murders. Witnesses who were potentially embarrassing to Buisson, "colleagues" who were too talkative or otherwise risked being a detriment to him. were simply killed in the middle of the night—his favorite place for this was the Senart Forest— and buried at the foot of the trees. More than a dozen individuals, most of them outlaws, who were with Buisson frequently and sometimes accompanied him in assaults, disappeared mysteriously and were never seen again.

To stalk and hunt down Buisson, Chenevier used all the Gallic guile and practical resources at his command, along with a dangerous ploy which, for sheer nerve and audaciousness, perhaps only a French police officer would attempt.

Chenevier first set about creating a "void" around Buisson. Gradually and inexorably as the result of special efforts conducted over a period of months, the police tracked down, killed, or imprisoned the majority of the other members of the gangster's band. Before long, Buisson was so isolated that he took to sleeping in the Boulogne woods. He had no other place to hide.

Chenevier's gradual encircling of Buisson went on, slowly, painstakingly, for two-and-one-half months even after the detective, through means of his own, had discovered Buisson's whereabouts. "All of my efforts were intended to give confidence to the one that I wanted to arrest for the third time," explains Chenevier. "Buisson was so intelligent, shrewd, cunning, hypersensitive, that a minuscule detail was enough to indicate to him that he was located or followed. He then fled and it all began again. This is how he had been able to resist the police for thirty-three months."

As if devising a script, Chenevier reflects, "His 'old friends' are all dead or in prison, his band broken up by recent arrests. Hunted everywhere, he hides himself. But he won't be able to hide forever. One day he will need money. . . . And that day, what will he do? He will look for someone for a holdup. He must be forced to come out of his haunt."

To lure him out, Chenevier employed a technique he had used to bring countless other criminals to justice. "I always used the same method, old as the world: that of the Trojan Horse. I send one of my informers into the bandit's surroundings, into a café that he goes to, for instance. But my man should not try to come in contact with him. On the contrary, the gangster must catch himself in the mesh of the net I have held out for him. Therefore, he has no reason to be suspicious. The operation is delicate, of course, but a gangster is still a man and it is painful for a hunted man, in a constant state of alert, abandoned by all, to be always alone."

In Buisson's case, the Trojan Horse was an ex-convict Buisson had known in prison. In the latter part of May 1950 Buisson committed his first mistake. He came into contact with the ex-con, struck up a conversation with him, and promised him a large sum in exchange for a car and a gun.

"I'll see what I can do," his old prison mate replied.

Moments after the conversation, Chenevier was informed of it. "Emile had taken the bait that I had set out for him," says Chenevier. "It was now a question of 'putting him into irons' gently."

Intentionally, Chenevier let three days go by; too quick a response might have given his go-between, his Trojan Horse, away. It was then that the detective took his biggest risk. Chenevier had received word that the fugitive wanted to be driven to an inn on the outskirts of Paris, where he would relax for a few days. The detective rented a car under his name from a garage in the eighteenth *arrondisement*, which he handed over to Buisson's former cell companion—along with a loaded Colt revolver.

Recalls Chenevier, "I had played all my trumps in the struggle, but I leave it to you to think about what would have happened if Buisson and his companion had come upon a police roadblock."

In fact, when Chenevier told his friend and police colleague, Gillard, what he, Chenevier, had done, Gillard was aghast. "Do you realize that you just risked your life, without mentioning the ridicule?" exclaimed Gillard. "If Buisson had been surprised and had made use of the weapon you had given him along with the car. . . . Talk about nerve. . . ."

Chenevier answered, "But, my friend, that is poker. Believe

me, we can have Emile only by risking the whole pack. And you don't know everything; I am the one paying his lodging at the inn."

Nevertheless, Chenevier's last wild card, as it turned out, proved enough to win all the chips. At 11:00 A.M. on June 3, Chenevier was informed that all had gone well, that Buisson was taking his ease in his new hideout, a small country inn on a Normandy road north of Paris.

Recalls Chenevier, "Then I asked Gillard to have two inspectors chosen by him to come to me, and I said to them: 'Gentlemen, I wanted simply to announce to you that at 1:45 P.M., June 10—seven days from now—we are going to arrest Emile Buisson."

Chenevier was in no hurry. He wanted his man to feel increasingly safe in his new surroundings.

The climax to Chenevier's script was carried out with all the detailed orchestration of a professional stage production—except for the fact that it was a real-life drama in which one miscue could have triggered wholesale bloodshed.

Early on the morning of June 10, Chenevier drove to a spot three kilometers from the inn, on a road leading to Deauville. The *commissaire* left his car, made his way through a forest by foot, and reached a dense thicket across the road from the inn. There he waited to be joined by his chief inspector, Monsieur Hours. Shortly before noon, Gillard, who bore the rank of chief commissioner, accompanied by his inspector general, Borniche, and the latter's wife, arrived at the inn in a luxurious Delahaye limousine, which in fact had been the main attraction of the last Paris auto show. All three were casually dressed in sports clothes. The two disguised detectives carried no guns; the telltale bulges would have been immediately obvious to Buisson's ferret eye.

Buisson was already at his usual table alone. He noticed the two men in shirtsleeves and especially the pretty woman who accompanied them. Probably tourists, thought Buisson, and besides cops don't drive around in limousines. For all his travails as a fugitive, Buisson had not lost his admiration for beautiful cars and the focus of his attention went to the Delahaye. From his seat, he could hear the carefree trio in the adjoining dining room.

At a prearranged moment, Inspector General Borniche asked the waiter, "Could you call the reception desk of the Hotel Normandy in Deauville for me? I should like to speak to them about my reservations."

The waiter approached the telephone, which was near Buisson, and called Deauville. A few seconds later, he advised the customer that he had his connection. Borniche left his table, passed by Buisson without looking at him, picked up the telephone and said, "Is this the reception desk? This is Dr. André from Paris. I would like to confirm my reservations for my wife and me. We will arrive tonight for a week."

At the other end, the hotel clerk answered, "Just a moment, sir."

"Fine, fine," said "Dr. André." "How much do you charge for a double room with bath?"

The desk clerk continued, "I'm sorry, sir, I cannot find a reservation under your name."

"André" interrupted, "That's fine. We're bringing some friends with us, Monsieur and Madame Forestier. Can you reserve them a room?"

Disconcerted, the clerk protested, "Please, sir, there is no . . ."

"Yes, a double room, too, and next to ours if possible."

"Monsieur Forestier," Gillard in reality, came to the door and asked, "Jacques, were you able to get a room for us?"

At that instant the two men jumped Buisson. The gangster did not even have time to go for the gun he was carrying, though it was loaded and cocked. The charming Madame Borniche, who had followed the scene with admirable coolness, produced a whistle and blew an ear-splitting signal to Chenevier across the road.

With the dramatic timing worthy of Emile Zola, the *commissaire* strode into the room and clicked the handcuffs onto Buisson. Astounded, the gangster exclaimed, "You again?"

Chenevier looked at his watch, smiled, and said, "It is 1:47 P.M., I am sorry to say, I am two minutes late for the meeting I had scheduled."

The colloquy that ensued reflected the quintessence of Gallic aplomb.

Said Chenevier, "I myself have had no lunch. The walk across the woods has made us hungry." He and Chief Inspector Hours sat down and chose their order. Pointing out a chair to the manacled Buisson, Chenevier invited, "Sit down, Emile, you've got time to have some coffee and cognac if you want."

Buisson hissed, "Why not some rum?" (a reference to the fact that in France a condemned person, on the morning he is to die on the guillotine, is offered a cigarette and a small glass of rum).

Buisson watched Chenevier with a murderous grimace while the *commissaire* and his assistant ate with appetite. Seeing Chenevier order some strawberries, the gangster said to the detective, "Do you know where they come from, these strawberries? I picked them myself this morning in the garden!"

"Really?" replied Chenevier. "They are very delicious, as a matter of fact."

Buisson smiled thinly, "If I had known that you were going to eat some, you can believe that I would have sprinkled them with rat poison."

Chenevier laughed and asked Buisson what fooled him so completely in the policemen's act. The ex-fugitive thought for a moment and said, "I think it was the car. Cops have never been seen riding in such a car."

Chenevier got up. "Let us be off, Emile! It is time now to think of serious things."

Buisson chose a cognac for his afterlunch drink in the country inn before he was led away, evidently saving his ration of rum for that cold dawn on February 28, 1956, in the courtyard of Santé prison, when the blade of the guillotine lopped off his head.

3

Teacups and Calling Cards

At 3:30 P.M. on January 26, 1948—a bleak day in Tokyo, with occasional flurries of snow—a slim, middle-aged man with cropped hair, identifying himself as a government health official, politely pushed his way past the clerk who was about to close the door of the Shiina-machi branch of Tokyo's Teikoku Bank. Courteous in manner, the visitor was dressed in a loose-fitting white coat over a brown suit, with an official armband stamped "Sanitation." He wore red rubber boots and carried a small black satchel.

With the tellers all busy checking the accounts, the clerk, briefly noting the man's calling card, ushered him into the bank manager's office. The visitor politely bowed to Acting Manager Takejiro Yoshida, exchanged calling cards, and informed him that his visit was a matter of urgency.

He told Yoshida that he was from General Douglas Mac-Arthur's occupation headquarters with orders to immunize the bank employees immediately because of an outbreak of amoebic dysentery in the neighborhood spread from a polluted public well. He explained that he had come directly from MacArthur's GHQ in advance of the sanitation squad and police to administer preventive medicine. A military jeep was to follow shortly.

The dysentery report came as no surprise to Acting Manager Yoshida. He had been informed that morning that one of the bank's neighborhood customers was ill with dysentery. The regular manager, Senji Ushiyama, had been stricken that morning with a stomachache and had gone home. Yoshida was aware that an outbreak of dysentery was possible.

"I understand, doctor," Yoshida said with a nod.

But what surprised Yoshida was such prompt action by occupation authorities, although he had been informed that the Americans were sticky about speedily enforcing health and sanitation regulations. Furthermore, during the Allied Occupation no one questioned orders from the headquarters of General Douglas MacArthur, conqueror of Japan and referred to by some Japanese as *Shogun* (samurai general) MacArthur.

After listening to the visitor's explanation and what he wanted done, Acting Manager Yoshida had the bank employees, including even the janitor and his family, put aside their work or whatever else they were doing and assemble in his office with their teacups.

"Is everyone present?" the caller asked.

Yoshida took a head count and reported, "Yes."

The visitor explained why he was at the bank and told them that they were to be given two anti-dysentery medicines which must be taken quickly, one after the other. He pulled out two bottles, which he said were from GHQ, and a medical syringe from his bag.

"The drug is very potent," he continued. "Gulp it down quickly and be careful that it does not touch the enamel of your teeth. Just stick your tongue out a little and cover your lower teeth as you swallow." He demonstrated with an empty teacup. "In less than a minute, wash it down with the second dosage."

The man proceeded to squirt a dose of liquid from the syringe, extracted from a dark violet bottle marked "Number One," into each employee's teacup. He surveyed their faces and the teacups they held in their hands, then gave the command, "*Dozo* [Please]." The bank employees quickly drank in unison and extended their cups for the second dose. Some began to gasp and cough as the liquid burned their throats.

"The second medicine will make you feel better," the man calmly stated as he squeezed, with a steady hand, a small portion from the syringe taken from bottle "Number Two" into each cup. Again they gulped it down. A male employee, rubbing his throat, asked: "May we gargle some water?"

"Yes," the imperturbable stranger replied.

Miss Masako Murata was waiting in line to reach the water fountain when someone standing behind her suddenly collapsed. Sprawled on the floor, flat on his back, his eyes open, gasping, was accountant Hidehiko Nishimura. Masako, alarmed, rushed back into the manager's office, screaming for help—only to discover others on the floor, moaning and groaning in agony and pain. Then she, too, collapsed.

The visitor in white calmly watched his victims, writhing and sinking to the floor. With the bank's entire staff immobilized, he quickly scooped up 164,400 yen in cash and an uncashed check for 17,405 yen, walked out a side exit with the total equivalent of 600 U.S. dollars—a tidy sum at the time for a Japanese—and disappeared into the cold late afternoon.

An hour later, Miss Murata regained consciousness. Aghast at what she saw around her, she crawled over prostrate bodies and staggered out the back door of the bank. She managed to cry for help in an incoherent voice. Two female passers-by, startled by her call, notified a police officer who hurried inside the bank. He too was shocked at a scene of horror—men and women lying on the floor, some frothing at the mouth, some moaning, others lifeless. The officer grabbed a desk phone and dialed the local precinct police station.

By the time ambulances and police cars arrived, ten of the victims were dead. Two others died later. There were four survivors, including Acting Manager Yoshida and Miss Murata.

A hasty check of the dregs in the teacups, some still clutched in the hands of the dead, drew suspicion that the "medicine" was some kind of deadly drug. But this was not automatically considered to be the case since food poisonings were common in postwar Japan, with its economic, political, and social confusion, and it was not unusual for hundreds working at the same place of employment to be stricken at the same time.

At 6:30 P.M., approximately three hours after the impromptu

Japanese Artist Sadamichi Hirasawa, handcuffed and in ceremonial robe, arrives in court in Tokyo on last day of his trial for the murder of twelve persons in Japan's bizarre poisoned-teacups bank robbery. (*Asahi Shimbun*)

teacup ceremony, medical examiners at a hospital reported that the fatalities were no ordinary cases of food poisoning. Doctors had pumped out the stomachs of the survivors and discovered that the drug was potassium cyanide.

Japanese Super Sleuth Tamegoro Igii, who nabbed Hirasawa after superiors in the Tokyo Metropolitan Police Department had exhausted thousands of other possible leads, is shown in a recent photo. (*S. Kimura*)

The Teikoku Bank massacre and robbery was Japan's major postwar crime, a diabolical, chilling, and sensational mass murder that triggered a nationwide manhunt that took seven months to reach its conclusion.

Authorities initially assigned Inspector Shigeki Horizaki, chief of the homicide division of the Tokyo Metropolitan Police Department, to handle the case—considered a direct challenge to Japan's law enforcement system recently reorganized under American supervision. Assisting Horizaki was Chief Public Procurator Umezo Takagi. Yet, for all the investigatory teamwork involved, one man was most responsible for cracking the crime: a quiet, doggedly determined detective sergeant whose dedication has made him as famous in Japan as the case itself—Tamegoro Igii. To colleagues and personal friends alike, Igii is known as a policeman of impeccable manners and inscrutable acuity of perception.

It wasn't until late that night, based on what the bank's Acting Manager Yoshida and the three other survivors told investigators, that the first inkling of what had happened became known. Police, however, found no fingerprints on the teacup the "doctor" had held in his hand for demonstration purposes, and which he had left behind, or on the calling card he had exchanged with the bank manager.

Working as a team on the case were six police detectives with Horizaki as "captain," who stationed himself at headquarters to maintain close liaison with the public procurator. This postwar practice in Japan still prevails. No single detective, regardless of his record, is assigned to any case alone.

The investigators were soon to learn that three months earlier, on October 14, 1947, a similar incident had occurred at the Ebara branch of the Yasuda Bank in a Tokyo suburb across town. There, a man, also dressed like a government health and sanitation official, had handed a calling card to the bank manager. The card bore the name: "Dr. Shigeru Matsui, Welfare Ministry Specialist." The visitor said that he had orders from occupation general headquarters to disinfect the place and to administer antidysentery medicine. He lined up twenty bank employees and bank Manager Toshio Watanabe and gave them what was described as medicine to drink just as had occurred later at the Teikoku bank. But nothing untoward had happened, and the man promptly left. The incident may have been a rehearsal.

On January 19, 1948, seven days before the mass teacups poisonings, a man with a calling card identifying him as "Dr.

Jiro Yamaguchi," a technical expert of the Welfare Ministry, had called at the Nakai branch of Mitsubishi Bank. However, he had fled when his legitimacy was questioned by bank Manager Taizo Ogawa and other employees.

The previous two incidents were not reported to police headquarters until the Teikoku case. Precinct police lamely explained that there had been no robbery, and that the visitor's motive was not clear at the time.

On January 27, the day after the poisonings, the police lost a possible chance to nab the mass killer when a careless bank teller at the Itabashi branch of Yasuda Bank cashed the stolen check for 17,405 yen, which had been made out in the name of Toyoji Goto. By the time the bank manager spotted the check with the forged endorsement, the man who cashed it had disappeared.

As police pondered the case, Horizaki decided that the calling cards offered the most promising clue and that it was the same man who had presented the cards at all three banks. Police soon learned that the card bearing the name Dr. Jiro Yamaguchi, which had been presented at the Mitsubishi Bank, was printed in a small shop near the Ginza in Tokyo. But no man by that name—which is as common in Japan as John Smith is in the United States—could be found who had ordered the cards from the shop.

Dr. Shigeru Matsui, a reputable physician living in Sendai, northern Honshu, voluntarily called at the Tokyo police headquarters. He identified the card bearing his name, which had been presented at the Yasuda Bank, as one of his, but reported that he had not presented it at the Yasuda Bank, and had been nowhere near Tokyo when the mass murders at the Teikoku Bank took place.

"I definitely remember ordering one hundred of these cards," Dr. Matsui told police. "They were printed in Sendai prior to a medical meeting."

Dr. Matsui recalled handing out ninety-six cards, which are ordered in lots of one hundred. He had only four left.

Exchanging personal cards in Japan is still a tradition and common practice, an act of respect and courtesy, especially for business and professional men when they meet for the first time. The cards, known as *meishi*, are often kept—some in carefully indexed files—for future reference.

Descriptions of the mass murder given by witnesses to the police left little doubt that "Dr. Yamaguchi" and the man who pretended to be "Dr. Matsui" were one and the same. The man had a mole on his left cheek and a scar under his chin, and witnesses agreed that he was past middle age. From this description police made a composite likeness which was circulated throughout the Japanese archipelago.

For weeks, Police Inspector Horizaki and his detectives checked the information given them by Dr. Matsui of Sendai. It was at this point that Horizaki called in Sergeant Igii.

Assigned at the time to briefing newly recruited police investigators at Tokyo Metropolitan Police headquarters, Igii, forty-three, had gained respect for his interest in and knowledge of calling cards, and indeed had made himself something of an expert on them. Some of his police colleagues even jokingly accused Igii of being an advocate of prognosticating with calling cards, a charge he denied.

Igii says that he joined the police force because he wanted to make a contribution to society by helping alleviate crime, but once he became a policeman he discovered that that is much easier said than done. "I was ready to quit shortly after I became a policeman," he recalls, "but I had signed a five-year contract so I stayed on. Then the war came."

After returning from the war, he found that men who had joined the police force at the time he did had earned promotions while he was in the service for three years. "During my absence," Igii explains, however, "the police department looked after my family, so I felt an obligation when I returned. I made up my mind to remain, determined that I would catch up with my colleagues."

During their tortuous investigation of the poisoned teacups case, the police were to question more than 8,000 persons, and eliminate them one by one. They had Dr. Matsui go back over the calling cards he had received in exchange for his, from the time his cards were printed to the day of the bank murders.

Among his batch of received cards was a *meishi* with the name "Sadamichi Hirasawa," an artist, whose address was given as Otaru, Hokkaido. The card listed Hirasawa as president of several art societies and a recognized artist whose works were accepted by salons without having to be approved by an examining committee.

Dr. Matsui recalled meeting Hirasawa on a ferry between Aomori and Hakodate on a trip back from Hokkaido, Japan's northernmost main island. Matsui said that he had been impressed by the artist, who was carrying a painting titled "Spring is Near," which he said he had painted and was to present to the Crown Prince in Tokyo.

Making a routine check, Horizaki asked the Otaru police to call on Hirasawa at his Hokkaido home. The Otaru police reported back that they found the artist to be in his fifties (an earlier description had said he was in his forties), timid, and a gentlemanly sort of person, an unlikely man to be linked with the bank massacre. After questioning Hirasawa, the Otaru police added, they had cleared him.

The probe dragged on. By April, the investigators had run into a stone wall. Police inspectors from all over Japan gathered in Tokyo to review the case. They sifted through all the data obtained so far and reexamined all the evidence. Once again, a query was sent to Otaru to question Hirasawa, but again the Otaru police reported that they had cleared him completely.

Many of the investigators were ready to commit the case to the "unsolved" file, but Sergeant Igii was determined to battle the odds. A tough, patient detective, he was already known for his bulldoglike tenacity. Once he got his teeth into a case, he refused to yield until he was satisfied that there were no further paths to probe.

As details of the poisoned teacups murders unfolded, Igii recalls telling himself, "This is going to be a tough case that will tax one's patience and ingenuity." The sergeant, a judo expert, was determined to unmask the cool and cunning killer. He decided to go over the case again, step by step, focusing on the calling cards. (He was later to be accused by the defense of being obsessed with calling cards.)

On June 3, Sergeant Igii headed north, his briefcase stuffed with records of the bank poisoning case. At night he strapped his briefcase to one of his legs as a precaution against the records' being stolen while he was asleep.

Igii first set about visiting many of Dr. Matsui's acquaintances, their names drawn from the doctor's file of calling cards. He then called on Hirasawa, although Igii was well aware that the gentle-appearing artist had been removed from the suspect list.

"I had a hunch, call it a premonition," Igii says, "and I simply couldn't get it out of my system."

He arranged to meet Hirasawa through the artist's brother, Sadatoshi Hirasawa, who operates a dairy in Otaru. Igii asked the brother what Sadamichi Hirasawa, the artist, was doing.

"He is home doing nothing," Sadatoshi Hirasawa replied, as he escorted Sergeant Igii to the artist's house. Sadatoshi Hira-sawa asked Igii to wait at the entrance. Several minutes later, the brother returned and ushered the police sergeant upstairs, where he found Sadamichi Hirasawa with his parents. The latter both looked healthy. This was most unusual, Igii thought, since the artist had earlier told his wife and the police in Tokyo, where he maintained a second residence, and where he was also interviewed by the authorities, that he was returning to Otaru because his parents were sick.

Through the sliding door of the next *tatami-* (straw mat) strewn room Igii saw art materials scattered about, paint brushes and canvases, as if Sadamichi Hirasawa had been painting. And yet the painting on the easel looked dry, as did the paint brushes. "He wasn't supposed to be doing anything," Igii reflected to himself. "Why was he trying to pretend?"

Igii recalls that he was particularly impressed by Hirasawa's appearance. Although fifty-seven years old at the time, he looked no more than forty-eight and, to Igii, bore a striking resemblance to the man in the composite police drawing that Igii had brought along from Tokyo. Most striking of all, Hirasawa had a mole on his left cheek and a scar under his chin.

"Strange and more unusual," Igii says, "was the fact that Hirasawa, without being asked, offered an alibi by discussing his whereabouts on the day of the mass murders."

According to Igii, Hirasawa said that he was in Tokyo at the time, where he daily attended a United States-Japan Goodwill Water Color Exhibit held in the exhibition gallery of the Mitsukoshi Department Store at Nihonbashi from January 21 through 28. On January 26, Hirasawa purportedly said, he visited the art exhibit in the morning, called on his son-in-law, Izuo Yamaguchi, at the Maritime Board in Marunouchi in the afternoon and couldn't possibly have got to the Teikoku Bank in Shiina-machi at the time of the robbery-murders. He said he learned of the crime from radio newscasts after reaching his home late that day.

Because Hirasawa had been cleared by the local police of Otaru, Igii, out of deference to them, did not question him further for the moment. The sergeant continued his trip through Hokkaido, asking questions that might lead him to the criminal. Nevertheless, on June 12, Sergeant Igii, before returning to Tokyo, again called on Hirasawa. "There was something about the man," Igii says. "I just couldn't put my finger on it."

The interaction between the Japanese detective and his suspect became a polite test of wills, with all of the formalities being observed.

Igii invited Hirasawa out to dinner, to return courtesies, and asked him for a photograph but was told he didn't have any. That struck the Japanese detective as rather odd, an artist without any photographs of himself. So Igii took some pictures of Hirasawa "as a souvenir."

The detective again asked about Hirasawa's meeting with Dr. Matsui. The artist remembered the meeting aboard the ferry and declared that the doctor had taken a fountain pen from his pocket and written an address on the card that he gave Hirasawa.

Igii asked to see the card. The artist replied, "Sorry, but my wallet was stolen in Tokyo by a pickpocket soon afterward and Dr. Matsui's card and about 11,000 yen were lost."

Igii dropped by Sendai enroute back to Tokyo, and informed Dr. Matsui of Hirasawa's story about the card and Dr. Matsui's supposedly writing on it. The doctor frowned and seemed puzzled. "I never carry a fountain pen," he said.

Another thing that surprised the sergeant was Hirasawa's

knowledge about chemicals, including potassium cyanide, which he had mentioned in casual conversation. "The artist was so well informed on chemicals," Igii said, "far beyond what was needed for a tempera painter, that it was frightening."

Back in Tokyo, Igii submitted his report and photographs to his superiors. Nevertheless, after an exhaustive review and a series of conferences, they again ruled out Hirasawa as a suspect. Homicide Chief Horizaki told Igii that up to that point more than 2,000 suspects in the bank poisonings case had been arrested, questioned and cleared. This had touched off a storm of criticism in the Japanese news media and the general public demanding that the police respect civil rights—an ideal unheard of in prewar Japan. Under the nation's new democratic constitution, police had to act with extra care to avoid being accused of using prewar militant tactics. Japanese police therefore had become extremely sensitive about any charge of ignoring personal rights or of otherwise being undemocratic. In Hirasawa's case, Igii's superiors concluded that Hirasawa was a reputable artist, with no criminal record. Moreover, in contrast to Igii's opinion, top investigators insisted that the photographs of Hirasawa's face did not resemble the features of the "wanted man" in the composite likeness circulated throughout the country.

Igii was crestfallen. He was told, however, that if he wished to pursue his line of sleuthing in the case he could do so on his own, so long as he did not embarrass headquarters. His superiors said frankly that they were backing off from the case, but promised that if Igii uncovered fresh evidence they would reopen the investigation.

Igii took them at their word. He was confident that he was on the right track. Since then he has disclosed that he was, at the time, even about to sell his house for 350,000 yen (about 1,000 dollars) to cover his expenses. Police headquarters, however, moved by his stubborn determination, agreed to give him an allowance of 70,000 yen, enough to last him for seventy days. Then he was on his own.

"I was convinced I was finally tracking the right suspect," Igii says, "so I decided to go it alone."

After more long hours of additional homework on the case

at headquarters, Igii decided to keep watch on Hirasawa's Tokyo house. He also commenced a painstaking checkup on the artist's friends and mode of life. He questioned Hirasawa's neighbors, filling a pocket notebook with names, places, and events, noting in particular his movements. Igii even called on the artist's wife, Masa Hirasawa, and his daughter. The painstaking investigator also obtained samples of Hirasawa's handwriting from postcards and letters and had them checked and compared by a handwriting expert with the signature on the check cashed the day after the teacups murders. They were adjudged to be the handwriting of the same person.

With this and other evidence in hand, Sergeant Igii once again approached Inspector Horizaki to report his latest findings and to ask for a warrant of arrest. Igii had also unearthed two important facts:

One: On February 9, Mrs. Masa Hirasawa had deposited 44,500 yen in her husband's bank account. Until two days before January 26, Hirasawa had been unable to pay even a 150-yen bill or to meet his dues to an art society. She explained that her husband had given her a total of 69,000 yen in three installments.

Two: Hirasawa was keeping two mistresses and they were pressing him for money.

Sergeant Igii got his arrest warrant and on August 20, armed with it, he left Tokyo for Otaru. There, almost seven months after the teacups massacre, he arrested Sadamichi Hirasawa.

Igii had the artist handcuffed to two fellow detectives who had accompanied Igii on his mission. He attempted to bring Hirasawa back in secrecy, but the news media learned of the artist's arrest and ignited renewed criticism about alleged violation of human rights guaranteed in the new constitution.

There was criticism about Hirasawa's being handcuffed. Igii points out that he was responsible for bringing Hirasawa safely back to Tokyo. To be sure, the detective concedes, under postwar jurisprudence Hirasawa was innocent until proven guilty. But, Igii adds, he had to prevent the possibility that the artist might suddenly decide to take his own life by jumping off a ferry or train.

A huge crowd turned out at Tokyo's Ueno Station to catch a

glimpse of Hirasawa, while public opinion for and against the artist began building up. Some said he was a victim of a miscarriage of justice and was being railroaded in disregard of his civil rights, that such a gentleman could not possibly have been involved in such a nefarious crime as Japan's mass-poisoning case.

Yet the evidence continued to build. After obtaining a search warrant, police later found in Hirasawa's Tokyo home a brown suit and a loose-fitting white coat similar to those worn by the poison-murderer, and a small, black leather bag resembling the killer's kit. Two of the poisoning survivors positively identified Hirasawa as the killer.

At police headquarters Hirasawa continued to maintain his innocence. Igii asked Hirasawa where he got his money, purposely not mentioning what money he, Igii, was trying to trace.

"From the president of Iino Industrial Company, Mr. Uzo Hanada," Hirasawa replied.

"When?" Igii asked.

"Last October," the suspect responded. That was three months before the bank murders and robbery.

Igii pulled out his pocket notebook, flipped the pages, suddenly whirled around to Hirasawa and demanded, "How could that be? Hanada died in August."

Igii recalls that Hirasawa's face paled. He stammered and was unable to explain the discrepancy in his story.

Hirasawa later described Sergeant Igii as an *onikeiji*, or "devil detective," with the cunning of a cat. The artist insisted that he had been tricked by the detective's wiles and pretensions of being a friend.

While in custody, Hirasawa made three attempts to commit suicide, including slashing his left wrist with a pen snatched from a police officer's desk and by taking an overdose of pills for hemorrhoids.

Hirasawa finally confessed. At the time, the artist offered prayers for the dead, explaining that he was bothered by their ghosts which made it difficult for him to sleep. He also asked that he be killed with potassium cyanide.

Nevertheless, his lawyers later repudiated the confession, claiming that it was extracted from Hirasawa under duress, and denied that he said anything about ghosts or potassium cyanide.

On October 12, 1948, Hirasawa was charged with robbery, attempted murder, forging official papers, and premeditated murder.

The police had spent 6 million yen, or the equivalent of 17,000 U.S. dollars—more than had been expended to apprehend any other single criminal suspect in Japan's history—before Hirasawa was charged. Police had also questioned and cleared 8,796 persons.

The trial opened on December 10, 1948, in the Tokyo lower court before a panel of three judges and no jury.

A legal sensation of postwar Japan, the trial was the first major case brought before the Japanese court system since General MacArthur had had Japan cast off its system of French jurisprudence, adopted during the early 1900s.

During the trial, which lasted fifteen months, Hirasawa denied all charges and declared he was innocent. He told the court that his confession had been forced out of him by brutal police investigators. "I felt as if I'd been hypnotized," he protested. His lawyers also demanded psychiatric tests because Hirasawa was suffering from Korsakov's syndrome, which was said to have been caused by anti-dog-rabies injections he had been given in 1925. Psychiatric tests were dutifully made, but the court said that Hirasawa had been found sane.

Public Procurator Takagi entered as evidence an 8-mm film made of Hirasawa demonstrating to police investigators how he assertedly administered doses of potassium cyanide in the teacups that were gulped down by his victims.

The prosecutor thundered, "Neither heaven nor earth could forgive a man who had undertaken such a dastardly crime after two unsuccessful attempts."

The defense, summing up its case in a four-day presentation, insisted that all evidence submitted by the prosecution was circumstantial.

"The defendant, Hirasawa," the defense said, "lacks the moral and intellectual elements necessary for such a crime as he is charged with, for his is a most loving heart and alien to the callous cruelty that was required to do what he is alleged to have done."

The defense attorneys added, "He is most considerate to his parents and is known to have been a loving father. Moreover, he is an old man of 57 without any strong desire apart from painting, a timid and fainthearted person.

"The poison used must be the most powerful evidence in a poisoning case but the prosecution has failed to show just how the alleged poisoner obtained the potassium cyanide.... The judgment of the handwriting expert regarding Hirasawa's supposed hand on the check is not scientifically tenable."

Hirasawa, dressed in an olive-drab *kokuminfuku*—the national wartime civilian uniform—sat through the marathon arguments impassively.

On the final day of the trial he changed his dress. He appeared in court in a ceremonial masculine *kimono*, consisting of a dark formal *haori* coat with the family crest, dark *hakama* skirt, white *tabi* socks and zori sandals. The ceremonial costume did not help him. Hirasawa was found guilty and sentenced by Presiding Judge Kiyoo Eriguchi to death by hanging.

When the verdict was read, Hirasawa startled the crowd of 100 jammed into the small courtroom by jumping up and shouting, "A frameup! A great wrong has been done!"

His eyebrows were raised and his face twitched.

Judge Eriguchi, in a 150-page decision, noted that Hirasawa had "achieved a certain renown as an artist, having had his works accepted for the coveted *Teiten* [a noted art society] exhibition a dozen times."

Added the judge, "When he began to slip owing to a brain disease [Korsakov's syndrome] occasioned by a rabies-preventive injection in 1925, he took to deceiving other people and himself with all sorts of lies.

"Even when his works began to be rejected and no one would buy them, he told his family and mistresses (he kept two) that he had rich patrons and had considerable income. In order to keep up this pretense, he thought he would get rich quick by staging a bank robbery or something."

By chance, the judge continued, Hirasawa obtained a name

card from Dr. Shigeru Matsui, "and this he used in his first
attempt at potassium cyanide poisoning at a bank and quick get-
away with the booty." He failed in two attempts, the judge said,
but succeeded on his third try "to take twelve innocent lives.
Four survived to tell the tale."

Hirasawa, continuing to denounce the trial and the sentence
in Oriental hyperbole, later told newsmen through his lawyers
that "if the trial were fair my innocence would have been established." "The court and the police," he added, "displayed their
fangs. . . . They tried to melt the snow of purity and innocence
and, instead, exposed their own ugly character. But the flames of
justice will not be extinguished." The true criminal, the artist
vowed, would be caught by the "grace of Buddha."

After exhaustive reviews of the case and appeals by Hirasawa,
the Tokyo Higher Court on September 29, 1951, rejected Hirasawa's appeal, as did the Supreme Court of Japan on April 6,
1955, after reviewing 71,200 pages of testimony.

But even though two decades have passed, Hirasawa's death
warrant—for reasons that have never been spelled out—has not
been signed. Nor has it been stamped with a seal by the justice
minister for official authorization to clear the decks for his hanging.

Today, Sadamichi Hirasawa, now more than 80 years old, still
sits in his cell in a prison in Sendai, northern Japan, a short
walk from the gallows. The *Guinness Book of World Records*
lists his case as the world's slowest execution.

Hirasawa spends his time composing poetry and painting still
lifes, which some compare to the works of Paul Cézanne. He has
painted more than 850 works in prison, which have been circulated by a Tokyo-based "Save Hirasawa Society" seeking his release. Although a Buddhist, Hirasawa reads the Bible. He continues to insist he is innocent, hopes some day to leave prison a
free man, run in general elections for the Upper House of Parliament, and to fight, he says, for men like himself, convicted of
what he calls false charges.

Mrs. Masako Murata Takeuchi, one of the two women who
survived the poisoned-teacups robbery, who sounded the alarm,
maintains that Hirasawa was not the man who walked into the

bank that wintry day and ordered those present to drink from teacups containing cyanide. (Weeks after the crime, she married Riichi Takeuchi, a reporter for the Tokyo newspaper *Yomiuri Shimbun*, who sneaked into the hospital room in which she was recovering disguised as an intern for an interview that resulted in a scoop.)

After Hirasawa was charged in the bank murders case, Igii was promoted from the rank of sergeant to that of police inspector. He was transferred to the Ikegami precinct station in April 1949 and was then made an instructor at the police academy. In April 1952 he was recalled to the Metropolitan Police Department's homicide division.

Inspector Igii, who retired from the Tokyo Metropolitan Police Department on March 20, 1964, says that he has no doubt of Hirasawa's guilt. "It was my toughest case," Igii reminisces. "It was especially difficult because my superiors were reluctant to acknowledge my findings," which, he points out, forced him to battle opposition among his police colleagues, shore up his confidence in himself, and go it alone until he dug up and pieced together what he considered to be conclusive evidence.

Hirasawa was not a repugnant fellow, Igii says, but "he was clever, too clever, and you had to be constantly on the watch that you didn't let your guard down."

"I had confidence and faith in myself," Igii says. "Both are invaluable factors in police detective work, even today despite computers and modern-day scientific methods. Other factors that make a good detective are a probing mind, tenacity, being articulate, legwork, and maintaining a cool presence at all times."

Since his retirement, Igii has been almost as busy as when he was on active duty. He is often called upon to give lectures to police officers, and writes occasional articles for investigative community professional magazines.

Igii's philosophy is never to take things for granted, never take another man's word as such. "Find out for yourself," he advises.

"The first time I met Hirasawa," Igii recalls, "I didn't feel that he was the killer. I didn't assume that he was. My job was to start from the beginning. Hirasawa was innocent until I dug up evidence that indicated he wasn't."

The inspector adds, "Detectives before me assumed that Hirasawa, being an artist, did not have any knowledge of potassium cyanide. They investigated but did not probe deeply enough. I was determined to find out how much he knew about potassium cyanide and what I learned from Hirasawa himself indicated that he was no amateur in his knowledge of poisons."

Summing up the case of the teacups and calling cards, the Japanese super sleuth reiterates with firm conviction, "There was no mistake. I am confident that the calling cards were the key factor in solving the case, and I am convinced that Hirasawa, although I feel sorry for him, was guilty of the mass murders."

4

Archives of Hell

THE ARGENTINE *colectivo*, a dilapidated city bus, ground to a halt at a street corner in the suburb of Buenos Aires. It was mid-May. The work-weary passengers stepped off into the chilling air of a fall evening in a land where the seasons are reversed from those in the Northern Hemisphere. Standing in the gloom, illuminated only by flickering street lights, they waited until the *colectivo* lurched away on its run.

One of the passengers started walking toward his nearby home, a starkly bare brick structure which housed his German wife and children. In his mid-fifties, the man appeared older than his years. His droopy-nosed face was marked by hollow cheeks that betrayed years of living in terror.

In the dim light, the solitary figure never saw the speeding sedan until it was too late. The car screeched to a momentary stop. Two pairs of powerful arms seized the man and hurled him into the vehicle, which roared away before the startled victim could even yell for help.

Hours later, coming out of a drug-induced sleep, Adolf Eichmann gazed with fear into the eyes of his Israeli captors. "Which one of you" he is said to have asked plaintively, "is Tuvia Friedman?"

Tuvia Friedman was not among the secret agents who kidnaped Eichmann that chill evening in Buenos Aires. But the commandos knew well the man who had plotted for fifteen years to hunt down Adolf Eichmann—the former *Schutzstaffel* (SS) colonel who was Hitler's chief executioner of Jews during World War II.

Eichmann was spirited aboard an Israeli airliner and clandestinely flown to Tel Aviv, where he stood trial before the world and was hanged for his role in Nazi Germany's extermination of six million Jews.

Before his execution Eichmann told acquaintances that he had lived in constant terror of being killed, but had never dreamed of being kidnaped. Since the war he had constantly been on the move, traveling from country to country, from city to city. He changed jobs, he changed names. His few friends said that he saw assassins around every corner. He grew gaunt, nervous, bald. He tried to shroud his life in middle-class obscurity. His oldest son thought Eichmann was his uncle.

"As the years rolled by," one acquaintance related, "Eichmann began to cling more and more to the hope that he would be forgotten. But his terror never really subsided."

And Adolf Eichmann never could banish from his mind the spectre of his most tenacious enemy—Tuvia Friedman.

A Polish-born Jew, Friedman survived a concentration camp to dedicate the rest of his life to being a special brand of detective with a singular mission—the search for an elusive army of former black-uniformed SS and Gestapo officers who had annihilated two-thirds of all European Jewry. Over the course of his career, Friedman has been credited with tracking down more than 7,000 Nazi war criminals and bringing them to justice, either in prison or at the end of a rope.

Eichmann was Friedman's prize catch. But he also hunted

down, among others high in Hitler's hierarchy, the deputy of Gestapo Chief Heinrich Himmler, and one of the most powerful state secretaries of Nazi Germany. Friedman declares that he can smell Nazi criminals like a trained dog can smell hashish.

Friedman has been called a fanatic, obsessed, cruel, vengeful, judicious, tender, driven, egotistical. There is, however, no one word that sums up this detective who hunts his prey around the world. Friedman is a tangle of fierce emotions and uncanny ability that astonishes his admirers—and keeps Nazi criminals on the run.

Nazi Hunter Tuvia Friedman, who was responsible in great part for the collection of evidence that resulted in charges of genocide being levied against Eichmann, is pictured in the Haifa, Israel, Documentation Center of Nazi War Crimes, of which Friedman is the director. (*Wide World*)

Friedman is a short, wiry man with intense, deeply recessed blue eyes. He has a low, flat forehead and a bald pate. He has been bald since his early twenties when he lost his straight blond hair after a bout with typhus.

His personality is intense—one moment jovial, quick-talking and light, the next minute submerged into a quiet reminiscence of things past. When he is aggressive, it is the aggressiveness of a small man who has to prove he is as good as the big guys. When he is quiet, it is the quiet of a small boy lost in reflection on a cruel childhood.

To understand Tuvia Friedman, why he devotes his life to hunting Nazis, and why he has been so successful, one must understand his origins and his experiences under the Germans.

Friedman was born in 1922 in Radom, Poland. His father was a printer, his mother a seamstress. He was seventeen years old, fresh out of high school, when the Nazis invaded Poland and plunged Europe into another world war. The Jews of Radom were kicked out of schools and their professions and pressed into a ghetto.

Tuvia Friedman was taken away and forced to work as a slave laborer for the SS on the Russian front, building fortifications. After a year, he escaped and returned to Radom, only to be forced to work for the Wehrmacht, loading trucks with food and medical supplies for German troops. The Wehrmacht (the regular Germany army) was not as cruel as the SS. Friedman was able to receive his food without the beatings he had received at the front.

Friedman's father contracted typhus and died. Tuvia tried to get permission to bury him, but the Germans refused. Jews were meant to rot unburied, the Germans told him. They also told the youth he had better not miss any work.

Friedman worked twelve hours a day, while his mother sold all her sewing machinery to have enough money to buy her food.

One day, while Tuvia was at work, the Germans rounded up his younger brother and sister and his mother, and sent them to the Treblinka concentration camp where they died. Friedman came home to find only his older sister Bella, a nurse, alive. The Nazis allowed her to continue working at a Jewish hospital, and

Tuvia continued to load food and medical supplies until the spring of 1943.

Then the Nazi occupiers received orders to round up Jews in earnest for deportation to the death camps. The "final solution" was in full swing.

The Nazis used many excuses to lure Jews out of their homes and make them report to the local train station. Promising them they were being shipped to Palestine, or pledging that they were exchanging Jews for German soldiers in British prisons, they cut down the Jewish population in Radom from 30,000 to less than 5,000 in a few months.

Friedman and his sister were ordered to report for one of the Nazis' "prisoner exchanges" in the early summer. Tuvia and Bella boarded one of several buses—their bus was the second in the convoy—and proceeded toward the train station.

But when they arrived at an intersection where they would have had to turn right to go to the station, the buses turned left and drove out into the countryside. The caravan of buses proceeded for a half hour until they reached a point approximately thirty kilometers from Radom. There, the buses stopped. An SS colonel named Kappke ordered everyone out of the first bus. The Jews were ordered to strip off their clothes and line up in front of a ditch.

Then the shooting began—machine guns, pistols, rifles. Hand grenades were also used.

With the first busload of Jews dead, the SS men came to Friedman's bus and ordered everybody out. Bella jumped out and pleaded with Kappke to allow them to live. She was a nurse, she said, and her brother a laborer.

Kappke stood her off to one side and told her he would see when the shooting was finished. It was all over in twenty-five minutes. Friedman, his sister, and eighteen others were taken back to the Radom concentration camp and told that their lives were saved as a present from Hitler. The Führer had had a birthday, Kappke explained.

Bella was put to work in a refinery while Tuvia loaded coal, meal, and potatoes in sacks weighing 200 pounds for twelve hours a day. Tuvia twice tried unsuccessfully to escape. A third attempt was successful. He and a few other inmates tunneled out of the camp and tried to join Polish partisans. But the Poles turned out to be viciously anti-Semitic. The escapees learned that if it was discovered they were Jews, the Poles would turn them over to the Nazis for a reward of twenty-five grams of bread.

Tuvia lived in the woods for weeks. Meanwhile, the sound of advancing Russian guns on the eastern front grew louder. Near the Nazis' forward lines Friedman was captured again by the Germans but he killed his guard, slicing his throat with a concealed bayonet. He escaped once again.

The Russians liberated the Radom camp. Friedman wandered through the tableau of destruction that was once his home town of Radom. He went to the Soviet military authorities occupying Poland and asked to be sent to the war front inside Germany, where the Nazis were making their last-ditch stand around Berlin. Instead, the Russians sent him to Danzig to learn the art of hunting down Nazi war criminals.

In Danzig Tuvia was put in charge of a bureau overseeing several other investigators under the command of Soviet General Gregor Koczinsky. The job of the bureau was to weed out Nazis hiding in the area and arrest them. While in Danzig, utilizing captured German documents and the sworn testimonies of eyewitnesses, Friedman prepared conclusive cases against 5,000 Nazi war criminals, among them SS General Kurt Becher; his deputy, SS Lt. Col. Wilhelm Blum; and Danzig's Roman Catholic Cardinal Splet, an intimate acquaintance of Hitler. It was in Danzig too that Friedman caught up with SS Colonel Kappke and arrested him. The Russians later tried Kappke and hanged him.

Friedman's methods of investigation combined explosive emotion with mechanical efficiency. He sometimes lost control and beat his suspects—he even moved into the local prison where Nazis were being held in order to perform his duties faster and more efficiently. At other times he would coolly dispatch his findings to his Russian commanders, knowing that the results spelled Siberia—or worse—as the Nazis' last destination.

By 1946, Friedman felt he had had enough of Nazi-hunting

in Poland. The war had disfigured the memories of his homeland and destroyed his allegiance. As a Jew, he decided that his place was in Palestine helping in the struggle to create a Jewish state.

Friedman resigned from his investigative post with the Russians in April 1946 and went to Vienna where he contacted agents of the Haganah, Israel's pre-state underground army. Asher Ben-Nathan, later Israel's ambassador to France, gave Friedman two jobs. The first: to work as an agent, spying on Arab arms movements. The second: to continue his work hunting down Nazi war criminals, as a service to his fellow Jews.

It was in Vienna, in that same year 1946, that the hunt for Adolf Eichmann began.

Friedman recalls, "Asher gave me a list of the 700 most-wanted Nazis. He told me, 'Please find as many as you can.' From that list, I found 250. But the most important for me was Eichmann."

With the rank of SS colonel, Eichmann had been placed in charge of carrying out Hitler's "final solution" to the Jewish question. It was Eichmann who had issued orders for roundups, deportations, slave labor, mass shootings, and finally the gassing of Jewish victims. It was Eichmann who had ordered the construction of the infamous Auschwitz death camp. And it was Eichmann who had directed that the hair of Jews be cut off and used to stuff mattresses, that Jews' gold teeth be yanked out and melted into bars, and that the body fat of Jewish victims be boiled down and made into soap. In all, Eichmann was held responsible for the murder of four million Jews.

Working out of Vienna, Friedman spent months searching for clues to Eichmann's whereabouts. He interviewed former German prisoners in American, French, and Russian prisoner-of-war camps. He went to movies showing dated newsreels of high-ranking Nazi officers visiting their death camps, hoping to catch a glimpse of a man whose face Friedman had never seen.

The first break came when Austrian police gave Friedman a document bearing Eichmann's signature. The document not only put the initial piece of a jigsaw puzzle in place, but amounted to a piece of concrete evidence against Eichmann. The document had authorized the deportation of 50,000 Hungarian Jews to a Polish death camp.

Friedman still had little idea what Eichmann looked like. Nevertheless, Tuvia knew an industrialist friend who had bargained with Eichmann for Jewish lives in the early years of the war, and so knew that he could get verification if he could find a picture.

Friedman finally obtained a photo of his prey in 1947. The means by which Tuvia did so were characteristic of his cunning. While interrogating Eichmann's former chauffeur, Joseph Wiesl, Friedman discovered that one of Eichmann's numerous mistresses lived near Linz. In all probability, Tuvia conjectured, she had a photo of her SS lover. Friedman dispatched a German-born Israeli agent to "befriend" her. He was young and handsome, and the woman, a Frau Missenbach, was still an elegant, curvacious female in her forties.

They met in a cafe, and soon the agent became a regular caller at her home. One day she showed him her photo album. There was a picture of her with a thin, aquiline-nosed SS officer.

"Who is that?" he asked.

"Oh, someone I knew during the war. He is not important," she replied.

The agent telephoned word of the photograph to Friedman, who arranged for the police to conduct a secret search of her home. During the search, they removed the photograph of Eichmann without her knowledge.

Tuvia's industrialist friend verified the fact that Eichmann was the SS officer in the picture. It had been taken in 1939. Surely Eichmann's appearance had changed since then but at least there was something to start on.

The search for Adolf Eichmann lost momentum temporarily as the reality of Israel's statehood drew closer, and with it the threat of an Arab-Israeli war. Friedman suspended his Nazi-hunting to devote full time to espionage operations against Arabs buying arms in Vienna. When war broke out in the Middle East in 1948, Friedman was instructed to stay in the Austrian capital and continue his work for the Israeli secret service.

Thus, when the war ended in 1949, Friedman was no closer to finding Eichmann. The Nazi mass murderer seemed to have vanished more completely than ever.

Nevertheless, Friedman doggedly resumed his search. In 1950 he discovered that Eichmann's wife and three children were living in the Austrian resort town of Bad Ausee—an exciting and promising revelation. Tuvia suggested to Asher Ben-Nathan an audacious and cold-blooded plan: kidnap the children and kill them unless Frau Eichmann revealed her husband's whereabouts. Ben-Nathan rejected the scheme and instead sent a team of Israeli agents to monitor the movements of the Eichmann family.

Friedman claims that the agents were clumsy and harassed the family to the point that they mysteriously disappeared. Friedman had lost his most important lead.

He continued his hunt for Eichmann for two more years but was then replaced in Vienna. In 1952 Friedman married and moved to his new homeland of Israel.

There, Friedman and his bride found life far from easy. The fledgling country was poor, crowded with immigrants, and still trying to pull itself out of the trauma of the 1948 war. Jobs were at a minimum, and more than half the population was living in tents. Tuvia tried to join the police force but was turned down. Finally, he got a job as director of the Haifa branch of the Jerusalem-based Yad Vashem Memorial to the victims of the Nazi holocaust.

With national problems of development, living standards, and security to worry about, government and popular interest in Israel in tracking down Nazi war criminals was waning. There was a country to be built and many Jews, while never forgetting the ashes of the past, wanted to embark upon their new lives. Not so Tuvia Friedman. Restless and irrepressible, driven by the nightmare-memories of his experiences under the Nazis, he resumed his pursuit of Eichmann.

Friedman was fired from his Yad Vashem position because he used his office to continue his hunt. Yad Vashem's purpose was to honor the six million, not to avenge them, he was told.

Frustrated with the "short memories" of his own people, and notwithstanding lack of cooperation from the Israeli government, Tuvia refused to be deterred. He started what he called the Haifa Documentation Center for the purpose of amassing further evidence against the Nazis. His wife, Anna, an eye surgeon at a Haifa clinic, supported him while Friedman carried on his investigations, compiling more documents and more pictures, and following new leads.

Eichmann continued to be Friedman's special target. He appealed to the Israeli government for funds, part of which would be used to offer a reward for information leading to Eichmann's capture. But Tuvia's old Haganah boss, Asher Ben-Nathan, now a high-ranking foreign ministry official, turned Friedman down.

In 1959, the West German government opened its Central Office for Prosecution of Nazi War Crimes, headquartered in Ludwigsburg. Friedman quickly established contact with the director of the office, Dr. Erwin Schuele, sent Schuele documentary evidence, reports, files, photographs, affidavits, eyewitness testimonies—all to be used by local prosecutors in German courts who were preparing cases against former SS and Gestapo officials.

Friedman later described his relationship with Schuele. "He would write, asking if I had evidence against specific Nazis charged with murders in certain cities, especially in Eastern Europe. I would send him, in most cases, the full information he required. When I did not have the information he needed, I would have the [Israeli] newspapers publish a notice reading, in effect: 'If you were in city X during the years 1941 to 1945 and can furnish information about war crimes committed at that time, contact the Haifa Center for the documentation of Nazi war crimes.' Then there would follow letters, phone calls and personal visits from survivors of concentration camps and ghettos, which I carefully screened, put together and rushed to Ludwigsburg. My office bulged with statements and affidavits, far more than the number of Nazi criminals who were being brought to trial."

While Friedman and Schuele worked together to convict many lesser Nazi criminals, there were still no new leads on Eichmann. Then, later in 1959, Friedman received a tip that Eichmann was living in Kuwait. Tuvia had no proof that the story was true but decided to leak it to the press. It was an election year in Israel, and if he could arouse public opinion enough to make Eichmann's capture an issue, the government might renew its efforts to find Eichmann.

The story did indeed inflame Israel's populace. Israelis suddenly wanted to know why nothing was being done to capture the Nazi monster. Foreign Ministry officials belatedly invited Friedman to give them a report, while simultaneously asking him to stop publicizing new developments in the Eichmann case. Friedman gave his report but refused to keep quiet. In the fall of 1959, speaking at a pre-election rally in Tel Aviv, Friedman entreated Prime Minister David Ben-Gurion to throw the government's resources behind a drive to capture Eichmann.

Then, acting on his own, Friedman published notices in the world press announcing that the Israeli government would pay $10,000 to anyone offering information leading to the capture of Adolf Eichmann.

"My mail was filled with letters from every part of the world," he later recalled. "An anonymous postcard in a bold hand from Germany said, 'You'll never get Eichmann, never, never!' It was signed with a series of Xs. Someone in New Zealand wrote to me saying that there was a man living in a hilltop house, all alone, who never ventured out of his home, never talked to anyone, and he must surely be Eichmann. I read and reread my mail, and sorted the letters. It was like a poker game: here was a good card for you, and a bad card for another. Possible straight, possible flush. Possible. Possible."

Then Friedman received a letter, dated October 18, from Buenos Aires, Argentina.

Eichmann, the letter said, "does not live in Kuwait, but in the vicinity of Buenos Aires under an assumed name with his wife and children, in a house of his own, where he very cautiously, with much money and clever maneuvering, has managed to keep out of the public eye."

The letter concluded, "I am in a position to furnish your institute with precise dates and exact material, and I stand prepared to clear up this case completely, provided, however, the strictest secrecy is observed. . . . Sincerely, Lothar Herman."

Friedman contacted the Israeli secret service and made arrangements with Herman, a blind Jew whose daughter was dating one of Eichmann's sons, to hand over the information to an Israeli agent who would visit Herman soon.

A long period of silence followed. On March 28, 1960, the blind man wrote to say that he had received an Israeli agent at Christmastime and turned over his details on Eichmann.

Two months later, on May 23, 1960, Israel announced that its secret agents had captured Eichmann and flown him to Israel to stand trial for crimes against the Jewish people.

After fifteen years, Friedman had finally put Eichmann behind bars.

In December 1961, the gaunt, fear-ravaged Nazi was found guilty of mass murder. Five months later he was executed. His trial had taught an entire generation of young Israelis the horrors of the holocaust, put 2,000 years of Jewish persecution into perspective, and sent Jewish soldiers into the 1967 Mideast war with an unmistakable picture of what their defeat could mean.

Friedman considers his next-greatest success the apprehension of SS General Karl Wolf. Wolf at one point during the war headed the Gestapo and, under orders from Himmler, ordered the transportation of Jews to death camps.

Friedman brought about Wolf's demise by pursuing an enigmatic clue: a series of documents signed with a mysterious "W." The first, dated August 13, 1942, was a letter sent from the Führer's headquarters to the chief of German railways, Dr. Albert Ganzenmuller, expressing "joy" that during the preceding two weeks, a train filled with 5,000 members of the "chosen people" had been sent daily to Treblinka. The letter added the observation that "cattle trucks are good enough for Jews." It was signed "W."

Friedman linked "W" to Wolf by uncovering a second, earlier letter, dated July 28, 1942, informing SS *Obergruppenführer* Wolf that 5,000 Warsaw Jews were being transported daily to Treblinka.

Friedman checked out Wolf in a "black book" that had been maintained by the Nazis containing the names of 15,000 officers of the SS and the Gestapo. Wolf was there, No. 47 in the SS hierarchy, just two numbers below Hitler's own deputy, Martin Bormann.

Then, by dint of painstaking checking, Friedman found Wolf's name in the Munich telephone directory. The ex-SS officer was alive and free, living in a villa outside the city in the suburb of Kempenhausen. Wolf's villa contained a private park and a private lake. As a retired general, he received a monthly pension of 5,000 marks from the West German government.

Friedman decided that, since Eichmann's capture, public opinion could be of great importance in a case such as Wolf's. Wolf would have to be publicly compromised. The German public would learn that he had been a general in the SS, not the "fighting general" he passed himself off to be.

Friedman dispatched a young Israeli journalist, Uri Dan, to Munich armed with Friedman's entire file on Wolf. Dan telephoned Wolf for an interview, explaining only that he was a foreign newsman and had come a long way to talk with him. Wolf was amenable. Dan arrived with a photographer and met the general as he emerged from a morning swim in his lake.

The reporter then revealed that he had come from Israel and that he wished to hear details about the extermination of Jews by the SS.

The general paled visibly, excused himself, and hurriedly retired to his villa, promising that he would dress and return to answer questions.

When he emerged, Wolf denied any knowledge of the Nazi exterminations and asserted that he had been a fighting general on the Russian front and had had nothing to do with Jews.

Dan subsequently wrote a story for the West German magazine *Stern*, describing the feelings of an Israeli who had visited Germany for the first time. He told of his visit with former SS General Wolf, and cited Friedman's documents to show what the general had actually done—how he had aided Nazi genocide by obtaining trains for transporting Jews to the death camps, how he had also been involved in arranging Jewish slave labor for the I. G. Farben munitions factories and the Auschwitz concentration camp.

Then he described the general's quiet, idyllic life in his private villa, presented to him by Hitler.

The public outcry was explosive. Wolf was arrested in January 1962, tried, and sentenced to fifteen years' imprisonment.

Tuvia Friedman feels that his greatest defeat is his failure to capture Gestapo Chief Heinrich Mueller. Friedman unearthed what was believed to be Mueller's grave in Germany, but discovered that the corpse in the casket was not Mueller's, but that of a Wehrmacht private.

"Mueller is smarter than me. He's more clever ... stronger," Friedman says. "I haven't the slightest notion of his whereabouts. He's simply vanished."

Still, Friedman says, he has lain awake many a night wondering about Heinrich Mueller.

Another disappointment is Joseph Mengele, the monstrous "doctor" of Auschwitz. It was Mengele who decided who was to live and who was to die, as he sorted out arriving Jews for the gas chambers or the work camps. It was Mengele who carried out such experiments as attempting to change brown eyes to "Aryan" blue.

Friedman claims that he knows where the phantomlike Mengele is and could have him abducted from his South American hideout if the Israeli government would only pay $50,000 to the informants.

The Israeli government has taken the position that one Nazi war crimes trial is enough, and has refused to help in Mengele's capture. Nonetheless, a wealthy American who was a victim of Mengele's barbarism and a Jewish organization have both offered to pay the reward, and Friedman refuses to comment further on his hunt for Mengele.

Martin Bormann? "As far as I'm concerned, he's dead," Friedman says. "I agree with the German report that he died near Hitler's bunker during the last days of Berlin."

Friedman is also distressed with what he regards as the light sentences that Nazis receive from West German courts. "These men are responsible for the murder of millions of people and they get a few years in jail. You call that justice?"

What are Tuvia Friedman's methods of investigation? How has this diminutive Polish Jew managed to track down and help convict so many Nazi criminals? Does he think of himself as a detective?

He most definitely considers himself nothing if not a detective. He points out that he was trained formally in criminal investigation by the Russians in Danzig immediately after the war. In Israel, he is known as one of the most thorough and hard-working investigators concerned with the continuing search for Nazi war criminals.

"My principal method is maintaining a very strong will," Friedman says. "Secondly, I have a magnetic attraction to Nazi criminals. The second I sense him, I'm running after him. Some people have talent to be good doctors, businessmen, or lawyers. They have it in their fingers. I'm luckier—I have my talent in my whole body."

To make his cases against Nazis, nevertheless, Friedman must have more than a sixth sense. He must have proof—such tangible proof as documents, photographs, and, most importantly, eye-witness testimony. He received many of his documents from the Allies after the war, others he had to search for all over the continent of Europe—in offices, homes, and in the ruins of battle. He uses to good advantage the central registration office in West Germany—where every West German is registered. Yet, because many Nazis have familiar German names, more legwork is required to find out, for example, which "Wilhelm Blum" is the correct one. Friedman also gathers photographs—from film clippings, family albums, World War II historical societies, newspapers and feature agencies, and private photographers.

Eyewitness statements are the hardest to come by, Friedman says. Many witnesses to Nazi brutality are dead, and many survivors are reluctant to come forth to testify for fear of reviving in their minds the horrors of their experiences. One woman witness died and scores collapsed in hysterics while testifying at Eichmann's trial.

Still and all, through lists of survivors compiled by the Allies and the Israelis, and by word-of-mouth and public announcements, Friedman's Haifa Documentation Center bulges with the sworn testimony of concentration camp survivors. When Friedman concludes that he has enough evidence to convict a Nazi suspect, he compiles his information and sends it off to the prosecutor seeking extradition or conviction.

Interestingly, many of Friedman's tipoffs come from former Gestapo and SS men—as in the realm of common criminality, where detectives often receive their tips from the underworld. Nazi criminals, Friedman maintains, turn in their friends so they won't have to go to prison alone.

"They like to stick together," he says.

"Sometimes they are so stupid, so cowardly. I've had Nazis crying on their knees before me, pleading for mercy. And if you happen to touch one of them, he literally shits in his pants. After they are caught, they are like children."

Commenting on his own complex motivations, Friedman insists, "It's not revenge. If I wanted revenge, I would go to their homes and hideouts and kill them myself." Yet he has described his investigations for the Russian Colonel Koczinsky as "working for revenge." And, when reminiscing about his year in Danzig, he repeatedly mentions "beating my prisoners, like they beat me," and the "fine feeling I would get after a day's work."

But then there is Tuvia Friedman, the idealist, the Pole who miraculously lived through it all and still cannot understand or accept why it happened, why his family died—and why he lived. He admits the guilt of the living.

"There are still nightmares," he says.

Then why does he continue? What makes this man bury himself in archives of hell?

"I tried other work, but I always came back to this. I tried being a reporter, but it just didn't work. . . . It is my right. Someone has to do it, and I am the one. I can't forget what happened and I must remain true."

But Friedman's chosen wish for the Chosen People still has its problems. In addition to the immense ground he must cover in locating documents, witnesses, informants, and photographs, he complains that he receives insufficient cooperation from the West Germans and the Austrians in compiling evidence against Nazis. In the Eichmann case, the Germans claimed that Eichmann was Austrian and the Austrians claimed that he was German. In 1947, the Austrian police closed their files to Friedman, telling him frankly that they could not afford to assist in Eichmann's capture because, if they did so, the Allies would link Austria with Nazi crimes and prolong the postwar occupation.

Friedman's biggest problem is money. The Israeli government

gives him no assistance. He must rely on private donations to support his hunt.

Will it ever end?

"Not until justice is done," Friedman vows. Is he still seeking justice three decades after the war's end, or is his hunt for Nazi war criminals a vengeful obsession? Commenting on Tuvia Friedman, Israeli journalist Moshe Meisels concludes, "He's sane but he's obsessed."

5

Mr. Homicide and Father McCreadie

SOUTHERN CALIFORNIA IS A LURE for young women, especially those who are pretty, ambitious, and rootless. They come west from the dairy farms of Wisconsin, the hard-scrabble soil of Arkansas, the hills of Pennsylvania, and the tenement flats of New York and Boston. They pour in by car and bus, by train and plane, and by thumb. Often they come with little promise and less hope. Still, Southern California means Los Angeles and Los Angeles means Hollywood. Never mind the stories of those who didn't make it. Hollywood is still a mecca, still the tinsel-town of fan magazines, glamour and fame, long cars and short skirts and tall drinks by the pool of the Beverly Hills Hotel—the town of dreams of overnight success where even bus tours through the neighborhoods of the stars can be an industry.

The mystical glow exuded by Hollywood was especially magnetic in the 1930s and 1940s. There was a quality of unmatched excitement about this suburb of the City of the Angels. This was, after all, where actresses such as Mary Pickford and ex-chorines such as Joan Crawford achieved instant and worldwide stardom. This was where, word had it, you could be "discovered" by sitting on the right stool at the right drug store counter at the right time. And even the word "discovered," with its connotation of having been lost before, was no discouragement. After all, wasn't this where an elevator operator became the glamorous Dorothy Lamour, where a Spanish dancer named Rita Cansino became Rita Hayworth, Love Goddess of a nation?

Hollywood. Where you could sit in a restaurant and watch a movie star lunching at a table nearby. Where you could play in the playgrounds of the famous—Ciro's, Mocambo—and dine in their restaurants—the Brown Derby, Romanoffs, Chasens. A city of premiere-night searchlights sweeping the sky. A city of men with money and connections. A city where a smart girl could, if only in her mind, have a chance at the top. That was the million-to-one shot: to shine amid the brightness, even for a minute in a movie crowd scene, even in the background behind a movie queen.

Such things would never be possible in places like Medford, Massachusetts, where Elizabeth Ann Short grew up.

Elizabeth was one of the girls who fell under the spell. She was pretty, with jet-black hair. Her skin was porcelain white, just like in the soap ads. Oddly, she almost always wore black, perhaps because it set off her milky complexion. She liked men and flashy convertibles.

In high school, back east in Medford, Elizabeth had been shy and retiring, a girl who stood out in no one's mind. In the bleakness of industrial New England, Southern California must have seemed a bright jewel indeed. So Elizabeth, as so many other young women, went west while still in her teens.

In 1943 she was working in the post exchange at Camp Cooke, an Army base near Santa Barbara, 100 miles north of Los Angeles. At the camp she was remembered as a blushing, sweet thing, but that may have been only a surface impression. For the following year, still underage, she was arrested for drinking with soldiers and shipped back to Massachusetts by juvenile authorities.

She didn't stay long; the lure of Hollywood was too great. After the dark night of World War II, the movie capital glowed brighter than ever. The Swing Era was in full swing. People were dancing to Tommy Dorsey, Harry James, and Benny Goodman. New cars were rolling off assembly lines for the first time in a half-dozen grim years. Superhighways were becoming longer and wider, creating a new and mobile way of life suited for girls like Elizabeth. She went back to Southern California, to the night clubs and the men, to the Sunset Strip, Muscle Beach, and Hollywood and Vine.

On the morning of January 15, 1947, the spotlight finally found Elizabeth Ann Short, by then twenty-two years old. She was "discovered"—but not in a drug store. Her naked, milk-white body was found in a vacant lot in southwest Los Angeles, bisected with surgical precision.

A reporter, learning of her penchant for black, dubbed her "The Black Dahlia."

Harry Hansen, tall, dapper, and one of the most formidable detectives in the history of the Los Angeles Police Department, was assigned to the case. Hansen also had a nickname. They called him "Mr. Homicide."

And for good reason. In more than two decades with the Los Angeles police force, Harry Hansen had investigated and solved literally hundreds of murders, among them several of the most celebrated in the bizarre criminal annals of Southern California.

Yet the case of the Black Dahlia was to be his most frustrating. In the career of virtually every detective there is the one crime that defies his most expert investigative skill, his most intensive efforts to bring the perpetrator to justice. Such cases are often more important to a detective than those he has solved, since the unsolved crime stands as a continuing challenge to his professional proficiency—and, in fact, he is likely to classify it not as "unsolved" but rather as "still to be solved." Moreover, the "still-to-be-solved" case is frequently more fascinating to the public, representing as it does an intangible mystery that remains to be unraveled.

Such, to both Detective Harry Hansen and the public, has been the case of the Black Dahlia murder. After more than a quarter of a century, the question of who carved Elizabeth Ann Short in two—and why—remains unanswered. Thus, to Hansen,

Elizabeth Short (*left*), who was to become "The Black Dahlia" murder victim in Los Angeles, is shown here on a beach with a friend. This picture was found in Miss Short's album after she was butchered. (*Wide World*)

it is an endless assignment; to the American public, it is a tantalizing enigma.

Harry Hansen, now retired but still active in police circles, was—and is—a master detective, a patient man of breeding, taste, and wit who used psychology, native intelligence, and a gentle manner to elicit information in an era when intimidation and fear were more the norm among police. "You have to be a student of behavior," he says. "You have to size a guy up and listen to him talk, then start putting two and two together."

Starting his police career as a uniformed patrolman in 1926, Hansen performed so well that, two years later, he was transferred into the Records Bureau where he quickly showed a knack for tracing fingerprints. Hansen identified William Edward Hickman, the killer of a little girl, from a single fingerprint taken from the rear-view mirror of a Chrysler roadster used in a holdup and shooting.

From the Records Bureau, Hansen moved to the Auto Theft Unit for a year, then to Robbery Investigation and the Burglary Squad.

While in the last, Hansen would meet trains at the Los Angeles station to intercept eastern gangsters bent on expanding their operations to the West. "We'd tell them we wanted to see them out of town by tomorrow morning," Hansen recalls with a chuckle. "That's how it worked in those days."

In 1936 Hansen was moved into the Homicide Squad. There is a saying among police that there is "no home in homicide," but for Harry Hansen the murder detail proved to be his niche.

At first, his work in Homicide consisted largely of being stationed at Los Angeles' Receiving Hospital, where he would interrogate victims brought in with gunshot and stab wounds and take down dying declarations. Gradually he was given more demanding assignments.

For much of his forty-two-year career, Hansen was teamed with Jack McCreadie, a friend from days at L.A.'s Manual Arts High School. They both reached the rank of sergeant together in Homicide, both retired the same year, and both have moved to Palm Desert, California.

McCreadie grew up in San Francisco and moved to Los Angeles, where his brother was a police officer, in 1919. By the time he put on a Los Angeles police uniform, McCreadie was nearly thirty years old, but he rose fast through the ranks—Traffic, Vice, the Metropolitan Division, and finally, Homicide in 1941. McCreadie shared not only many of Hansen's adventures, but also his philosophy. Like Hansen, McCreadie looks like a man to confide in, an aspect that also earned him a nickname: "Father McCreadie."

Working side by side, "Mr. Homicide" and "Father Mc-Creadie" became a fabled pair in the Los Angeles Police Department.

As is essential for detective-partners, Hansen and McCreadie functioned well together. Once, interrogating a suspect for more than two hours, they noticed that the man had a way of coughing before telling what they knew to be lies. "Suddenly it dawned on us," Hansen says. "Cough, cough meant he's going to lie. Without discussing it, we just looked at each other and read each other's meaning." Hansen and McCreadie gave the man a key question and he coughed. "You're lying," the two detectives said. The man replied, "I give up," and confessed.

It is the kind of teamwork, and shared intuition, that makes for successful partnership in the detection of criminals.

Moreover, working singly or as part of a team, it takes years of experience to become a capable homicide detective, a fact that Hansen believes is little appreciated by the public. "A person doesn't go into the police department and the next day go into Homicide as a detective," he explains. "You have to have background. You have to be pretty well schooled in various types of criminal activity—robbery, burglary, know how a good stickup-man works, know about con men. Then you pool your information, put it in your index file—in your sconce, as we say—and you draw on that when you start working murders."

Hansen continues, "You must know thieves, people that hang out in skid row, you must have already instilled a large amount of trust in them. If a murderer goes down in skid row, a person like Jack McCreadie, who had terrific contacts down there, would make a phone call or two, put the word out that he wanted certain information, and nine times out of ten, he would get a phone call that would give him the information he wanted and then hang up. The person calling him might not even know him."

Such rapport with informers on the fringe of society is not easy to achieve. A detective can easily get the reputation of being a bully, but Hansen and McCreadie's image was just the opposite.

McCreadie once had a "connection" on skid row, a man who

was always in trouble with his wife and children and who seemed always to be calling the detective for advice about family matters. "I was having coffee in the police cafeteria one morning with Hansen and received a phone call from this man," McCreadie recalls. "He says 'Jack, I'm in trouble. I just heard a radio broadcast that I'm wanted for murder and that I was armed and dangerous and they're looking for me.'" McCreadie hadn't known of the "wanted" bulletin and checked on it. It had been issued by the county sheriff's office. "Sure enough," McCreadie relates,

Detective Harry Hansen (*right*), who was in charge of the long and frustrating Black Dahlia murder investigation, is pictured at a Los Angeles police station with another officer. (*Wide World*)

"they wanted this man for murdering his wife. And I said 'He just called me.' Well, they immediately wanted to get the shotguns and the machine guns and bring this man in. So I said, 'Well, he's going to call me back in twenty minutes and I'll let you know.' The man called back and I verified that he was wanted. And he says he's scared they might kill him. So I found out where he was, way in the south end of town in a motel, and I went and picked him up." The man went to trial and McCreadie was called to testify. There were two hung juries and the third found him innocent. McCreadie would never say whether he thought the man was guilty. "Someone had killed her," he'd say. "But that's the way we made our contacts, informants."

In rare cases, Hansen admitted, some excessive force was used but he and McCreadie never believed in that. "If we couldn't outthink them and come up with the evidence to counteract any story or alibi they had, we'd say the hell with it. Why should we start beating up somebody? It wasn't in our makeup."

For all their sensitivity, Hansen and McCreadie were hardly the sort of cops who were sociologists first and law enforcers second. Both have strong feelings about the U.S. Supreme Court's Miranda decision of the 1960s that obliges an interrogator to warn, "You have the right to remain silent; you have the right to an attorney. . . ." And they believe strongly in the death penalty as a deterrent to murder.

In support of the maximum punishment, Hansen cites the case of Louise Peete—one of his most famous—as one in which the death penalty was applied too late.

Louise Peete was a Louisiana girl, born before the turn of the century, a vamp who held fatal attraction for men. Her charm masked a nature that was at once cold and cunning. Abandoning the bayous of Louisiana, she headed north, to the sophistication of Boston, posed as an heiress, and became Mrs. R. H. Bosley. Such flimsy facades, however, have a way of crumbling. Realizing that the masquerade was nearly over, she left Boston for Dallas. In Texas, Mrs. Bosley teamed up with a hotel clerk named Harry Faurote, who courted her, but Louise wearied of him and he committed suicide.

Next, Louise appeared in Denver and captured another heart,

that of Richard C. Peete, a quiet salesman. Husband Bosley had by then been legally shed, and Louise became Mrs. Peete.

That pairing did not last long either. Boredom overtook Louise and she left husband number two. As young Elizabeth Short, "The Black Dahlia," would do years later, Louise Peete headed for the more scintillating life of Los Angeles. She wound up as a housekeeper for one Joseph C. Denton, a wealthy Arizona miner whose wife and baby had died before a house he had purchased for them was ready. Mrs. Peete leased the house, and Denton became a boarder. The arrangement, begun in May 1920, had lasted about one month when Denton disappeared. While the search for him was still on, Mrs. Peete had a sudden change of heart, subleased the house, and returned to Denver as the dutiful wife of still-smitten Richard Peete and mother to their four-year-old daughter.

That September, Jacob Denton was dug up from a crude grave in the basement of his house, a bullet hole in his head. Police went after Mrs. Peete, returned her to Los Angeles, and put her on trial for murder. It was as sensational a trial as any newspaper of that era could want. For once her charms over men failed Louise, and an all-male jury convicted her of murder for money. Still, no woman had ever been executed in California up to that time. Louise went to San Quentin as Prisoner No. 35672 under a life sentence. Husband Richard put a bullet through his head, the second man to kill himself over the vivacious Louise.

During her trial, Mrs. Peete's little girl was cared for by Mrs. Margaret Logan, a woman so gentle that she could not believe the soft-spoken Southern belle could have committed such a heinous crime.

In 1933, Mrs. Peete was transferred to the newly opened California Institute for Women at Tehachapi and became "Queen Louise," the star boarder. All the time she was filing applications for parole. Her tenth application was successful, and in 1939 Louise walked out of Tehachapi and, subsequently, into the career of Detective Harry Hansen.

In October 1943 Mrs. Peete became a companion-assistant to Mrs. Logan, who twenty-three years before had taken care of Louise's child. The daughter, by then grown and herself a mother

of four, was living in Canada. Mrs. Logan had a real estate business and owned a home.

Moreover, romance found the irresistible Louise again. She
met Lee Borden Judson, a sixty-seven-year-old former advertising
man and newspaper reporter, and they were married in May 1944.
Their honeymoon room was in Mrs. Logan's home.

Later that month, Mrs. Logan vanished. Louise explained to
her husband that the elderly woman had gone away for a while.

Harry Hansen recounts, "Everything seemed to be going along
fine. The parole officers were checking the parole reports and
they noticed 'Hey, that isn't Margaret Logan's signature.' So they
called in a handwriting expert, who compared the signature with
known handwriting of Margaret Logan, and it was definitely a
forgery. So now we had a big, hairy mystery on our hands."

"Thad Brown, who was captain of homicide then [and who later
became chief of detectives], assigned Lt. Vaughan and myself on
the thing and he went with us. We went out to the house in
Pacific Palisades where Margaret Logan was living and we looked
through the venetian blinds and here is Louise Peete going
through her strongbox, going through the goodies. And we
knocked on the door. She came to the door, very pleasant. We
asked to speak to Mrs. Logan. And she says 'Oh, that poor dear
is in the hospital having plastic surgery. Her husband went berserk
and practically bit her nose off and I promised I wouldn't tell
anyone where she was. But I go to see her every day and I'll tell her
you were here. What is it you want?'"

At that moment, another detective gave a signal from the back
of the house. In the yard outside Louise's bedroom window was
a slight mound topped with potted plants. The detectives removed the plants and started digging. With a third shovelful of
dirt, they unearthed Mrs. Logan's body. She had been shot
through the head. Years later, Hansen could still express surprise.
"Can you imagine that, buried right outside Peete's bedroom?"

Then the detective work began. The house was searched, a
gun was found. A forensic chemist was called in and he and Hansen went over the walls of the house with a fluoroscope. Imbedded in the wall by a hallway telephone stand, head-high, was
the bullet. It proved to have been fired from the gun found in the
house, which turned out to be Louise's gun.

More checking uncovered the fact that Louise had called a carpet man to remove the bloodied floor covering, and had had a carpenter and plasterer come in to fix the wall. According to Hansen, there was nothing to tie her new husband to the crime. "But we filed murder on Louise."

This time her luck ran out. On April 11, 1947, at 10:13 A.M., Louise Peete Judson died in the gas chamber at San Quentin as coldly as she had killed. Seventy-nine witnesses and twelve prison guards saw her go. Harry Hansen was one of the witnesses. "She walked into that gas chamber with a spring in her step," he remembers. "You'd think she was going to sit down and have her hair done or something, gonna go to a party that night. She sat down in that chair. She looked out and saw me, recognized me and I read her lips. She nodded her head and said 'Thanks for everything.' "

Although Harry Hansen continues to feel that the death penalty in certain cases is richly deserved, he never wants to see another execution.

No matter how savage a criminal, a detective must try to avoid emotional involvement in a case. Rage can blind an investigator to clues that he might otherwise see. Friendships can get in the way. Harshness in questioning a suspect can make him or her fearful and uncooperative.

"In working the sort of cases McCreadie and I worked," Hansen reflects, "we had to more or less steel ourselves against becoming emotionally involved. We would have to look at a dead body, a body that is mangled, disfigured, as an inanimate object, and approach it from a professional attitude. We couldn't start talking about, 'Oh, look what he did, he cut out her liver and he put it in the waste basket.' We had to take a distant, independent view of the whole thing, because if we didn't, we wouldn't last any time at all. Two or three fellows were transferred into our division. They were highly successful detectives in other fields, but they're out on their first dead body—and it's anything but pleasant—and they go into the captain and say, 'I can't take this; I want a transfer.' "

McCreadie remembers a case that stands out in his mind because of the brutal murder of two women. "This man was a good burglar," the detective recalls. "You'd be asleep in your room and he'd go in and prowl your house. Strictly money, no jewelry. He was involved in some two hundred to three hundred burglaries in the Westlake area of Los Angeles. So we found the body of this one woman early one night. It was called the 'Bird of Paradise' case. She worked at an art studio out on Beverly Boulevard. Very brutally murdered. Her head was smashed in completely, and she had been sexually molested also. We found the MO [method of operation] similar to a burglary that had happened down the street. He had a habit of picking up a woman's purse and turning the contents completely out, and taking the money. Right after this murder, the burglaries stopped, so we were working with the burglary detail and we felt there was a connection. It wasn't until several months later that we found the second murder, Miss Lindsay, who had been killed in her home. She had a wooden box outside the fireplace that went out into her yard, which would have been a means of entry, because there was no forced entry shown. So we had our fingerprint men out there and a very thorough man found a partial palm print, just the upper part of the palm. He removed the section of board and took that in and photographed it and developed this palm print—the only physical evidence we had."

Miss Lindsay had been brutally beaten, carried from one couch to another and sexually molested. In McCreadie's mind, it tied in with the methods used in the Bird of Paradise case. "We figured," he recounts, "that our burglar was working again. So we put a stakeout in the Westlake area, had a van out there and a couple of young officers from the metropolitan squad. They saw this man approach an apartment house and start looking at mail boxes, searching for the names of single women—his usual targets. Then they noticed that he also was barefoot. They started to get out of the van and apparently made some noise. He saw them and started to run. They took out after him, and he tried to cut through a vacant lot where he stepped on a nail."

One officer fired, and hit the suspect in the arm. But the nail in the foot stopped the man. When McCreadie started interrogating the suspect, McCreadie did not yet have the palm print. But the burglar, who carried a pair of gloves when arrested, did not know about the print. "I took him up to the photo lab," Mc-

Creadie recounts, "and had this picture taken with the glove partially off to show this part. I never mentioned the print to him but he immediately got the message because he wore his gloves turned down at the cuff. I talked to him a bit, took him past the scene of the two murders, asked if he'd been there before. 'No, never been here, never been in the neighborhood at all," the former detective mimicked the suspect. "The guy wasn't sharp enough to say 'Yeah, I was there the night before, I burglarized the place the night before the murder.' "

McCreadie got a surprise when he arranged to have the man appear in a lineup, to be viewed by victims of other burglaries and rapes. McCreadie remembers vividly how one victim reacted. "She was a single woman, divorced, who played the organ in a church in the neighborhood—a nice woman. And he came in and burglarized her place. She slept in the nude, and the next thing she knew there was a gun at her side and this man is there with her. Fortunately, she didn't scream, or she would have been the third victim like the other women. She talked to him very nicely and told him not to harm her, and she'd do anything he wanted.

"He even let her go into the bathroom, but kept the door open, of course. So then they came back to the bed and he proceeded to rape her. But she told me he was very gentle, very quiet. Matter of fact, she was rather impressed with him. He was a very handsome young man. On the way out he took her handbag and dumped out the contents. This made her very unhappy, after being so nice and everything. So she reported it to the police. And she was the one to identify him."

Something about McCreadie's quiet, piercing questions bothered the suspect. He begged to be booked for burglary. The suspect later asked McCreadie, "That woman out in the audience tonight identified me?" The detective said "Yes." "Would she have to testify in court?" he asked McCreadie. The cop realized the man was smitten with the woman he had violated and had tried to call her for a date a few nights later. He told McCreadie he was concerned about putting the woman through the trauma of testifying. He did not realize the detective was booking him for murder as well as rape. The suspect distrusted McCreadie, and asked to talk to another detective in Burglary. During the interrogation, McCreadie listened in over a loudspeaker in another room. The suspect finally confessed both murders. "He was crying, and it was all down on tape," McCreadie remembers. "He confessed to everything."

A good homicide detective not only has to be a good investigator, and a psychologist, but also a lawyer. Hansen recalls that many times he would be sitting next to the district attorney at a trial, and the D.A. would turn to Hansen and ask, "What do you think about this? Should we put this guy on now? Should we skip this one?" A detective learns the law not just on the street, but by sitting in a courtroom day after day as the case he has been working on is presented.

In any murder investigation, Hansen explains, nothing is more important than the scene of the crime. It is there that an intimate knowledge of the physical aspects of violent death is vital. The investigator must know, for example, that blood settles to the lowest point of gravity in the corpse. Thus, if postmortem lividity—a deep purple discoloration caused by the settling of blood—is seen on the front of a body that is lying on its back, it is evident to an expert that the body was moved at least several hours after death.

At a shooting-death scene, the detective's technical expertise regarding weapons comes into play. If a witness, for instance, contends that his companion committed suicide, the witness will be asked to reenact the scene. Perhaps an automatic pistol was used, in which case the ejected cartridge would be thrown approximately ten feet backward unless deflected. It would roll or slide or stay in place, depending on whether the floor was slick or carpeted. Once the investigator locates the cartridge—if it hasn't been moved—he knows where the weapon was when it was fired, and therefore would be in a position to confirm or challenge a witness' story.

In cases of murder-suicide, observes Hansen, detectives "have to be particularly accurate in our investigation because of the matter of life insurance, double indemnity that might apply to who died first. Suppose you find two murders and a suicide. Which died first? Lots of angles, tricky aspects." Such cases emphasize again the crucial nature of the preliminary investigation, that all-important first hour on the job.

Hansen and McCreadie were so proficient in their investigations that they became two of only three detectives who were qualified as expert witnesses in homicide cases in Los Angeles Superior Court.

Hansen summed up what he considers to be the traits of the effective criminal investigator. "Your appearance, your personality, your ability to project yourself, to sell yourself, to instill confidence in someone that you want to help him, that you're not here to harm him. All these things combined. You can't open a book to page three and say 'Now I must follow those rules, number one, number two.' Throw the book away. You play it by ear. It is something you develop gradually, don't even notice it yourself. You develop every day. You take on a little more polish, if you will, expertise. You walk in and you're obviously the man in charge. You can't be a shrinking violet and wait for Henry to do it or let George do it."

Detective Harry Hansen would need all the experience on which he could draw in the hunt to find the killer of Elizabeth Ann Short—"The Black Dahlia." Moreover, in the Black Dahlia murder Harry Hansen came to feel a sense of mission, to see the search as his alone.

At the time he received his most famous and baffling case, Hansen and his partner at the time, a fellow detective named Finis Brown, had just completed investigating the death of a man who had evidently succumbed of natural causes in a quiet section of Southwest Los Angeles. Hansen and Brown were awaiting the arrival of the coroner when a call came in from Homicide Captain Jack Donahoe.

"Red [as Hansen was sometimes called because of his red hair] we've got a rough one," said Donahoe. "Drop what you're doing, have a uniformed officer stand by there for the coroner, and you and Brown get over to an empty lot on Norton, between 39th and Coliseum Street."

Almost as an afterthought, Donahoe added, "It sounds bad, Red. . . . Damn bad. It's going to be a rough one."

It *was* a rough one—one that was to plague Hansen for the

rest of his working life. For twenty-one years, until his retirement in 1968, Hansen painstakingly sought a diabolical slayer whose identity is not known to this day. Even now, on his own, Hansen continues to take a personal and active interest in the case. The murder of Elizabeth Ann Short, the Black Dahlia, stands as the most celebrated unsolved crime in California's history, but not for lack of skill or effort on Harry Hansen's part.

He and his partner arrived at the scene in the Leimert Park section of Los Angeles. It was mid-morning. Sprawled in the weeds of a vacant lot, just a few feet from the sidewalk, was a nude female body, cut in half. She had also been stabbed repeatedly. Her face was unrecognizable. The mutilations of the body were bestial. But the most bizarre aspect was that the corpse had been professionally cleaved and scrubbed. The natural speculation was that the killer had studied surgery. Even to two veteran policemen such as Hansen and Brown, the sight was grisly beyond belief.

Hansen unlocked his eyes from the bisected corpse and gazed around. Looking on, horrified, was a knot of reporters, photographers, and plain citizens. They included eleven-year-old Bobby Smith, a kid from down the block, astride his bike taking in a sight he'd never forget, a man who'd been walking his dog, and the uniformed police who had responded to the first call.

The morbid tableau was set amid land that one day would become streets of pleasant houses with lawns, palm trees, and people who would recall that this is where the Black Dahlia was found. But in 1947 there were only vacant lots covered with weeds, with telegraph poles and wires the only demarcation lines. The sky, once bright with sunshine, had by now turned bleak.

No one who has ever seen a cadaver dumped like so much rubbish is ever likely to erase the sight from his mind. The presence of death, especially violent death, has an awesome effect. People speak in hushed tones and move quietly, as if afraid to disturb a pitiful but precious presence. There is nothing more I can do for you, twenty-two-year-old Elizabeth, but I can mark your passing with reverence. Harry Hansen went about making his report, mechanically, but what was in his mind was clear. This killer, this maniac, must be found.

A police department, especially a top-notch one like the Los Angeles Police department, can be a marvel of efficiency. Disparate teams come together. Identification. Pathology. Method of Operation. Files of known criminals. Men who know the criminal mind and men who know the criminals. By late afternoon, the autopsy had been performed, fingerprints taken, and now Hansen knew that the carved-up body had once been Elizabeth Ann Short.

He was to learn more about her. She had maintained several residences, all at the same time. She had had a room in the Las Palmas Hotel near Hollywood Boulevard. She had rented another room in the Congress Hotel and an apartment in Long Beach. From time to time she had stayed overnight in a private home on San Carlos Street in Hollywood.

The first night passed without finding her killer.

Now Hansen concentrated on the tip that had brought police to the corpse. It had come from a woman who had sounded frightened. After telling the dispatcher about the body, she had hung up without giving her name. Could she have seen more? Could she have known more? Was there a chance that she had observed something, anything, that could provide a clue? Local radio stations were asked to broadcast requests for the woman to contact police.

Hansen, meanwhile, was spending his second straight day—without rest—at headquarters. As the chief detective on the case, he received all the various reports. He had also contacted police back in Medford, Massachusetts, to find out additional details about the brief and tragic life of Elizabeth Ann Short.

Hansen reviewed the photographs and other evidence relating to the scene of the crime. In the Black Dahlia case, there was no doubt about the circumstances of death. It had been a butcher-block method, if anything, involving a complete severing of the body and, it was rumored, a rearrangement of the ovaries. The on-site inspection of the body had yielded one interesting, if not surprising, clue. There was dew beneath the body, still wet, meaning that she was probably slain elsewhere and carried to the Norton Street location.

In a city the size of Los Angeles, murder is an everyday occurrence. The death of Elizabeth Ann Short, even the bizarre way she was sliced up, might have escaped public notice, or been quickly forgotten, had it not been for the facile phrase-making of a reporter named Bevo Means of the now-defunct *Los Angeles Express*. On the day after her corpse was discovered, Means went to Long Beach to interview Elizabeth's landlady there, and learned about the young woman's strange habit of dressing in black. He nicknamed the victim, in his ensuing story, "The Black Dahlia"—and the name and the murder caught the public's attention. Across the nation, newspapers and magazines became curious about the grisly discovery on that vacant lot, and sent their best crime reporters out to see for themselves. It was not yet the era of television where fictionalized crime is often more bizarre than the real thing. People paid more attention to actual criminal cases. In fact, the Black Dahlia killing took place one week before the debut of Los Angeles' first television station.

A detective, speaking for the department, told the press, "The big push is on. Our men are fanning out now to bring in the killer." Harry Hansen himself believed the investigation was going well. Leads and clues were pouring in. Early on, Hansen told his wife, Norma, that he expected to have the slayer in hand soon.

There was good reason for optimism. An envelope arrived at police headquarters containing the victim's black address book. The envelope also held her birth certificate. But whoever sent them had gone to great pains to hide his or her own identity. The envelope was addressed with letters cut from advertisements—a technique possibly learned from dozens of kidnap movies.

As promising as things initially looked, the days went by without the apprehension of the Black Dahlia murderer. A city-wide roundup brought in suspects who were questioned closely and released. A man claiming to be the killer telephoned Jimmy Richardson, city editor of the *Los Angeles Examiner*. The caller's account was filled with details, including some that only the real murderer could know. He told Richardson he wanted to watch the police try to find him for a few more days—apparently enjoying the game of hare and hounds. Then he would give himself up. Richardson had the impression that the man was pleased with himself, not so much for the murder, but for having out-witted the police despite their best efforts.

Any well-publicized murder brings out the phony confessors, individuals who for one compulsive reason or another show up at police stations or newspapers to volunteer their false guilt. The Black Dahlia murder lured them in droves. Day after day, as stories about Elizabeth Short's unhappy end and police activi-ties aimed at finding her killer appeared on front pages of Los Angeles' four daily newspapers, the confessors appeared.

The confessors are a problem. Mostly they turn out to be innocent—persons who come into the case with only the scant facts they can glean from the newspapers. Still, how is one to know if a man or woman who shows up at a police station and says, "I did it" is the actual perpetrator? There is always a bare chance, and each story must be checked.

Hansen recalls another confessor, a soldier at Fort Dix, N.J., who insisted after prolonged questioning that he was the culprit. "He held out for ten days saying he did it," Hansen recollects. "We checked his army record and found he was here, in Los Angeles, at the time. There'd be edition after edition of the papers every day. Get one thing new and they'd come out with a new edition. So this soldier had access to all this. The one thing he didn't have was the answer to the key question. With practically every murder there's a key question and we don't let that come out in the public eye or give it to the press, for obvious reasons. This guy finally copped out. He says, 'What the hell, I'll tell you why I admitted it. My wife left me and I couldn't find her, and I figured if I copped out to something like this, I'd hit the papers all over the country and she'd feel sorry for me and come back.' Why had he finally admitted the truth? 'It looks like she's gone for good, so the hell with her!' "

Hansen hadn't believed him from the start because "you get an intuition, like when you get someone and even though they deny, deny, deny, something tells you that you've got the right one. If you stay with it long enough, you'll come up with the answer."

In the Black Dahlia case, nevertheless, a month had gone by and there was still no answer. The murderer had been busy, though, taunting Hansen and his fellow police. The mail brought a steady flow of Elizabeth Short's belongings to the Los Angeles newspapers. There came another black book in which Elizabeth had recorded the names and addresses of seventy-five acquaintances. Hansen checked them all out, to no avail. The sender of the articles, presumably the killer, had continued to stay busy with scissors, putting together a note made from the headlines. "Here's Dahlia's belongings. Letter to follow." There was no letter, but there was a postcard. "I have changed my mind. You would not give me a square deal. Dahlia killing was justified."

Justified? How? The writer never said.

The woman who found Elizabeth's body was finally located by Hansen, and he interviewed her. She and her daughter had been walking along Norton Street when the child, a few steps ahead, called out, "Mommy, look, there's someone lying down there." The woman had no further details, another brick in the blank wall.

But now Hansen was on the trail of RM, twenty-four, the last person known to have seen the Black Dahlia alive. Hansen got onto M, a Huntington Park hardware salesman, through interviews with the victim's friends in San Diego. M was found but at first denied even knowing the Black Dahlia. Then he broke down and admitted that he had arranged to pick her up in front of a bus depot in San Diego, had taken her back to where she had her belongings, had stayed with her in a motel, then dropped her off the following afternoon in front of the Biltmore Hotel on Pershing Square in downtown Los Angeles. That was on January 9, six days before her body was found. San Diego to Los Angeles is a trip that normally takes three hours at most by automobile, and the overnight stay added to police suspicions. For two weeks they questioned M.

Hansen remembers that M was "the one that looked good. We had a hell of a time finding him. He didn't want his wife to know that he was 'chipping' a little. He'd picked up this gal and they had stayed at a motel on the way up, and what made me think he was lying was that he said he'd had no sexual action with her at all. She slept in the bed and he slept in the chair."

Hansen had a theory. "If they lie once, they lie again." He asked M whom he thought he was kidding, but M insisted he was telling the truth. "After we got into her background, I had to believe him," Hansen concedes. "She wasn't a pushover. She was a tease artist."

M was later administered sodium pentathol, the truth drug which Hansen calls "silly syrup," and it verified M's story. He was cleared.

M had run dry as a lead, but there were others. By now, more than forty persons had come forward and announced that they had slain the young woman with the cameo complexion. In time, the story moved off the front pages, and the confessions slowed to a trickle. They included farmers and soldiers, bums off skid row, even clergymen. Some were charged with making false police reports; others were remanded to mental institutions.

Harry Hansen went on to other murders, but the Black Dahlia remained on his mind. There is no such thing as closing the book on a murder that is "still to be solved." Especially to a detective like Hansen.

So even after the public had shifted its fickle attention to other things, even while he was on new cases, Hansen continued working on the Black Dahlia. Over and over, he read stacks of love letters found in her apartments. Over and over, he pondered the names in her address books. He questioned more suspects, more confessors. Eventually, his file on Elizabeth Ann Short grew to more than 6,000 typewritten pages.

Persistent newspaper reporters, still running down their own leads, had their theories. Jimmy Richardson, the city editor of the *Examiner* who had received the telephone call from the man who may have been the killer, eventually concluded that the man had died, perhaps prematurely, as had his victim. Richardson's reasoning: the murderer had exhibited such an inflated ego— witness his telephone call and the early series of mailings— that he would not have been satisfied with anything less than full credit, and that would have taken exposure. Since the killer had not fully exposed himself, Richardson argued, he too must somehow have expired.

Aggie Underwood, a top crime reporter on the *Examiner* who

succeeded Richardson as city editor—the Dahlia was her last reportorial case—thought that the killer was a man, and expressed suspicion about one who was questioned in the case and released. The man, whom she refused to identify, also is no longer alive. Reporter Bevo Means, who first christened Elizabeth Ann Short "The Black Dahlia," doubted that the case would ever be unraveled. "She had too many phony connections; she was so damn secretive that even her friends never really knew where she was. She was always with a different guy. She just made one of them mad."

One early report alleged that Elizabeth moved around in the lesbian world. This allegation was pursued by reporter Sid Hughes. He visited every known lesbian hangout in the city, and he and Harry Hansen compared notes. Hansen remained convinced that there was nothing to the homosexual angle. Bevo Means disagreed strongly. He believed in the homosexual theory, basing his belief on a certain undisclosed aspect he learned about the autopsy.

By 1968, when he retired, Hansen's red hair had turned snow white. He still had the booming voice, the big laugh, the takeover personality that made him a favorite storyteller at police functions. The Los Angeles City Council passed a resolution "in highest praise for distinguished service." Official Los Angeles knew Harry Hansen for the hundreds of cases he had solved; to Harry Hansen himself, he was the man who had tried and failed to find the killer of the Dahlia.

What has happened to the Black Dahlia killer? There is only speculation. Hansen agrees that the murderer may no longer be alive because "by now, he would have done something, said something that would have attracted attention. If he's still alive, he's got it made unless he just completely slips and blows it."

Many years have passed, making it difficult now to prove a murder charge, even if the killer were found. Hansen is certain that he never met the killer face to face, that he did not slip through with the other 500 or more suspects. "We considered the possibility of his coming right in, making a confession, then cleverly sidestepping the key question," is how Hansen puts it. "We watched for that, took measures to expose him in that event. We never underestimated the guy. You'd never believe the amount of checking we did on this case; we followed everything as far as it would go and then we'd turn right around and walk through it again."

To the day he retired in 1968, Harry Hansen would hear one question over and over. "When are you gonna catch the Black Dahlia killer?" He did not need the question to remind him that he had not apprehended his elusive quarry after nearly twenty years of searching. In the back of his mind was locked another question, the "Key Question"—the one fact or set of facts about any case that the public never hears—the question that only the real slayer, not the false confessors, can answer.

And the confessions still came, although in decreasing numbers, right up to the day Harry Hansen departed from the force for his retirement home in Palm Desert. Even in retirement, he has never left the case. "I recently had a call from a lady in San Diego about the Black Dahlia case, says she killed her," Hansen reports. "So I go to San Diego and I ask her "How many times did you shoot her?' 'Three times,' she says. Well, you see, she wasn't shot at all. I shouldn't be so tricky."

For confessors like that, the Key Question isn't needed. But it was asked more than 500 times of other suspects by Hansen and his fellow detectives. More than a quarter of a century after Elizabeth Ann Short met her untimely and horrible death and was discovered in that weed-grown lot, police still won't say more about the Key Question except that it deals with some fact having to do with the condition, appearance, or attitude of the Black Dahlia's body at the time it was discovered. For years there was a rumor that the victim's ovaries had somehow been switched around by the killer, but Hansen says that there was no basis for the rumor. There were a series of odd markings on the corpse that could have been the killer's work—a fact that went unpublicized. Was that the Key Question? Hansen says it wasn't.

The files of the Black Dahlia case, filling a five-foot-high steel cabinet to the bursting point, are locked and in storage. Two filing experts spent six months organizing them. Inside are the 6,000-plus pages of typewritten reports, photographs of the milky-complexioned, raven-haired victim walking arm-in-arm with suitors, her address books and bundles of her love letters.

Always Hansen looked for someone with medical finesse. He also went on the theory that the killing seemed to be based on unbelievable anger. "I suppose sex was the motive, or at least the fact that the killer was denied sex," Hansen conjectures. "From all accounts, Elizabeth Short liked to tease men. She probably went too far this time and just set some guy off into a blind, berserk rage. I suppose I allow myself to lean slightly toward the theory of a male murderer, someone with medical training. I based that merely on the physical aspects of the case. Still, you have to have an open mind to anything, can't close your eyes to any evidence. In other words, it may have been somehow possible that the killer didn't have any medical background. We had to keep that in mind despite the evidence. All you have are facts and evidence; all you can do is fit them and see if they dovetail. Nothing we ever had did."

Hansen became more familiar with the brief life and times of Elizabeth Short than he ever did with the victim in any other case in his long career.

For all his determination, Harry Hansen remained professionally objective about finding her killer. Hansen put the case away when he got home at night and brought it out again the next morning—the way any professional detective does. But he says, "Being objective didn't mean that we didn't want that killer. I never wanted anything more. Every now and then there'd be some new development, a lead would pop out of nowhere and we'd think, here it is, this is it. But it never really was."

The Black Dahlia murder was the kind of killing that catches the public fancy, that the public nurtures and never forgets and never ceases to speculate about who the perpetrator was.

Harry Hansen, master detective and super sleuth, did his best to solve the Black Dahlia murder. He is satisfied that he brought to bear everything he could, everything his experience had taught him. And yet he too still has to wonder who it was who slew Elizabeth Ann Short so viciously and why. Is the murderer walking around today, still harboring his or her dark and bloody secret? Like Hansen, we may never know. Yet, apropos of the tantalizing mystery of every still-to-be-solved murder, maybe some day we will.

6

Murder at the Opera

IT WAS LATE in the afternoon of March 12, 1963, in Vienna. Inside the ornate Vienna State Opera House, one of Europe's most famous stages, preparations had begun at 4:00 P.M. for that evening's scheduled performance of Wagner's foreboding musical drama, *Die Walküre*. At 5:05 P.M., twenty-two-year-old Gertrude Galli, who was employed by the opera company as a hairdresser, entered the ladies' shower. It is situated in a remote upstairs area of the theater, in a section that also harbors the dressing rooms for extras and ballet members, as well as rehearsal rooms for the choir. Since the opera *Die Walküre* does not feature any choirs, walk-ons, or dancers, this area of the building was virtually deserted.

In the stillness, which contrasted eerily with the stage bustle below, Fräulein Galli came upon a horrifying and heartrending sight. On the floor of the shower anteroom lay the body of a preadolescent girl, partly nude and soaked in blood.

The hairdresser ran to notify a co-worker and the janitor, who called the theater doctor. The physician confirmed that the child was indeed dead, from what was evidently a multiplicity of stab wounds.

Thus was discovered one of the most notorious crimes in modern Austrian history and one that stirred worldwide attention.

The victim was identified as the ballet student Dagmar Furich, ten years of age, who had been a member of the Opera Ballet School for two years. Pretty, slender, and frail, with long blond hair, Dagmar and her sixteen-year-old sister Sylvia lived with their mother, Isolde Furich, an employee of the magistrate council, an administrative office for their district of Vienna. The dead girl's father, Franz Furich, a contract employee of Austria's Federal Ministry for Trade and Reconstruction, lived away from his family.

On the tragic afternoon, Dagmar, who attended Vienna's *Realgymnasium* for Girls, had left her home at Boltzmanngasse 22/9 to dance in a ballet rehearsal scheduled at the opera house for 5:00 P.M. She would never arrive for the rehearsal.

True to theatrical tradition—and perhaps particularly so in the Austrian capital, where music has held a place of honor since Vienna's Imperial Court Orchestra was founded in 1498—the show went on. The audience was admitted as scheduled beginning at 5:30 P.M., and in spite of the agitated state of the cast, the performance of *Die Walküre*, with its brooding tale of murderous gods, began at 6:00 P.M. Seated in the glittering opera house, the audience was unaware that a real murder had just been committed backstage, and that, pending investigation, the body had not yet been removed.

As the opera progressed on stage, police began their probing behind the back curtain. Among the first to arrive on the scene was a tall, silver-haired, distinguished-looking man who could have been a diplomat. Nevertheless, he was more interested in clues than in protocol. The imposing gentleman was Dr. Friedrich Kuso, chief of the Vienna State Security Office and Austria's most renowned living detective.

Son of middle-class parents, Kuso was born in 1917 in Vienna. After graduating from high school he enrolled in the University of Vienna as a student in law and government science. There he received a law degree, which entitles him to be addressed by the Austrian honorific of "Court Counselor."

During World War II, in August 1943 while serving as a first lieutenant with Rommel's Afrika Korps in North Africa, Kuso

Little Dagmar Furich, ballet pupil and victim of the savage murder in the ornate Vienna State Opera House.

was captured. He spent three years in American prisoner-of-war camps in Concordia, Kansas, and in Indiana. While in the POW camp at Concordia, Kuso became interested in the general subject of law and order, and began reading books and magazine articles about the FBI. He was especially impressed by the Anglo-Saxon tradition of trial by jury, and wrote an essay on the subject. With the help of the camp administration and the YMCA Kuso managed to borrow legal research files from Kansas' state library. He recalls, "It was a marvelous thing for a prisoner to be able to keep busy. I was on my way to becoming a fighter for law and order." The essay, entitled "Uncertain Judgments in Anglo-American Law," was later accepted by the University of Vienna, and today forms part of the library of the university's Professor Dr. Roland Grassberger, one of Central Europe's leading experts on crime.

Kuso returned to Vienna in 1946, and at first wanted to become a district attorney. After working for a year at Vienna's state court for criminal affairs, he came to the conclusion, as he puts it, that solving a crime is more interesting than formally trying the caught criminal. Kuso says, "I wanted to dig into the unknown quantities of criminal investigation, to be in the front lines of the police. My aim was to deal with the person at the place of the crime regardless of whether he or she was the criminal, the victim, or the witness."

In 1947, the year he was married, Kuso became a police commissioner and was assigned to the Vienna State Security Office, which is the center for the control of crime in the Austrian capital. "There," Kuso recounts, "I had my first major successes in the clearing up of complicated and difficult murder cases. In 1955, against my wish, I was made head of police for the largest precinct in Vienna. But in 1959, because of my talent [Dr. Kuso is too forthright to be overly modest] I was called back to the Security Office as chief of the investigation division for all capital crimes."

It was in this capacity, as head of the special branch that handles the gravest offenses, that Kuso cracked some of his most spectacular murder cases. None was more chilling than the savage slaying of little Dagmar Furich in Vienna's State Opera House.

Kuso unhesitatingly terms it his biggest and most important case. He adds, "In the first place it was a crime that took place on the most important cultural site in Austria. Then, the victim was, after all, a girl of the age of ten. Also the way the murder

Dr. Friedrich Kuso, Austria's most renowned detective, who painstakingly wove the web of evidence that clinched the confession of the slayer of 10-year-old Dagmar Furich, stands on the steps of Vienna's Belvedere Palace.

was committed enraged me. Furthermore, this criminal case stirred the greatest interest in the Austrian public and abroad. And last but not least, this case was a matter of prestige for the entire Viennese criminal police."

Thus a classic crime was confronted by a classic investigator. Contemplating the pathetically small, blood-spattered corpse of the ballet pupil, Dr. Kuso had reason for his personal sense of rage. Only a human animal could have been responsible for the sight that greeted the detective's eyes.

The little girl's corpse lay on its back, legs slightly pulled up. The left arm was stretched out. On her left wrist was a watch made of yellow metal; the watch was still working. The right hand lay between two legs of a tipped-over stool.

The upper part of the body was dressed in a blue blouse with white mother-of-pearl buttons and a pink undershirt. Both had

Joseph Weinwurm, center, is led away following his arrest on suspicion of stabbing a 64-year-old Vienna woman with a fork and committing a series of knife attacks on other women in the Austrian capital. After lengthy and intensive questioning by Detective Kuso, Weinwurm confessed to the slaying of Dagmar Furich. (*Wide World*)

been pushed up and were soaked with blood. Below, white underpants, black bloomers, light-brown tights, and beige stockings had been pushed down to the ankles, leaving the lower part of the body bare. The feet were in brown buckled shoes. A blue knitted cap, a blue pleated skirt, a blue cardigan, and a multicolored scarf were on the floor to the left of the body. A gray winter coat with a brown fur collar hung from a clothes hook. In a coat pocket were a ticket for city bus No. 6 of March 12, 1963, and a key. A plastic handbag, containing sweets and a pair of woolen gloves, was on a bench.

The tiny entranceway was spattered with blood. Several patches of crimson splotched the left side of an adjacent row of radiators. Above the nearby bench on the wall were five blood marks. Below an inside door bolt, on the light switch, and next to it were wiped blood smears. There was a large puddle of blood below the body.

The left side of the child's chest had been stabbed seventeen times through the clothing. Of these, thirteen stabs had pierced or touched the heart and the left lung and had penetrated the back wall of the chest. The fact that the stabs were so close together led to the conclusion that the slayer had not even pulled out the murder weapon after each major stab before making another thrust.

Ten of the seventeen stabs had penetrated the back of the rib cage as well as the back of the clothing. Seven of the stabs even damaged the floor underneath the child, four of them going completely through the floor covering.

According to the autopsy, all seventeen of the chest stabs were dealt while the victim was still alive. The girl had also been knifed five times in the left temple, three of the thrusts penetrating the skull, the face, and the brain. The latter five stabs were probably administered after the child had already died from the seventeen stabs in the chest.

There were eleven more stabs in the area of the girl's genitals. Two of the thrusts penetrated into the abdomen, ending only at the coccyx. One of the stabs had opened the bladder.

Based on traces found on the forehead and in the pelvis, the conclusion was that the murder instrument had to have been a hunting knife or similar weapon with a firm, fairly long and slim blade.

An inspection of the body, and the autopsy performed at the University of Vienna Institute for Legal Medicine, indicated that the little girl bled to death as a result of the numerous knife wounds in the chest. Preceding the fatal wounds, there had been strangling and blunt use of force against her face and head. Dagmar had not been raped or otherwise sexually molested.

Clearly the killer was a psychopath. But how to track him or her down? The question set in motion one of the most massive, painstakingly meticulous probes in the annals of criminology.

As Kuso was only too aware, the psychopath, with a peculiar cunning tending to surpass that of the one-time perpetrator of a crime of passion or the cold-blooded professional killer, frequently blends more indistinguishably into the "normal" populace when not on a murderous rampage. The individual who commits a crime of passion is apt to suffer a visible guilt reaction or, conversely, to boast of the deed. The hired assassin is often traceable through his underworld associations. By contrast, the psychopath in many cases bears no perceptible guilt and has no evident motive.

Compounding Kuso's dilemma was a paucity of clues. Even as the opera was being performed, Kuso's Security Office and specialists from the Institute for Legal Medicine launched their investigation backstage. The slayer had left behind not a single fingerprint. They did, however, piece together some interesting traces and recollections that would later prove to be of vital importance.

The impression of a rubber sole was found on the floor of the shower room. Streaks of blood were found on the French double-doors of the main floor of the opera house, and on the inside of the glass of the stage door leading to Kärntnerstrasse. To try to sniff out any additional clues, Kuso's security team searched the opera house with police dogs. The search went on for more than a day, without success. Exits from the opera were guarded. As the investigation at the opera house continued, teleprinter messages were dispatched informing all Vienna police stations and all security offices in Austria of the murder.

On the night of the slaying, other ballet students, among them eleven-year-old Susanne Fichtenbaum, were questioned. Susanne said that she had gone up the staircase of the opera house at 4:15 P.M. In front of the glass door on the second floor, she had seen a man. She had greeted him with *"Grüss Gott."* The man had turned and come toward her down the steps, answering her greeting in the same way. She had passed him and looked down at him from the third floor because the man had seemed "nervous and frightening." She noticed that he was coming up the stairs again. She described the man as approximately forty-two years old, about 1.72 meters tall, with dark-blond wavy hair, combed back, and an oval face with marks on it "like my Uncle Peter has" (acne scars). He was dressed in a gray suit and carried a black briefcase under his arm. He gave Susanne the impression that he was an office employee.

Subsequently, several persons reported to the police that, at the approximate time of the murder, they had seen a man leave the opera house at the Kärntnerstrasse exit. Among the descriptions was that given by a salesman, Ludwig Kovacs, who stated: on March 12, 1963, at around 5:15 P.M.—he could not give the exact time—while he was driving behind the opera house a young man had run across the street "like crazy" from Kovacs' right to his left, that is, from the direction of the opera. He was small, thin, without an overcoat, apparently dressed in a suit, and had "protruding eyes." He had paid no attention to the heavy traffic and had narrowly escaped being hit by a taxi.

Kuso and his investigators set about trying to reconstruct little Dagmar Furich's last movements. As the ticket found in the victim's coat pocket showed, she had boarded bus No. 6 at 4:15 P.M. and had gotten off the bus at the Kärntnerstrasse opera house stop at approximately 4:31 P.M. Therefore, Dagmar should have reached the opera house at its Kärntnerstrasse entrance at around 4:33 P.M. Using a girl of the same age, Kuso's Security Office reconstructed Dagmar's walk from the bus stop to the washroom. The investigators concluded that Dagmar must have met her murderer at the latest at 4:38 P.M.

The condition of the victim's clothes, the fact that her coat was on the hanger and that the hooks and zipper of her pleated skirt were not torn, as well as the way her handbag had been placed on the bench, led to the conclusion that the victim had taken off her clothes herself. This indicated that the little girl had probably accompanied the slayer into the room voluntarily.

The location of the crime was such, Kuso further concluded, that the assassin had to be familiar with the surroundings. The murderer, therefore, could have been a member of the opera company, or an outsider who had managed to procure information about the opera house. Inquiries revealed that there was a lack of control over entry into the building that could easily have enabled strangers to familiarize themselves with its interior. There had also been group tours through the opera house. They started at the entrance on Operngasse, continued over the staircase on the second floor—past the scene of the crime—and ended at the exit on Kärntnerstrasse.

Employees of the opera revealed that, during the guided tours, male visitors not infrequently separated themselves from their groups and were later caught peeping at female artists in the showers, lavatories, and dressing rooms. This had never been reported to the police by the opera.

For these and other reasons, Kuso decided that the investigation could not be limited to the opera personnel.

Still, the employees of the State Opera—approximately 1,900 individuals in all—could hardly be ignored. Kuso and his investigators interviewed each and every one of them. They ranged from the artistic personnel (soloists, chorus singers, ballet dancers, extras, orchestra and philharmonic players) to technical personnel (stagehands, wardrobe handlers, hairdressers, makeup experts, common laborers, ticket sellers, and the fire and building protection staff), to the opera's administrative personnel (members of the federal theater administration and the federal buildings administration).

Also questioned were personnel of firms participating in the reconstruction of the State Opera*, and employees of several firms that were engaged, both at the time of the murder and

---

* The State Opera, almost destroyed during an Allied bombing raid in World War II, was sufficiently reconstructed to be reopened in 1955, but the renovation had continued.

before its occurrence, in street construction work in front of the opera.

The investigation likewise encompassed checking known sexual deviates (rapists, sadists, clothes slashers, exhibitionists, animal torturers, and arsonists).

A check was also made of mental health and nursing institutions for any new patients and an evaluation of those released on good behavior, as well as escaped mental patients. In this aspect of the probe Interpol was asked to inquire abroad.

Inquiries were made in prisons about volunteer admissions and newly admitted criminals.

Dry-cleaning establishments were questioned about blood-stained clothes, and cutlery stores about the suspect knife based on the measurements of the wounds and the supposed shape and form of the murder weapon.

In addition, checks were made on possible suspects reported by the public. The crime had drawn such wide publicity that hints and suggestions were pouring in.

All told, Kuso and the sleuths under his command carried out no fewer than 14,000 inquiries, checkups on alibis, and evaluations of statements. (One chief inspector, Rudolf Rothmayer, even died, in all probability, as a result of the pressures of the case. In spite of a high fever he refused to interrupt his participation in the probe, and subsequently succumbed to a heart attack.)

Still the spoor of the psychopathic killer of little Dagmar Furich remained elusive.

Kuso's Security Office called on well-known psychological and criminological experts for advice that might illuminate the personality of the slayer. Contact was made with the head of the Rosenhuegel mental institution of the city of Vienna, Professor Dr. Herbert Reisner, and with the chairman of the psychiatric neurological clinic of the University of Vienna, Professor Dr. Hans Hoff, to obtain a personality profile of the murderer from a psychological point of view, and at the same time to seek the identities of patients of both institutions who might fall under suspicion.

Moreover, Kuso conducted an exchange of opinions with the

chairman of the institute for criminology at the University of Vienna, Professor Dr. Grassberger. Professor Grassberger confirmed the view that tracking down a murderous psychopath is among the most difficult and near-hopeless tasks of the criminal police. Pointing to three famous cases in Germany—those of Haarman, Kuerten, and Luebke—Grassberger recalled that these culprits had committed a series of murders before they were captured, and that they were apprehended only as a result of accidents. Grassberger expressed the opinion—which was in conformance with the pessimistic prognostication of Kuso's Security Office—that in spite of the massive search that had taken place so far, the real question was, "When and where will the next offense occur?"

The path of the slayer had been partially reconstructed, but then the trail had run into sand. The evidence that had been collected so far provided not a single conclusive clue. While never letting up in their intensive investigation, detective Kuso and his colleagues wearily conceded that Professor Grassberger might well be right. The murder of the girl in the State Opera, it appeared, could not be solved until the killer struck again.

Unfortunately, Kuso and his colleagues did not have long to wait.

On June 17, 1963, at approximately 6:00 P.M., a twenty-six-year-old female student, Waltraut Brunner, together with her friend Liselotte Fremuth, went to the cinema on Vienna's Graben. As the two entered the darkened movie, Fräulein Brunner felt a blow near her thigh, just as a man passed her and ran toward the exit. A woman usher, Herta Wendler, thinking that the fellow had thoughtlessly pushed the girl aside, chased him but was not able to catch up. Fräulein Brunner and her girl friend took their seats. Only then did Miss Brunner notice that her dress was becoming soaked with blood. An ambulance was called, and at an emergency station, a cut measuring 1.5 centimeters deep was discovered in Miss Brunner's thigh. The injured woman related that her attacker had been around 1.75 meters tall, but could give no other description of him. The woman usher described him as approximately 1.65 meters tall with strong build and dark, wavy hair. He was dressed in a dark ski jacket and dark trousers.

As the Austrian summer wore on, it became all too evident that a Viennese Jack the Ripper was on the loose.

On July 30, 1963, at around 3:40 P.M., a twenty-two-year-old American student who was on holiday in Vienna, Virginia Chieffo, visited the church of St. Augustine on Augustinerstrasse. She had arrived in Vienna from Salzburg the day before and was living at the city-sponsored Youth Inn in Potzleinsdorf.

While Miss Chieffo was sitting in a back pew, a man approached her from the high altar, coming up the right-hand aisle. He seized one of her breasts and punched her above the right eye, knocking her glasses to the floor. Then he picked up the glasses, threw them at her, and ran toward the exit. The terrified young woman fled toward the interior of the church from the pew toward the high altar. But then the assailant turned around, came back, caught up with her, and stabbed her several times with a knife, without saying a word. Then he fled.

In response to her cries, a tourist guide, Jakob Wiellandt, and a woman who was waiting to be guided through the Hapsburg burial vaults, hurried to her aid. While the woman took care of the wounded girl, Wiellandt ran outside to find a policeman. The assailant, however, had escaped.

Miss Chieffo was taken to ambulance emergency station No. 1. Detective Kuso was immediately notified, and at the request of his Security Office, the chairman of the University of Vienna's Institute of Legal Medicine, Professor Dr. Leonard Breitenecker, hurried to the emergency ward and inspected the American girl's wounds even before a physician had treated them. In this incident the injuries were considerably more serious: a contusion from a blow on the right outer eye, a cut through the right earlobe, a puncture in the area of the right collarbone, a puncture in the left breast, and two punctures in the right back. One of the stabs barely missed the heart.

A search was launched for the assailant, whom Miss Chieffo described as twenty-eight to thirty years old, nice-looking, 1.75 meters tall, slim, with crew-cut blond hair combed back, and a slightly tanned face.

Even as the police investigation intensified, a third knife assault on a woman occurred. An August 2, 1963—the attacks were now coming with greater rapidity—a forty-one-year-old saleswoman, Frau Maria Brunner, closed her tobacco stand on Pra-terstrasse shortly after 7:00 P.M. On her way home she paused in Vienna's Stadtpark, a lovely green oasis in the heart of the city, to rest. She had been sitting for approximately forty-five minutes when she suddenly felt a blow on her neck. In the dark-ness, Frau Brunner thought that she had been hit by a ball.

A little later she got up and walked toward the park exit that leads in the direction of Weihburggasse. As she passed another woman who was sitting on a bench, the woman told Frau Brun-ner that she was bleeding. The woman, seventy-three-year-old Frau Rosa Tourkoff, also pointed out a man not far away who was heading for Weihburggasse. Only then did Mrs. Brunner realize that she had been stabbed. She was taken to the city's General Hospital, where doctors found an eighteen-centimeter-long puncture in the right side of her neck which had also per-forated the lung.

The man leaving the park was described as around twenty-five years old, approximately 1.72 meters tall, slender, with dark-blond hair combed upward, and dressed in a dark suit, green shirt, and pale necktie. Frau Tourkoff completed the description by adding that he was nice-looking, "like a clean-cut student."

Notified of the latest stabbing, Kuso dispatched carloads of detectives to scour the area. But the phantom knife wielder was nowhere to be found.

By now, alarm began to grip the storied city of the waltz and the Wiener schnitzel. Where would its Jack the Ripper slash again? Viennese—especially women—walked more carefully and looked warily over their shoulders at strangers. Security Chief Kuso, for his part, ordered reinforced patrols in parks, and re-doubled his efforts to round up and question sexual deviates and other men about whom his investigators had received informa-tion. Yet the knifer continued to roam free.

As Kuso had anticipated, nevertheless, the assailant would ultimately trip himself up on one of his own crimes. And, as fate would have it, the fugitive's undoing—much like that of The Lavender Hill Mob in the film—was brought about by a re-doubtable elderly matron.

On August 6, 1963, at approximately 4:50 P.M., a sixty-four-year-old pensioner, Frau Emma Laasch, arrived home and entered the hallway of her residence at Tuchlauben No. 3, in Vienna's First District. As she opened her purse to get out her keys, a hand reached from behind and clamped itself over her mouth. At the same time she felt what later turned out to be a stab in the right side of her neck. She wrested herself free and found herself confronting a man who was holding a dinner fork in his hand.

He yelled, "Money!" In spite of her age, Frau Laasch managed to elude him and, in a loud voice, called for help. The assailant fled, but Frau Laasch sprinted after him and saw him run into the next house, Tuchlauben No. 5.

She told passersby what had happened, and one of them notified a traffic policeman, Johann Kowarik. Officer Kowarik entered the house. Between the second and third floors a man met him, flushed and perspiring. When the officer questioned the man as to why he was in the house, he gave suspicious answers. He was taken into custody and turned out to be one Josef Weinwurm, an Austrian national who had been born in Haugsdorf on September 16, 1930, which made him not quite thirty-three years old. He identified himself as a salesman.

Was the fork-wielding mugger the same man as the knife-flashing assailant—and was he in turn the murderer of little Dagmar Furich? There were certainly similarities in the modes of operation, but Security Chief Kuso was far too careful an investigator to jump to conclusions. Moreover, there were those who did not believe that Weinwurm, who was suspected of trying to rob for money, could be the random knifer who evidently stabbed for thrills. Kuso and his team of fellow detectives began a painstaking check of Weinwurm's background, and discovered a series of interesting patterns.

Weinwurm was in fact a jobless, homeless, unmarried drifter and ex-convict. His family had come from Haugsdorf in lower Austria. One of his brothers had been killed in the World War II invasion of France, another brother was in government service, and two sisters were married. Weinwurm had attended elementary school in Haugsdorf. Because of the wartime bombing attacks on that city, he was sent to a youth camp in East Tyrol, where he remained until the end of the war. The family later moved from Haugsdorf to Vienna, and began operating a store selling food and incidentals in Währing, a district of Vienna. Young Josef Weinwurm worked as an apprentice in his parents' store.

But he soon began showing antisocial tendencies. During the austere postwar years, Weinwurm began stealing from his parents' store and dealing in Austria's then flourishing black market through a woman he had met. Through her boyfriend he obtained a pistol.

On March 21, 1947, Weinwurm was supposed to take food stamps from his parents' store to an accounting office that was housed in a girls' school. There he threatened a girl with his pistol and attempted to force her to undress in a toilet. When she screamed he fled, but he was caught in the school building. This incident, however, did not go down in his criminal record. The youth court of Vienna declared him guilty but, on the basis of a psychiatric report, did not fix any penalty.

Weinwurm returned to work at the family store, but friction developed with his parents because he persisted in staying away from classes at a trade school he was supposed to be attending. After an argument with his mother and father, he ran away from home and wandered about the center of the city.

On January 22, 1949, he attempted to rob a woman on Vienna's Wildbretmarkt by putting a pair of scissors to her breast. When she cried for help he ran, only to be seized by the police in the upper floors of a house in Kurrentgasse. Brought before the Vienna State Court, he was given another psychiatric examination and again declared not responsible for his deed. However, he was placed in a rest home. On April 29, 1950, after a court commission decided that he no longer needed institutional care, Weinwurm was released and returned to his family.

To Kuso, both of these early offenses clearly had sexual motives. Nevertheless, because of the disposition of the court proceedings against Weinwurm in those two cases, and because of the nature of his later crimes, Weinwurm did not show up in the police files as a sex offender but rather as a burglar. All told, he was to be cited seven times for burglary, and occasional and habitual theft, and had drawn three convictions in connection with these offenses.

On January 22, 1953, Weinwurm had been arrested, according to the police, after he had committed no fewer than eighty-two burglaries, most of them in Vienna's First District. This time the Vienna State Court sentenced him to four years at hard labor. On October 5, 1955, Weinwurm was released on parole from the Stein prison.

Less than two months later—on November 22, 1955—he was again arrested for burglary, and was again sentenced to four years at hard labor. He was released from Stein prison on probation on March 11, 1961. Yet, after only a few weeks of freedom, on April 18, 1961, Weinwurm was once more jailed on charges of burglary. He was sentenced to ten months in the penitentiary. On March 5, 1963, he was released from Goellersdorf prison.

While Weinwurm was behind bars his father had died, and his mother had had a leg amputated. No longer able to run the family grocery, she had given up the store. Frau Weinwurm had moved from Währing into Vienna's Twenty-second District where her son Josef had visited her shortly after his release from prison. She had heard nothing from him since. His sister, Gertrud Rupp, had occasionally helped her brother out. But she maintained no regular contact with him, on orders of her husband.

Checking into Weinwurm's record, Kuso's investigators discovered that the police had received a lead on him in the immediate wake of Dagmar Furich's slaying, but he had slipped through their fingers. Among the tips from the public that had streamed in had been two messages from Goellersdorf prison. One was from the widow of a watchman of the penitentiary, Maria Zehetmayer, and the other from the prison superintendent, Johann Hubeny. Both messages contained approximately the same information.

They concerned an inmate of the penitentiary named Josef Weinwurm, who had been released on March 5, 1963. At the time of his release, two knives that had been among his few belongings when he entered the prison were handed back to him. Hubeny believed that one of the knives, a jackknife, was similar to the presumed murder weapon, a duplicate of which had been pictured in the Vienna newspaper, *Kurier*. In the Goellersdorf penitentiary release file investigators discovered a note: "Jack-knife was handed over."

Inquiries made at the time to Weinwurm's mother produced the information that her son had spent only a short time with her after his release; she thought that it was only two or three days. He supposedly had taken a job in a lime pit but had given it up. She had later evicted him, had had no further contact with her ex-convict son, and did not know where he was. This did not seem unusual to her since he had often disappeared for longer periods.

As required by Austrian law, Weinwurm, as an ex-convict, had registered with the police, but no new registration had followed after he had moved out of his mother's apartment. The checkup on his whereabouts could not be completed, and it had remained among the numerous potential leads—given the multitude of tips that had been received—still to be examined.

Nevertheless, the fact now remained that the ex-convict who had allegedly tried to mug an old woman with a fork had been in possession of a knife that could fit the opera house murder committed seven days after his release. This understandably stirred Dr. Kuso's interest in Josef Weinwurm.

Delving deeper into Weinwurm's background, Kuso discovered a fascinating pattern in the arrested man's misdeeds. From court records it was discovered that Weinwurm had carried out many of his burglaries in dressing rooms and checkrooms. Among them: the dressing room of a skating club, the actors' dressing room of the Löwinger Theater, the checkrooms of the Gösser-Bier-Klinik, the dressing rooms of the Kleines Theater, the checkroom of the Opernkino cinema, the employees' dressing room at the Heiner pastry shop, and the directors' rooms at the Pfundmayer Modeling School.

With these two circumstantial arrows (his possible possession of a knife and his penchant for carrying out criminal activities in dressing rooms) pointing Weinwurm to the savage murder of the girl ballet pupil, Kuso began to suspect that he might have his man. Nonetheless, Kuso is too shrewd an investigator to reveal such potential trump cards prematurely. In their initial interrogation of Weinwurm, the police carefully avoided any reference to the murder at the opera house, but instead confined their questions to the series of assaults on women that had occurred since then.

In the immediate case at hand of the attempted fork holdup of Frau Emma Laasch, Weinwurm denied having committed the deed. However, a black pullover belonging to him had been found in the house next door at Tuchlauben No. 5. When Weinwurm, dressed in the pullover, was brought before the victim, Frau Laasch declared categorically that he was the culprit.

On August 7, the day after the attack on Mrs. Laasch and the apprehension of Weinwurm, the American student, Virginia Chieffo, was released from the hospital. A lineup of suspects in the assault on her, not including Weinwurm, was shown to Miss Chieffo but she eliminated them. She also looked through various categories of police photograph files, without result. The following day, however, surveying another lineup that included Weinwurm, Miss Chieffo positively identified him as her assailant.

Other witnesses identified Weinwurm as the man seen leaving Vienna's City Park after the stabbing of Maria Brunner.

The movie box-office clerk, Herta Wendler, picked him out as the probable man she had chased after the knife attack on the female student, Waltraut Brunner.

Yet, confronted with these damaging denunciations, Weinwurm continued to protest his innocence. He maintained that he had lived with a girl friend whose name he did not want to reveal, and conceded that he had not registered his residence with the police. Beyond that, he refused to give any information about his whereabouts from the day of his release from Goellersdorf penitentiary until his arrest.

Like a hunter in hot pursuit, Dr. Kuso now bore down on Josef Weinwurm. With the consent of the judicial examining officer, Weinwurm was interrogated daily including Saturdays, Sundays, and holidays. He still denied the assaults on the women and still refused to give any detailed information about his movements after his release from Goellersdorf.

Utilizing the press, radio, and television, Kuso appealed to the public for help. Appearing personally before television cameras, the celebrated criminal investigator asked Austrian citizens to come forward with any information they might have about the life of Josef Weinwurm. The plea proved successful.

Two waiters from a cafe recognized Weinwurm from a published photograph as a regular television-viewing customer. They also provided a tip about a frequent companion of Weinwurm's. The latter was found to be a fifty-four-year-old waiter, Ernst Gschellhammer, who had a police record for homosexual offenses. Picked up and questioned by Kuso, Gschellhammer admitted that he had met Weinwurm in Stein prison in 1960, and that, since the preceding Easter, Weinwurm had been living with him without registering with the police. Gschellhammer further said that the two had sustained a homosexual relationship.

Although the waiter himself lived as a roomer and had only one bed, he had given Josef Weinwurm lodging every night for approximately four months without the landlady's knowing about it. Weinwurm had played hide-and-seek with the landlady, leaving the apartment after the woman, who had a regular job, had gone to work, and returning after she had retired. To Gschellhammer, Weinwurm had explained that he worked during the day for a wholesale firm—a lie, as it turned out.

Asked why he had not reported Weinwurm's living with him to the police, Gschellhammer said that he had been shocked by the arrest of his friend and had hardly slept that night. Then, Gschellhammer added, he decided not to report voluntarily in the hope that Weinwurm would not betray him. The waiter was sentenced to sixteen days' arrest for violating the duty to report to police.

Under further questioning, Weinwurm declared that following his release from Goellersdorf he had begun working in a limestone quarry in Ernstbrunn but had had to give up the job after a few days because of a skin disease. On his own, he added that on March 12, 1963—the day of the opera house murder—in the early afternoon, he had taken the train to Salzburg, and that his ultimate destination was West Germany, where he was going to start a new life.

Now that alibi underwent examination. Tailoring the investigation to the story, Kuso assigned one of his detectives who had worked at Austrian border control points and who was familiar with their procedures to pursue this aspect of the probe. Inquiries at the national railroad revealed that Weinwurm could have taken one of three trains on that day: the Orient Express (which left Vienna at 2:00 P.M.), the Rot-Weiss Kurier (which departed at 3:00 P.M.), and the Wiener Walzer (which left Vienna at 8:00 P.M.). On March 12, the Wiener Walzer arrived at Salzburg ten minutes late at 11:55 P.M. Kuso's investigators established, from the hotel's registration records, that Weinwurm had arrived at Salzburg's Hotel Elmo after midnight.

Weinwurm continued to deny the series of attacks on women. Now he also denied, when Kuso casually inserted the question into the interrogation, that he had had anything to do with the murder in the opera house. Throughout long days and nights of questioning, Weinwurm remained a stubborn, resistant prisoner.

Kuso decided that the time was now ripe to bring his prisoner to terms with reality. The results of the investigations in Salzburg, as well as other discrepancies in Weinwurm's story, were shown to him.

The effect was dramatic. Weinwurm was visibly shaken. He finally said that, if witnesses had testified against him, he may have been capable of committing the crimes without remembering them, that he suffered from mental disturbances. He added that he had to straighten things out with himself, and he asked for time to think things over.

On August 27, 1963, Weinwurm requested a confidential meeting with a certain detective who had manifested sympathy toward him. To the detective, Weinwurm confessed the assaults on the women—and also confessed to the murder of little Dagmar Furich.

Kuso's painstaking interrogation of Weinwurm had embodied a drama all of its own, climaxed by the prisoner's detailed admission of his act of horror.

As often happens in such cases, the confession came suddenly. For the second time in one evening, the green prisoners' van rumbled from the Gray House, as Vienna's city prison is called, to Kuso's Security Office.

Josef Weinwurm, tired, pale, obviously stretched to the end of his rope by Kuso's implacable questioning, was once again, for the umpteenth time, brought to the bare office in which he had already been interrogated for countless hours. A short time later, police reporters raced to the nearest telephones, and in editorial rooms urgent bulletins clattered from typewriters: Weinwurm had capitulated. On that Tuesday evening he admitted having slain the ten-year-old girl ballet student in the State Opera.

Kuso's "victor" in the duel between the police and the stubborn criminal was an experienced district criminal inspector, Blasko, a member of Kuso's murder squad. Weinwurm picked Blasko out as the preferred listener after the ex-convict declared himself ready "to tell it as it really was," and babbled out the confession.

Kuso and his detective team let Weinwurm tell it as he wished, interrupting his macabre stream of consciousness only to check Weinwurm's account against the official report from the murder scene. Weinwurm described the deed with details that only the real slayer could have known. The man was clearly telling the truth. He also divulged things that were not in the official report but that fitted perfectly into the circumstantial picture of the murder.

As with most if not all murderers, Weinwurm demonstrated that confession is good for the soul. In the wake of his initial admission of guilt, he became more relaxed and talkative. He went on to expand his confession, giving the police a meticulous description of his movements and activities that preceded the opera house murder.

Already a specialist in burglarizing theater dressing rooms, Weinwurm had sneaked into the opera house four days earlier, on March 8, and had stolen a purse containing 40 schillings from the room of a choirmaster.

Weinwurm spent the night of March 11 in his mother's apartment in the Kagran district of Vienna. The next morning, he had an argument with the sorely tried woman. His mother had evidently told him again that he should look for a respectable job. As Weinwurm explained it, the argument revived in him a hatred toward all women that he had long harbored. He decided to seek satisfaction by murdering a female. Who the unfortunate female was did not matter.

Teeming with rage at his mother, Weinwurm headed back to the Opera House, where he had been only a few days before, initially with the intention of committing a robbery, which he did. Once he was inside the opera house's nearly deserted upstairs, however, the notion occurred to him that here would also be an ideal place to carry out his compulsion to kill some woman or girl at random.

Thus, he later returned to the opera house, this time with the firm intention to kill, only to discover that he had left his jackknife at home. He went back to his mother's apartment, got the jackknife, and returned once more—his third time to slip into the State Opera that day.

According to Weinwurm, he lay in wait at first for a woman who went to the toilet. "Just then a man in a gray coat came by and sized me up from head to foot. Although I stood there in the corridor with drawn knife, the man noticed nothing and I got out of there."

Then a young girl came up the stairway, and Weinwurm saw in her his victim. She was little Susanne Fichtenbaum, who got a good look at the stranger and who was later to provide a description of him. Fate intervened in Susanne's behalf. The knifer was stopped from culminating his compulsion upon her by the presence of more girls who came up the stairway.

Minutes later, ten-year-old blonde Dagmar Furich came up the stairs alone. Weinwurm accosted her, pretended to be a doctor, and lured her into the out-of-the-way shower room. He explained to the unsuspecting girl that the ballet was dressing elsewhere on that day, and led her through the door through which she would not leave again alive. In the shower room, Weinwurm told his victim to take off her clothes and asked, "Have you, by the way, been examined yet?"

His next action was the ferocious attack and murder.

Now all of the evidence that had been so painstakingly pieced together by Kuso and his squad of investigators came into play. "After the murder Weinwurm did just as the police had reconstructed for March 12," declares Dr. Kuso. The detectives had determined that the murderer fled down the stairway and through the long, ground floor corridor of the opera house in the direction of Kärntnerstrasse. Drops of blood on the glass door in front of the exit had been the basis for the police theory, which was now confirmed by Weinwurm's confession.

Statements of witnesses collected by police at the time of the murder also bore out Weinwurm's account.

Corroborated was the account of a taxi driver who, moments after the slaying, almost ran over a man hurrying nervously across the street adjacent to the opera house. Fleeing with his blood-soaked coat over his arm, Weinwurm was nearly hit by the cab. This likewise confirmed the report given by the salesman-motorist who had seen the near-accident.

Weinwurm continued down Fürich Street, where he maintains that he had a coffee in an expresso bar. Later he strolled slowly toward the Schweizer Gate and the Hofburg, Vienna's former imperial palace, where he slipped into the Batthyanyi staircase and, on the second floor, hid his bloody coat and gloves behind a box. They were found there by the police. This was the last piece of evidence that linked Weinwurm inextricably to the murder. Without such tangible proof—Weinwurm's coat and gloves which he had worn during the deed—he would always have been able to deny his confession.

Weinwurm then went to the West Railroad Station, where he caught the eight o'clock express to Salzburg. The next day he continued on an excursion ticket to Munich. There he discarded the jackknife and his papers and reported to the local police under a false name. In the meantime, back in Vienna, hundreds of police were searching for the opera house murderer.

As the motive for his crime, Weinwurm declared, "I hate all women." A diagnosis confirming the fact had been made by a psychiatrist after Weinwurm's first sexual assaults as a youth. Declared the knife slayer, "I have hated women since I was fifteen years old. Why, I cannot say."

Weinwurm also indicated where he had thrown the knife he had used in the attacks on Virginia Chieffo in the St. Augustine church and on Frau Brunner in the city park. He had discarded the weapon while running from the park. The knife had been found by a woman, and as a result of a newspaper description of the weapon, she had turned it over to the police. She had discovered it in the place designated by Weinwurm.

Dr. Kuso concluded, "Through the inquiries of the Security Office it has been possible to prove the crimes of Josef Weinwurm in such a way that even if, at a later date, the confession should be refuted, the evidence held by the Security Office cannot be changed." Weinwurm's confession had been nailed down by the facts.

Reflecting on the Opera House murder, Kuso unhesitatingly concedes that "The case certainly gave me the most headaches of my career." Kuso adds, "A criminal investigator with my responsibilities always has big cases. Fortunately, most of them can be solved; others cannot. The opera house murder was most certainly my biggest."

Even though the slaying of little Dagmar Furich was solved, Kuso says that he will think of it all his life, "because a criminal case like this one happens only once in the career of a crime specialist."

As for his methods of investigation, Dr. Kuso observes, "The most important thing for a detective is to be able to build a human bridge to the suspect. The person who has been arrested but has not yet made a confession should not see me as an enemy. Again and again during an investigation I try to awaken an understanding of and to concentrate on the person. Detectives, priests, and psychiatrists are people who are able to look into the depths and secrets of the human soul. I try to understand the action of the criminal, even though I cannot excuse it.

"I always repeat in my lectures that our kind of work does not stop at the confession but the work begins again, namely to support the confession with evidence. And, by the way, I oppose any kind of force.

"My big secret is the good relationship that I and my subordinates have with the underworld. We always try to have our fingers on the heartbeat of criminal happenings. We cultivate information and the informers. We try to have contact with prisoners during their prison terms so that after their release we can count on possible cooperation from them. Also in each case

I concentrate on the crime as though I had committed it myself. With this I try to discern not only the motives of the criminal, but also his methods.

"I consider myself the visual type of crime specialist. I do not rely on reports. The best reports and the best photographs cannot replace my own impressions. I therefore go immediately to the scene of the crime and form my own picture. And following that I am constantly kept informed of every small detail of an inquiry or report so that I am hardly ever surprised by a sudden change in developments. At least not by those things that are already known to the criminal police."

Austria's famed super sleuth concludes on a note of real-life realism. He says, "The lonely detective, cast in the way Sir Conan Doyle created the figure of Sherlock Holmes, is pure fiction. The truth of the matter is that criminal police function through a well-experienced team with one person at the head. Good ideas for me are not tied to rank. My colleagues are extraordinary men and very able. No crime specialist in the world can continuously be the only successful one. One simply needs good assistants, and those I have. But the decisions and the responsibility for success and failure are mine."

7

The Legend of Le Cocq

THE MOST FEARED MAN in the Rio de Janeiro hillside slum, or *favela*, known as Red Clay was a cold-blooded killer named José Alfonso de Jesus. "Mino," as Jesus was called, had wrought terror in Red Clay. He robbed workers as they came home on pay day, raped teenage girls, and had murdered several of the slum dwellers. Mino's principal source of income was money he extorted from the owners of Red Clay's small stores. Acting as a one-man Mafia, he demanded from each owner a share of the day's receipts in exchange for peace and quiet.

One day Mino appeared in a selected shop to demand his usual cut from the storekeeper, Enias Teixeira, who had been among Mino's frequent contributors. Explaining that business had been bad, Teixeira opened the till and showed Mino the pitifully small

amount of money in the drawer. To divide it, the shopkeeper
ventured, would hardly be worth the trouble. Unmoved, Mino
declared he would be back at 8:00 A.M. the next morning to pick
up his customary payoff, and swore to kill Teixeira and his entire
family (an eight-month pregnant wife and two children under
ten) if he did not produce a healthier sum.

Mino was understandably hated in Red Clay *favela*, and as he
left the shop some daring inhabitant threw a rock at him from
behind, striking Mino in the back. Thinking that the culprit was
Teixeira, Mino turned around to deal once and for all with an
uncooperative source of revenue. The terrified shopkeeper fled
out his back door, jumped over a low wall, and ran to the nearest
police station for help.

There, Teixeira poured out his story to Brazil's most famous
detective—a slight, deceptively casual looking cop with the in-
effable name of Milton Le Cocq de Oliveira. Le Cocq listened
to the extortion victim's tale of terror and coolly instructed him
to return to the slum, assuring Teixeira that everything would be
taken care of.

As familiar with Rio's *favelas* as the *favela*-dwellers themselves,
Le Cocq knew the labyrinthine pathways of the hillside slums
like the backs of his rather delicate hands. That evening he
slipped into Teixeira's small store in the slum without being seen
by Mino's local informers. Le Cocq was accompanied by two of
his colleagues, detectives Euclides Nascimento (nicknamed
"Garatoa" or "Big Boy") and Anibal Beckman (nicknamed
"Cartola" or "Top Hat"). In colorful Brazil, detectives sport
nicknames as well as the hoods they pursue.

The three lawmen spent the night in the store owner's living
quarters, which were separated from the store by a curtain. The
next morning, Le Cocq and Nascimento took up a position just
behind the curtain while Beckman went out to cover the only
possible escape route. Teixeira was instructed to go about his
business as usual. The stakeout was set.

At 8:00 A.M. a small boy who lived nearby announced the local
nemesis' approach with the shout, "Mino is coming!" Seconds
later Mino appeared, walking around a curve in the dirt path
leading to the store. Sinisterly attired, wearing dark glasses and

a black beret pulled low over his forehead, he seemed in no hurry. His hands were stuffed casually into his pockets. The fellow hoods accompanying him were a pair of holdup men. "Paraibinha" ("The Little One from Paraiba State") and Iva "Gaguinho" ("Little Stutterer"). Paraibinha was a dangerous

Milton Le Cocq de Oliveira, who reigns in death as he did in life as Brazil's No. 1 super sleuth. After bringing countless murderers and other criminals to justice, Le Cocq was gunned down by a petty hood in Rio in 1964. But, says a colleague, "It will be a thousand years before there is another Le Cocq." (*O Globo*)

outlaw who specialized in robbing and killing tourists in remote sightseeing areas. Gaguinho was a minor crook.

As Mino drew nearer, inhabitants of the adjacent huts hurriedly closed their shutters and locked their doors, like a scene out of a Brazilian version of *High Noon*. Trying to feign normalcy in the front of his shop Teixeira began to perspire and whispered that he was leaving because he did not want to die. From behind the curtain, Le Cocq hissed to Teixeira to stand firm. By now, both Le Cocq and Nascimento had drawn their .45s.

Mino entered the store. He demanded the money.

"Please forgive me," stammered the quaking storekeeper, "but this is all I could get together."

He placed a small stack of cruzeiros on the counter.

As Mino gathered up the bills, Beckman yelled an order to surrender, and Le Cocq came through the curtain, .45 in hand. Mino hesitated for a second, then went for his gun.

In the blazing shootout that followed, all three outlaws opened fire. Le Cocq fired once, felling Mino. On his way down, Mino got off two shots that went wild. Paraibinha and Gaguinho managed to flee. Officer Nascimento went over to the prostrate Mino, stooped down, and felt for his pulse. The murderer of Red Clay *favela* was dead.

The inglorious end of José Alfonso de Jesus, and the methodical efficiency with which he was dispatched, was a typical example of the cunning and courage that has made the name of Milton Le Cocq de Oliveira a modern police legend, not only in Brazil but throughout South America. Le Cocq himself was to die in a 1964 shootout at the age of 44. Yet, fascinatingly enough, he is as much or more an influence in death, not only on Brazil's police circles but on the country's public opinion, as he was in life. Rightly or wrongly, Le Cocq has become the inspiration of an aggressive and controversial law and order movement in South America's largest country. Le Cocq's life inspired the best from his colleagues. His death, it is widely if erroneously believed, has helped inspire Rio de Janeiro's legendary Death Squads—said to be bands of off-duty policemen who take the law into their own hands and summarily execute suspected criminals.

Le Cocq, as he is universally called by his former colleagues, the press, and his widow, was born in the city of Jacarepagua near Rio. Like many Brazilians, he came from a mixed family background. Le Cocq's father, Luiz Vitor le Cocq D'Oliveira, was the son of a Brazilian engineer and an Englishwoman, and became an architect and diplomat. He was Brazilian consul in New York and in China during the government of Brazil's President Nilo Pecanha. Le Cocq's mother was a Brazilian-born descendant of Italian immigrants. Because of his European blood and partly foreign name, Detective Milton Le Cocq was sometimes called "the Gringo"—in Brazil, which knows few social distinctions, Europeans as well as Americans enjoy the status of "gringos."

Detective José Guilherme Godinho Ferreira (nicknamed "Sivuca") worked closely with Le Cocq and was one of his most ardent admirers. Sivuca recalls that, as a teenager, Le Cocq read a book about a real-life French detective whose last name, coincidentally, was Le Cocq. The French investigator made a lasting impression on the Brazilian youth, which was reinforced by the similarity in names. Young Le Cocq also developed an admiration for famous fictional sleuths. Sivuca adds, "He always wanted to be just like Sherlock Holmes."

Against the wishes of his parents, Le Cocq wasted no time in pursuing his dream. When he was seventeen, he joined the Brazilian army and became a military policeman. Deciding that that offered little future in detective work, he entered the civilian police force after his discharge and soon found his niche: the *delegaciao de vigiliancia*, a branch in which the assignments were tough and the work was in the streets.

Le Cocq studied police science on his own in order to become *detetive* ("detective" in Portuguese) a rank that he attained in 1954 and held until his death. A high school graduate, he had planned to study law after his retirement and become a trial lawyer. Many policemen in Brazil have law degrees, including the majority of Le Cocq's closest circle of colleagues. This makes them eligible for advancement to the rank of police commissioner. Le Cocq insisted that he would get his law degree only after he retired, because he did not wish to be promoted out of active police work to the administrative post of commissioner. He wanted to stay a sleuth.

By 1958, crime had become so rampant in Rio de Janeiro that

the head of the Police Department (in what was then called Guanabara State, where Rio is situated), a general with the James Bondian name of Amaury Kruel, gave the go-ahead for the creation of a special crime-fighting force. La Cocq and seven of his colleagues were chosen to form the mobile squadron of the special police unit. They soon began sweeping Rio's hillside slums for criminals in hiding. While in the motorized squadron of the *Policia Especial*, Le Cocq was acknowledged to be the best motorcyclist in the outfit.

Le Cocq's abilities soon became known throughout Rio's police department. Before long, when lesser operatives failed in their attempts to capture a suspect or curb a crime wave, Le Cocq was called in to give advice—and increasingly to take over the case. Le Cocq was allowed to choose those whom he wanted to help him, and eventually the job got done. His reputation grew accordingly. The press got wind of his exploits and quickly made Le Cocq a household name not only among *cariocas* (inhabitants of Rio) but among much of the Brazilian population.

Le Cocq became a special legend in the fetid *favelas* that, like a brooding and accusing presence, overlook the modern center of Rio de Janeiro. Astride a wheezing motor scooter, he would ascend into the hills regularly, the putt-putt of its engine bringing reassurance to poverty-plagued dwellers who were being harassed by petty crooks. Le Cocq rarely wore a uniform, except when there was a specific reason to do so. His ensemble consisted of dark civilian clothes that made him less of a target at night, topped off by a black beret. With his unsocked feet inside old, misshapen shoes, and wearing a rumpled sports shirt and wrinkled trousers, Le Cocq looked very much like the men he was out to capture. Under his shirt, which always hung out over his pants, he carried two .45s stuck into his belt.

Le Cocq used them dozens of times, even though he preferred not to. If possible, he would approach the bandit he had caught up with and try to convince him to surrender. Le Cocq did not wish to shoot first. But if fired upon, he was ruthless— and deadly accurate.

A meticulous investigator, Le Cocq was not above using disguises. He would dream up a disguise that fit into any scheme.

Dressed in that manner, he would casually draw out those who could tell him about the habits of the fugitive he was pursuing. He would spend weeks or months observing the houses, businesses, and streets that the criminal was known to frequent, all the while studying the traffic flow in the area, making sure that no school children would be in the line of fire at a given time during the day, and noticing how well-lighted the neighborhood was at night.

No one case catapulted Le Cocq to fame. He was responsible for solving countless crimes, one as difficult and as sensational as the next. Many of the thugs he captured boasted colorful nicknames that make the Mafia's sobriquets seem dull by comparison: "Padlock," "Toad," "Bad Thing," "Mother's Plague" (so-called because he raped his own sister), "Russian Baby," "Coca-Cola George," "Dry Meat," "Island Jack," and "Billy Goat," to name just a few.

Le Cocq's most important and celebrated triumph was the capture of a nefarious criminal known as "Buck Jones."

An ex-bus driver in a Rio suburb, Buck Jones had abandoned his chauffeur's job for a new career: organizing a gang of bandits that harassed a *favela* known as "Monkey's Slumhill" (*Morro do Macaco*).

Buck Jones was a pitiless and probably pathological killer. If someone looked at him the wrong way, Jones had been known to whip out his .45 and shoot the offending person in the feet or in the chest, depending on Buck's mood. He also specialized in raping slum women, whether they were teenagers, married, or pregnant.

When he was hungry, he would often seek out a house whose owners bred chickens or pigs, and command, "I want that pig (or those chickens) baked for me and my friends. We will be back in two hours."

The terrified family did not hesitate to obey. They knew that if Buck Jones returned and the feast was not served, the whole family would very possibly be killed. The Jones boys made their money by robbing garages, gas stations, and grocery stores.

Victims had complained insistently to the police, but efforts to capture Buck Jones had long gone for naught. For six months soldiers from the military police, aided by civil policemen, had searched Monkey's Slumhill with the help of German shepherd dogs, but Jones' gang of outlaws had always managed to flee.

One afternoon, Le Cocq was at home when a friend of his, a garage owner, called on him. The garage owner complained that his garage had been held up by Buck Jones, who had also sworn to kill one of the employees, a car painter named Osmar.

Le Cocq went to the garage and talked to Osmar, who confirmed Jones' threats, adding that the outlaw had also sworn to kill the family of one of Osmar's neighbors, a man nicknamed "Pardal" ("Sparrow"), who worked in a textile factory. Osmar and "Pardal" both lived on the fringes of Monkey's Slumhill.

The next day, Le Cocq dropped by Osmar's home to pursue the investigation. While Le Cocq was inside the house, Osmar strolled out onto his front porch. Suddenly Buck Jones appeared with his men. Fulfilling his deadly promise, he drew a bead on Osmar, shot him in the heart, and fled.

By the time Le Cocq reached the scene, it was too late: Osmar lay gasping on the ground, blood flowing from his wound, and his murderer had escaped.

Osmar murmured to the detective, "I am dying, Le Cocq."

Le Cocq tried to comfort him. "Nonsense! An ambulance will be coming soon, and when you leave the hospital, he will already be in jail."

Osmar died before the ambulance arrived.

Incensed by the cold-blooded slaying, Le Cocq vowed to get Buck Jones. He set about doing so even as the victim's body was being hauled away. So totally did Le Cocq throw himself into the case that he was not to return to his own home for a month— until after he had singlehandedly captured and killed Buck Jones.

Le Cocq did so by means of a scheme that was almost peasant-like in its simplicity. By now he knew that the bandit frequently passed by Osmar's house. Surreptitiously, Le Cocq opened a small hole in the wall of Osmar's cabin and covered the hole on the outside with a transparent tissue paper of the same color as the house.

The aperture was perfectly disguised. It was impossible to see it from the street but, from a dark room inside, Le Cocq could see through the tissue paper and had a clear view of the area. He took up temporary residence in the dead Osmar's home. Le Cocq had to work alone; too many people in the victim's dwelling might tip off Buck Jones' gang.

Patiently, Le Cocq noted the hours that Buck Jones habitually passed, the number of henchmen who accompanied him, the number and calibre of the guns that the bandit and his friends packed, where they carried their weapons, whether there were children or other innocent persons who could be hit in a shoot-out, and an infinity of other details.

Finally deciding that the moment was ripe, Le Cocq went to the precinct station where he made his headquarters and issued himself a submachine gun. He slipped it into Osmar's house by hiding the weapon among vegetables in a grocery bag, a method Le Cocq frequently employed to conceal tommyguns for stake-outs.

His machine gun at the ready, Le Cocq took up his vigil at his observation post and patiently waited for his man.

It was not long before Buck Jones appeared, approaching the house on foot behind his gang from the brow of a nearby hill.

Le Cocq slipped out onto the front porch, drew a bead on the outlaw, and when he was within range shouted, "Hands up, Buck Jones! It's the police!"

The bandit went to his gun; Le Cocq fired, aiming at Buck Jones' legs to avoid killing him. Jones pitched to the ground, while his friends fled back up the hill.

One of the machine gun bullets, however, had severed an artery in Buck Jones' groin, and as the detective reached him, the notorious criminal was breathing his last.

Le Cocq gazed down at the dying man.

"Why did you draw the gun?" Le Cocq asked. "I did not want to shoot you."

The outlaw gasped fatalistically, "That's the end of every bandit, anyhow."

By the time an ambulance reached the scene, Buck Jones was a dead cowboy.

Residents of Monkey's Slumhill celebrated the demise of Buck

Jones with a feast. A crowd of relieved slum dwellers drank beer, played the samba, and danced throughout the night. The guest of honor, hailed as a hero, was Le Cocq.

Although Le Cocq stood only five feet six inches tall, he was lean, muscular, and well-coordinated, and, most importantly, as shrewd as his quarry. His fellow policemen remember that when Le Cocq looked at you with his intense blue eyes, you felt that he was looking through you. His widow contends that Le Cocq authentically did not fear danger, that through a kind of philosophical imperturbability he accepted the threat of danger in much the same way he accepted peace and quiet.

Sivuca says of Le Cocq, "He had an astonishing ability to reason. He was never at a loss. He always found a way to deal with touchy situations. He was an authentic and natural leader. He wasn't vain and he never left the station with the intent to kill."

Where possible, Le Cocq preferred to apply ingenuity in dealing with malefactors. A case in point was that of one "Mineirinho," who dedicated himself to extorting money from grocery stores. Mineirinho possessed a curious idiosyncrasy for a criminal: he was devoted to Saint George, whom he called his protector saint.

If Mineirinho arrived at a grocery store and saw a statue of Saint George in the establishment, he would turn around and leave, and never bother the place again.

Once, while in custody after having been arrested by Le Cocq, Mineirinho divulged his peculiarity to the famous detective. Le Cocq tucked away this nugget of information in his mind. Later, after Mineirinho had served his time and was embarking again on his life of crime, Le Cocq promptly visited countless grocery store owners and advised them to display statues of Saint George in conspicuous places. Those who followed Le Cocq's advice were never harassed by Mineirinho.

Le Cocq would often display an uncharacteristic—for a police-man—compassion for criminals he had brought to justice. Such was his attitude toward one Ze Felipe, who had become a bandit at fourteen after murdering a priest and a pregnant woman.

After Ze Felipe had run up an unconscionable string of

robberies and slayings, Le Cocq received orders to track down the young outlaw. Le Cocq learned that Ze Felipe frequented a bar where he would boast publicly about his past exploits and his future plots.

Disguised as a Roman Catholic priest, in a long black cassock and carrying a big Bible, Le Cocq seated himself at the bar and ordered lunch. Ze Felipe was there. While Le Cocq ate, the bandit expounded loudly on his plans for his next robbery.

The following day, Le Cocq arrested Ze Felipe, who was sent to prison for a long stretch.

Years later, before dawn one morning, while Le Cocq was at home sleeping, someone rapped at his door. His wife, Lili, answered the knock. It was a man.

"What do you want?"

"I would like to talk to Doctor Le Cocq."

("Doctor" is a distinguished appellation in Brazil, applicable to anyone deserving great respect or adulation.)

"He is sleeping. Can you not wait until tomorrow?"

"It is very urgent. Please tell him it is Ze Felipe."

Le Cocq got up and went to the front door. He immediately recognized the former outlaw, who had been freed.

"What now, Ze Felipe?"

"A terrible thing has happened to me, Doctor Le Cocq. I was arrested by a vigilance station. They retained all my documents and told me they would return them only if you ordered it personally. I need my documents because I plan to get married tomorrow. Help me, Doctor Le Cocq, please."

"All right," Le Cocq answered, "I will go with you, but under the following condition: you do not get into trouble anymore. If I ever hear that you have done anything wrong again, I will find you wherever you may be hidden."

Ze Felipe swore that he would go straight. Le Cocq liberated his documents.

Fifteen days later, Ze Felipe (who was still single) killed a man. Le Cocq promptly went up to Turano Slumhill, where Ze Felipe was hiding out, and put him back behind bars.

From time to time, Le Cocq would take it upon himself to help care for the mothers of hoods he had shot. His explanation was that it wasn't the mothers' fault that their sons had turned into criminals.

Le Cocq demonstrated pity for the prisoners detained in the spartan cells of his precinct station. He would keep old newspapers to give those locked up so that they could cover themselves to keep warm.

Le Cocq gave inspiration to his colleagues. This was a result not only of his bravery but of his intelligence. He never broke open a door by charging through it, thus exposing his body. He lay down to one side and kicked the door open. Once Le Cocq and several fellow policemen were engaged in a shootout with a much-sought hoodlum. In the midst of the gun battle, Le Cocq is said to have whispered to one of his colleagues that he should be careful because he had already fired four times and had only two bullets left in his gun. With all of the shooting that was going on, it was little short of incredible that Le Cocq had been able to keep track of such a minute detail—a feat that many a director of a Hollywood Western has had trouble matching.

Duty always came first. One day Le Cocq arrived home so exhausted that he nodded off to sleep in the bathtub. A short while later, several of his detective colleagues showed up to call him on an urgent mission. After yelling futilely to him through the bathroom door, and with Mrs. Le Cocq standing by helplessly, they had to break down the door—an exercise in which they were all too experienced—to wake him up. He climbed out of the tub, got dressed, drank a cup of coffee, and went back to work.

Like many a dedicated cop, Le Cocq would spend his days off and holidays working on a case. Says his widow, without any trace of rancor, "He lived more for his work than for his home life."

In order to permit him to sleep, his wife sometimes tried to muffle the telephone by placing it under a pile of blankets and pillows. Her husband would invariably hear the faint ring and wake up, telling her, "Do not ever do that. It could cost a man's life."

Le Cocq would sometimes spend one, two, three months without letup on the trail of a fugitive. Nevertheless, in order to be sure of his evidence, he never liked to hasten a capture.

For all his prestige, Le Cocq worked as hard, while on a case, as any of his subordinates. Recalling a six-month manhunt with Le Cocq that led to the capture of a father and his four sons who formed an especially dangerous gang, a police companion reports, "We would spend nights in stone quarries or in slums staking out the fugitives' movements. Once we spent fifteen days in one place. The only things we had to eat were hot soda pop, hard bread, and greasy sandwich meat."

Nor did Le Cocq abuse his authority by special self-treatment. Although as exhausted as everyone else after a chase, Le Cocq would put his men's comfort before his own. For example, if a prisoner had to be brought back from São Paulo to Rio de Janeiro, a distance of 250 miles, Le Cocq would send all but one or two of his assistants home on a plane, and set off in his police car with the prisoner in the back.

Second to duty, Le Cocq cared about the men under his command. Whenever a young policeman was tempted to risk his life needlessly, Le Cocq would counsel him, *"Mareco novo nao mergulha."* ("Young ducks do not plunge too deep.")

Indeed, he was like a father to his men. He worried about their personal problems and from time to time even tried to resolve their family difficulties.

Le Cocq would help anyone who asked him, not just policemen. He would even use his influence to help deserving individuals get jobs.

In addition to his wife, Le Cocq supported his mother and two sisters. Moreover, he was a soft touch, constantly dipping into his own modest salary to make loans to those with more need. Not surprisingly, Le Cocq never seemed to have any money of his own. When he himself was in financial straits he would take out loans from the police department. With one such loan Le Cocq purchased the plot of land on which he built his home.

A veritable Renaissance man, Le Cocq was a skilled carpenter, bricklayer, plumber, house painter, and electrician. He restored and repaired virtually everything in his house himself.

Le Cocq's personal life could scarcely have been more exemplary. He didn't drink, attended mass every Sunday, liked cats and house plants, and was unabashedly faithful to his wife. Latin men are notorious for cheating on their mates, and the more *macho* the man's job (according to Brazilian policemen, who consider themselves in a very *macho* profession) the more extramarital activities are indulged in. This was just one more area in which Le Cocq stood out from his colleagues. And, interestingly enough, instead of their thinking less of him for it, his conjugal "nonconformism" only increased their respect.

Le Cocq was also a thoughtful husband. When he got home, usually early in the morning, he would sit down with Lili and recount to her at length what he had been doing, in contrast to many policemen who prefer not to share their work in the underworld with their wives.

Furthermore, Le Cocq was always punctual—almost as un-Latin a trait as not being a philandering husband.

Although serious of mien, Le Cocq, when at ease taking coffee with friends, was not above indulging in a childlike practical joke: he would touch the arms of his friends with a hot coffee spoon.

Above all, he had that quality which often seems increasingly rare in human beings—humility. Le Cocq never attempted to embellish his or his group's feats.

A man of intellectual depth, Le Cocq also had a social awareness, and believed that society's problems were his problems, too. To him crime was principally a social ill and this could be alleviated through reforms such as better education and improved opportunity. At the same time, he felt equally strongly that if because of society's imperfections there had to be a police force, it should be composed of persons of the highest calibre who knew how to do their jobs and to do them honestly. Le Cocq would cite Brazil's numbers game (called *jogo do bicho*) as essentially a social problem rather than a police problem. Yet since not enough had been done to eradicate the socioeconomic conditions that led to widespread betting on the numbers racket, he pointed out, the police were forced to intervene in the criminal problems that resulted.

Only if policemen do their jobs responsibly, Le Cocq wisely counseled, would they enjoy the public's respect, confidence, and support. While on patrol with Le Cocq, his long-time partner, José Godinho Ferreira ("Sivuca"), recalls, he would suggest occasionally to Le Cocq that they stop an individual at random to check his identification. Brazil being Brazil, the man was more often than not black. Le Cocq, says Sivuca, would respond that if they were going to spot-check blacks they had better check whites, too, because Le Cocq—who was white—had found that as many whites as blacks were criminals. Such racial evenhandedness, Le Cocq believed, was of enormous importance to the police force.

As is often the policeman's lot, Le Cocq had been to court dozens of times to defend himself against murder charges growing out of the killing of suspects. He was invariably exonerated. Such was the case in the killing of the bandit Mino in the Red Clay *favela* shop. Le Cocq and his two detective companions, Nascimento and Beckman, were absolved by a judge after it was proved that they had indeed acted in self-defense.

Ironically, prudence in using his gun was to prove Le Cocq's undoing. He died in a gun battle with a pug-nosed thug called Horseface ("Cara de Cavalo").

Horseface's real name was Manuel Moreira. A petty crook whom Le Cocq and his colleagues had picked up many times, Horseface had always managed to get out on some technicality or spend only a few days behind bars.

Le Cocq was preparing to go on vacation and, characteristically, wanted to leave a clean desk. Thus he happened to be at his police station house when he received a telephone call from an informant telling him of the whereabouts of Horseface, who was again wanted by the police. Le Cocq interrupted his vacation plans to round up the criminal.

Although menacing to his victims, Horseface was usually a coward before policemen. His previous arrests by Le Cocq had always been without violence. In fact, Horseface had great respect for Le Cocq, whom he called "Doctor Lescopio." The semi-literate Moreira was unable to pronounce the detective's foreign surname.

Le Cocq and three fellow officers left the precinct house in Detective Helio Vigio's Volkswagen "Beetle." Vigio was at the wheel; Le Cocq beside him. Detectives Anibal "Cartola" ("Top Hat") Beckman and "Jacare" ("Alligator") occupied the back seat. Approximately ten minutes later, they arrived at the area mentioned by the tipster, a working-class district in the northern part of Rio. Suddenly, a taxi carrying a single passenger crossed an intersection just ahead of them.

"Isn't that the child?" (Horseface's other nickname), Cartola asked.

"It seems so!" Le Cocq answered, "Speed up, Vigio!"

A soccer game had just ended at Maracana Stadium, which seats 150,000 people, and traffic in the area was becoming heavy.

The taxi, an ancient black American car, attempted to ease its way through the jammed traffic. Horseface was evidently aware that he was being followed.

Le Cocq's fellow cops wanted to open fire. Horseface would have been an easy target. Le Cocq stopped them. "Take it easy so as not to scare him. He may not be the bandit. No shootings. I do not want violence."

The snarled traffic finally forced the taxi to a halt. The Volkswagen screeched up and stopped beside the taxi's left side, as Le Cocq opened the door to get out.

Horseface leaped from the taxi drawing the two .45s he habitually packed in his belt. Le Cocq did not draw his guns, thinking, his companions said afterward, that he could persuade Horseface to give up without either of them getting hurt. It was a fatal error in judgment. Horseface started shooting. One slug hit Le Cocq in the chest, another in the jugular vein. As the famed detective fell, a third bullet struck him.

Cartola was also wounded. Never expecting Horseface to fire, the other three detectives found themselves trapped inside the small car.

In the confusion, Horseface fled.

The detectives arrested the taxi driver and rushed Le Cocq to a hospital, where he died that night at 10:30 P.M. The date: August 27, 1964.

The final confrontation with a criminal which cost Le Cocq his life seemed, in a way, his ultimate moral legacy. His companions agreed that Le Cocq could easily have shot Horseface first, but he had preferred to act the humanitarian toward the petty hood. Le Cocq's widow, Lili, is certain that Horseface did not know Le Cocq was one of the four men in the VW pursuing him. Had Horseface known, she is equally sure, he would have given himself up.

In any event, his widow said later, Le Cocq was always prepared to die and was not afraid of the ultimate moment. She commented, perhaps displaying Le Cocq's own fatalism, "That's just life, right? His time had come."

A typical epitaph from those who worked with Le Cocq was uttered by a cop nicknamed "Guaiba," " 'Gringo' died yesterday and he'll always be my teacher and idol."

Needless to say, Horseface was in big trouble.

Grief-stricken and furious over the slaying of Le Cocq, his fellow policemen launched a relentless hunt for Manuel Moreira, who instantly became the most wanted man in Brazil. At Le Cocq's massively attended funeral, his colleagues swore revenge on Horseface Moreira.

Indeed, in the wake of Le Cocq's death the Rio de Janeiro police came close to getting out of control. After swearing vengeance at the "Gringo's" grave, many cops did not go back to their stations, but instead set out on their own to hunt down Horseface. Revolvers cocked, hatred in their eyes, each wanted to be Horseface's executioner.

Concerned, Brazil's Secretary of Security, Colonel Gustavo Borges, appealed for calm. "I hope the policemen manage to capture him [Horseface] without a scratch," Borges declared, "because it is important that justice tries him and gives him the penalty of law."

It was too much to expect. The police of Rio de Janeiro teamed up with their companions from surrounding Guanabara State, and the chase began.

Working around the clock, detectives scoured Rio de Janeiro and its suburbs.

The toll of hoods who got in the cops' way was appalling. As the pursuit quickened, bullets of rage began to fell other criminals; one was shot down after being taken for Horseface during a raid in the northern section of the city. Among those who died in the wake of Le Cocq's murder was "Paraibinha," the notorious murderer of tourists who had escaped Le Cocq's ambush of José Alfonso de Jesus ("Mino"). Paraibinha was killed during an operation carried out in the full-scale search to find Le Cocq's murderer.

Horseface, in his desperate flight, changed hiding places repeatedly. Several times he encountered his pursuers but managed to elude them. On one occasion, Horseface was located in a cheap hotel near the São Carlos *favela* in downtown Rio. The place was instantly surrounded by police, but the fugitive murderer of Le Cocq escaped by taking the hotel manager as hostage.

It was not only the criminal element that suffered the effects of the passions that drove many Rio policemen to extremes. "Perpetuo" de Freitas, considered one of the best detectives on the Rio police force—as good as Le Cocq, some say—was killed by a colleague while trying to capture Horseface alive.

"Perpetuo," as he was called by his fellow cops and by the press, had many informers in the underworld and liked to work alone. On the morning he died in the Skeleton Slumhill (*Favela do Esqueleto*), he had an appointment with a certain person who, it was said, would arrange for Horseface to surrender.

Like Le Cocq, Perpetuo was widely known for the protection he guaranteed criminals who were under his responsibility. Nevertheless, there was little doubt that Horseface had already been condemned to die, at least unofficially. Perpetuo was not to be permitted to capture the slayer of Le Cocq alive.

The news that Perpetuo was about to arrest Horseface spread fast. A group of policemen led by a young detective, a newcomer to the force, went up the hill to stop Perpetuo.

The young detective and his team met Perpetuo at a bar and, following an exchange of angry words, Perpetuo was shot to death.

The slaying of detective Perpetuo de Freitas in Skeleton Slumhill had great impact on public opinion, and focused even greater public attention on the pursuit of Horseface Moreira, the killer of detective Milton Le Cocq.

The policemen now hunted in silence.

On October 3, 1964, thirty-six days after the slaying of Le Cocq, the chase reached its grim climax.

The police received a tip that Horseface was hiding with a family in a modest cottage in a remote area of Cabo Frio, a fashionable resort town fifty miles north of Rio de Janeiro.

At dawn a band of men surrounded the bungalow.

Suddenly a yell broke the stillness of the sultry Brazilian morning.

"Come out, Manuel! Come out with your hands up! It is the police!"

Guns at the ready, the waiting cops could hear Horseface jump out of bed and start stumbling about the darkened house, knocking over furniture.

Silence again.

Flattening himself against a wall of the cottage, detective Euclides Nascimento tapped on one of the windows with the barrel of his M-1 rifle.

"Open, my boy. We want to arrest you alive!"

From another half-open window, Horseface opened fire. "Fire, you dogs!" he screamed, "Shoot to kill! Before dying I will take one more to hell with me!"

Crouched low, the outlaw rushed from room to room inside the house, trying desperately to cover all the doors and windows. At one point, he attempted to flee through the back door, but was blocked by detective Ivo Americano who foiled Horseface with a burst from an Elliot Ness-like Thompson submachine gun.

All the while, the owners of the house—one Pedro Januario Luz, his wife, Clotilde Alves da Costa, and their daughter, Vanilda Alves Luz (Horseface's girl friend)—were quaking under their beds, praying loudly for divine protection.

Horseface reloaded his guns and kept firing.

As the battle increased in fury, detective "Jacare" got carried away by a brave idea: tossing his machine gun aside, he stood up and called out, "I have thrown away my weapon, Manuel! I want to go inside the house to talk to you!"

Horseface cackled hysterically and directed his fire at an easy target. He missed.

The other policemen kept the desperado pinned down inside the cottage with an unremitting barrage of bullets, riddling the doors and windows.

The family occupying the house loudly implored the police to let them out. Officer Sergio Rodrigues ordered a cease-fire, yelling to Horseface,

"Manuel, throw your gun away and come out! We want you alive. Do not be afraid because I will protect you."

Horseface merely laughed and broke off his shooting momentarily to look around for more ammunition.

As he did, detective Luiz Mariano dos Santos, nicknamed "Paulista" (native of São Paulo State), sprinted to the front door, his machine gun cocked.

His move was covered by detectives "Chocolate" Helio Vigio, Le Cocq's close friend Sivuca, Guaiba, and Eloi.

Paulista kicked in the door and invaded the house. Horseface opened fire at the cop but the slugs went awry. The detective machine-gunned the desperado.

Mortally wounded, Horseface crumpled to the floor and crawled to one side of the room, still holding onto his gun.

Other policemen burst into the house and riddled the criminal's body with bullets. Horseface had lost his last race.

In a most uncharacteristic display of emotion for detectives, the executioners embraced each other, alternately sobbing and laughing. They fired their guns into the air and shouted, "Le Cocq, you are revenged! You see, Gringo, we knew we would catch the beast that killed you!"

A few hours later the Cabo Frio police station received an anonymous phone call. "There's a present for you on Kilometer 23 of the Buzios highway."

The "present" was the corpse of Manuel (Horseface) Moreira, the killer of Le Cocq. Perforated by more than 100 slugs, it was turned over to a bewildered coroner.

Le Cocq's death has led to the creation of the *Scuderie Detetive Le Cocq* (Detective Le Cocq Emblem), an organization that is dedicated to paying homage to Milton Le Cocq de Oliveira. "The principles defended by Le Cocq himself—brotherhood, solidarity, and friendship," says his old friend and fellow policeman Sivuca, "are the basis of the *Scuderie*. He died and we took it upon ourselves to imitate him." Says another member, "We follow in the footsteps of Le Cocq. He meted out justice and we do, too."

The *Scuderie*'s shield, which is often seen on the back windows of cars, is the subject of much debate. Indeed Le Cocq himself, were he alive, might well have reservations about the symbol. At the top of the shield's round center is the name of the organization. In the middle is a skull with blood-red eyes and crossbones. At the bottom are the letters "E.M.," which means, say the *Scuderie*'s members, *Esquadrao Motorizado* (Motorized Squadron), referring to the mobile unit Le Cocq served in early in his career. Nevertheless, many are convinced that the initials really stand for Rio's notorious *Esquadrao da Morte* (Death Squad), reputed to be composed of police who take the law into their own hands and execute criminals. The emblem has often been linked to skull-and-crossbones drawings with the initials "E.M." standing for "Death Squad" found near bodies dumped in remote areas of the city.

Scuderie members emphatically deny any relation between their institution and Brazil's so-called "Death Squads." They attribute the confusion to their own negligence in counterattacking the rumors at the very beginning, which they say have resulted in misunderstandings as to the real objective of the organization.

"We would not bring our wives and kids to this house (the *Scuderie* headquarters) if it were frequented by pitiless and dangerous executioners," they argue, explaining their reasons for choosing the skull emblem thus: When Le Cocq was a motorcyclist in the motorized squadron of the *Policia Especial* (Special Police Corps) at the beginning of his career, he wore a black leather coat bearing a red-eyed skull with crossbones on the back. The choice of that emblem by the *Scuderie* was, then, both a tribute to Le Cocq and a symbol of the policeman's risky profession.

Furthermore, the expression "Death Squad" had first entered the Brazilian vernacular in 1958, long before Le Cocq's death. Coincidentally or otherwise, many hoodlums began turning up dead. Such slayings continued, and the reasons for them varied. Some of the victims were indeed crooks "eliminated" by individual policemen who took the law into their own hands. Other victims were murdered by criminal bosses who blamed the slayings on the police. Brazil's Death Squad model spread from Rio to other cities: Belo Horizonte, São Paulo, Niteroi, Vitoria, Santos, Bahia. In all, the Death Squads are said to be responsible for more than 1,000 killings.

Once in a while, a sharp increase in the number of Death Squad-attributed crimes, or in the sophistication of the atrocities committed, has shocked public opinion and spurred officials to order special investigations.

Two scandals are good examples.

The first, which occurred in the early 1960s, involved a number of policemen who set about "cleaning" Rio de Janeiro of its beggars by killing them and dumping the corpses into the already-polluted Guarda River, which flows north of the city. The massacre was revealed in January 1963, thanks to one of the intended victims, a woman named Olindina Alves Jupiacu. A swimming champion in her youth, Jupiacu, who had become mentally disturbed and a beggar, managed to escape her executioners (who thought she was dead) and swim for safety despite a bullet wound.

Agonizing in a public plaza, she told her tale to a group of astonished bystanders. The press broke the story, and after a lengthy series of investigations and trials, a group of policemen from the beggar-woman's municipal department were condemned to sentences that totaled more than 1,000 years in prison.

In 1968, a group of Rio de Janeiro policemen organized a Death Squad that, with macabre management efficiency, employed the services of a "public relations" man to announce the victims. On May 6 of that year, for the first time, a man who identified himself as "Red Rose," the Squad's public relations representative, telephoned Rio's newspapers advising reporters that there was a body to be found in the district of Barra da Tijuca.

The male corpse, which had been dumped on a deserted road, had been the object of a particularly brutal "rubout." The victim's arms were tied behind his back; a nylon rope still around his neck had strangled him; the coup de grace had been administered in the head. Next to the body, on a piece of cardboard, were scrawled a roughly drawn likeness of a Volkswagen and the inscription: "I was a car thief."

The newspapers received many other calls from "Red Rose." The situation became so serious that Brazil's President Emilio Garrastazu Medici ordered a full-scale investigation that resulted in the arrest of several more policemen.

What Le Cocq might have thought of the Death Squads can only be the subject of conjecture. It is highly probable, however, that he would have condemned them as strongly as he did the criminals he fought. Le Cocq's principles were diametrically opposed to the Death Squad style of dealing with malefactors.

Those principles are enshrined in the *Scuderie Detetive Le Cocq*, which was founded on August 27, 1965, by thirteen of Le Cocq's closest and most loyal friends, among them detectives Euclides ("Garatoa"—"Big Boy") Nascimento, Helio Guahyba Nunes ("Guaiba"), José Guilherme Godinho Ferreira ("Sivuca"), and Luis Mariano dos Santos ("Paulista"). The *Scuderie* drew the support of other policemen, and grew in membership and goals. One of the objectives was to unite all Brazilian policemen under the principles of "companionship, friendship, solidarity, faithfulness, spirit of union, comradeship and masculinity," as is stated in the publication of *O Gringo* ("The Gringo"), the *Scuderie*'s official voice.

Another of the *Scuderie*'s goals, in the words of *O Gringo*, is to "draw the portrait of the policeman before public opinion, revealing how he is and not how many people, erroneously for lack of information, think he is."

To this end, the *Scuderie* has promoted advertising campaigns and has sponsored courses for its police members aimed at broadening their intellectual awareness in order to enhance the performance of their professional duties.

Membership in the *Scuderie* is open to anyone, policeman or non-policeman, man or woman. To be admitted, however, one has to be proposed by two members and has to undergo three types of investigations: one must have a clean police record, must demonstrate a good relationship with neighbors and debtors (the latter stemming from Le Cocq's easygoing ways with those who owed him money), and finally must be free of charges of unethical political activity.

With nearly 2,000 members—not including their families—

in its Rio de Janeiro headquarters alone, the *Scuderie* enjoys an intense social life, promotes get-togethers for adults and parties for children, educational film sessions, soccer tournaments, and other constructive activities in addition to daily meetings.

"It is a kind of masonry," explains Nelson de Carvalho, a former *Scuderie* spokesman and still an active member.

The *Scuderie* has branches in eight Brazilian states, and has even gone international. It has representatives in Argentina, Portugal, the United States (in Miami and New York City), Great Britain, West Germany, and Italy. It also maintains permanent contact with police organizations all over the world, including Interpol, Scotland Yard, and the FBI.

Thus the legend of Le Cocq lives after him.

The people of the *favelas* loved detective Le Cocq because he was their defender. A crowd of more than 1,500 persons accompanied his funeral procession. Concludes colleague Sivuca, "It will be a thousand years before there is another Le Cocq."

8

Chicago's "Crime of the Century"

THE WOMAN'S OUTCRY was piercing and shrill. An unusual sound for the South Chicago neighborhood known as Jeffrey Manor, an island of relative tranquility in a surrounding area that has the reputation of being one of the more turbulent sections of the Windy City. The South Side of Chicago: where Al Capone set up shop, where speakeasies bubbled up in a sea of illicit Prohibition-era hootch, where Leopold and Loeb killed for the sheer thrill of it.

The cry that warm and humid Thursday morning of July 14, 1966, attracted the attention of neighbors residing in a cluster of town house units in the 2300 block of East 100th Street. Before anybody could come out to the street to investigate, the cry was heard again, more clearly.

"Help me! They're all dead!"

Mrs. Alfred Windmiller, a housewife, and Miss Judy Dykton, a nurse, emerged from their homes at opposite ends of the block. Both heard the pitiful wail again.

"Everyone is dead . . . Oh, God . . . he's killed them all. . ."

They saw a petite, dark-haired young woman in a multicolored shift standing precariously on a narrow, second-floor ledge outside the window of an apartment that was being used as a residence for nursing trainees at nearby South Chicago Community Hospital. Miss Dykton recognized the distraught girl. She was Corazon Piezo Amurao, a twenty-three-year-old Filipino.

"I'm the last one alive on the *sampan!*" she cried to Miss Dykton, who by now had reached the sidewalk ten feet below. "Everyone else is dead. . . ."

Mrs. Windmiller had also hurried to the scene. "Don't jump!" she yelled up to the panic-stricken young woman on the ledge. "Go back inside and take the stairs. . . ." But Miss Amurao remained frozen on her perch.

In the meantime, Miss Dykton approached the apartment's ground-floor living room window and peered inside. What she saw made her blood run cold. A girl's nude body lay sprawled face-down on the couch.

Miss Dykton ran two doors away to the residence of the nurses' housemother, Mrs. Laura Bisone, and telephoned the police. The first officer to arrive on the scene was patrolman Daniel R. Kelly. Miss Dykton and Mrs. Windmiller related to him what little they had heard and seen. Kelly could see for himself the young woman still cringing on the ledge, whimpering with fright.

Pausing only long enough to radio for assistance, he hopped out of his patrol car and shouted to Miss Amurao, "Stay there. I'll come inside and help you."

Kelly found the front door locked, but when he went to the rear of the building he discovered the back door open. He also noticed that a screen had been removed from a ground floor window, which was likewise open.

Revolver drawn, Kelly entered the apartment house. He went into the kitchen, and saw nothing unusual: dirty dishes and glasses in the sink, a bag of garbage on the counter. He passed through another door into the living room. The floor was strewn with papers, books, and personal belongings. What caught his immediate attention was the left side of the room and the same spectre seen through the window by Miss Dykton—the nude female body on the two-cushion orange couch.

Kelly dashed over to check the young woman's condition. The body bore no marks, but a strip of white cloth was knotted tightly around her neck. The policeman looked at the face and was horrified. He recognized the pretty brunette as Gloria Jean Davy, twenty-three, whom he had dated before his marriage to another nurse. The policeman even knew her family, which lived

Detective Sergeant John Murtaugh who was in charge of the murder investigation—the "crime of the century." (*David Jackson*)

in Dyer, Indiana, just across the state line but still part of Chicago's greater metropolitan area. Miss Davy had obviously been strangled, and was dead.

Kelly's shock and consternation were interrupted by a familiar voice outside calling up to Miss Amurao not to jump. It was that of another patrolman, Leonard J. Ponne, who had just arrived.

"Hey, Lennie!" shouted Kelly, opening the front door, gun still in hand. "Get in here. A girl's been strangled. The killer may still be in the building. We've got to check the place."

Pulling out his own revolver, Ponne raced in to check the basement as Kelly went up the stairs to the second floor. Ponne found nothing, but Kelly did. At the top of the stairs he was stopped by a pair of feet sticking out of the bathroom into the hall. They belonged to a young woman, who was clad only in panties. Her breast and neck had been slashed. She too was dead.

An open door on Kelly's right now took him to a front bedroom. He walked into a triple horror: three more girls' corpses, two on the floor, one on a bed. One of the young women on the floor had been gagged and her wrists tied; there was a strip of cloth around her neck, possibly torn from a bedsheet, and there was also a jagged wound in her neck. The body lay partly over the other victim on the floor. The latter's wrists were tied behind her back and the same kind of cloth was wound tightly around her throat. Kelly spotted a trickle of blood from a stab wound in her neck, but he could detect no sign of life. The third corpse, on the bed, was bound hand and foot, and her throat was slashed. The three could not have been dead for long because the color had not yet drained completely from their faces, and one was still bleeding.

Kelly now set about rescuing the girl on the ledge, but he realized that he could not reach her from the front bedroom window. With his gun still cocked and finger on the trigger, he went back into the hall and entered a second bedroom. Again, he was halted by a scene of numbing horror—the slashed and strangled bodies of three more young women. One's wrists were tied and a cloth twisted around her neck; another's left breast had been punctured by what might have been a knife, and she was also strangled; the third victim had been stabbed in the back, in the back of the neck, and in the left eye.

From where he now stood, Kelly could see Miss Amurao framed in the bedroom window, still frozen on the ledge. The

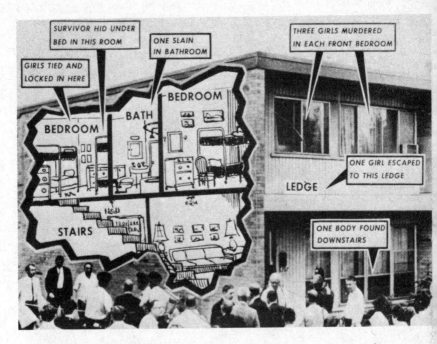

This photo/drawing outlines the happenings of July 14 when the eight student nurses were massacred in their dormitory on Chicago's South Side. (*Wide World Photos*)

policeman skirted the three corpses, reached out the window, and yanked the terrified young woman into the room. He led her into the hall.

"Do you know who did this?" Kelly asked. The Filipino girl, trembling and sobbing uncontrollably, stammered, "One man . . . I don't know who he is . . . He kill all my friends. . . ."

"Can you describe him, tell me what he looks like?"

The policeman pressed her as gently as he could. He sensed

that at any moment she could lapse into hysteria and not be able to answer questions coherently.

Miss Amurao gasped a description. "He was young man, maybe twenty-five, about a hundred and seventy-five pounds . . . his hair very short." She couldn't recall the color exactly, either brown or dark blond. He wore a dark waist-length jacket over a white T-shirt and dark trousers. "I don't remember anything else about him . . . please take me away from here. . . ."

Patrolman Ponne escorted Miss Amurao down to the first floor while Kelly checked the rest of the second floor. There were no more bodies beyond the seven that he had seen there and the one on the couch downstairs. Eight victims—which made it the worst mass murder in Chicago history.

Only once before in that violent city had there been anything approaching such a wholesale slaughter of human beings. That was the 1929 St. Valentine's Day massacre when seven gangsters

Richard Speck in the Cook County Jail Hospital after his arraignment on charges of killing the eight nursing students. (*Wide World Photos*)

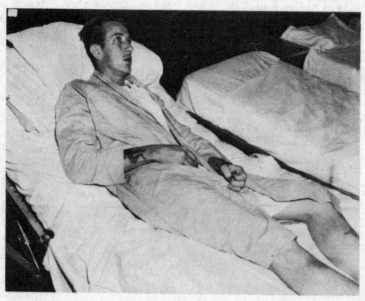

were lined up in a garage on Clark Street and executed by four rival underworld gunmen. Even so, that had been pretty much a businesslike operation, carried out for rational—if cold-blooded —reasons of power and profit. The massacre in the nurses' quarters was a crime of a different nature, a classic case of senseless savagery.

The sound of sirens growing louder could be heard outside the house of carnage on 100th Street. One of the unmarked cruisers speeding toward the scene was carrying a tall, heavyset, boom-voiced veteran sleuth who would be in charge of the investigation. He was Sergeant of Detectives John Murtaugh.

In his twenty-one years on the Chicago police force John Murtaugh had investigated more than 1,000 homicides, but none as chilling as this one.

"I'd handled more multiple murders than I can remember," Murtaugh reminisces, "but no case even came close to this one. I had cases in which there were as many as four dead . . . that is, three persons murdered and the fourth one, who committed the killings, taking his own life. But eight bodies at one time— never."

Murtaugh continues. "It had been a quiet night, unusually quiet, and warm. Ordinarily we would have been jumping, but there was not that much activity that night in the whole area. We got a call. The policemen on the scene said there were five bodies. Later, they called back, said six. Later, while I was enroute, they said eight."

Several of the homicide detectives who would join the probe had met the victims while conducting investigations that involved visits to South Chicago Community Hospital. "We knew these girls personally, being in homicide," observes Murtaugh. "In any investigation, you derive a certain amount of self-satisfaction. It keeps you on your toes. But here it took on a personal touch because you knew them personally. They were high-quality girls."

Murtaugh, normally an easygoing, philosophical man, turns bitter when he reflects on the savagery of the crime, and what he is convinced is the leniency that in recent times has contributed to violence. He says, "It takes all types of people to make up this world, and in my career I have run into a lot of kooks. People commit murder for the sake of two pennies, or for the sake of an extra drink out of a bottle. One of the reasons for the increase in homicide is that there is no capital punishment. What the hell, you don't get any more for murder than robbery. If you get rid of the witnesses, there is less chance of being convicted for robbery. Hell, this [sic] is quotes from their [the perpetrators'] own mouths. It is easier to beat a homicide rap than a robbery. This is their thinking. Eliminate your witnesses, cut down your chances of conviction.

"The whole trend of penologists, the social studies in colleges, is toward leniency to the criminal. Today it is not society that is being protected, but the criminal. The individual takes precedence over the whole of society. Today, what the hell, give the individual criminal all his rights.

"Seventy percent of those in prison are repeaters, and there is no rehabilitation as far as callous murders are concerned. Society is far better off eliminating them. I am a firm believer in capital punishment. The animal doesn't change."

Detective Sergeant John Murtaugh adds, "To me, a child demands discipline. Part of loving is to discipline. If a child doesn't get it, he feels unwanted. Same with society. If it is not disciplined, people, groups, individuals—they can do whatever the hell they want. I say that we should revert back to where society disciplines itself and its individuals."

But there was no time for such reflection on that muggy morning of July 14, 1966. An unspeakable crime had been committed and it cried out to be solved. Murtaugh's car squealed up to the town house on East 100th Street. A crowd of women with sweaters and coats pulled over nightgowns and pajamas had clustered on the sidewalk. Men in sleeveless undershirts had gathered. The curious looked on silently, or murmured to each other in hushed tones.

"I assumed full charge of the scene," Murtaugh relates. He then went about the enormous task of setting in motion what would be the biggest manhunt in Chicago history. "All police work is a lot of canvassing," he says, "a lot of asking questions. It's the only way you get anywhere."

Murtaugh was accompanied to the scene by two subordinates, detectives Byran Carlisle and Jack Wallenda. All were from the Homicide and Sex Crime Unit, at Area 2 Detective Headquarters only a short distance away at Ninety-second Street and Cottage Grove Avenue. Also arriving at the house was Commander Francis Flanagan, chief of Chicago homicide detectives who, it turned out, lived only three blocks away. Patrolman Kelly related the events in sequence from the moment he had arrived.

"How bad is it?" Flanagan asked.

"Very bad," the patrolman replied. He led the detectives into the living room and pointed to the nude body on the couch.

"There are seven more upstairs," Kelly said.

"Seven more girls?" Flanagan exclaimed, stunned.

"I know it's hard to believe," Kelly replied. "You'd better see for yourself."

Murtaugh, with more than fifteen years investigating Chicago homicides, had taken personal pride in his work, striving, along with other dedicated police investigators, to wipe out the stigma that had been stamped on Chicago almost two generations before when it was known as the crime capital of the world.

Yet, despite all his experience, Murtaugh was confronted here with a case the likes of which he had never before encountered. He looked at the carnage in the town house and shook his head disbelievingly.

Not long afterward, news of the mass murder was flashed on radio and television. Newspaper headlines that morning had featured the imminent launch of astronauts John Young and Michael Collins aboard *Gemini 10* for a three-day journey into space. The nation's attention suddenly turned from Cape Kennedy to Chicago, as word of what had happened on the South Side raced across the land. Headlines changed from "Gemini Pair Get the Go-Go" to "Eight Student Nurses Slain in Chicago."

It was a terrible crime and it commanded nationwide attention.

The question now was: how would it be solved? Above all, Murtaugh resolved: the killer must not be allowed to get out of town, which could make his escape permanent.

All leaves in the Detective Division were canceled. Sixty

police investigators were ordered to report for duty at Area 2 Detective Headquarters at eight o'clock that morning. Another eighty detectives from other squads around the city were sent in as backup.

The Area 2 headquarters building, with a sprawling second floor and a large assembly room, was designated as the command post for the investigation. Extra telephones were installed to receive calls from the public and underworld tipsters who might have leads or clues to the killer. The probe was to be total.

By 8:00 A.M.—less than two hours after the killings were reported—the army of 140 detectives called into the case gathered in the assembly room. They were split up into twenty-man teams and directed to conduct a saturation canvass of the South Side. Several teams were assigned to start in the city limits on the Indiana state line; they were to work their way north. Others would work to the east, west, and north of the East 100th Street block in a wide perimeter. They were ordered to check taverns, restaurants, pawn shops, theaters, rooming houses, hotels, motels, gas stations, and other places that might conceivably have been points of contact for the killer.

The intruder's description provided by Miss Amurao was distributed to the assembled detectives. It was also put on police Teletype machines and transmitted to law enforcement agencies throughout the United States, Canada, and Mexico. It read:

WANTED: MALE, WHITE, 25, 6 FEET, 170 POUNDS, SHORT HAIR, BLACK COAT WAIST-LENGTH, DARK TROUSERS, NO HAT. STATED HE WANTED MONEY TO GO TO NEW ORLEANS. MAY BE ARMED WITH REVOLVER OR KNIFE.

Sergeant Murtaugh eventually would be in charge of the most significant aspects of the investigation and would be committed to carry it to a satisfactory conclusion. In the meantime, in the early first minutes and hours, many other investigators were at work.

Now it became Dr. Andrew J. Toman's turn. Toman was the Cook County coroner, and he arrived on the scene with six pathologists as well as a caravan of huge mobile crime labs with their crews of police technicians.

The coroner's men filed into the house accompanied by a male employee of South Chicago Community Hospital who had been brought in to help identify the victims. Already inside the town house were Daniel T. Dragel, director of the Chicago Police Department's Crime Laboratory, and ten of his technicians. They were conducting dozens upon dozens of dustings for latent fingerprints, along with a minute search for other clues that the killer might have left behind.

Glancing at the first victim on the couch, the hospital employee calmly called out her name, "Gloria Jean Davy." Detective Carlisle wrote it down in his notebook. The identifying witness was taken upstairs to the second floor, and stepped over the outstretched legs of the panty-clad girl. Trying not to look at the ghastly wounds on her breasts and neck, he called out, "This is Suzanne Farris."

Police would learn that she was twenty-one years old, the daughter of a Chicago Transit Authority supervisor, and engaged. Athletically inclined, she had worked the previous summer as a Chicago park system recreation leader until she went into nursing.

Led to the first front bedroom, the witness' composure was shaken further by the sight of one corpse sprawled on top of another and the body on the bed.

"Awful," the hospital employee murmured as he peered at the girl on the bed, bound wrists and ankles with her throat slashed. He identified her as Merlita Gargullo. The twenty-two-year-old Miss Gargullo would become further known as the "beautiful, lovely, and shy" daughter of a Philippine physician, a graduate of the Arellano University School of Nursing in Manila the previous year, and one of three Filipino exchange students who had arrived the previous June fifth for graduate nursing studies and training at South Chicago Community Hospital.

A second of the exchange students was Miss Amurao, a native of San Luis on Batangas Island, who had miraculously survived the butchery and was now being interviewed by Commander Flanagan two doors down the street.

The third exchangee from the Philippines was quiet, attractive Valentina Pasion, like Miss Amurao, twenty-three, and like her a graduate of the Manila University School of Nursing. Miss Pasion was the girl on the floor from whose neck Patrolman Kelly had noticed a trickle of blood, but it was no longer flowing.

The young female whose body had either fallen or been pushed over that of Miss Pasion was identified as Nina Joe Schmale, twenty-one, who came from one of the oldest families in Wheaton, Illinois, thirty-five miles west of Chicago. Miss Schmale was a tall brunette, a former beauty queen who was also engaged and who had planned to pursue a career in psychiatric nursing.

The identifying witness from the hospital was escorted into the adjoining bedroom where the last three corpses lay.

"Pamela Wilkening," he pointed shakily to the girl on the left side of the room who had been stabbed in the left breast and strangled. The twenty-four-year-old daughter of a Lansing, Michigan, steamfitter, Miss Wilkening had a zany sense of humor—she smoked cigars at the opera for laughs—but she was also deadly serious. On her application for nurse's training she had written, "I have always wanted to be a nurse because I never liked to see people suffer."

As Sergeant Murtaugh and his two detectives continued to compile the list of names, the hospital employee sidestepped the body beside Miss Wilkening and went to the right, identifying the remains of Patricia Ann Matusek, daughter of a Chicago tavern owner. The twenty-year-old Miss Matusek had been a champion swimmer and member of the water ballet class at Fenge High School. In her application for training at South Chicago Hospital, she had written, "The joy in helping cannot be taken away."

The witness was led to the one body that remained to be named. "This is the last identification you will have to make," he was assured.

Shaking his head, the fellow hospital worker said, "I'm sick . . . I can't look any more. . . ." But he forced himself to make the identification. "She is . . . Mary Ann Jordan. . . ." Murtaugh was to learn that Miss Jordan's inclusion in the carnage was particularly ironic. The twenty-year-old victim normally lived at home with her family while attending nursing school. On the previous evening, however, she had obtained permission to stay in the town house with her friend, Suzanne Farris, whose body lay sprawled on the bathroom floor. It was more than a bond of friendship between the two girls; Mary Jordan's brother was the man Suzanne Farris had been engaged to marry.

Reported one newsman, "You couldn't walk anywhere without getting blood on your shoes."

With the victims all identified, the search for evidence was stepped up. One team of experts, the coroner's men, examined each body, hoping to learn from probings of the fatal wounds what kind of weapon or weapons were used. Another team of experts, the crime lab technicians under Director Dragel, searched for flesh scrapings or strands of hair under the fingernails of the victims, in case they had fought the killer.

Yet nothing would prove as valuable in the investigation as the memory of the only eyewitness to the events preceding the mass murder—Corazon Amurao. Sergeant Murtaugh joined Commander Flanagan in questioning Miss Amurao, who had been taken to the residence of the housemother, Mrs. Bisone. Miss Amurao had been sedated by a physician from South Chicago Community Hospital. The doctor had found that although she had not been injured physically by the killer, she had suffered minor bruises and scrapes on her wrists and elbows which she had inflicted on herself while struggling to work free of the bandagelike bedsheet strips the intruder had also tied around her wrists.

"I will tell everything I know," she said. "I did not see the whole thing because I was hiding much of the time. But what I saw I will tell. . . ."

Miss Amurao told Murtaugh and her other questioners that she was preparing to go to bed late the night before, Wednesday night. She wasn't certain of the exact time, but it might have been around eleven o'clock. Six girls were in the house, all upstairs. Patricia Matusek, Pamela Wilkening, Nina Schmale, and Valentina Pasion were in the front bedroom on the right, lounging and talking. Miss Amurao was in her own bedroom, the smallest one, in the back of the house. She had just changed her clothes and was chatting with her friend and roommate, Merlita Gargullo, who had just come home from duty at the hospital.

Suddenly they heard a rap on the back door. Miss Amurao

went downstairs to answer it. She thought it was one of the other girls who might have forgotten her key. But when she opened the door—a fatal mistake—Miss Amurao was startled to see a tall young man standing there, a knife in his left hand, a revolver in his right.

"I'm not going to hurt you," she remembered he said immediately. "I need your money to get to New Orleans."

As Miss Amurao backed away in fright, he lunged across the threshhold. "I'm not going to hurt you," he repeated, closing the door. "I just want your money."

Then he motioned Miss Amurao through the kitchen and living room to the stairs leading up to the bedrooms.

"The first thing I noticed about him was the strong odor of alcohol," Miss Amurao recalled.

At the top of the stairs, the intruder held Miss Amurao at bay with the gun and thrust his head into the small bedroom where Miss Gargullo was. "Get out here!" he commanded. She came out.

"Down there," he directed, and herded the two girls to the front bedroom where he could hear the chatter of the four others. He motioned the two Filipino girls into that room. As the girls inside looked up startled, he snapped, "Everybody lie face down on the floor."

Terrified by the gun and the knife, the girls obeyed without a peep. He pulled a sheet off a lower bunk bed and tore it into strips with his knife with expert precision. He then proceeded to tie the girls' hands and stuff gags into their mouths.

The last of the six girls, Miss Pasion, had barely been tied before the voice of Gloria Jean Davy was heard downstairs. She was on the phone in the kitchen reporting to the housemother that she was home safe from her date. That was the rule: every girl had to check in with Mrs. Bisone. The housemother's record showed that Miss Davy had called at 11:20 P.M.

Miss Davy came upstairs and was confronted by the man with the knife and gun. He ordered her into the room and made her lie beside the rest. She did and he bound her wrists.

Then he talked to the girls. His voice was slow, soothing, reassuring. "I'm not going to hurt you," he kept saying. While he was talking, the front door opened. Suzanne Farris and her future sister-in-law, Mary Ann Jordan, who was going to visit overnight in the town house, walked in.

Unaware of what was going on upstairs, the last two girls went into the kitchen and telephoned the housemother. Then they went upstairs and into the left front bedroom, still not knowing that their sister-students in the next room were lying bound and gagged, and ordered under knifepoint to remain still.

"We were all too afraid to move or to make noise," Miss Amurao said.

The intruder quickly bounded into the room Miss Farris and Miss Jordan had entered, forced them to lie down, and tied them up as he had the others. To the last two victims also, the young man repeated his assurances that he was not going to harm his captive harem. That may not have allayed the women's fright, but it did curtail their panic.

"All I want is money.... I've got to have money to get to New Orleans," he continued to repeat.

Whether the other female prisoners believed his line is something no one will know; Miss Amurao did not. She was petrified and her only thoughts concentrated on trying to escape. But how?

For a half hour after he had finished tying up everyone, the intruder went about ransacking the house. Miss Amurao could hear him going from room to room. Finally he returned and said, "All right, I'm taking all of you out of here."

Ordering them to their feet, he herded the girls into the small back bedroom where he again made them lie face down on the floor. Then he took Miss Davy out of the room. From the direction of their footsteps, Miss Amurao determined that they had gone downstairs.

Some twenty-five minutes later, he came back for Miss Pasion. By this time Miss Amurao was convinced that everyone's life was in peril. There was nothing else she could do to help the others, but she could do something to save herself. Though her wrists were bound together, she managed to roll over on the floor and squeeze under a bunk bed. She went as far as she could, huddling against the wall. Now she was out of sight.

In minutes the man returned to lead still another girl from the room—who she was, Miss Amurao could not see from under the bed. She held her breath until he left again. Although none of the girls whom he had taken out so far had been heard to scream, Miss Amurao sensed that something terrible was going on.

After an inordinately long period of time had passed, it dawned on Miss Amurao that she had not heard any more sounds, not even breathing. And the man had stopped coming back to the room. Yet she still did not dare move—not until she was jarred by the ringing of an alarm clock in one of the other rooms. That told her it was 5:00 A.M. The clock went off every morning at that hour to awaken some of the student nurses who had to report to the hospital at six.

As the clock rang, Miss Amurao used the covering sound to struggle out of the bedsheet shackles around her wrists. And after the alarm ran down, she waited motionless for at least another half hour in her hiding place. Then she finally decided that it might be safe to crawl out.

Police theorized that the killer had not sought out the surviving nurse either because he had lost count of how many girls were in the house, or had never counted all nine to begin with.

Walking on tiptoes into the hall, she stopped dead in her tracks as she spotted Miss Farris' legs protruding from the bathroom.

"When I see Suzanne is dead," Miss Amurao told Sergeant Murtaugh and Commander Flanagan, "I know other girls must be dead too."

Her worst fears were realized when she looked into the front bedroom on the left and saw the bodies of Miss Schmale, Miss Pasion, Miss Gargullo; then, in the bedroom on the right, three other bodies.

Miss Amurao panicked. She jumped over the last three corpses, kicked out the screen of the front window, and clambered out onto the two-foot-wide ledge. It was from there that her hysterical screams told the world of what was to become known as Chicago's "Crime of the Century."

As the widespread search for the killer got under way, detectives who had been tracking down initial clues and leads began to report their findings. Detectives Carlisle and Wallenda, for example, were able to brief Sergeant Murtaugh on what they had come up with in their examination of the slain nurses' residence. The wild disarray of the bedrooms—clothing and personal belongings strewn about the floor—had most probably been the result of the killer's search for money rather than of a struggle by the victims. None of the girls' pocketbooks and purses had any money in them. How much was taken could not be determined, but Miss Amurao told Murtaugh and Commander Flanagan that her own purse had contained thirty-one dollars—and that cash was now missing.

The preliminary examination of the bodies at the scene by Dr. Toman and his team of pathologists determined how each of the girls had been slain. In most, multiple stab wounds had been the cause of death; others had been both stabbed and strangled. Only Miss Davy was not stabbed; strangulation alone had been enough to kill her. The doctors also took vaginal smears, which determined that the girls had not been sexually molested.

The most significant clue developed during the pathological examination was the determination of how the killer had knotted the strips of bedsheets around his victims. Detective Carlisle, who with his fellow sleuth, Wallenda, had watched the doctors remove the bonds from the girls' wrists, advised Sergeant Murtaugh about a characteristic common to all the knots.

"They were good square knots," Carlisle reported. "Nobody could open them and he had their hands tied behind them the right way, with the backs of the wrists against each other and the palms facing the sides."

"It's the way police handcuff prisoners," Wallenda pointed out. "If you tie the hands with the palms straight down, they can work them around and twist their fingers enough to get at the rope."

"Not the way this guy did it," put in Carlisle. "He must have been arrested in his time. A convict, probably. And he surely has been around rope."

This suggested that the killer might be a seaman. And that in turn pointed to a distinct avenue of inquiry. For less than a half block down the street from the town house, just across the next intersection to the east, at 2335 East 100th Street, was a hiring hall for the National Maritime Union.

Murtaugh lost no time relaying this possible lead to his superiors. Immediately a detective team composed of Edward A. Wielosinski, John T. Mitchell, Edward A. Boyle, and Eugene Ivano was dispatched to the hiring hall with Murtaugh at their head.

Earlier, the same team had picked up another possible lead. They had stopped at the CTG gasoline station at 100th Street and Torrence Avenue, near the Indiana state line, and described the suspected killer to the owner, thirty-year-old Richard Polo.

"Yes," Polo told the detectives, "I saw such a man on Tuesday afternoon. He was carrying a brown plaid flight bag and a small brown overnight case. He said he had gone to Indiana to get a job, but didn't land it. He came back and was looking for a place to stay."

The service station owner added that the young man was very talkative, soft-voiced, and spoke with a Southern accent. Polo also said that the man related that he had slept on the beach along Lake Michigan on Sunday night and in a rooming house on Monday night. But when he returned Tuesday from Indiana, he found that his room had been rented to someone else.

"He asked to leave his bags here and I let him. Then he returned yesterday, took the bags, and said he was on his way to the Ship Yard Inn where he had managed to rent a room."

The detective team hurried to the Ship Yard Inn, a rundown rooming house on Avenue N overlooking Chicago's Calumet Dry Dock, which caters mostly to transients and seamen. The clerk confirmed that a young man matching the description had checked in, paid nine dollars for a week's rent, then just as suddenly checked out that very morning—Thursday. Although the clerk could not say where the man went, the clerk did remember that the guest had telephoned a sister, who lived in Chicago.

With Murtaugh leading the way, the probers now descended on the Maritime Union hiring hall.

"It was pay dirt almost from the first moment," Murtaugh

recalls. "We were told that a man matching the description had been in on Monday looking for a job. It certainly got us excited, but nothing like when the hiring agent told us that the fellow was looking to get on a ship for New Orleans."

The hiring agent, William O'Neill, said he had told the young man that the only opening was on a Great Lakes ore boat sailing out of Indiana Harbor. The man decided to try for the job. But he had returned to the union hall on Tuesday and reported that he had gotten there too late—someone else had been hired. There were no other openings that day and he was told to come back on Wednesday. He did, but again the hiring agent could not place him.

"He was told to keep coming back, that we would try to find something for him," O'Neill related to Murtaugh and his team of sleuths. "He had filled out an application. But his qualifications weren't much and it didn't seem likely he'd find work because most maritime jobs require experience."

Application? Where was the application?

It was at O'Neill's fingertips. Murtaugh scanned it avidly. The name of the job-seeker: Richard F. Speck. Description: Age, 25; Height, 6 feet; Weight, 170 lbs; Color of hair, brown.

Moreover, the application provided Murtaugh and his men with the most precious lead of all: a small, passport-sized photograph of the suspect.

They hurried back to Area 2 Headquarters and reported their find. The police photography lab turned out two dozen copies of Speck's picture in less than an hour. By 2:00 P.M. on the day that the murders ·were discovered, each team of detectives assigned to the manhunt on the South Side was furnished with a photograph of the suspect.

Meanwhile, plans to trap Speck at the Maritime Union hall if he should return for a job were painstakingly laid. That aspect of the investigation now assumed critical proportions because the sophisticated electronic archives at Central Headquarters had not set any red lights flashing when Richard Speck's name and photograph were run through. He had no police. record in Chicago.

The Ship Yard Inn and Speck's sister's house were by now

also under surveillance. The authorities had no way yet of knowing where else Speck might be found. Without a dossier, he was a stranger to the police. But to Detective Sergeant John Murtaugh, if Speck was indeed the killer, he had to be caught—and soon. A man who had murdered eight women without provocation was not likely to hesitate to kill again.

The detectives supervised by Murtaugh returned to the Maritime Union hiring hall, whipped off their jackets, took off their ties, opened their collars, and rolled up their shirtsleeves. They were now "hiring agents" for the Maritime Union, a pose that they hoped would help them seize Speck if he should return seeking a job.

At 2:30 P.M., detective Wielosinski telephoned Speck's sister, Mrs. Martha Thornton, thirty-eight, wife of a Chicago railroadman. Posing as an NMU agent, the detective asked Mrs. Thornton where her brother was. She said she didn't know. "Well, tell him to call the hiring hall as soon as he gets in touch," Wielosinski said. "We've got a job for him."

At 3:10 P.M., a telephone rang in the hiring hall. William Olsen, a union employee, answered.

"Do you have a job for me?"

"Who is this?" Olsen asked.

"Richard . . . Richard Speck. . . ."

"Yes," Olsen said, signaling to Wielosinski and the other detectives on stakeout at the hall. "I have a job for you on the Sinclair Great Lakes. Where are you?"

"Downtown at Ruthie's."

"How long will it take you to get here?"

"About an hour."

Murtaugh advised Commander Flanagan of the development. Twenty more detectives were rushed into the area and staked out in strategic spots around the hiring hall.

The wait was in vain. Speck never showed up. Whether he suspected anything when he spoke earlier to Olsen—perhaps an anxiety in the voice, the easiness of the offer of a boat berth—was difficult to ascertain.

But the stakeout at the hiring hall was not without its rewards. Murtaugh and his team had extracted valuable fragments of in-

formation from some of the seamen. A couple of them remembered Speck. One had seen him arrive Monday morning in a car
driven by a woman. Someone else remembered seeing Speck
after he had been turned away from the hall. The informant
reported observing the suspect walk along Crandon Avenue to
Luella Park, a half block away, and then sit on a bench sunning
himself, watching children at play on the seesaws and swings.

From that same bench he also had an unobstructed view of the
back of 2319 East 100th Street, the house in which the eight
student nurses lived.

Other witnesses supplied still more pieces of the rapidly ma-
terializing jigsaw puzzle depicting Speck's movements. From the
park he had returned to the hiring hall, found that there still
was no ship for him, and had gone to the gas station at East
100th and Torrence where the owner let him leave his brown
plaid flight bag and small overnight case. Then he had walked
back to his rooming house, a sleazy place called Pauline's. Still
no rooms, but he was offered the couch in the lobby. Speck
settled for that.

On Wednesday morning Speck left Pauline's, went to the
Ship Yard Inn, found a room there, went back to the gas station
for his bags, then returned to the Ship Yard Inn. After settling
in his room, Speck went to the bar downstairs and spent the day
drinking.

But now the police, who had pieced together his movements
from Sunday night through Wednesday afternoon, began to have
difficulty reconstructing Speck's subsequent trail. And this seg-
ment was the most important—the critical hours just before and
during the mass murders.

Nevertheless, Murtaugh and his men succeeded in finding a
witness who claimed to have seen Speck approximately an hour
after the killings were discovered, at 7:00 A.M. on Thursday. At
that time Speck had assertedly been in Pete's Tavern on Ewing
Avenue, eleven blocks from the scene of the nurses' slaughter.
The witness was William Kirkland, a twenty-two-year-old laborer
who had met Speck some four months earlier. As Kirkland re-
counted it, "We started talking over drinks. He was drinking
whiskey and beer, and after a while he took out a hunting knife

which he said he had bought in Vietnam on a voyage aboard a ship he was working as a seaman."

The knife, according to the witness, had at least a twelve-inch-long blade.

"I asked him if he wanted to sell it," Kirkland told the detectives. "I offered him a dollar and he handed me the knife."

Kirkland was asked for the knife. He went up to his room and brought it down. The police sent it to the laboratory.

A bartender at Pete's Tavern, Raymond O. Crawford, had a vivid recollection of Speck that Thursday morning.

"He had started talking about the knife," Crawford said. "Until then he had just been joking around at the bar and buying drinks for other customers. He had spent about eight dollars. All at once he picked up the knife off the bar, walked behind me, grabbed my neck with one arm and put the edge of the blade against my throat. He was trying to show me how to kill a person. I remembered he said, 'This knife has killed several people . . . and that's how I like to kill 'em.' "

During that episode, another acquaintance, Robert ("Red") Gerrald, who once worked on an Inland Steel ore boat with Speck, had come into the bar; Speck borrowed two dollars from Kirkland and left the tavern with Gerrald. The detectives were told by Gerrald, "We hit three or four more bars. In one of them we heard the news about the murders. Speck said to me, 'It must have been a maniac who did it.' "

After departing from the last tavern, Speck had checked out of the Ship Yard Inn and left in a cab. That was at 7:45 A.M. on Thursday.

From that point, Speck's trail was again lost. The police set about trying to find the cabbie who had picked up the suspect. By Friday morning their doggedness paid off. Murtaugh's sleuths located the taxi driver, who said that he had driven his passenger to the 1300 block of North Sedgwick Street. Speck paid the $5.90 fare and let the taxi go.

Police canvassed the neighborhood where Speck had left the cab, searching for anyone who might have seen a man answering his description. Before long they encountered Mrs. Jo Holland, who lived on the twelfth floor of a high-rise apartment house in the 1100 block of North Sedgwick. Mrs. Holland told an incredible story.

She had been sitting at her window shortly before 8:00 A.M. on Thursday, listening to radio bulletins about the murders, and watching the street with field glasses. Through the binoculars, she saw a cab stop in the 1300 block of North Sedgwick and observed a tall blond young man with two bags get out, pay the cabbie, then stroll back to the 1200 block of North Sedgwick. He walked east, and she followed him through the binoculars until he turned south into Dearborn Street and out of sight.

Then Mrs. Holland offered a spectacular example of long-distance observation.

"I was able to read the writing on his arm . . . on the tattoo. I could see it as clear as your face. It said, 'Born to Raise Hell.' "

There was little doubt that the arm was that of Richard Speck. Background on him by now obtained from the Coast Guard listed identifying marks on his body. They included tattoos, and one was of a serpent on Speck's left forearm that bore the legend: "Born to Raise Hell."

Although by now some twenty-four hours had passed since Mrs. Holland had spotted the suspect through her glasses, Murtaugh and his immediate superior, Lieutenant William McCarthy, agreed that Speck must have headed for one of the hotels or rooming houses on Dearborn Street or on Clark Street.

"Let's hit every one of them," snapped McCarthy. Murtaugh, in turn, dispatched teams of detectives on a building-by-building manhunt.

As the on-scene search for Speck picked up renewed momentum, developments broke on other fronts. At South Chicago Community Hospital, Corazon Amurao had slept through the night and awakened considerably improved. She could be questioned, and she could also tolerate the ordeal of sifting through 177 mug shots of known criminals who either resembled Richard Speck or were believed capable of committing the atrocity perpetrated on the eight nurses.

Not until the last photograph was placed before Miss Amurao did she evoke any sign of recognition.

"This!" cried Amurao. "This is man!"

"Are you sure?"

"Yes, this is him!"

The picture was that of Richard Speck.

It was now 1:00 P.M. Friday. Murtaugh had unleashed a dozen sleuths along Dearborn and Clark streets, and before long they began making heartening progress in the area, best known as Chicago's vice trap, so typical of the wretched road that Richard Speck had been traveling since Sunday—through gin-mills and flophouses, all on the wrong side of the worst parts of town.

Now he was in all probability somewhere in the most savage jungle of Chicago, where knives flash and men fall bleeding in toilets or on barroom floors, where prostitutes are at a man's beck and call, where drug addicts jam needles into their scarred arms, where the nerve-jangling jukebox music and the ten-cent beer help ease the aches of desolation of lost souls. This was the last outpost. And Speck was there.

But where?

Still, Murtaugh's noose was inexorably tightening. He recalls, "We were just one step behind him."

The Twist Lounge was a long, shabby saloon on North Clark Street. Its name celebrated the early 1960's dance popularized by Chubby Checker. Now, in mid-1966, the Twist was about as popular as the Roaring Twenties' Bunny Hop. The dance may have been dead, but the Twist Lounge was not. With its seventy-five-foot-long bar and its atmosphere reeking of urine, vomit, and bad breath, it was doing a land-office business even though the bouncer kept whacking the disorderly blacks,. Mexicans, and Indians, male and female, who patronized the place.

"Sure he was in here last night," the bouncer told one of Murtaugh's detectives who showed the bouncer Speck's mug shot. "He was sociable, real sociable. He stood over near the jukebox, most of the night, playing records and drinking. He didn't give anyone any trouble. He had this sweater on, that's why I remember him, this white sweater with red and blue stripes."

When did he leave, where did he go, the officer wanted to know. The bouncer had to think. It had been a very busy night.

As the bouncer searched his memory, some of the patrons sat on silver beer barrels against the back wall. The tables up front were packed. Everybody was talking, yelling, cursing. It wasn't easy trying to remember what had happened the night before in the Twist Lounge. One night blended into the next in a Hogarthian continuum.

Suddenly, the bouncer remembered.

"Yeah. It was around two o'clock this morning. This guy in the picture started talking to one of the broads. . . ."

She was a heavyset blonde. Her name was Mary. But sometimes she called herself Sylvia. Or Tomi. By whatever name, she was always available.

At approximately 3:00 A.M. Speck and the blonde had left the Twist Lounge.

It was barely mid-afternoon on Friday when Murtaugh's men received this information from the bouncer. The sun was too high and too bright for Mary or Sylvia, or whatever her name was, to be out on the street. The detective went to her flat, in a rotting boarding house down the street.

"He was here with me," she readily admitted. "About an hour. He was a cheap one. He only paid me three dollars."

She didn't know where he was staying. But she remembered that he had told her he was going back to get another beer and "maybe find me another broad."

The detective took time out to report the results of his investigation to Sergeant Murtaugh.

"Go back to the Twist Lounge and see if you can find out what happened when he got back," Murtaugh ordered.

Now one of the bartenders in the Twist Lounge recalled the man in the photograph. The bartender also remembered watching the man leave with a middle-aged black prostitute.

Did the bartender know who she was? He did. The detective had little difficulty finding her.

The man in the picture, she confirmed, was the same one she had met at the bar and had "entertained" until 7:00 A.M., when he paid her five dollars and left.

Where had they gone for their fun?

To the Raleigh Hotel. As the detective started to leave, the woman called out, "Hey! If you don't believe me, just ask the desk clerk about me. I'm the one who told them this guy had a gun in his room."

The detective hurried to the street and reported what he had learned to Sergeant Murtaugh, who was in a parked squad car nearby serving as the command post for the vice district sweep. Other detectives on the search were summoned back and alerted to the development.

Murtaugh proceeded to the Raleigh, six blocks away on Erie Street: a six-story third-rate hotel that was advertising rooms for two dollars and up. The desk clerk checked the register. "There it is," he exclaimed, pointing to the name. Speck had checked in Thursday morning at nine o'clock and paid a week's rent.

"He was here up until thirty minutes ago," the detectives were told. "He went out with a bundle. Said he was going to a laundromat."

Murtaugh assigned several detective teams to stakeouts on the street in front of the Raleigh and in various parts of the hotel. One team of detectives went up to the room Speck had rented. They entered with a passkey and searched his meager belongings in the two bags.

Among other items they found a black jacket, black pants, and a T-shirt—garments that fit the description of those that Miss Amurao said the killer had worn. All were on hangers and all had been freshly laundered.

Murtaugh and his fellow detectives settled down to wait for Richard Speck's return.

In the meantime, details obtained from Speck's Coast Guard application for maritime duty had been run through the FBI files in Washington, and a wealth of information amassed.

The FBI had learned that Speck was an ex-convict with a long history of trouble with the police, beginning at the age of sixteen when he was living in Dallas, Texas. The record showed that his most recent brush with the law had occurred in Dallas in 1963, when he was convicted of forgery and sentenced to three years in the state's maximum security prison at Huntsville.

Paroled in January 1965, Speck got in trouble again for

felonious assault upon a woman he had threatened with a knife. He was returned to prison for parole violation, but because of a mixup was released prematurely from serving the full time he owed.

The record listed Monmouth, Illinois, as Speck's birthplace. His father had died when Richard was still a young boy. His mother had taken him to live in Dallas. The dossier also reflected his record of employment as a seaman, working on Great Lakes ships, but always briefly.

For all the energy, sleepless nights, and brilliant sleuthing that went into tracking the spoor of Richard Speck, the Chicago police had committed at least one blunder that received little notice amid the turmoil and terror generated by the atrocity.

It is, of course, easy to second-guess. Police, no matter who they are or where they are, are only human. Like all of us, they can exercise questionable judgment at times, especially after tragedies of such proportions as Chicago's "crime of the century," which had the ingredients not only to stir the deepest wrath but also to upset the keenest senses.

It came as a shock and embarrassment to Sergeant Murtaugh to learn during the stakeout at the Raleigh Hotel that Richard Speck had been questioned by police earlier that Friday morning. It happened this way:

By 6:00 P.M. that Friday Speck had not returned to his hotel. A police lieutenant asked the desk clerk whether anyone knew where Speck might be. The clerk was curious as to why police were so anxious to find Speck when, after all, the cops had already given him "a clean bill," as the clerk put it.

The lieutenant was startled. "What cops . . . what are you talking about?"

"Well, I'll tell you how it goes," the clerk began. "You may not know it, but one thing about this place is that we run it strictly legal. And early this morning when this woman came down from Speck's room and told me that he had a gun up there, do you know what I did? I called the police right away."

"What police?"

"The Chicago Avenue Station."

"And what happened?"

"Oh, they sent a car down and a couple of cops talked to the guy."

The Chicago Avenue Station was checked immediately. Yes, someone said, there was a report, all right. It had been turned in by the patrolmen sent to investigate the call. The report indicated that the man readily admitted there was a gun in his room and brought it out for the patrolmen. It was a .22 calibre revolver, according to one account given out by authorities. In a later version, it was called a starter's pistol. He also had six cartridges.

Speck had claimed that the gun and bullets weren't his—that they belonged to the woman who had just left. The officers confiscated the gun and ammunition; they were inventoried at the police station at nine o'clock Friday morning.

"What's the name on the report?" the station house was asked.

"Richard Speck," was the reply.

Sergeant Murtaugh and his team of detectives had come up with Richard Speck's name more than twenty-four hours earlier at 1:00 P.M. Thursday, and less than seven hours after the eight nurses' bodies were found. Murtaugh had promptly alerted his superiors at Area 2 Command. All afternoon not only Speck's name, but his photograph too, could have been circulated to every precinct in the city. Instead, they had been put in the hands of a relatively few detectives because of the danger of a libel suit if Speck had happened to be the wrong suspect.

Had the name of the wanted man been read to the patrolmen at muster before going on their beats, had the photograph been posted on every station house bulletin board, then every cop in Chicago would have had his eye out for Richard Speck. Instead, some eighteen hours later, a pair of patrolmen who could not be blamed for not recognizing him had run smack into Speck— with a gun, to boot—and had simply bought his story that the weapon belonged to a prostitute.

Now Murtaugh could do little else than continue to wait for Speck at the Raleigh, convinced more than ever that he was the sadistic mass murderer the law was seeking.

That conviction was reinforced later that evening when fingerprint charts flown from Washington, D.C., were compared with the prints turned up in the town house. They matched on at least twelve points. Richard Speck unquestionably had been inside the dwelling where the eight nurses were slain.

At ten o'clock Saturday morning, when Speck still had not returned to his room at the Raleigh and had not been seen in any of the bars patrolled all night by detectives, Superintendent of Police Wilson called a press conference. He was now convinced that Speck was not coming back to his room and, armed with the evidence amassed by Murtaugh and his teams of sleuths, had decided to seek the public's help.

Wilson announced that the police had enough evidence to convict Speck of the killings, that Corazon Amurao had identified his picture. Displaying a blowup of Speck's photo, the superintendent declared, "I am sure this is the right man."

Sergeant Murtaugh could hardly have asked for a greater vote of confidence.

The picture was published in Chicago's newspapers and in hundreds of others across the United States. To guard against Speck's fleeing the city or state, U.S. Attorney Edward Hanrahan went before U.S. District Court Judge Julius J. Hoffman and obtained a fugitive warrant. That placed the case under federal jurisdiction as well, and opened the way for the FBI to participate officially in the search.

In Chicago, Murtaugh pursued the hunt for Richard Speck relentlessly. Squads of detectives and uniformed policemen watched railroad stations, bus terminals, airports, and the waterfront. Messages were flashed to ships that had sailed into the Great Lakes out of the Chicago area during the hours since Speck was last seen. Weary detectives plied the streets of the tawdry North Side, checking every flophouse, beanery, bar, and cheap movie house. They searched drifters found leaning against doorways or stretched out in drunken stupors on sidewalks and alleys. But there was no sign of Speck.

The whine of sirens on a Saturday night in Chicago's North Side is not an unusual occurrence. So on that Saturday night of July 16th, when an ambulance siren sounded along West Madison Street shortly after midnight, it was largely ignored. No one got excited when the small van, called a "squadrol," pulled up in front of the Starr Hotel at 617 West Madison.

The Starr's night clerk, William Vaughan, had called the

police about one of the guests, a young man who had registered earlier that evening as B. Brian. He had been found bleeding in his cubicle on the fifth floor, evidently having attempted suicide by cutting a vein in his left arm and right wrist. Such an incident was so routine in the city's skid row hotels that it was all part of the night's work for the two patrolmen in the ambulance, Eugene Krause and Michael Burns.

The inside of the Starr Hotel was a familiar and miserable setting to them. They knew all its depressing fixtures—the sign stenciled above the bilious green tile walls: "No drink is allowed on these premises"; the seedy front desk where a key for the night cost ninety cents; the pictures of Lincoln and Kennedy in the lobby; the elevator run by an old man and the sign inside that warns: "Enter at your own risk."

The two ambulance patrolmen were told as they came in that the bleeding guest was on the fifth floor. His cubicle would have no air conditioning and no sanitized-for-your-protection drinking glasses. It was merely an eight-by-six foot arrangement with a wire mesh over the ceiling, a four-legged wooden stool, a black metal locker, and a sheetless cot with sagging springs on a concrete floor. They call the cubicles at the Starr "cages" for good reason.

The young man was lying on his back on the cot in Cage 584, his arms dangling over the sides, his blood spilling onto the floor. Patrolman Burns quickly tied a tourniquet around the man's left arm.

Patrolman Krause turned to Vaughan and asked whether he knew what had happened. The night clerk explained that he had been called upstairs by the man in Cage 582, whose name was George. The latter was with the bleeding man when the cops came in.

"I didn't want to talk to him at first," George told the patrolmen. "He came in here last night with a couple of bottles of wine and holed up in his cage. Once in a while he began calling over to me. But I didn't want to be bothered. Goddam hillbilly. He finally fell asleep. Then this morning, around ten, he went downstairs and returned with more bottles of wine and the newspapers. He went to his cage. Late this afternoon I heard him calling for water. I told him to shut up. 'I need water,' he kept saying. He was out in the hall. Then I heard him say, 'Please, a beer. I'll give you anything for beer.' I told him to get out of there and stop bothering me. Then I heard him go by, heading for the men's room. A few minutes later he came by and fell up against my door, busting through it. I was in here trying to read *True Detective* and I was ready to belt the bum. But I looked up and saw the guy bleeding like a stuck pig. I took him back to his cage and laid him down. Then I ran to get help. When I got back I gave him some booze and told him to be quiet."

"What's your name?" the patrolman asked the young man on the cot.

"Brian . . . B. Brian," he replied.

"Address?"

"No address . . . I'm staying here. This is my address."

"How did you cut yourself?"

"Who the hell knows . . . all I know is I'm cut."

Patrolman Burns was told by another of the hotel's occupants that there was a broken bottle in the men's room. Evidently that was where the young man had cut himself.

The two patrolmen lifted him up and Burns walked the young man out of the cubicle to the elevator. Krause looked around the room and gathered the injured man's belongings; a tube of toothpaste, a pack of razor blades, a bottle of after-shave lotion, a jar of men's cologne. On one of the pale-green metal walls the patrolman noticed one of the literary masterpieces that adorned some of the Starr's cages. It was scrawled in pencil: "I will pay $5 for a guy who is young (25) and has dirty sweating feet. . . ."

Beneath it at the foot of the cot lay a copy of the Chicago *American* with a banner headline, "Strangler Hunt Stymied, Police Admit."

The man with the bleeding arms who had told the ambulance policemen that his name was B. Brian was whisked to Cook County Hospital. Brought into the emergency room, the patient commanded the immediate attention of Dr. Leroy Smith, the twenty-six-year-old resident surgeon. After a quick assessment of the nature of the wounds, Smith took the patient into the trauma ward for treatment.

Assisted by nurse Kathy O'Connor, the doctor began to clean the blood from both arms. He noted that the patient had a cut in the crease under the elbow of his left arm from which there was free bleeding from a severed vein, as well as a superficial cut on a bony part of the right wrist.

But the doctor's attention was also drawn to the patient's face. An hour earlier, Smith had read a newspaper story about the search for the slayer of the eight student nurses, and he had studied the fugitive's photograph. The physician turned the patient's head for a better view, then whispered to the nurse, "Bring me the newspaper."

As Miss O'Connor went out, Dr. Smith wiped more blood from the patient's left forearm. Part of a tattoo became visible. The physician could discern the letter "B." He cleaned more blood away and saw "B-o-r-n." Then, as he cleaned the entire forearm, Dr. Smith read the telltale legend: "Born to Raise Hell."

Even before the nurse returned, Dr. Smith knew the patient's identity. So when Miss O'Connor walked in with the paper, the doctor said quietly, "Get hold of the police." The nurse hurried out again and summoned the patrolman on duty in the hospital.

Meanwhile, Dr. Smith did some preliminary interrogation of his own.

"What's your name?" he asked.

The patient stared blankly at the doctor.

"Are you the man police are looking for?"

The man shrugged resignedly.

"What's your name?"

"Richard," the patient said. Smith waited. "Richard Speck," the man blurted.

The patrolman summoned by Miss O'Connor arrived in the emergency room and made the arrest. After completing the emergency treatment, Dr. Smith turned and walked away.

The search was over. The relentless pressure of Sergeant John Murtaugh's probe had finally flushed its quarry. "He tried to commit suicide," reflects Murtaugh. "I believe he had an idea that he had been identified. The papers had said that he was wanted. When we hit the pad on North Park we found clippings. He apparently was following the papers."

The time was 12:45 A.M., Sunday, July 17, approximately sixty-seven hours since Corazon Amurao had struggled out of her bedsheets bonds, clambered over the corpses of her roommates, and climbed out to the ledge, screaming, "Help me! Help me! They're all dead!"

Nine months later, a jury in Peoria, Illinois' third-largest city, returned a verdict of guilty against Speck. The eight-week trial was held in Peoria County because the defense did not believe that Speck could get a fair trial in Chicago. It took the veniremen just forty-nine minutes to reach their verdict, which condemned Richard Franklin Speck to die in the electric chair.

Yet Speck did not go to the death ordained by his his twelve peers, thanks to the U.S. Supreme Court's view (in 1972) that capital punishment, as then applied by the states, was an unacceptable form of retribution for the taking of a life—or even of eight lives.

So the man who was "Born to Raise Hell"—and did so by engaging in an orgy of mass slaughter on a scale never witnessed before or since in Chicago—beat the chair. For whatever consolation it may be to Sergeant John Murtaugh and the scores of other sleuths who toiled to avenge the savage murders of the eight young women, Richard Speck was at least permanently removed from society when his death sentence was commuted to life imprisonment. That is little consolation to Murtaugh. He says, "Pigs like Speck. No question in my mind, he should have been executed."

9

A Noble Professional

THE SUMMER OF 1956 was a bad time for jewelry stores in Toronto. Beginning with the disappearance of two ladies' diamond rings from Gray's Jewellers on Yonge Street, rings and watches worth tens of thousands of dollars were being stolen from the better establishments in the Canadian metropolis.

Evidence indicated that they were being shoplifted during regular business hours—either during busy periods or during slack times when few salespersons were on hand—from windows or display cases at the front of the stores. From the accounts of shop owners and clerks, it appeared that members of a gang would enter a store, singly or together. While one or more of the group would keep salespersons occupied at the rear of the floor with queries about merchandise, other members would spot where they were going to make "the sting."

Into the case stepped the Toronto Police Department, whose

forces included a young detective who was to become one of the most highly respected operatives in the history of Canadian justice. He is James Mervyn Noble.

If Great Britain's Scotland Yard embodies the Anglo-Saxon police tradition of maintaining order through civility, and pursuing investigations through patience, Canada's law enforcement institutions represent the western extension of this custom. The polite but dogged determination of the Royal Canadian Mounted Police to get their man is well known, but this trait also defines Canadian lawmen on other levels. From the small towns of Canada's bleak north to the booming cities of the country's east and west, no one is more typical of the Canadian police officer—or more effective among Canadian criminal investigators—than detective Jim Noble. Gentle, thoughtful, and courteous, he is at once a painstaking professional and an unassuming humanist.

Son of a Northern Ireland carpenter who brought his family over from Whiteabbey, near Belfast, when Noble was four, Jim Noble grew up on Toronto's Shaw Street, in what he calls an "ordinary workingman's neighborhood." He adds, "Because everybody was poor, we didn't realize we were poor. There wasn't much crime. It was a kind of nice time to be growing up, in spite of the Depression."

After finishing twelfth grade of school, Noble volunteered for the Royal Canadian Air Force at eighteen. He won his wings as a pilot officer in December 1944, but never got overseas during the remainder of World War II, to his immense frustration. After leaving the RCAF in late 1946, he found that "I couldn't settle down to a routine civilian job. I wanted something with a little bit of action, a little bit of excitement."

His father brought up the subject of Jim's career with a police inspector friend, who suggested that young Noble, then twenty-two, come in for a talk. "When my dad mentioned that at the dinner that night," Noble recalls, "he probably got his biggest laugh from me." After two lengthy sessions with the inspector, nonetheless Noble "decided that I would give it a try."

Noble spent six months pounding a beat as a uniformed policeman in midtown Toronto, then was assigned to a patrol car with another officer on a 7:00 P.M. to 3:00 A.M. shift. They handled the "usual cases: fights on the streets, drunks, domestics, robberies." It was the kind of schedule that wreaks havoc with a policeman's digestion and private life. After working their overnight shift, Noble and his partner would have to appear in court four or five mornings a week to present evidence, which meant that they had time for only a brief nap, a wash, and a bite to eat before being called as witnesses for sessions that lasted from a half hour to an entire day.

At the time, the Toronto force gave no special training in crime detection; nor was there a systematized selection process for detective candidates. "The detective sergeant in the division would be on the lookout for an officer who was able to 'make a

Toronto detective James Mervyn Noble (*The Toronto Star*)

good pinch,' as we call it," recalls Noble. "There was just on-the-job training."

In his spare time—which was precious spare—Noble studied the Criminal Code, and took police briefs on old cases out of the station's archives ("a pretty good education in itself"). Nor was the time he spent waiting for his cases to come up in court wasted socializing in the corridor. "I learned a lot there, not only when I was working. My partner and I would always listen to other cases being heard."

Among other things, Noble observed in court that many lawyers have almost a set routine. "You know what the next question is going to be. You can develop your own investigative techniques knowing what the questions will be. Of course, that's the acid test of any police officer: how does the case go in court?"

Noble regards his commitment of time and self as nothing out of the ordinary for a dedicated policeman. Noting that he was single at the time, he points out that "You gain a lot being a policeman, but you have to give up a lot, too. Your old friends get tired of calling you up to go to a party or go fishing, and finding that you can't go. After a while, in a good number of cases, they just stop calling. So a lot of policemen develop their little circle of friends with other policemen, which I don't think is really the best thing."

Noble was picked to fill a detective vacancy at No. 5 station, and moved up to the rank of divisional detective. "As a divisional detective, you get housebreaking, frauds, sex offenses, robberies, a little bit of everything," he explains. Noble recalls one of his cases at No. 5 station, a brief of which was retained by Noble's former divisional partner Jack Foster ("seven years and never a cross word") and personally conveyed to Noble. The case attests to the alertness and ingenuity that have marked the investigative mind of Jim Noble from the earliest years of his career.

The principals included a woman who owned a ladies' wear store and her boyfriend, who perpetrated an insurance fraud by hiring a group of young men to stage a break-in of the store. "We felt it was a phony from the outset," says Noble.

Working a 4:00 P.M.-to-midnight shift on a Saturday, Noble and his partner, Foster, happened to drive past the store at around 10:15 P.M., and noticed two youths loitering outside. Immediately suspicious, the two detectives parked their unmarked police car three blocks away, got out, and separated in order to keep the youths, who had been joined by two others, under better surveillance. After an hour, when a uniformed policeman came into view, the four youths got into an automobile and drove away. Before going off duty, Foster and Noble described the youths, and gave their car's license number to the policeman on the beat who went on duty at midnight.

At 12:25 A.M. on the same night, trying the rear of a shop next door, the beat patrolman saw a young man run out of the back of the ladies' wear store and managed to arrest him after a chase. Shortly afterward, at 12:40, Detective Foster went off duty but decided to drive past the shop on his way home. Seeing the constable with the captured youth and learning that the expected break-in had occurred, Foster scoured the neighborhood and arrested another suspect, who proved to be a brother of the first.

That was only the beginning. Initially, Noble recalls, the woman shop owner said that nothing was gone from the store. But on the following Monday she produced eight foolscap-sized pages listing clothing allegedly stolen and valued at $9,500. "That's when we really figured that the break-in was a phony," says Noble. Still, although Noble and Foster went to Toronto's Don jail where the accused brothers were held, the officers could not break the brothers' "sense of honor" and persuade them to talk.

At the youths' trial, the shop owner maintained that none of the clothing, on which the insurance company ultimately paid a reduced valuation of $5,130.66, had been recovered.

"What had happened," Noble says, "was that she and her boyfriend came back on Sunday and removed the clothing. Later on, that started to filter back into the store."

As a result of the circumstantial case that had been put together by Noble and his colleagues, the two brothers were convicted of the break-in. "All of a sudden," recalls Noble, "as they were being taken out of court after sentencing, they had a change of heart about confessing." As a result, the police got enough additional evidence to convict the woman and her boyfriend.

By March 1961, Noble was transferred to the homicide squad, an assignment of which he is justly proud. Says Noble, "Most policemen consider murder investigation the acme of police work." He became the squad's deputy head in November 1969, and its chief in January 1973, at which time he was also promoted to the rank of inspector.

Headquarters for the Metropolitan Toronto Police Department are in midtown, at 590 Jarvis Street, in a nondescript postwar red-brick office building that was assigned to the police in 1967. The fourteen-man homicide squad occupies a third-floor corner section. One member of the squad doubles as a police artist, sketching the likenesses of wanted persons. (He also draws the squad's annual Christmas card. One year it showed a gowned defense lawyer, waving a gun in a courtroom, helping the accused to escape. A detective is saying, "I admit he didn't do much during the trial but he certainly came through when his client needed him.")

The chief of the squad occupies a small corner office, strictly utilitarian, with gray metal furniture and buff walls.

On the job, Noble—who has since left Homicide and been promoted to staff superintendent in charge of a police district covering one-fourth of metropolitan Toronto—is cool, organized, and decisive, a clean-desk man, giving guidance deftly, and diplomatic in his dealings with outsiders. Serious when work demands, he also possesses an almost irrepressible sense of humor. "If you didn't have a sense of humor in this job," Noble wryly observes, "you'd go squirrelly after six months."

By way of confirmation, a Canadian magazine once published the following description of Noble's involvement in a particularly messy murder investigation:

She was murdered in May, but the body wasn't found until September, buried under the coal down in the basement. The two homicide detectives, Jim Noble and Norm Hobson, were to spend six full hours down there with that rotting corpse, gathering the evidence that would convict her husband. They didn't faint, and they didn't vomit, but at one point they started out for coffee and a sandwich. "How," one asked the other, "are we going to force ourselves to come back down here?" So they stayed.

When Jim Noble got home that night, he undressed in the

garage. His wife tossed out a pair of shorts for him, and he burned all the clothes he had on save his suit, which was new. He took a hot bath and a hot shower and then another hot bath, but he still felt unclean. Days later, reading a newspaper, the smell came back to him; it was imprinted in his subconscious. He sent the suit to one cleaner, and then another, but he hardly ever wore it again.

The case of the slain wife in the basement is but one of more than 100 murders Noble has investigated in a police career that spans more than a quarter of a century, a dozen years of which were on the Homicide Squad. The imperturbability of his approach to the dilemma of the decomposed female body was in keeping with his style.

In addition to the stench, the dampness of the basement added to the unpleasantness. The corpse was found near the mouth of the coal bin, but that was only the start of the distasteful—yet unavoidable—investigatory task that confronted Noble. He and his partner had to spend six hours in the basement because of the necessity to comb it for evidence. There was no other way.

The job required them to shift the coal, piece by piece, and to sift the ashes in the coal-burning furnace. Eventually, their laborious efforts paid off. Picking through the ashes, Noble and his partner found a wrist watch and a brooch that, it turned out, the woman's husband had tried to burn. He was charged with noncapital murder and convicted.

Thoughtful and articulate, given to a vivid turn of phrase and the telling quotation, Noble is a lucid instructor in investigative procedure and the psychology of the criminal mind. He stresses the teamwork that goes into any investigation conducted by the Toronto police. "We try to play down the individual here. We have a good esprit de corps. We try to stay away from that prima donna aspect. There's never any quibbling here about who's going to make the arrest."

Noble also places great stress on the basics of homicide investigation. At the outset, there is the vital necessity of preserving the scene of the crime exactly as it was when the crime was discovered.

Noble reports, "Standard operating procedure with our department is that, for police officers and detectives who arrive at the scene, the first duty is to try to preserve life. We expect them, without disturbing the scene, to make a cursory examination to determine whether life is present. But then, if they're reasonably satisfied that the person is dead, we emphasize that their next most important duty is to preserve the body and scene as they find it. We take this literally. They must not risk contaminating the scene by adding to it in the way of lighting cigarettes, or picking something up on their shoes or clothing, or taking something away from the scene. When we get there, nothing should be disturbed."

All officers and detectives who become involved in the investigation are expected to take detailed notes. Adds Noble, "We are always in the position that we have to reconstruct these things either from our memories or notes, for the judge and jury later on. We never know what will be important at the trial. Something to which you didn't attach great importance may later assume major importance."

"I have always had a theory," Noble declares, "that I didn't need to interview a detective to know what kind of policeman he was. I could tell just by reading his reports."

Obviously, murder investigations require both care and infinite patience. "You get involved in a lot of information and misinformation," Noble points out. "You have a lot of things that funnel in, and you don't know which are good, bad, or indifferent. You may spend hundreds of hours trying to locate a person you think is a good suspect. And you may never find him. Or you may find when you interrogate him that you can rule him out."

In the questioning of a suspect, Noble observes, "It's a great leveler in itself when you announce your name and your rank, and that you are with the homicide squad." The experienced detective learns to look for certain telltale signs: "a darting of the eyes, the mouth becomes dry and there's a wetting of the lips, a throbbing of the artery in the neck. The person gets pale, he's trembling." Noble demonstrates a violent spasm of the leg that can occur.

"Quite often you see that he's reached the stage where he wants to tell us about it. The body starts to rack, the tears to flow. It's really quite a poignant moment in your investigation. The reaction is basically the same with people who have done 'big time' and with people who haven't done any time."

He notes that "There's almost a compulsion of people to confess, especially in murder cases. It makes them feel that they have salved their conscience to some degree by telling about it." And when a suspect is arrested on one charge, he frequently confesses to other crimes. "Quite often when a person is arrested, he'll say, 'You have got me bang-up on that offense, I might as well clear the slate.' "

Again, copious note-taking on confessions is insurance against a "tendency to either add to what the accused says, to delete something, or to take it out of context. The lawyers love that. It gives them a beautiful opportunity to shoot you down in flames." Returning with a confessed murderer to the scene of the crime, Noble and his colleagues take care not to lead him, but instead allow him to lead them as he reconstructs his actions.

Looking ahead to the trial, Toronto's homicide detectives, relates Noble, try to imagine themselves as the defense lawyer and ask, "What is his defense going to be?"

As a "classic example of looking ahead," Noble cites the case of a young man who was charged with killing a homosexual. The accused was picked up in a routine check while driving an expensive car, and found to have blood on his clothing. Police went to the car owner's apartment, to determine whether he had loaned his car, and found him beaten to death with a wrench. The arrested youth admitted killing the man. Nevertheless, the detectives on the case, suspecting that the killer might claim that his victim surprised him with unwelcome advances he tried to repulse, found two witnesses to previous homosexual activity by the accused.

Thus, when the defendant put on an act at the trial, claiming that the man had picked him up at the bus terminal on a cold winter night when the defendant had no place to stay, and said that the wrench just happened to be handy when he needed something with which to defend himself, the prosecution produced two surprise rebuttal witnesses who testified, as Noble delicately puts it, that "the accused was no stranger to vice."

Reflecting on the well over 100 homicides he has handled, Noble makes the point again and again that detection is painstaking work, requiring the piecing together of many strands of evidence.

The teamwork practiced by the Toronto homicide squad was illustrated by a case involving the brutal killing of a man named Therland Crater and a woman named Carolyn Ann Newman by a narcotics dealer, one Arthur Lucas (all were from Detroit) in 1961. Noble and his partner, Norm Hobson, were, as Noble puts it, "little" cogs in the investigation.

Investigating a distress call made by a woman to a Bell Canada telephone operator in the early morning of November 17, 1961, police went to a duplex apartment at 116 Kendall Avenue, and found two corpses. The male victim lay in the front hall, shot to death, and the woman was in the upstairs flat from which she had evidently telephoned, dead on the bed of a slashed throat. There was no sign of a gun or a knife.

Nevertheless, a flashy ring left on the bed provided the initial clue to the killer's identity, which was established by that same afternoon when two women, among a group of suspected black pimps and prostitutes from Detroit rounded up by Toronto police, separately identified the ring as belonging to Lucas. By then, Lucas was no longer in Toronto; Detroit police staked out places he was known to frequent there, and arrested him on the day after the killings.

The gun used to shoot Crater turned up in an unlikely fashion, thanks to an alert citizen. It was Noble who took a telephone call on the afternoon of the murder from a man who was somewhat embarrassed to be calling in, but who had heard of the murders, and thought that he had seen a gun lying on Burlington Bridge as he was driving to work in Hamilton that morning along the Burlington Skyway. The Ontario Provincial Police quickly found the revolver. Evidently the gun's owner thought that he had thrown it out over the open water into Hamilton Harbor, but his judgment and aim were off. Instead, the revolver had struck a girder and bounced back onto the bridge, and though the cylinder was missing, it was found in a search of the ground below the bridge the next day. Test-firing at the Centre of

Forensic Sciences identified the gun as the murder weapon, and through serial numbers and a description, the weapon was traced back to Lucas.

Lucas was also linked to the scene of the crime by another detective, who remembered having questioned Lucas, who was staying at a downtown hotel, a week or so earlier as to why he was in Toronto. Lucas had said that he was up to visit friends who lived at 116 Kendall Avenue.

"It's the old story," concludes Noble. "Individually, the pieces mean very little, but collectively it adds up to that nice rope of circumstantial evidence."

Arthur Lucas was one of the last two convicted murderers to be hanged in Canada, in December 1962. In a crowning irony, Noble was a pallbearer for both—"Not by choice."

The other murderer who walked the last mile was one Ronald Turpin, convicted of shooting a policeman who had stopped Turpin late one Sunday night in a routine check.

Noble and three fellow members of the homicide squad were pressed into service to act as pallbearers for Lucas and Turpin.

Noble explains, "Bodies of persons executed for murder were buried in unmarked graves in cemeteries, in the very early morning hours—in this case, around 4:00 A.M. Presumably one of the reasons would be that there might be some resentment by persons who already had a member of the family buried in that area of the cemetery, or who might be burying some member of the family at a later date. Such procedure would also preclude the possibility of a disturbance or demonstration by pro- or anticapital punishment groups or individuals. Pallbearers are not overly numerous in this situation—in particular at 4:00 A.M."

Teamwork also resulted in a quick solution to a 1964 case in which Noble played a key role.

At 10:45 P.M. on Friday, September 25 of that year, a woman was heard screaming on Collinson Boulevard, in the suburban borough of North York. She was found collapsed and gasping on the sidewalk, and was pronounced dead on arrival at Branson Hospital. An autopsy performed at the Centre of Forensic Sciences established that the victim, a waitress who had been on her way to work at a Mister Donut restaurant, had been stabbed six times with a sharp weapon, possibly an ice pick.

In light of the vicious character of the crime, and the public fear that such a murder could arouse, the entire homicide squad was called in.

Searching a vacant house a half block from the scene of the crime, police found the victim's purse and its contents, including identification, but no money, strewn over the bare floor of a room with a closet containing paint cans. The woman's husband was able to report that she had gone to work with some $70 in her purse, including two Canadian silver dollars, and was saving for a trip to her native England. It was obvious that in all probability she had tried to resist her attacker's attempt to steal her purse and had been killed in the effort.

There was no sign of a weapon either at the scene of the stabbing or in the vacant house. Approximately two blocks from the scene, however, an alert policeman discovered a suggestive object: a folded-over piece of belt leather wrapped with adhesive tape to form a sort of scabbard. Following prescribed procedure, he picked up the object, marked the spot where it was found, labeled it with his initials, and turned it over to Noble at No. 32 station, the neighborhood precinct, in the early morning. "We didn't know at the time if it had any significance," Noble relates, "but this goes back to police college, where we were told, 'If there's any doubt at all about taking something as a possible piece of evidence, then resolve the doubt by taking it.'"

Later in the morning, around 8:00 A.M., Noble exhibited the object to officers reporting on and off duty at No. 32. One policeman recalled that, several years before, he had arrested a youth in a stolen car, and the youth had had a similar object with him. Looking up the youth's file, Noble and his partner at the time, Detective Sergeant Jim Crawford, found that the young man, now twenty-four years old, had been released from jail, and was living some six blocks from where the waitress had been murdered. "Naturally, this perked up our interest," recalls Noble. He and Crawford went to the young man's home for a suspenseful interview.

"He was obviously nervous and distraught at our being there," Noble recounts, adding that after questioning him briefly, "we saw enough signs that we gave each other the eye."

They found him "vague" about his activities the night before, and continued to interrogate him for some time, asking him about the plots of the previous evening's television shows he claimed to have viewed (Noble recalls one of the shows was "Combat"). The two officers noted that when the suspect mentioned having gone out after watching TV to mail a letter, the errand took him in the direction of the crime.

Then they asked him how much money he had in his possession, and requested him to take out his money. The young man, who was wearing tight trousers, finally stood up and, saying that he had about five dollars, produced that amount from one pocket. Hearing the "clinking of heavy coins," the detectives asked him to take his money out of the other pocket, whereupon he drew out $60 or $70 in bills. "Any coins in your pocket?" he was asked, and he came out with two silver dollars. "I think from that point he realized the game was over," says Noble.

Explaining the situation to the young man's mother, they took him to the station for further questioning. There he gave way to tremors and tears, "took his hands away from his face and admitted that he had stabbed the woman with an icepick and robbed her."

After cautioning the suspect about his rights, the detectives took a formal statement from him, then set about corroborating it. "In this case," says Noble, "we drove slowly past the scene, and he said, 'Slow down, you'll have to go back. You've passed it.'"

The suspect showed them where the struggle had taken place. He pointed out the empty house to which he had fled, and told them about the paint cans. He related how he had taken the money, including the two silver dollars, and gone out the back of the house, down through the back yard and vaulted a wire fence topped by a two-by-four railing that had broken under his weight. Examining the fence, the investigators found a fresh break. "Taken with all the other evidence," Noble observed, "it's a pretty straightforward picture that he's telling the truth."

More crucial corroboration was to come. Up to that point, the man had been unable to recall what he had done with the weapon. When the officers took him back to the yard opposite that of the empty house, he suddenly remembered. He had planted the ice pick in a small round flower bed and had lightly covered the instrument with soil. Exploring with his hand the place where the suspect thought he had buried the ice pick, Noble brushed dirt aside and uncovered it.

The young man then showed the detectives the direction in which he had run when he got back into the street, and gave them a rough idea where he had discarded the homemade scabbard. In his home they found another portion of the belt leather from which the scabbard had been made, and the remainder of the roll of adhesive tape he had used, as the forensic laboratory confirmed.

Less than eleven hours had elapsed between the crime and the suspect's arrest on Saturday morning. He was charged with capital murder and convicted. He was sentenced to hang but the sentence was commuted to life imprisonment, and he is now free on parole. ("One of the farces to my mind of our life imprisonment," protests Noble.)

Not only the family of the victim, but also the family of the accused, tend to "lean" on the detectives in a murder investigation "for counsel and advice," Noble says. "It's an onerous position," he observes, in that "many times you develop a rapport with the accused and his family. It's surprising, to people who are not policemen, some of the things they tell us that they wouldn't tell their closest friends, spiritual advisors, or spouses." He adds that "It's not unusual for fellows on the squad to get Christmas cards from people they have had dealings with in the past."

Prisoners may send gifts they have made—items of petit point, wallets, fishing flies. Producing a copy of a letter from a convicted murderer thanking him and his partner in the investigation, Jim Read, for their kindness—Noble admits that there are not too many such missives—Noble declares with admirable understatement, "I think those are a real compliment to the way the fellows handle things."

He continues, "A lot of people get the impression that many detectives are sadistic and callous individuals, and I just don't think that's true. There are policemen and detectives who give people a break and go out of their way to get them a light sentence.

"You can do a good, honest job as a policeman, without losing a bit of humanity, and treat people decently."

At the same time, in common with probably most detectives, Noble is concerned lest liberalization of laws hamper the guardians of order in their duty. "As time goes on, the laws are changing, it seems to me, to the detriment of the honest, law-abiding citizen. More and more policemen are getting the impression that the laws are helping the criminals, and creating more criminals."

Noble believes that policemen have a responsibility to become "activist" with respect to law and order, "to convince people on the decision-making level that these things can happen here. Once they do happen, you can't remain in control. To what avail are all the nice things we enjoy in life if we're afraid to leave home in the evening?"

Noble points with approval to a *Toronto Star* editorial headed: "Violence Is a Crime Against Democracy."

Unsurprisingly, Noble voices concern that violence on the part of an individual may be repeated. He cites cases where killers have been released from mental institutions despite histories of violence, and deplores the ease with which parole is granted to convicted murderers.

Pointing to the case of a man who was picked up in Ontario and charged with a brutal rape, only to confess to an earlier unsolved murder, Noble says, "You just cringe to think that there are so-called human beings who would stoop to such a level. He is an animated argument for the retention of capital punishment." Noble reports that the man's pattern of behavior became obvious to police when he was nine years old. "It's a pretty tough thing to accept if you're not a policeman," Noble asserts, "but there are some people we just can't afford to have at large." He offers an additional thought-provoking point, "It's women who in many cases have no defense against these types of persons."

A case in point, which Noble was involved in solving, was the vicious murder of an eighty-nine-year-old female physician, Rowena Hume, who was believed to be the oldest practicing woman doctor in Canada. She was kicked, clubbed, and strangled to death on the second floor of her Toronto home. Her battered body was discovered on the day after the murder by a police constable summoned by a *Toronto Star* woman reporter who had had an appointment to interview Dr. Hume, but who could get no response when she arrived at the doctor's home on Carlton Street.

A clue to a possible suspect was discovered on a slip of paper with a Salvation Army letterhead found in a pocket of an apron the doctor was wearing. The paper gave her address, the date, and a man's name. On checking a nearby Salvation Army hostel, which operated a service offering to hire out its guests to do odd jobs, Noble and his partner Jim Read learned that the paper was an assignment slip, and that the man in question had been sent over at the doctor's request to do some cleaning for her; she may have decided that her house (which Noble remembers for its fine old furniture and rugs) needed to be spruced up for the interview. On file at police headquarters Noble and Read found a photograph of the man, which they took to the hostel for confirmation.

Two days after the murder, Noble and Read were driving through the neighborhood when Read spotted the wanted man. Noble got out of the car, told the suspect who they were, and that they wanted to speak to him about the murder. Recalls Noble, "He just blurted out in effect that he had killed her." The man said, "I don't know what made me beat her up like that. I've been walking around for two days trying to get up the courage to give myself up."

His account was a chilling portrayal of irrational rage. He was living at the hostel because he was separated from his family, and he became enraged when the doctor innocently asked him about his family. He struck her with his fist and knocked her down, kicked her about the head, broke her left arm my kicking it, throttled her around the neck with the cord from a portable electric heater, then left the body. A few minutes later, hearing her moan, he finally killed her by crushing her skull with a pair of exercise clubs.

Noble is on the job Monday through Friday from 6:30 A.M. until after 6 P.M. When two seventeen-year-old girls were found shot in a field on Friday, April 27, 1973, Noble, along with many colleagues, worked until nearly midnight on the Saturday and Sunday following, and put in extra time on the next weekend also.

He prefers to keep work and home separate. "I'm sort of a Jekyll and Hyde. I try to give it a good effort when I am here, but I always try to divorce myself from being a policeman when I am home. Many of the things you see and the people you are dealing with are unpleasant. So my wife knows very little about my police life. It's very seldom that I tell her any of the tales of the cases that I'm involved with, and it's very seldom that she asks."

English-born, Noble's wife Barb is dark-haired and attractive even in the passport photo that Noble takes out of his wallet, saying that she hates his showing it. He met her in 1960 in the aftermath of a case; she was office manageress for a chain of ladies' wear stores in Toronto, and Noble and his partner Jack Foster called on her to present her with a restitution check from the culprit in a forgery case. Foster pointedly told Noble, who was thirty-five and still single, that she was attractive, and Noble telephoned her a couple of days later. They were married on September 2, 1961.

They have a daughter, Elaine, in whom Noble takes enormous pride and pleasure. His wife is a gourmet cook, bakes and freezes in quantity, grinds her own spices to make curry, and handles both the flower and vegetable gardening while Noble takes care of the lawn and the hedge at their suburban home.

Noble is a skilled cabinetmaker, judging from a couple of examples of his craftsmanship in his recreation room. Wife Barb is a keen figure skater and daughter Elaine has taken up the art seriously, too.

Although Noble has been involved in more dramatic investigations, the early case of the gang that specialized in stealing jewelry during business hours sticks in Noble's mind. To him, the outcome was a quintessential illustration of the teamwork, alertness, and attention to detail that detectives must apply in order for a case to be brought successfully to trial. Herb Langdon, the Crown Attorney who handled the prosecution, called it the most intriguing case he ever argued in court.

"It was because of all these little threads of evidence that individually meant nothing but, woven together as the case came out, made a whole cloth," explains Noble. "These people were never caught in action," nor were any of the gang ever caught in personal possession of the stolen goods. Circumstantial evidence—and the memorable physical appearances of two of the thieves involved—enabled the police in several divisions working together to secure convictions of four members of the ring on charges of stealing and receiving jewelry during a five-week shoplifting spree in the summer of 1956.

Toronto police became aware of the ring, which was new to the city, as a consequence of a series of thefts at some of Toronto's better downtown jewelry stores. All betrayed a common modus operandi.

The initial theft, at Gray's Jewellers, was noticed shortly after the departure of two men who had kept the proprietor busy at the rear of the store, and a young blonde woman who had stood near the front display window. In some establishments, the thief or thieves got behind counters to reach into display cases and in one store cleverly managed to deactivate a buzzer intended to prevent unauthorized persons from opening the glass.

The investigation of the thefts was complicated by the fact that sometimes several hours elapsed before the disappearance of jewelry was even noticed. The thieves benefited, as Noble drily observes, because the sales personnel were often "so engrossed in what they thought was a valuable sales commission they could only see the dollar signs."

Explains Noble, regarding such robberies, "We try to establish when the item was last seen positively, who saw it at that time, and when was it missed and by whom. We try to narrow down the time element. This is always important when you question a suspect. They mostly have an alibi."

The police initially hoped for an early conclusion to the Toronto jewel thefts on hearing recurrent accounts of the two suspicious male "customers," along with the mysterious blonde. "One of these fellows was very tall and very slim, with a very prominent Adam's apple and a pimply complexion," Noble recalls. "Another was very self-conscious about his receding hairline. Instead of combing his hair back and flaunting his receding hairline as I do, he combed it forward into what I call a 'Caesar.'" When none of the "stung" salespersons was able to make an identification of either of the two men from the Toronto mug shot books, it became probable that the gang was from out of town.

What was to prove the first break in the case occurred when Detective Sergeant Edward Evans picked up a tall, thin man, whom we shall call "Skinny," and his common-law wife on suspicion of stealing a fur coat in a department store. Although the evidence did not justify laying a charge, Evans "surreptitiously," as Noble puts it, and foresightedly, removed from Skinny's person several photos showing him with the woman. They had been taken by a street photographer. Made into a composite print, the pictures were copied and distributed to the three downtown Toronto police stations where the better jewelry stores were concentrated, and to the police forces in neighboring cities.

Information came back from Hamilton, Ontario, police that Skinny was understood to have come east from Vancouver. And Alexander Gray, proprietor of Gray's Jewellers, identified Skinny from the print as having been in the store at the time of the first theft. Copies of the print, identifying Skinny as a shoplifting suspect, were then sent to all divisions in the city.

All the while, jewelers' losses continued to mount. On the afternoon of Monday, July 30, a salesman named John Calder noticed that a ladies' $4,500 ring had disappeared from the front window of the branch of Ostranders Jewellers at 1477 Yonge Street, along with the silver box in which it was displayed. On Thursday afternoon, August 2, the disappearance of $6,575 worth of ladies' rings and watches was discovered at the Bloor Street branch of the Gold Shoppe. That same afternoon, six men entered E. R. Conery's Jewelers at 4 Jordan Street together, one ostensibly in search of cuff links, and when they left, two watches valued at $925 wholesale were missing from the front window. And sometime between 9:00 A.M. and 8:00 P.M. on Friday, August 3, another twelve rings worth a total of $575 wholesale were stolen from a display window at the front of Howard's Credit Jewelers at 2525 Yonge Street.

At 5:25 P.M. that Friday—before the last theft was noticed or reported to police—an alert constable named Jack Shaw from No. 1 station, on traffic duty downtown, recognized Skinny at the wheel of a 1954 Ford heading west on Front Street. Shaw stopped the car, and took Skinny and a man with receding hair combed forward who was sitting beside him, to No. 1 station. There they were searched and questioned by Sergeant of Detectives John Gillespie.

The arrested pair denied any knowledge of any thefts. The man with receding hair, whom we shall call "Caesar," gave his address as 415 Lakeshore Road, Block 5, apartment number 314, in the then-suburb of Mimico. Skinny refused to say where he was living, but he had a key chain containing three house or apartment keys. And Caesar had on his person a small piece of paper bearing the words "Hotel Room 400" and a barely legible telephone number. The investigators set about pursuing these fragmentary leads.

Two detectives from No. 1 division, Edward Barclay and Donald Arnott, and Jack Foster of No. 5 Division, took Caesar to his Lakeshore Road apartment at 8:00 P.M. to search the premises. Behind some books in a clothes closet Barclay found a Walther P-38 semi-automatic pistol with the serial number 135. While they were there, the telephone rang. It was a moment for some investigatorial theatrics. By turning on a phonograph and clinking glasses, the detectives gave the callers the impression that a party was in progress, and invited them to drop by. One woman and three men turned up and were taken to No. 1 station for further investigation. One of the men, named Jones, was subsequently charged with the theft of the gun.

The registration of the car Skinny was driving proved false. On searching the car, Gillespie and detective Tom MacLeod found a ticket that had been issued against the vehicle a few nights before for illegal all-night parking on Bleecker Street. At approximately 8:00 P.M. Gillespie instructed two constables to go to the Bleecker Street neighborhood and try the keys in doors there. After several tries, the policemen found that one of the keys fit the lock in the back door of a building that faced 435 Sherbourne Street. When they described Skinny to the superintendent there, the latter identified Skinny as a man who had subleased apartment number 48; he had been living there with a woman and had been joined two days earlier by Jones. On searching the apartment, the officers found an ammunition clip for a Walther P-38 semi-automatic pistol on a small table; the clip bore the serial number 135.

A short time later, Noble and MacLeod pursued the little slip of paper with hotel room 400 written on it. The phone number proved to be that of a Front Street hotel (since torn down), the Barclay. At 9:30 P.M.—knowing that Skinny's Sherbourne Street apartment had just been located—the two detectives went to room 400 at the Barclay and found it occupied by a young woman from Vancouver, who had been living there for a week with a third man, B. During a cursory search, Noble and Mac-Leod discovered another slip of paper in a dresser drawer with the address of Skinny's apartment, and took the woman to the station for further questioning.

At 10:20 P.M. Skinny and Caesar were placed in a lineup and identified by personnel from Ostranders and the Gold Shoppe branches as having been in those stores at approximately the time that jewelry was stolen from them. The web of circumstantial evidence was thickening.

A major remaining problem was that of recovering the stolen jewelry. At 11:40 P.M., Skinny and Caesar were locked up in cells on either side of Jones. Concealing himself at the end of the cellblock near Skinny's cell, Foster listened as the suspects talked. First they covered the possibility of getting bail. Then Skinny asked Caesar whether he knew where some jewelry was, and got the reply, "Next block, separated by a steel wall (or walk)." When Foster, accompanied by Noble, surreptitiously returned to the cellblock at 12:50 A.M., the two policemen heard Skinny observe with belated hindsight, "I wonder why they put us all together. We'd better dummy up. This place might be bugged."

Back at the Barclay, the hotel's night detective, Wally Spear, was keeping an eye on room 400 for the police. When B, who had no room key, returned to the hotel, Spear stalled him by alleging that the staff was having difficulty finding another key.

Noble and Foster arrived at 1:00 A.M. to find B standing in the hallway and, after a bellhop let him in, arrested him in the room. At 3:00 A.M., after reviewing the overheard conversation among the suspects, Foster and MacLeod returned to the hotel and established that it was constructed in two blocks of rooms, separated by a steel hallway. Searching room 400 thoroughly, they found a diamond-and-platinum watch and ten diamond rings hidden behind the upholstery of an armchair; these were subsequently identified as part of the jewelry stolen from the Gold Shoppe on August 2 and from Howard's Credit Jewelers on August 3.

Although the $3,400 ring filched from Ostranders was not found, a link to Caesar turned up a few days later. After learning of Caesar's arrest, his employer at the advertising company where Caesar worked as a salesman went to his desk to look for some records, found a silver box, and turned it over to the police. Noble took the box to Ostranders' manager, established that it was marked with the branch store's number, and had contained the valuable ring.

The pistol, checked out with the Royal Canadian Mounted Police registry of firearms in Ottawa, proved to be registered to Hallam Sporting Goods Ltd., at 621 Yonge Street in Toronto, which had purchased the gun from its previous owner the preceding April 22. The pistol and its ammunition clip had been put on display a week or so later, and its disappearance from the store had never been noticed. A clerk remembered having seen Skinny, Caesar, and Jones in the store near the end of July.

At a preliminary hearing on September 20, Skinny, Caesar, B, and the woman were committed for trial on charges connected with the stolen jewelry; Skinny, Caesar, and Jones were arraigned for theft and possession of the gun. One key identification was that of Caesar by an Ostranders salesman, John Calder. The latter drew a laugh from the court when he declared that Caesar's aft-to-forward hairdo "resembled the swimmer Cliff Lumsdon emerging from the water after a marathon swim."

On September 29, by sheer coincidence, another aspect of the story was added by a housewife who resided with her doctor-husband in Block 6 at 415 Lakeshore Road. On the afternoon of that day, she brought a gold ring set with a diamond to be appraised at the Gold Shoppe on Bloor Street—the very store from which it had been stolen the previous August 2. Questioned by the police, she explained that she had found the ring on the driveway of her apartment complex on August 4. She had posted notices in the various apartment blocks about finding the ring, to no avail. Then, at the suggestion of the Mimico police, she had advertised in the local paper for the owner. She had originally intended to have the ring appraised at another jewelry store on Yonge Street, but had found traffic so heavy that she went to the Bloor Street store instead.

Satisfying the police of her innocence, she too testified at the trial the following January, at which Skinny, Caesar (now combing his hair straight back), B, and the woman he had been living with were convicted on jewelry charges. The gun charges against Jones were dismissed, and Skinny and Caesar were convicted only of possession of the weapon.

The case was to have a delayed "kicker": Skinny was sentenced to six years in the jewelry thefts and dispatched to the federal penitentiary in Kingston, Ontario. Less than two years later, a valuable set of earrings, worth $850 wholesale, turned up missing from Birk's on Toronto's Bloor Street. The salesgirl—who, according to Noble, was sharp-eyed and had made several identifications for the police over the years—described a man who had been loitering around the corner as being tall and skinny, with a prominent Adam's apple. Noble recalls, "Jack Foster and I looked at each other and started to kid her about having made a mistake. 'You booted this one because that guy's still in the bucket.'" Still, the two detectives telephoned Kingston, and learned that Skinny had been paroled after serving less than two years.

Picked up on another charge, Skinny was startled when he was confronted with the Birk's theft. Eventually, from jail he said that he would try to get the earrings back. He sent Noble and Foster a key to a subway locker. It proved to contain a package of earrings, with the original stones, but not the settings. Says Noble, "It goes to show that you cast your bread upon the water when you treat even the worst criminal fairly."

10

Even His Wife Didn't Know

MIAMI ATTORNEY SIDNEY ARONOVITZ glanced at his wrist watch, frowned, and turned to a secretary. "You'd better phone Ethel's landlord and have him look in on her," Aronovitz said. "I'm worried. We should have heard from her by now."

The concern was justified. For more than three hours on that Tuesday morning of December 15, 1959, Aronovitz had been wondering why his principal legal secretary, sedate, white-haired Ethel Ione Little, had not shown up for work. For all of the years that the frail, 115-pound, fifty-five-year-old spinster had been in Aronovitz's employ, she had never failed to telephone the office if she was going to be even slightly late.

But it was now 12:25 P.M., and there was still no sign of her. Thus, another secretary in Aronovitz's law firm in downtown

Miami placed a call to A. E. Banks, Miss Little's landlord who lived at 1220 NW 31st Street in a middle-class, predominantly white neighborhood whose residents prided themselves on the neat appearance of their modest yet comfortable homes, and on their meticulously manicured lawns.

Miss Little herself lived in a small, square, one-story stucco cottage some forty feet behind her landlord's larger one-family home fronting on palm-lined NW 31st Street. During the many years she had been his tenant, Banks had trekked countless times from the back door of his house to Miss Little's front door to give her a message or attend to some chore. Yet none of those other trips would stand out so vividly, so horrifyingly, as the walk he took on that early December afternoon in 1959 in response to the call from his tenant's worried employer.

Approaching the cottage, Banks was puzzled at once to notice that Miss Little, known as an early riser who delighted in reading the morning news at her breakfast table, had not yet claimed either her folded copy of that day's *Miami Herald* or the quart of milk that had also been delivered to her stoop. Banks rang the doorbell. There was no response. He knocked on the door, gently at first; then, when he heard no sound from within, he rapped urgently. Still nothing. Finally, he opened the lock with his landlord's passkey.

The front entrance led directly into the living room. Nothing alarming there. The settee and upholstered armchair were against the right wall as they had always been. The room was orderly and clean. Yet just beyond the far partition, whose opening led to the kitchen, Banks' eyes caught one slight sign of something amiss—spilled coffee grounds on the linoleum floor. That was strange for a lady as tidy as Miss Little. Banks also noted partly wrapped Christmas packages on the kitchen table and, next to the packages, a small, empty ice cream paper cup.

For a brief second, Banks' mind flashed back to the previous evening. At around 8:30 P.M., he had been sitting in his living room watching television when he heard the metallic clank of the lid on Ethel Little's mailbox, then the characteristic scrunch of her footsteps over the gravel path that led from the sidewalk to her cottage. Banks had told himself that Miss Little was home from work, and his concentration had returned to the TV show.

Now, he called out Miss Little's name before entering the third and last room of the cottage—the bedroom, which was accessible through a door halfway down the left side of the living room.

There was still no answer.

Miami Homicide Detective Mike Gonzalez, whose tenacious fourteen-year investigation of the mutilation-murder of spinster Ethel Ione Little finally led to its solution.

The landlord shuffled to the bedroom, whose door was wide open, and glanced inside. His eyes popped open in palpable horror as he glimpsed a sight more terrible than anything he had ever seen.

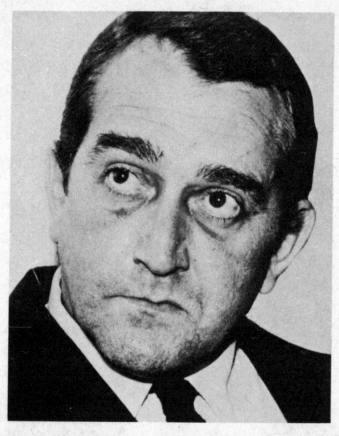

Vernon David Edwards Jr., confessed killer of Miss Little and waitress Johanna Block. According to sleuth Gonzalez, the slayer was psychopathically akin to Jack the Ripper. (*Miami Herald*)

On the four-poster bed lay the nude corpse of his kindly ten-ant. Her arms and legs were spread-eagled, each wrist and each ankle wrapped in cord and seemingly tied to the four bedposts. The chest and rest of the body bore numerous knife wounds. Banks was particularly petrified by one especially ghastly sight— the torn, mutilated, and bloodied flesh on one side of the chest where the victim's left breast had been cut off.

Banks had the presence of mind not to touch anything in the cottage. He even locked the front door. Then he raced back to his own house and phoned the police.

Among the first detectives from Miami's crack Homicide Unit to reach the scene was a young sleuth named Mike Gonzalez. Son of an Argentine-born father and an Italian-American mother, New York City-born Gonzalez could not have known it at the time, but he was on his way to beginning what was to turn out to be his toughest, longest, and most celebrated case, one that would make him famous in Florida police circles. It was a case in which he would ultimately play the key role in solving, thanks to thirteen years of tenacious determination and preparation that permitted him, when the big break came, to nail the real perpetrator.

By mid-afternoon, as the full savagery of the slaying became known, every detective in Miami's Homicide Unit was on the case. Off-duty sleuths volunteered their own time. The all-out response was prompted by the heinous nature of the murder of Ethel Ione Little:

Bruises and welts on her face indicated she had been severely beaten, possibly with clenched fists; a ligature around her neck suggested that she had been strangled; wounds in her chest indicated repeated stabbing with a knife, probably the bloodied knife detectives found on a chest of drawers in the bedroom; her missing left breast was found atop the dresser, and a drag mark on the mirror indicated that the breast had been placed or hurled against the glass, stuck there momentarily, then slithered down to the top of the dresser; a bloodied flashlight found on the floor had been used to commit a final savagery— chemical and smear tests indicated that the bullet-shaped end of the flashlight had been inserted into the victim's vagina.

Who could have committed such an unspeakable crime?

Why would anyone have wrought such brutality on a woman?

At the time Miami's Homicide Unit was using as a guide Dr. J. Paul DeRiver's *Crime and the Sexual Psychopath*, a widely read criminology text. Comparing DeRiver's study with the crime at hand, Gonzalez and his fellow sleuths concluded that the sadistic slasher who had murdered Ethel Ione Little must be psychopathically akin to the infamous "Jack the Ripper," who prowled London's fog-shrouded streets murdering women, before the turn of the century.

Dr. DeRiver's text pictured the "Ripper" as a classic example of the psychopathic killer:

"The disregard for all law, whether made by man or God, in his striving to gain his will to power, and the fantasy, actual or imagined, of the torture and pain of his helpless victim throws him into a state of clouding consciousness. . . ."

The detectives had studied and restudied those words. The paragraph spoke volumes about psychopathic killers who lust after the dead. At the same time, the book held out a word of warning for law officers endeavoring to apprehend such crazed killers: "The sadist often is very clever in carrying out his crimes and covers his tracks so that he will not be apprehended. . . ."

There was practically no doubt that Miss Little's killer was a sadist, especially after the homicide detectives had reconstructed the crime and the events leading up to it.

Ethel Ione Little, a fastidious, precise, pleasant woman who, among other social-civic-religious activities, taught Sunday school at Miami's Central Baptist Church, had been a bit embarrassed when she approached her boss, attorney Sidney Aronovitz, nephew of former Miami Mayor Abe Aronovitz, in the late afternoon of Monday, December 14. She was begging off from finishing a stack of legal papers because she wanted to do some Christmas shopping with her sister-in-law, Mrs. Jefferson Little, who lived near Ethel Little at 1153 NW 30th Street.

"But I'll be in at seven in the morning to finish the work," Miss Little promised.

Mrs. Jefferson Little had not been able to keep her appointment to go Christmas shopping with her sister-in-law. Ethel Little, disappointed yet determined to go ahead with her Yuletide buying, went shopping alone in downtown Miami. She returned home at 8:30 that night, her presence having been registered by her landlord as she stopped at her mailbox, then walked the gravel path to her door.

The next seven hours were obscure. It was obvious that Miss Little had begun her Christmas wrapping, but why she had abandoned the task of packaging her gifts in gaily colored paper with ribbons and bows remains unanswered. Perhaps she had grown tired after her long day of work and shopping.

From all the evidence, it appears that Miss Little's murder did not occur until approximately seven hours after her landlord heard her arrive home. One basis for that assumption was a statement by Alexander Snelling, a neighbor who got up at 3:00 A.M. to go on his milkman's route. He recalled hearing a muffled female voice, like a moaning, and also a low, angry male voice but without distinguishing any words. Thinking that neighbors were quarreling, Snelling did not mention the incident to anyone until the next afternoon when he heard of Miss Little's having been killed. He then volunteered his information to detectives canvassing the area for clues and leads.

Dr. Raymond DiJusti, the medical examiner, ruled that the cause of Ethel Ione Little's death was strangulation. She had not been strangled with venetian blind cord that was used to tie her wrists and ankles in a spread-eagled position to the four bedposts, but with a length of string that laboratory technicians determined had been broken off from the ceiling light fixture in the bedroom closet.

The autopsy was to reveal that none of the other brutalities visited upon the victim—the beating of her face, multiple stabs in her chest, cutting off of her breast—was the direct cause of death. All of these acts had been performed after Miss Little was slain.

There was no sign of a forced entry at either the front or back doors or at the windows of the dwelling. However, the jalousied kitchen door at the rear of the cottage was discovered to be unlocked. Yet the fact that it was unlocked did not necessarily mean that it was unlocked when the killer entered the cottage. Could Miss Little have admitted the murderer into the house? Could her murderer have been someone she knew?

That question would have to go unanswered, at least until the killer was apprehended. But the suspicion that a lover might have committed the crime was effectively removed from consideration.

"Ethel was an old maid," detectives were told by one of her two brothers, William Little, who lived at 2900 NW 22nd Street. "She never had a date that I knew about."

The murder scene was by no means devoid of clues.

For one thing, investigators on the case were virtually certain that the killer must have been an extremely tall person, well over six feet. They reached that conclusion after noting the height at which the cord used to bind the victim's wrists and ankles to the bedposts had been cut from the venetian blinds in the bedroom. The cord had been hacked at the very top, nearly six-and-a-half feet from the floor. In the absence of any stepstool or chair by the window, investigators reasoned that whoever cut the cord had to have been quite tall.

Even more solid than the speculation about the killer's height was a clear fingerprint of a double-loop pattern found imprinted in the blood on the flashlight, and a large palm print on the ceramic tile windowsill. The fingerprint on the flashlight was so clear that it was not processed by the conventional method of dusting for latent prints. Instead, the fingerprint was photographed—and thus preserved perfectly. Immediately afterward, along with the palm print, it was circulated to every law enforcement agency in the United States.

The palm print, detectives surmised, had been left on the windowsill when the killer moved the victim's bed away from the window on the left wall to give him room to wind the venetian blind cord around the bedposts on that end. Still, the palm print may not have been the killer's. It could have been left there by a repairman who might have been in the cottage in the recent past. Or it could have been the palm print of some visitor. In any event, one fact was certain—it wasn't the victim's. The impression on the windowsill was twice the size of Miss Little's palm.

There was no question that the fingerprint on the bloodied flashlight was the killer's. Medical examiner DiJusti and homicide sleuths agreed, after receiving the results of the laboratory tests, that the end of the flashlight which had been inserted into the victim's vagina by the killer almost certainly had to have been removed from the victim by the same person. Therefore, the fingerprint in the blood on the flashlight must certainly have been the slayer's.

One of the more perplexing aspects of the crime was the condition of the venetian blind cords that had bound Miss Little's wrists and ankles to the four bedposts. Peculiarly, they had been cut, as though the killer had decided to release his victim. Yet the fact that her limbs were still spread-eagled when her corpse was found hours later indicated that she was already dead when the cords were cut, a belated and vain emancipating gesture.

The autopsy revealed that Miss Little may not have been raped. The autopsy failed to turn up any evidence of semen, which did not necessarily mean that the killer did not have sexual intercourse with the victim. It merely left open the possibility that he had, but had failed to reach a climax, which raised two other questions: was the killer inebriated to the extent of not being capable of an orgasm, or was he intrinsically impotent?

Certainly there could be no doubt that he was a sexual deviate of maniacal magnitude. The mutilation of the victim also tended to indicate that the slayer was most likely a psychotic with an intense hatred of women—a character who leaped lifelike from the pages of Dr. DeRiver's *Crime and the Sexual Psychopath.*

The murder of Ethel Little stirred a groundswell of fear throughout the normally casual and carefree vacation city of Miami. It had been more than five years since Miami had had a crime even remotely comparable to this one—the 1954 sex killing of seven-year-old Judy Ann Roberts.

Within hours after the discovery of the spinster's body, the investigation had branched out in myriad directions. Teams of detectives were dispatched to canvass Miss Little's quiet neighborhood and determine if anyone had seen any strangers or prowlers before or after her murder. All known sex deviates in the city were rounded up—more than sixty of them—and questioned exhaustively. Their alibis satisfied authorities that none of the past offenders could have been involved in the slaying of Ethel Little.

One of the hottest early leads was turned up by detective Mike Gonzalez and a partner, William Bonner, who probed into the details of a violently sadistic assault that had been perpetrated on a woman in West Palm Beach a month earlier. Gonzalez and Bonner found many similarities, including tying of the hands and wrists and molestation of the vagina, but ultimately the sleuths could not establish a link to the brutal killing of Miss Little.

One aspect of the inquiry into her death was unprecedented, not only for Miami and Florida but for the entire United States: Miami's fourteen-member Homicide Squad embarked on a massive fingerprint identification campaign, the object of which was to take the prints of everyone they could find who had ever known the victim—relatives, friends, acquaintances, fellow employees, repairmen who had come to the cottage, deliverymen, and even members of her church congregation and Sunday school classes.

A small Northwest Section grocery store, Stanley's Market, at 1300 NW 12th Avenue, was transformed into a police identification bureau in the history-making attempt to solve Miss Little's killing. A team of detectives headed by Joseph Musial, chief of the Miami Police Department's Fingerprint Section, fingerprinted long lines of individuals that formed in the store and spilled out to the sidewalk.

Although more than 2,500 persons gave their fingerprints voluntarily to help police eliminate them as possible suspects, assorted civil libertarians denounced the authorities for "Gestapo tactics."

None of the prints matched the one found on the flashlight. Eventually, as police had promised at the outset, all the fingerprint cards were destroyed.

Time passed, and there was no progress toward identifying the killer. Weeks grew into months and months grew into years.

The detective who ultimately became the Miami Police Department's greatest single expert on the Ethel Little murder case was none other than Mike Gonzalez. Taking an obsessive interest in it, he steeped himself in the details of the case so thoroughly that whenever a suspect was picked up, or anyone offered to "confess" to the crime, Gonzalez would be called in to question the individual.

Suspects and confessors there were aplenty.

Gonzalez and his fellow investigators never ceased focusing their attention on any rapist, child molester, Peeping Tom, or other suspect who was hauled in in Miami for a sex crime.

During that time, too, authorities took no fewer than sixty "confessions" to Ethel Little's murder. Owing in great part to Gonzalez' expertise in the case, they were all proved to be false. For Mike Gonzalez, it became a matter of virtually simple routine to detect why each of the self-professed killers was not Miss Little's slayer.

"It never took long to unmask the fakers," Gonzalez explains. "I had just a few control questions, and that was all I needed to know that the man confessing the crime had nothing to do with it."

Among the key questions that Gonzalez asked were, "How did you molest her?" "What weapon did you use to kill her?" "What was the ligature you used to strangle her?"

The last question was especially important. Because the newspapers had erroneously listed the ligature at various times as venetian blind cord, a pajama top, a pajama bottom, a sheet, and a rope, none of those trying to convince Gonzalez that they had killed Miss Little ever mentioned the ligature that had actually been used to strangle her—the pull-string from the light fixture in a closet.

Over the years, all the detectives who had worked on the initial investigation retired until finally only Gonzalez and William McClure, who had initially been in charge of the probe, remained active in the department. McClure, however, moved up the ladder to the ranks of sergeant, lieutenant, then captain, which put him in administrative functions. This left Gonzalez in the primary role of tracking down Ethel Little's killer.

Gonzalez is slender and wiry, with a face that crinkles into a ready smile. His bearing is authoritative without being authoritarian. He was a "homicide rookie"—new in the squad— when he was assigned to the Ethel Little slaying case. Over the years, however, it became "Mike's case," and at the finish only Mike Gonzalez was left on it. Suddenly, that became crucially important, because by then there was no one else around who knew the case intimately enough to bring about its solution.

It was a role he stuck to with dogged determination. For Mike Gonzalez, none of the scores of homicides he had handled in the past, and the scores upon scores he would investigate in the future, commanded as much grim and grinding grit to solve as the savage sex murder of the innocent Sunday School teacher. Today, after more than twenty-five years with the Miami Police Department, Gonzalez views the Ethel Little murder investigation as the most important and intriguing case in which he has ever been involved.

The case he regards as his second most important—and one that would play a strange and significant role in the pursuit of Miss Little's killer—was the vicious murder of Johanna Block, an attractive, thirty-three-year-old, thrice-divorced mother of three who was found beaten, strangled, and stabbed to death in her apartment at 1721 NW 41st Street in Miami on May 25, 1961, some seventeen months after Ethel Little's slaying.

There were a number of similarities between the Block and Little killings. Although there had been no attempt to mutilate Mrs. Block's body, which had likewise been found nude, or to perform sadistic rituals upon it, the attack was comparable in its viciousness to that visited on Miss Little. Mrs. Block had been stabbed at least twenty times with a pair of scissors, which was found imbedded in her chest; she was strangled by hand; and she had also been beaten severely about the face.

But it still did not seem probable to Gonzalez, who was also involved in investigating the Block killing, that Miss Little's slayer had been the same person who committed that crime. He explains, "Ethel Little's murder was so hideous and so heinous, like no other crime that I or any of the other Miami homicide detectives had ever investigated, that it was simply too outrageous to compare Johanna Block's killing to the other. Too many of the ingredients in the Little case were lacking in the Block murder to warrant the thought that the same person committed both crimes."

Yet, as it turned out, both women had been killed by the *same* man in spite of the fact that his modus operandi was different in significant aspects in each case.

Furthermore, Gonzalez confesses, shaking his head in dismay, "While I was investigating the Block case, I came this close to grabbing the man who killed both Ethel Little and Johanna Block."

The detective holds up his right hand and sticks out his thumb and forefinger an inch apart. "I was that close to grabbing the guy," Gonzales goes on ruefully.

Such, however, are the vagaries of detective work, and they have to be taken philosophically in stride.

Johanna Block's corpse was found on the bedroom floor of her first-floor apartment in a two-family house, where she had lived alone. An investigation into her background disclosed that she had married a GI in Germany just after World War II, and had come to the United States with him in 1947 when she was eighteen. A few years later she was divorced from him, remarried, then divorced again. She went through divorce once more in the late 1950s. By early 1961 she had gone to work as a barmaid.

A torrent of suspects cascaded into the police dragnet, all of them boyfriends or ex-boyfriends of the victim. There were two prime suspects, each of whom appeared to occupy a special niche in her affections. Both men were truck drivers. One saw Mrs. Block week nights, the other saw her on weekends.

"Neither man knew about the other," Gonzalez relates. "Each in turn was shocked to learn of the other's role in Johanna's life."

The case took other twists and turns. Gonzalez discovered that Johanna had also been seeing a policeman for three years. Although the cop resided in Miami, he was a member of another police department.

"Between him, the two truck drivers, the guys at the bar, neighbors, other men she went with," adds Gonzalez, "I'd say together we must have had no fewer than twenty red-hot suspects in that case."

None, however, panned out.

As Gonzalez would learn later, the Johanna Block murder case also contained an ironic and tragic coincidence. From the outset, one of the most helpful informants in the Block case was Mary Alice Bratt, daughter of a retired Miami police captain, Fred Bratt, and a close personal friend of the victim. Miss Bratt was the person who informed Gonzalez about Johanna's two truck driver boyfriends.

Through Miss Bratt, Gonzalez recalls, not only were the police able to question the truck drivers, and eliminate them as suspects in the murder, but investigators were put onto several other men who figured significantly in Johanna Block's life. Each of those involvements was deemed deep enough to conceivably generate the intensity of blind rage that seemed so apparent in Mrs. Block's murder: the repeated jabs with the scissors, the strangulation with bare hands wrapped so tightly around the throat that they crushed neck bones, the frenzied walloping with fists which shattered the victim's cheekbone and nose.

One day, during the height of the investigation, Miss Bratt arrived at Gonzalez' office with still another item of information —about another truck driver who had been coming into the bar where Johanna worked, and who had had a violent argument with Johanna at the bar only a few days before her death.

"Sit down, Mary, and give me all the details you can," Gonzalez invited. Miss Bratt shook her head.

"I can't. I'm in a hurry.... My fiance is waiting for me in the car out front...."

"Your fiance?" Gonzalez remarked. "I didn't know you're going to get married. Congratulations!"

Gonzalez asked Miss Bratt to bring her boyfriend in.

"I'd like to meet him. Maybe he has some information to contribute to the case. Did he know Johanna?"

"Yes, he knew her, but not nearly as well as I did," Miss Bratt responded. "I don't think there's anything he can tell you about her private life. He didn't know her that well. He only saw her when he was with me ... when we stopped at the tavern for drinks and Johanna waited on us. Otherwise he didn't know her at all...."

It was now mid-1964. Four and a half years had passed since Ethel Ione Little's murder, three years since Johanna Block was slain. Both killings were still unsolved. Although he had gone on to investigate dozens of other murders since, Gonzalez had never relaxed his efforts to ferret out clues and leads in the Little and Block homicides. And that was why he suddenly decided to get in touch with Mary Alice Bratt three years later, in mid-1964. The arrest of a suspect in another case involving a serious assault on a woman commanded Gonzalez' attention. The man had been patronizing the same bar in which Johanna Block had worked. Gonzalez wanted to see whether there was a connection, and he acted immediately to contact his best source—Miss Bratt.

But to the detective's disappointment, he learned that the former Miss Bratt—now married—had moved with her new husband to another state. Gonzalez had the possible suspect checked through other sources, and the man turned out to have no connection to the Block murder. Thus there was no need to pursue Gonzalez' informant in her out-of-state domicile.

Eight more years passed. It was on Saturday, July 22, 1972, Detective Sergeant Mike Gonzalez (he had since been promoted) was sitting at his desk examining some interrogation sheets on a recent homicide that had been solved and was being prepared for presentation to the Dade County grand jury. The jangle of the phone broke his concentration. He picked up the receiver. The voice on the line was that of Lieutenant William McElroy of the DeKalb County Police Department in Decatur, Georgia, a suburb of Atlanta.

"We have a fellow here who's doing a lot of talking about two women he swears he killed in Miami."

"What names does he give?" Gonzalez asked.

"Says one of them's named Little."

"Ethel Little!" exclaimed Gonzalez. He was understandably excited. And, even though he had taken more than sixty phony "confessions" in the case in the preceding twelve-and-a-half years, Gonzalez had never approached any of those suspects with anything less than the hope that he was on the right track.

"You can never know which one among all the nuts you interview is going to be the one you're looking for," he would later say. "So, I never lost my enthusiasm, not ever, when it came to questioning suspects in Miss Little's murder."

Lieutenant McElroy also told Gonzalez that the name of the other victim was Johanna Block.

"Ever hear of her?" McElroy wanted to know.

"You bet," Gonzalez shouted. "I have the squeals [dossiers] on both cases."

All at once his mind raced back over the years, over the assorted crackpots and weirdos who had claimed to have been Ethel Little's killers. Perhaps only Gonzalez would have known a salient fact: not one had ever tried to confess Johanna Block's murder in the same breath.

"What's the guy's name?" Gonzalez asked.

"Vernon David Edwards, Jr.," replied Lieutenant McElroy. He proceeded to give Gonzalez a brief rundown on the suspect. Edwards, said McElroy, was thirty-four years old, born in Atlanta but had moved to Miami in 1958 when he was twenty-one, then in 1964 returned to Atlanta, where he was still living with his wife.

"He works as a house painter," McElroy went on. "And you should see the size of the fellow. He doesn't need a stepladder to paint the ceiling. He's 6 feet 6 and weighs 285. A genuine monster man."

The mention of Edwards' height stirred Gonzalez' interest still more. There had never been a question in the Miami detective's mind that Miss Little's killer must have been very tall.

Drawing on his long-time accumulation and preservation of knowledge about the case, Gonzalez fed McElroy a series of control questions. They were similar to those Gonzalez had asked over and over in the past in screening those who had sought catharsis through the "confession" of Ethel Little's murder. If the suspect was indeed who he said he was, he should be able to answer the key queries as none of the others had been able to.

A half hour passed. Gonzalez' phone rang again. This time detective Steve Baumglass, of the DeKalb County Homicide Squad, was on the line.

"Lieutenant McElroy says there's a damn good chance this guy Edwards is your man," advised Baumglass. "He scored very, very high on the questions you gave us."

That was all that Gonzalez needed to hear. He made reservations on the first flight to Atlanta out of Miami the next morning, a Sunday. Then he went to his files and pulled Case No. OF-243166 and all the musty—yet, to Gonzalez, still-pertinent—evidence the file contained, such as the photograph of the fingerprint impression in the blood on the flashlight and the palm print taken from the windowsill. These and other significant data Gonzalez would need to determine whether Vernon Edwards was indeed the killer. Gonzalez also gathered up the vital statistics on the Johanna Block murder case.

By the time Gonzalez arrived in the Atlanta suburb of Decatur, he found that DeKalb Police Captain James T. Stanley had amassed considerably more background on the suspect. Edwards had attended elementary schools in his native Atlanta and was graduated from high school in 1955, joined the army at seventeen, earned a year's college credits, and served three years; he was court-martialed three times for being off-limits. In 1959 he went to Miami, where his parents were living by then, and worked as a six-dollars-a-day mate aboard a drift fishing boat, *Seabreeze III*, which sailed out of Dinner Key Yacht Basin. "Big Ed," as he was known, handled tackle, cut bait, baited hooks, cleaned fish, and mingled with the passengers, lending encouragement as they cast their lines. Later, he went to work as a house painter.

In 1962, he married, and two years afterward moved back to Georgia with his wife, settling in a modest two-bedroom, one-family house at 1248 Peachtree View in Atlanta. Then he returned to his favorite occupation, house painting, when he went to work for Garland W. Miller, a paint contractor. To Miller, Edwards was "the most gentlemanly gentleman I ever seen. Nicest boy on two feet." To his next-door neighbor on Peachtree View, he was "just an ordinary man who drank—but quite heavily. He was never rowdy to nobody but his wife. He was real proud of her, real proud. He also fussed a lot with her when he was under the weather. You know, he's a very heavy drinker. He could shout louder than the TV set when he had a bag on. But he was good to her. He loved her. He never did her no hurt. I didn't think he'd ever even harm a fly. . . ." The Atlanta liquor store Edwards patronized reported that he indeed was a good customer. He bought five quarts per week of eighty-proof whiskey at $4.79 a bottle.

After a briefing on Edwards' background, Gonzalez finally came face to face with the towering suspect. Lieutenant McElroy introduced the two men. The moment of truth had arrived for detective Mike Gonzalez and his encyclopedic knowledge of the case. Gonzalez began by reading Edwards his constitutional rights. Then Gonzalez started the questions. He interrogated the suspect in a question-and-answer format that was recorded by a police reporter. The session resulted in the full—and corroborated—confession by Vernon David Edwards, Jr., to the celebrated sex murder of Ethel Ione Little.

"Is it true that you told your wife last night that you killed Ethel Little and that she advised you to turn yourself into the police?" Gonzalez asked at the outset.

"Yes, that's right," Edwards answered. "And then I told her to call the police. She did and they came and got me."

Q. What made you decide to tell your wife and to tell the police about killing Ethel Little?

A. I imagine you could say it was just an attack of conscience.

Q. Had you ever told anyone else in the past about killing Ethel Little?

A. No.

Q. Did you kill her?

A. Yes.

Q. Did you know her before you killed her? (The question was posed because, ironically, Ethel Little had been born in the same city in which her slayer was born—Atlanta.)

A. No.

Q. Do you know where she was killed?

A. Not the actual address but I know what street it was.

Q. Where did you live at the time?

A. Thirty-second and Thirteenth Avenue.

Q. Who were you living with?

A. My mother and father.

Q. Are you willing to tell me in your own words how the killing came about and each thing you did?

A. It started that day. The company I was working for was having a Christmas party that night, at the Eighty-Six Hundred Club, I think it was, and there was quite a bit of liquor there, which I more than consumed my part, and being drunk and short of money, on the way home I thought it would be a nice little place to break into to get some cash to continue drinking with. Miss Little was awakened when evidently she heard me making the noise. And when I saw she was awake and had seen me, I attacked her on the bed.

Q. How did you enter her apartment?

A. I got into the apartment by taking a glass jalousie louvre off the back door.

Q. What did you do with the glass jalousie?

A. I don't remember if I put it back into the door or put it on the ground. (The likelihood is that the jalousie had been put back into place, because when detectives reached the scene they found no evidence to indicate that such a panel had been removed from the door to the kitchen.)

Q. What time in the day or night did you arrive?

A. About 2:00 A.M.

Q. What was the first thing you did when you got inside?

A. I think the first thing I did was take my clothes off in the kitchen.

Q. What kind of apartment was this?

A. It was a kind of little cottage in the back of a big house.

Q. Had you ever been in this apartment before?

A. No.

Q. What happened next?

A. When she woke up I put a pillow over her face to start with and we wrestled around on the bed and I started strangling her. . . . Then I removed her clothes and got down some venetian blind cord and tied her. At this time I believe she was already dead. Going back into the kitchen, I got a knife and severed her left breast.

Q. Why did you do that?

A. I don't know. Crazy drunk, I guess.

Q. What kind of knife was it?

A. All I can remember was that it was some kind of kitchen knife. It could have been a steak knife or a kitchen knife.

The questions continued in rapid-fire fashion. And the answers continued to come back in shuddering details—details that only the real killer could know—that wove a tapestry of unspeakable horror.

Q. Did you stab her with the knife?
A. I think I did.
Q. How many times.
A. I don't know.
Q. Did you do anything to her other parts?
A. I don't think so.
Q. The breast that you severed off, was it part way off or all the way off?
A. Completely.
Q. What did you do with the breast?
A. I think I put it on the dresser.
Q. What else did you do to her?
A. I used the flashlight and penetrated her anus and vagina with it.
Q. What kind of flashlight was it?
A. Just a two-cell, silver flashlight.
Q. Which end of the flashlight did you stick in her?
A. The bottom.
Q. Do you remember what the bottom end or the back end of the flashlight looked like?
A. It seems like it was kind of bullet-shaped.
Q. Why did you put the flashlight inside her?
A. I don't know. I guess I was just crazy, drunk.
Q. Did you do this after she was tied or before she was tied?
A. After.
Q. How was she tied?
A. All I know is I tied her with the venetian blind cord and I don't remember what position she was in.
Q. What else did you do?
A. I searched the place for money, then I found about fifty or sixty dollars.
Q. Where did you find the money?
A. I believe it was in the dresser or chest of drawers.
Q. Did you take anything from her pocketbook?

A. I may have. If there had been any money, I would have.

Q. She was strangled by something tied around her neck. What was it?

A. (Long pause.) The only thing I can think of that it might have been was a piece of the venetian blind cord.

Q. Did you go in the closet while you were there?

A. Probably.

Q. Why?

A. Just looking, prowling.

Q. Do you remember anything from the closet?

A. I think there was some Christmas packages in there.

Q. Did you see any Christmas packages anywhere else?

A. Yes, I think there was some on the kitchen table.

Gonzalez asked the suspect whether he had any intention of having sexual intercourse with Miss Little.

Edwards responded. "That would be the natural assumption."

"Did you have sexual intercourse with her?" demanded the interrogator.

"No," was the response.

Q. Why not?

A. Too drunk.

Q. A pillow was placed somewhere else other than her face. Do you know where that someplace else was?

A. Probably under her rear end.

Q. Do you remember doing that?

A. No.

Q. Then why did you say probably under her rear end?

A. Cause that's the only other place I could think of.

Q. Why did you kill her?

A. Because she saw me. And living on that same street, if she had of ever seen me again she would have recognized me.

Edwards had lived with his parents exactly seven houses from Miss Little's cottage.

Gonzalez pressed on with his interrogation by asking Edwards whether the victim had resisted his attack. The response was that she had.

Q. How?

A. She wrestled, struggled, and bit me.

Q. Where did she bite you?
A. Thumb.
Q. Which thumb?
A. Right thumb.

Then came another of the many ironies in the case. According to Edwards, he had been interviewed at home by a policewoman at the time of the massive investigation following Miss Little's murder.

"I had a bandage on my thumb and she never noticed it or said anything about it," Edwards told Gonzalez. "Well, I thought she might say something since I was wearing a bandage on my thumb. . . ."

With a cunning often displayed by criminals, Edwards cleverly eluded the voluntary neighborhood fingerprinting campaign, although he gave everyone the impression that he had submitted to the test.

"I got in line outside the grocery store, but when I got inside I managed to slip off it," Edwards admitted.

Although there were severe bruises on the victim's face and body, Edwards continued to insist that he could not recall beating her. He also wasn't certain whether she was wearing a nightgown or pajamas, although he was inclined to believe (as was the case) that she was in pajamas.

Q. Do you remember anything about the mirror that was on the dresser?
A. Nothing in particular.

Gonzalez was probing for the suspect's possible recollection about either having pushed or thrown the victim's severed breast against the mirror.

Q. Was she alive when you cut her breast off?
A. No.
Q. How do you know?
A. She did not bleed.

Throughout the time that he killed Miss Little and performed the sadistic acts upon her body, Edwards said he had had his clothes off. He could not remember how he disposed of the knife (found on the dresser) but he did recall that he washed his hands in the kitchen before leaving and that he was in the cottage altogether for approximately a half hour.

There were a number of other aspects about the crime that Edwards could not remember, and there were some about which his memory was fuzzy. For example, when Gonzalez asked whether Miss Little struggled when the flashlight was put in her vagina, Edwards replied, "I think she was already dead. . . . That is just the impression that I have of it. . . ."

Nor could Edwards answer the important question of what he had used to strangle Miss Little. Gonzalez could not get Edwards to recollect that it had been the pull-string from a closet light. When asked what he had employed to snuff out the Sunday School teacher's life, all Edwards could say was, "I don't remember."

Nevertheless, the fact that Edwards did not recall everything —while remembering some things in brutal detail—had the ring of truth to Gonzalez. After all, Edwards had been drinking.

At one point during the investigation Edwards blurted out to the detective, "Man, you've been working on the case for years and trying to remember everything about it, whereas all I've done all these years is try to forget it. So I forgot a lot about it and you remember a hell of a lot about it."

Nevertheless, the hulking house painter remembered enough to convince Mike Gonzalez that he might have his man. It was a crucial decision for one determined detective: he had rejected "confessions" to Miss Little's murder by more than half a hundred other men. Acting on the basis of Edwards' replies to the questions, Gonzalez telephoned Miami's Identification Bureau and requested a check on the fingerprint and palm print of the suspect. Gonzalez read designs of ridges, loops, and lines on the phone, and they were compared with the prints found in Ethel Little's cottage. The answer: the prints matched.

Said Gonzalez to Edwards, "I'm putting you under arrest for murder."

"Yeah, I know," replied Edwards.

Gonzalez returned to Florida. He went into consultation with his police superiors and the prosecutor's office. Would Edwards fight extradition? The answer was no. He would return to Miami willingly and face his punishment.

Brought back to Florida by Gonzalez, Vernon Edwards was booked on the two murders to which he had admitted. One was Ethel Little's. The other was the killing of Johanna Block.

Reflecting on the case, Gonzalez observes, "No one who knew Vernon Edwards ever considered that he'd be a rapist or killer. That fact has stood as a good example for us. Anyone that's been around for a good deal of time knows that rapists don't look like rapists, killers don't look like killers. Especially sex-oriented killers.

"Because of the movies and TV, people have a kind of idea these guys have to look like creeps, they have to look kind of dangerous and weird. Actually they don't. They look like the guy next door a lot of times.

"Their particular problem is usually a very separate thing from their normal everyday life."

What would possess someone like Edwards to kill Miss Little and Mrs. Block?

Explains Gonzalez, "That was one of the things that was the biggest interest to me. The fact that we had a confession from Edwards in both killings was very satisfying, yet I was very curious to find out what had motivated him. I had worked on something like a thousand homicides and perhaps five hundred rape cases in my quarter century with the Miami Police Department. So I really wanted to know what ran through this guy's mind.

"I tried very hard to have him talk about his background—and he really tried. And I think it helped to give me a clearer picture, although I don't think he was totally aware of why he killed. Yet it did have something to do with his past. Of that I'm quite sure. . . ."

Gonzalez questioned Edwards extensively about his childhood and came up with many significant events that appeared to have been etched in the suspect's psyche.

"He grew up in the house of his parents," Gonzalez relates. "He seemed to have had a very happy home life when he was a youngster up until he was twelve. Then his father, who worked as an accountant for some big company, was accused of embezzling a large sum of money from the firm. He was arrested, prosecuted, convicted, and went to prison. And although young Edwards felt that his parents were very much in love at the time, his mother decided she didn't want the husband anymore after he was incarcerated and divorced him.

"That really shook up young Vernon Edwards. He wouldn't admit to me at first how traumatic that experience was for him. But after we talked at great length, he admitted that. You see, Vern Edwards is not a tough guy. He's like the average guy, he has a lot of *macho*, and doesn't want to relate to the feelings of a young kid. But eventually he told me how severely his parents' divorce had affected him. He lay in bed many, many nights crying over the whole conflict. He never believed his father embezzled the money: he thought his mother should have stood by his father: and he was outraged when his mother divorced his father."

Thus, according to Gonzalez, hostility built up in Vernon Edwards against his mother. "That kind of conflict can tear your head off," the sergeant points out. "It's a case of I love mama, I hate mama, all at the same time. And as Edwards remembered, he had this terrible hatred of his mother, yet he also loved her very much, and wanted things to go back to the way they were."

Just at the point when these internal conflicts had reached a peak in Edwards, he was taken to a country resort by his mother.

"It was there that a homosexual 'chuck' made advances to him," Gonzalez said. "That made a very big impression on his mind—it was very traumatic."

What with his father's imprisonment, the ensuing split-up of his parents, and his experience with the homosexual, Gonzalez suggested, Vernon Edwards became "twisted up." Indeed, his inner state was a classic example of the kind of psychological conflicts that can create a sex offender. Moreover, as if those unsettling experiences were not enough, there occurred still another one.

"While his father was in prison," Gonzalez adds, "Vern Edwards wanted to go visit him—but his mother wouldn't let him. So the very first and only other crime he ever committed was as a youngster, when he stole a car and drove the car to the prison to visit his father. He had a compulsion to visit his father because young Vern always loved his father."

On his way to the prison, Vern Edwards was arrested and prosecuted for driving a stolen car; he was committed to a juvenile detention home for several months.

"That was the only other crime he ever committed," Gonzalez reflects. "Stealing a car to visit his father in prison."

All of these tortured pressures came to a head on the night that Vernon Edwards killed Ethel Ione Little.

According to Edwards' confession, for the preceding year or more he had peeked into Miss Little's bedroom window on numerous occasions and watched her undress for bed.

Gonzalez relates, "I had pointed out to him that anything he could remember about the case to tell us about it, that it might help us on other rape and rape-murder cases. We told him that if he could tell us about his feelings and all that, we might be better able to understand sex offenders and others like that. He understood what we said to him.

"He had gone to a Christmas party for the company he was working for. During the party, he was drinking heavily, and he was also taking amphetamines, actually Dexetrines. At the party he felt slighted by an elderly employee of the company. He didn't remember the details but he recalls that he had been talking a great deal with her and giving her a lot of attention. Then something happened, he was put down for doing that. He became very emotional, very upset. And the next thing he remembered was walking into Ethel Little's apartment."

Sergeant Gonzalez is convinced that Edwards was motivated in the killings by the hostility he had built up against women as a result of the problems between his mother and father.

"I really wanted to find out what made him tick," Gonzalez says. "I figured it would help us in the future on such cases. I had many long talks with Edwards—he has even written to me from prison—but I could never really get into his head as completely as I wanted."

Vernon Edwards' recollection of the Johanna Block murder was much more vague than his memory of the Ethel Little killing.

Even on that night of July 22, 1972, when, gripped by pangs of conscience, he confessed the killings to his wife in Atlanta, Edwards was far more hesitant in talking about Mrs. Block, because, in a note of high irony, his wife happened to have been the victim's girl friend.

Rarely, perhaps, has a girl friend of a murdered woman unknowingly married the killer.

Mrs. Edwards had been the same Mary Alice Bratt, daughter of the former Miami police captain, who was Gonzalez' prime informant in the Johanna Block case. The same Mary Alice Bratt who had told detective Gonzalez that her fiance, waiting outside the police station, couldn't be of much help in the investigation because, "He didn't know her that well. He only saw her when he was with me ... when we stopped at the tavern for drinks and Johanna waited on us. Otherwise he didn't know her at all. . . ."

On the night of May 25, 1961, Edwards said, he took Mary Alice to the tavern where Johanna Block worked. After several drinks that were served by Johanna, Edwards, according to Gonzalez, took his wife-to-be home, returned to the tavern, took the barmaid home, and killed her.

"He was never able to tell me why he committed that murder," reports Gonzalez. "In fact, if it wasn't for a couple of little things that he knew about that killing—things that even the police weren't aware of until Edwards pointed them out—you could hardly believe that he did it."

Thus, Mike Gonzalez' storehouse of knowledge, gained and preserved from having stuck with the two cases over the years, was a critical factor in solving both crimes. True, Edwards stepped forward to confess. But unless Gonzalez had known instantly and factually the right questions to ask, and the right answers to expect, about a crime thirteen years old, Edwards' confession could conceivably have been rejected or ignored.

Actually, Edwards' admission of the barmaid's slaying wasn't even required to remove him from society. His confession to Miss Little's slaying was all that was necessary. Judge Paul Baker, sitting in Miami's Dade County Court, accepted the defendant's plea of guilty after a hearing, thus avoiding a trial. Baker sentenced Edwards to life imprisonment, and he is now serving that term in Florida State Penitentiary at Raiford.

11

The Great Persuader

IT WAS THE NIGHT of July 20, 1970, a Monday. In their fashionable Cape Cod home at 36 Shinnecock Lane in East Islip, on New York's Long Island, Mr. and Mrs. Francis Kohr were becoming increasingly concerned about their pretty brunette daughter, Adele, who was long overdue from her late-hours nursing job at the Suffolk State School, an institution for mentally retarded youngsters in neighboring Melville.

It was totally out of character for Adele to be late. Her job was only eighteen miles from her home, and the drive at night was almost nonstop between Melville and East Islip since the route is paved with six-lane parkways. Adele's tour at the school ended at 11:00 P.M., and her parents had come to expect her home no later than 11:30. Yet on that night of July 20, as the clock ticked toward midnight, Adele had still not returned. By 1:00 A.M., her parents were on the verge of calling Suffolk State to determine whether their daughter might be working overtime.

Suddenly the front door chimes sounded. Adele's father opened the door and found himself facing two policemen. They had come to deliver a strange—and ominous—report about Adele Kohr.

Her 1970 blue Ford Maverick automobile had been found on the Sagtikos State Parkway at the approaches to Heckscher State Park, near an unmanned toll booth, approximately a quarter of a mile from her home. The driver's door was open, the motor running, the headlights on.

The policemen explained that they thought that, for some reason, Miss Kohr might have walked home. They were trying to spare the parents greater fright. The two officers did not tell Mr. and Mrs. Kohr at the time that the driver's window of their daughter's car had been smashed. The window obviously had been broken from the outside while the door was still closed. That determination was reached because glass slivers were scattered over the front seat and the floor. There were no dents or scratches on the rest of the car. Clearly the vehicle could not have been in a collision.

Nor did the policemen mention a cryptic and foreboding message, penned in a shaky hand, that had been found in a small blue spiral notebook on the car's front seat. The notebook was discovered lying under a tan leather pocketbook that was on the far side of the front seat from the driver. The pocketbook contained a wallet with fifty dollars in cash, some additional small change, and other valuables, leading to the conclusion that Adele could not have been a robbery victim. Only when police examined the small notebook did they begin to suspect the young woman's fate.

The first seven pages of the notebook had been used to keep a meticulous record of the car's gasoline mileage. Adele had noted every tankful of gas and entered the mileage driven and gallons of gas consumed. She had kept the record since early January, when she bought the car. Adele was proud of her new car, and maintained the daily log on fuel consumption so that she could boast to friends how well the car was performing. She was also keen on economy. Moreover, according to family and friends, she was an habitual record keeper.

What was chillingly significant about the notebook, however, was that, on four of the seven pages, handwriting was super-imposed over the previously entered notations. Scrawled errati-cally with a blue-ink ballpoint pen, the message read:

"A man in a car pulled alongside me ... on the Sagtikos ... he wants me to stop ... he is following me in same lane and I can't pull away ... doing 65 ... he is alongside again ... beard ...

Pretty Adele Kohr, who was abducted from a lonely Long Island, New York, parkway at night while driving home alone from her job at a hospital for retarded children. The young woman was yanked from her car, beaten, raped, and strangled by her killer—then run over with his car. (*New York Daily News Photo*)

glasses ... long hair ... hippy type ... blue shirt ... the car is a Tempest ... light green ... T-37 ...."

The message apparently had been scribbled while the car was being driven. An occasional word was written over. The end of the frantic message, on the last page, consisted of two words

Robert Meyer (*right*) in custody at Suffolk County police headquarters following his arrest. Meyer was convicted of the brutal crime and sentenced to twenty-five years to life. (*New York Daily News Photo*)

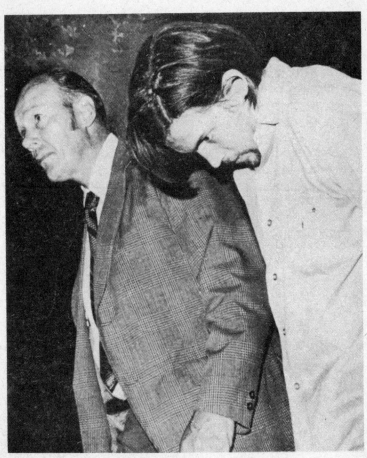

that stood all by themselves. These were written in what seemed to be a trembling, almost shivering hand,

"Dark . . . pants. . . ."

The last word trailed off the page.

Since Miss Kohr could not have identified dark trousers worn by the man while he was driving in his car, it became evident that she had made her final entry in her notebook after she had stopped her car near the toll booth, which was unmanned after dark, and the man had gotten out of his car and approached her.

Adele was described as five feet two inches, 120 pounds, brunette-haired, green-eyed, fair-complexioned, slender and shapely; all in all, strikingly good looking. From a photograph that her parents provided investigators, you could see that she had a sweet, wholesome-looking face that could have stamped her as "the typical American girl." She wore her hair with a part on the right side and combed down to the shoulders in a soft flip. She had dated a number of young men, but had said nothing to indicate any serious intention of getting married.

Oddly, if explainably, Miss Kohr had left home wearing a two-piece yellow print bathing suit under her blue nurse's uniform, and white moccasins. She taught swimming to her retarded students as part of their therapy, and according to her parents, she almost always kept her bathing suit on throughout her tour of duty, and wore it home with her nurse's uniform on top.

To Detective Sergeant Thomas Richmond of the Suffolk County Homicide Squad, who was dispatched to the scene, Adele Kohr's mysterious disappearance had all the smell of a murder. Within hours, Richmond's premonition was to be tragically confirmed. At 11:00 A.M. on the morning after the young girl's disappearance, two children at play on Webb Avenue, a dead-end street in the village of Patchogue, some eighteen miles east of the Heckscher Park toll booth, found a nude female corpse at the edge of a small woods.

The body was that of a shapely young brunette. It was sprawled on its back in a sandy clearing at the end of Webb Avenue. The face was beaten beyond recognition. The victim's eyes were puffed and blackened, the lips cut and swollen, the nose flattened. The direct cause of death had been strangulation.

But there were also black marks forming a distinct grid pattern on the victim's white flesh—tire tracks. The killer had not only beaten and strangled the young woman, but had also run over her with a car.

Moreover, semen was found in her vagina, indicating that she had been raped.

Although detective Richmond had the photograph of the miss-

Detective Tom Richmond, "The Great Persuader," whose county-wide check of eighteen light-colored T37 Pontiac Tempest automobiles, plus his adroit encouragement of suspect Meyer to tell all, were instrumental in cracking the case.

ing nurse, provided by her parents, in his pocket, he could make no comparison. The face of the young woman lying dead before him was unrecognizable, so merciless and savage had been the beating inflicted upon her.

Nevertheless, Richmond established identification by alternative means. One clue was the victim's jewelry. The killer had left a copper bracelet on the victim's left wrist, a gold cross on a gold chain around her neck, a Timex wristwatch on her right wrist, a double-heart-shaped diamond ring on her left ring finger, and a birthstone ring and a small diamond ring on the third and fourth fingers of her right hand—all items that checked with what her parents told police Miss Kohr was wearing when she had left for work that afternoon. Some seven feet from the body, at the fringe of the woods beyond Webb Avenue, Richmond and his fellow detectives found a yellow, two-piece bikini bathing suit; five feet further on they came upon a blue nurse's uniform and, next to that, a pair of white moccasins.

There was now no doubt: the murdered girl was the missing pretty young nurse, Adele Kohr.

In an era when the Women's Liberation Movement was beginning to become a serious force—and when violence against women was becoming an ever more serious public issue—the brutal rape-slaying of Adele Kohr, and her courageous efforts to write a description of her abductor, aroused widespread feeling in the Greater New York area.

To detective Richmond, now a lieutenant and executive officer of the twenty-three-man Suffolk County Homicide Squad, the Adele Kohr sex-murder case still stands as the most challenging and intriguing case of the more than 300 homicides that he has personally investigated in his police career. Burly and black-haired, standing six feet two inches and weighing 225 pounds, the fifty-year-old Richmond looks like a football player, and evinces a quiet, sardonic sense of humor. Brooklyn-born, Richmond graduated from Bishop Laughlin High School in Brooklyn, won a degree in criminal justice from the State University of New York at Farmingdale, and a degree in mortuary science from the American Academy of Mortuary Science. He served in the U.S. Navy during World War II and in the U.S. Army during the

Korean conflict. He is married and has two daughters. Richmond began his career as a mortician but later switched to police work.

Actually, Richmond found that holding a degree from the American Academy of Mortuary Science can have its advantages. For one thing, his mortician's degree enabled Richmond to "moonlight" as an embalmer during off-duty hours, bringing in extra income that helped pay the mortgage on his Long Island home and ease his burdens as the breadwinner for a wife and two daughters. More significantly, the training and experience that Richmond received as a mortician has provided an added dimension to his work as a homicide detective. He has developed a deeper insight into and a broader perspective about death, whether it is induced by natural forces or delivered by the wicked hand of a human being.

Once, soon after Tom Richmond was assigned to Suffolk County's newly formed homicide squad in 1963, one of his earliest assignments was to a seemingly unspectacular case involving an apparent drug overdose death. The victim was a sixty-two-year-old widow who had collapsed in the doorway of her home in East Islip. Before lapsing into unconsciousness, the woman whispered that she had taken too many sedatives.

A physician was summoned. He searched for vital signs, found none, and pronounced her dead. He then went back to his office, leaving the body for the "meat wagon" from the morgue.

Because it was believed that the woman had died of other than natural causes, homicide was notified, and detective Richmond responded with his then partner, detective Jack Shilling. At the widow's home, they were received by a grieving, middle-aged woman who identified herself as the victim's niece.

While Shilling spoke with the niece, Richmond kneeled beside the body, lifted the sheet, and glanced at the face.

"Jack! For Chris' sake!" Richmond cried out. "Call a doctor and a resuscitator . . . this woman's alive!"

A physician from the vicinity rushed to the home, injected adrenalin into the widow's heart, and had her taken to a hospital.

"Young man," she smiled later at Richmond from her hospital bed, "how did you ever know that I wasn't dead?"

"I do a little embalming on the side," Richmond chuckled, "but when I looked at you after you'd been left for dead, I could see you weren't ready for that kind of preservation just yet. Especially not after I saw your face twitch."

"No one detective is a homicide genius," Richmond philosophizes as he stands before 150 students at Half Hollow Hills High School in Dix Hills, Long Island. "It takes many detectives to solve a case." His talk is part of a lecture that Richmond gives under a county-wide program that endeavors to inform secondary school students about law enforcement procedures and practices.

Richmond, who also lectures as an assistant professor of criminology at Long Island's Suffolk Community College, is self-effacing about the many homicides he has helped solve. His philosophy is that, behind the solution of every murder, there are any number of experts at every level of the investigation: fingerprint men, laboratory scientists, and pavement-pounding sleuths who contribute to the total picture of arrest, indictment, prosecution, and conviction.

"What good is it to arrest a suspect if you cannot prove the charges in court?" asks Richmond. "That's why homicide work is a team effort and not a one-man show. It takes the specialists who have training and experience in their particular areas of investigative procedure to put a case together for successful prosecution."

All the same, even in the sophisticated, modern law enforcement community there is still room for those with individual talents, and Tom Richmond is a good example. In addition to his other abilities, Richmond is known in Long Island police circles as "The Great Persuader" because of his ability to elicit information from the most uncommunicative suspect.

A case in point involved another killing that occurred, coincidentally, one week after the murder of Adele Kohr. On the afternoon of Tuesday, July 28, a tiny woman whose face was etched with terror showed up at the Suffolk County Police Department's First Detective Squad in Babylon. Her hands trembled. She was Mrs. Janice Rench, and she had come to complain about a man who, according to her, had threatened her life.

"I'd been dating him," explained Mrs. Rench, a thirty-eight-year-old divorcée, "but then I broke off with him. Since then he's been coming to my house repeatedly and trying to reconcile. I told him I didn't want to see him, but he has refused to stay away. Today he came back and told me he had heard I was going out with another man. He demanded to know who I was seeing and he said if I didn't tell him he'd kill me. I am terrified. I believe he will kill me. . . ."

Her lips began quivering and tears welled in her eyes.

"Please," Mrs. Rench pleaded, "won't you do something?"

The precinct call sheet revealed at least three prior complaints by Mrs. Rench against her suitor, and two responses by patrol cars to her home in Babylon to break up disturbances reported by neighbors. Each time the trouble was stirred up by arguments between the suitor, Manuel Salvatore Llauget, and Mrs. Rench. In each instance, Mrs. Rench had been advised to take court action against the forty-two-year-old Llauget, but Mrs. Rench had never gone that far.

"If you want this man to stop bothering you," one of the detectives in the First Squad told her on her July 28 visit, "swear out a warrant for his arrest. But you must do that yourself. We can't do it for you."

However, Mrs. Rench once more chose not to seek the warrant for Llauget's arrest. And, some five hours after her visit to the First Squad, she was found fatally shot in her car on a Long Island highway.

At the outset, the information was vague and sketchy. But several statements by Mrs. Rench's fourteen-year-old daughter Deborah were significant enough to point to Llauget as the prime suspect.

"My mother left the house with my brother a little after six o'clock tonight," Deborah was quoted as saying. "She was going to drive him to the Bronx."

The victim's daughter told detectives that her mother was to have taken her brother, Rudy Kloiber, twenty, who was born to Mrs. Rench by a previous marriage, to Llauget's apartment at 211 East 233rd Street.

"Rudy has been living with Salvatore," Deborah said. "They

had come here together around noontime to see my mother. Salvatore and Mama had a big fight and I think she went to the police station to have him arrested. When she came home, he had already left."

Deborah said she had overheard her mother telling Rudy that she would drive him to Llauget's place because she "wanted to have a talk with him."

However, Rudy Kloiber had not been found in the car in which his mother was shot.

Again, as in the Adele Kohr case a week earlier, Detective Sergeant Richmond was assigned to conduct the investigation. That night he received a telephone call from the neighboring Nassau County Police Department.

"I thought you might be interested to know that I've got a guy named Rudy Kloiber in Central General Hospital with a couple of bullet wounds."

It was Mrs. Rench's missing son.

Richmond's detectives found Kloiber in excellent condition. He had been grazed by two bullets, on a buttock and the lower back. The slugs, later investigation showed, were two that had passed through his mother's body.

The youth was asked to tell what had happened.

"My mother was driving," Kloiber related. "All of a sudden we had an accident with this other car. It was really nothing but the other driver got very mad. He forced my mother off the road and he jumped out and came at her with a gun. He shot her and then he came and dragged me away to his car."

From that point on, Kloiber's story dovetailed with what detectives had learned from other sources: that Kloiber had come to the attention of a group of teenagers driving along Round Swamp Road in Plainview, a few feet from an exit of the Long Island Expressway. He was sitting on the curb, waving frantically to passing motorists. The youths stopped and asked what was wrong.

"I've been shot," he told them. They drove him to a county police booth a mile away, and a patrolman took Kloiber to the hospital.

The physician who had treated Kloiber assured the detectives that he would suffer no ill effects if he were removed to the homicide squad's headquarters in Hauppauge. Kloiber was taken there for further questioning.

Sergeant Tom Richmond took the youth into one of the squad's private offices.

"Rudy," Richmond said in his most persuasive tone, "cut the shit. You know who shot your mother to death. And you know if he'll kill your mom, he'll kill you, too, if he has too. . . . Now tell me the truth."

Kloiber still seemed hesitant to talk.

"All right, Rudy," Richmond smiled, "I'll tell you who did it— it was Salvatore Llauget. He had a big fight with your mom, isn't that right?"

The mention of Llauget's name was the key. Kloiber looked at Richmond and nodded.

"Yes," he said, "it was him."

Was Kloiber ready now to make a full statement, Richmond wanted to know? The answer was yes.

In his statement, Kloiber narrated details of the fight between his mother and Llauget earlier in the day, adding, "I live with the guy in the Bronx, and he's been wonderful to me. He's given me money when I needed it and he has taken good care of me. He's been like a father."

Kloiber also described to Richmond what had happened on the highway.

"I guess he was following us," Kloiber said. "He came alongside our car and forced Ma off the road. Before I knew what was happening, Sal came up to the window on my mother's side and said to her, 'Jan, why can't I meet this guy you're going with—just once?' He had been trying to find out the name of the man my mom was going out with and she wouldn't tell him."

"Mom just looked at Sal and the next thing I heard was Mom saying, 'What have you got there, a gun?' "

Kloiber said Llauget didn't answer but merely triggered off three quick shots.

"I heard Mom scream and then I felt the sting of the bullets and I yelled, 'I'm shot.' Sal ran over to my side, opened the door, put his hands around me and said, 'Gee, kid, I wasn't trying to hurt you . . . I didn't mean it . . . I would never do that to you. . . .'

"He said he was going to take me with him and he pulled me out of the car and took me into his. We drove to the expressway and after a while he looked at me and said, 'You aren't hurt bad, kid, so I'm going to drop you off.' But he told me not to call for help until he had a chance to get away."

Kloiber said that he had waited nearly three hours before beginning to wave to motorists to pick him up.

Did Kloiber know where Llauget might have gone, Richmond asked?

"He could be anywhere," Kloiber answered. "He might have gone home, but I don't know if you'll find him there now."

Hours earlier, Suffolk County's homicide squad had received a report from detectives of the Bronx Homicide Squad that they had not found Llauget in his flat on East 233rd Street when they went there to pick him up after the alarm was issued on Long Island.

With the incriminating statement signed by Kloiber, Richmond went to Suffolk County District Attorney George Aspland. Aspland, who is today a New York State Supreme Court justice, recalls, "Whenever I received a case from Tommy Richmond, I knew there'd never be a problem. He is thorough, meticulous, complete. In my opinion, he's one of the best homicide sleuths I've ever seen."

It took the grand jury only minutes to return an indictment after Richmond's evidence had been presented.

But Llauget was still a fugitive, and there wasn't the slightest clue to his whereabouts. Richmond decided on a ruse that, he reasoned, might succeed in smoking Llauget out of hiding. He telephoned Rudy Kloiber and asked him to come to police headquarters. When Kloiber showed up, Richmond asked him flatly whether he had seen Llauget since the crime.

"I swear I haven't," Kloiber replied. "I haven't seen him or talked to him since then. I don't have any idea where he is."

"Okay," Richmond said, "but if you happen to be talking to him, just tell him that we're looking for him as a murderer. We must assume he is armed because he used a gun to kill your mother. That means, if we run into him, there could be shooting."

Richmond sucked in a deep breath.

"You know," he said with an ominous tone, "Sal may even get killed."

The very next day, on August 28, exactly a month after the murder, a New York City attorney, William Erlbaum, phoned the district attorney's office in Riverhead.

"Salvatore Llauget has retained me as counsel and has asked me to surrender him," the attorney said.

Llauget accepted an offer from the district attorney to plead to a lesser charge of manslaughter, thus avoiding the ordeal of a trial and a possible maximum sentence on conviction of twenty-five years to life. Llauget was sentenced to serve five years in prison.

Richmond's talents as "The Great Persuader" were likewise to play a decisive role in the solution of the Adele Kohr slaying. First, however, there was the hair-splitting investigative work to be done. Richmond and his men focused first on the tire tracks, the tread impressions left in the sand before and after the killer ran over the body.

Examination indicated that the car in which the young nurse had been brought to the sandy clearing was driven off the macadam road, stopped, turned, and departed at high speed. That conclusion was reached after laboratory experts studied the mounds formed by the churned-up sand.

"The driver ran over the body after he made his turn," said one investigator. "Then he took off in a big hurry. These tracks tell a very accurate story."

To preserve that horrendous etching of murder, Richmond's sleuths photographed the tire tracks and made moulages (impressions) of the treads, which are in effect the tires' "fingerprints." The detectives also concluded from the impressions in the sand that the tires were relatively new, and were comprised of six treads. The tread design and the newness of the tires would be invaluable evidence once the killer's car was found. Detectives could then make actual comparisons and satisfy themselves that the tracks left in the sand had been made by the tires on the suspect's vehicle.

The next target for Richmond was finding the suspect's vehicle. If the T-37 green Tempest, a car produced by Pontiac, could be located, Richmond would ostensibly be just one step from the identification and arrest of the killer. Richmond dispatched detective Gerard Gozaloff to Riverhead, the county seat, to cull the auto registration files of all late-model Tempests, not just green ones but those in the beige and blue family as well. Richmond had eliminated any search for black, red, and other dark-hued models because Miss Kohr obviously had seen a light-colored car and described it as such. But because the Sagtikos State Parkway is illuminated by color-distorting gas-vapor lights, her impression of light green could have been in error. Therefore, Richmond decided to have Gozaloff check the gamut of light-colored Tempests, and not just green alone.

Gozaloff returned from the seventy-mile round trip to Riverhead with a list of eighteen registrations for Tempests fitting the specifications of color and design that Richmond had designated for the search.

Richmond split the list in half, giving the first nine names to detectives Thomas Mansel and Richard Dean, the remainder to detectives Gozaloff and Conrad Alt, and dispatched them to track down the owners for questioning.

Gozaloff and Alt telephoned a running series of reports to Richmond as they visited one after another of the registered Tempest owners whom they were checking out. None fitted the description of the suspect. Some were too old. Some were women. One balding husband was terribly embarrassed; he confessed to the two detectives that, yes, he *had* been driving his wife's Tempest on the previous evening, and had used it to take another woman to a motel.

But Mansel and Dean had a different report to offer when they phoned in. They had struck out on their first stop, but then they visited the hamlet of Central Islip, which adjoins Adele Kohr's East Islip community. The address in Central Islip was 185 Hawthorne Street, and the registered owner of the Tempest being checked out was listed as Linda Meyer.

The detectives found that the address was a garden apartment complex. They checked the directory, found Linda Meyer's apartment listing, and went to her door. Their ring was answered by a slender, pretty brunette who corrected Mansel when he asked if she were Miss Linda Meyer.

"It's Mrs. Meyer," she said. "I was married in April."

"Are you the owner of a light green 1970 Tempest T-37?" asked Mansel.

"Yes, I am," she responded.

"Who besides yourself drives the car?" Mansel wanted to know.

"Oh, my husband does," came the reply.

"Where is your husband now?"

"He's inside."

"Would you please ask him to come to the door," Mansel said.

The young woman turned into the foyer and called out, "Bob, can you come here, please?"

Almost immediately a tall young man came into view. The instant Mansel and Dean caught sight of him, they nudged each other. For what they saw told them that the search for Adele Kohr's slayer could well be at an end.

He had a beard, had long hair, and wore glasses—the key identifying features Adele Kohr had jotted in her book.

"We'd like you to come with us to headquarters and answer some questions," Dean said. Robert Meyer went along unhesitatingly. When he was led into the homicide squad's offices and Richmond spotted him, a smile creased the sergeant's face. He turned to his men.

"If it takes you more than ten minutes to get a confession out of him I'm going to ask you to turn in your shields," Richmond taunted.

Actually it did not take ten minutes. No sooner had the twenty-three-year-old suspect been settled down in a small office, than an anguished plea issued from his lips.

"I'm sick . . . very sick," he stammered. "I need help."

"But before we can do anything for you," Alt put in, "you've got to tell us what happened . . . do you know what I'm talking about?"

Meyer glanced at the detectives with a vacant look.

It was a key moment. Would he confess, or clam up? If not handled just right, he might do the latter.

"What you must tell is when it happened . . . how it happened," Richmond, monitoring the conversation, casually put in from the doorway.

The suspect turned and looked at Richmond with a frown. Richmond walked over to Meyer, put a hand on his shoulder, and asked softly but firmly, "It happened last night, didn't it...?"

Meyer nodded. "Yes," he replied.

Richmond patted the suspect's shoulder. "Atta boy," he said. "Now you level with my two friends here ... tell them everything ... and we're going to get you all the help you need...."

"I'll tell you everything," Meyer said.

Richmond read Meyer his rights. The confession began pouring forth. He had spotted "that young woman" driving along the Sagtikos State Parkway ... had pursued her until he forced her car to a stop at the toll booth ... tried to open the door of her car but it was locked ... went back to his car, got a jack, went back to the Maverick and smashed the window ... opened the door as she screamed out pleas to be left alone ... dragged her out, put her in his car, and drove to the end of Webb Avenue ... she resisted as he tried to remove her uniform and bikini bathing suit ... he beat her with his fists and when she no longer fought back he raped her ... then he choked her with his hands, threw her out of the car ... then ran over her.

The rest was almost routine. Meyer signed a statement admitting the crime. He was fingerprinted, photographed, and booked for murder. Then, before being led away, he was allowed to talk privately with his wife (who had followed him to the station house), with her mother, and with his mother.

The three women spoke with Meyer for some thirty minutes. Then before leaving, Meyer's wife and the two mothers converged on Sergeant Richmond. The defendant's wife spoke.

"I want to thank all of you for the way you handled yourselves in this arrest. My husband is a sick man and I don't believe he has any business being on the outside. You have done your duty well...."

Says Richmond, "That was the first time I ever heard any relative of a murder suspect in all the years I've been on this job actually thank detectives for making an arrest. It almost floored me and the other guys." Moreover, Richmond reflects, "Adele Kohr, in death, helped us catch her own killer."

Richmond and his fellow sleuths discovered that Meyer had a record of three previous arrests for assaults on women, that he had served two years of a three-year prison term for one of those attacks, and that his description matched that of a man sought for the recent rape of a young woman abducted from the vast Walt Whitman Shopping Center in Huntington, Long Island. The twenty-three-year-old victim of that attack was brought to the county jail, where Meyer was confined after his arraignment and held without bail. She identified him as the assailant, and Meyer was processed once more, now for sodomy, rape, kidnap, and robbery.

Robert Meyer did not get off lightly, even though his attorney sought and was granted a change of venue. His trial, for second degree murder, was held in Queens County. In spite of a defense of temporary insanity, Meyer was found guilty and sentenced to serve twenty-five years to life for the killing of pretty Adele Kohr.

12

The Hunter and the Hunted

IT WAS HOT for April, even in Rome, and Italy's Deputy Police Commissioner Angelo Mangano sweltered in the back seat of his chauffeur-driven Fiat as the driver weaved his way through the city's rush-hour traffic to Mangano's house on the outskirts of the capital. Mangano was only dimly aware of the cacophony of horns and the shouts of the drivers, for he was thinking ahead to the welcome he would receive at home from his two small children and his wife, who had prepared a pasta dinner as only the Sicilians can.

From the expression on Mangano's face it would have been impossible to tell that his mind was filled with pleasant thoughts. He wore the haunted look of the hunter who is constantly aware that his prey may turn on him in ambush. Mangano's prey were mafiosi, whom he had tracked down from Sicily to Genoa during a police career of eighteen years that had been so successful that he was known as Italy's "Super Policeman."

Among the many Mafia figures he had sent to prison was one of the country's most notorious criminals, Luciano ("The Faceless One") Liggio. Known as "The Godfather of Corleone," the Sicilian mountain town where he was born, Liggio was in fact the head of the Mafia for all of Sicily. He had escaped from custody and was on the loose again. Mangano had vowed to put him back in prison.

In his one-man war against the Mafia, Mangano was often just as ruthless as were the criminals he sought. The strong-arm tactics of the big detective, who stood over six feet, had led many small-time criminals to surrender without a fight when Mangano closed in on them. His appearance alone was enough to frighten some.

He had short, thick gray hair over a deeply furrowed forehead and prominent cheekbones that tapered to lean jaws and a Vandyke beard. The face was dominated by large green, piercing eyes that could look daggers into criminals but crinkle in laughter at the antics of his children. It was the children he was thinking about as his friend, Domenico Casella, eased the Fiat to a stop in front of the locked gate of the driveway to Mangano's house.

"I'll open it," Mangano said, sliding from the car with the keys already in his hand.

"Very well," responded Casella, who normally performed the task himself but realized that his friend was especially anxious to see his children on this night.

As Mangano approached the gate, a car shot out of a nearby street and screeched to a halt at right angles to the Fiat. Three men with sawed-off shotguns hopped out. Casella went for his pistol, realizing instantly that the attackers were mafiosi bringing *Il Bacio della Lupara* ("The Kiss of the Wolf")—death to those who have gone against the Mafia—and named after the sawed-off, double-barreled gun used to hunt wolves in the mountains and fancied for years by mafiosi as a painful, disfiguring weapon for disposing of enemies.

A blast from one of the guns struck Casella in the face and

chest before he could draw his weapon. Mangano, who had turned at the sound of the car, was struck in the head by a

Deported U.S. gangster Frank (Three Fingers) Coppola (*left, wearing tinted glasses*) is dwarfed by one of his Italian body-guards. (*Keystone*)

load from one of the shotguns and knocked flat. He struggled
to reach his pistol and get a look at the assailants through the

Italian Super Sleuth Angelo Mangano strides into a courtroom.
(*Keystone*)

blood gushing over his eyes. He didn't make it. Another blast
and pain seared Mangano's chest, leaving him helpless to do anything but feign death.

"Make sure he is finished," Mangano heard one of the men say in Sicilian dialect. "The driver too."

Two rapid blasts from the shotguns and again Mangano felt the searing pain, this time in the arm and the hand. He was vaguely aware of slamming car doors and squealing tires as the gunmen fled.

Waves of pain swept over Mangano. Miraculously, he was alive, and conscious. He could not understand why someone did not come from a nearby house to help them. They were probably afraid the gunmen would return, he thought. In his own house, perhaps they had not heard the shooting. All the better, Mangano thought. He had always been careful to shield members of his family from his work and he did not want them to see him looking like a butchered pig. Painfully, Mangano crawled to the passenger side of the car and opened the door. His friend was slumped over the steering wheel. Blood covered his forehead. Mangano whispered, "Casella?"

A few seconds of silence, then Casella replied weakly, "I am alive, Angelo."

Mangano crawled into the seat beside his friend. "The hospital," he whispered.

For the first time Casella turned to look at Mangano. "The hospital? The nearest hospital is five kilometers away."

"The hospital," Mangano repeated.

Casella was in no condition to argue. He attempted to start the car but discovered he could not move his legs. They had been riddled with shotgun pellets. He could move his arms. With Mangano handling the brake and the gas and Casella steering, the two men eased the car through the streets to the hospital's emergency entrance, where they passed out.

The next day the Italian newspapers screamed the story: ITALY'S SUPER POLICEMAN, AIDE, MIRACULOUSLY SURVIVE MAFIA ASSASSINATION ATTEMPT; SUPERCOP TURNS SUPERMAN TO GET HIMSELF AND DRIVER TO HOSPITAL AFTER BEING LEFT FOR DEAD; MAFIOSI FAIL IN ATTEMPT TO DELIVER KISS OF THE WOLF TO SUPER POLICEMAN; ASSASSINATION ATTEMPT MEANS MANGANO IS AGAIN HOT ON THE MAFIA TRAIL.

Scores of detectives stood guard at the hospital and outside the rooms of Mangano and Casella as they fought for their lives. Hospitals were not off limits to Mafia hit men. Two years earlier three mafiosi had entered a Palermo hospital dressed as nurses to finish a hotel owner who was recovering from stab wounds suffered in an earlier Mafia attempt on his life. This time the Mafia made sure. They walked into his room in their white nurses' gowns, took out their submachine guns and riddled the man with bullets as he lay in bed.

As soon as Mangano and Casella were out of danger they

Detective Mangano testifies in a Florence court on how gunmen ambushed and shot him outside his Roman home in 1973. In the defendant's dock, Frank Coppola, charged with engineering the murder attempt, gestures angrily. (*United Press International*)

were moved to a secret retreat to begin their long recovery. During the period after the assassination attempt, which came on April 5, 1973, neither Mangano nor Casella spoke to newsmen. But one high Mafia figure was talking. He was doing so to take the heat off himself and put it on Mangano.

The man was Frank Coppola, who had been deported from the United States to his native Italy as an "undesirable alien." Mangano had been trying to go through Coppola, who had retained his Mafia connections, to get Liggio. Coppola at one point told Mangano he would help bring Liggio back to justice. In fact, he was keeping Liggio informed of the policeman's every move. When Mangano got too close, the detective tasted *Il Bacio della Lupara*. Police quickly linked Coppola to the shooting. That is when he started to talk—against Mangano.

Coppola charged Mangano with demanding fifty million lire ($80,000) from the Mafia to erase from tape recordings of telephone conversations the names of politicians and judges who were sympathetic to the Mafia. Mangano had been authorized to bug the phones in tracking down Liggio.

Smear tactics against high-ranking policemen had become part of the game of the "new" Mafia, of which Liggio was the founder. He had led the organized crime syndicate into international smuggling and dope dealing, and into legitimate businesses and the "protection" of those the Mafia didn't own. He was thought to have originated the idea of the smear campaign such as the one Coppola was using against Mangano.

As he recovered from his wounds, Mangano, the center of this swirling controversy, could not have helped but yearn for the simpler days of Mafia hunting when he had gone into the Sicilian mountain town of Corleone by himself to hunt down the man who was so elusive that he was known as "The Faceless One."

For as long as he could remember, Angelo Mangano had never wanted to be anything but a policeman. He was always big for his age and in his native Sicilian village, San Giovanni di Giarre, near Catania on the east coast, he was "The Authority" among his friends. He settled all disputes and righted all wrongs, but he dreamed of bigger things, of catching Mafia cattle thieves and kidnappers who roamed the island at will and committed almost any crime without fear of capture because of *La Codice da Omerta* ("The Code of Silence") that is engrained in Italian life, especially in Sicily.

Omerta means that no one talks to authorities about a crime he has witnessed or knows about. Those who break the code are rewarded with *Il Bacio della Lupara*. Even as a youngster, Angelo dreamed of changing this, of making the mafiosi pay for their crimes.

Born in 1920, Angelo grew up in the turbulent years of the rise of Mussolini and was deeply affected by the nationalistic cause *Il Duce* espoused. As a young man, Mangano volunteered for the Italian army, to serve on the African front. But in a few months he knew he had made a terrible mistake. He deserted and returned home to fight with the Italian underground, first against the German allies of Italy, then against the German occupiers as Italy changed sides.

As soon as the war was over, he joined the Italian National Police force and married his childhood sweetheart. After graduation from the police academy, Mangano immediately used his almost limitless energy and tough tactics to make a name for himself, first in La Spezia, then Rome, and later in Reggio Calabria, the area of Italy that is in the toe of the Italian boot and is renowned as the worst Mafia stronghold outside Sicily.

They called him *Manganello*, or "Little Mangano"—in irony of his height, prodigious working habits, and fearless ways. In Reggio, he once went three days and three nights without sleep as he tracked a Mafia leader to his lair in the mountains.

As Mangano's reputation as a "Super Policeman" grew, the reputation of another Sicilian was also growing, but on the other side of the law. It was that of Luciano Liggio. Born five years after Mangano on another Sicilian coast, Liggio was earning a name as the most ruthless of the ruthless Mafia figures. Liggio's family had a farm near Corleone, a city of 14,000 in the mountains near Palermo. Liggio spent long, lonely hours tending sheep in the mountains and dreaming of rising above the poverty and hunger in which he lived. He drank goat's milk as it came from the animals, with whatever germs it contained, which was to lead to tuberculosis of the bone that plagued him through-out his adult years. The disease corroded his spine and he was forced to wear leather girdles laced with steel so that he could stand upright.

Liggio turned eighteen just before the American forces in-vaded Sicily and he came down from the mountains to find he could make as much in a day stealing American supplies and selling them to his countrymen as he could make from his sheep in a year. But no one was alone in the business of stealing, Liggio quickly found out. A man named Giulliano was in charge of stealing from the Americans around Corleone, and Liggio had to take his stolen goods to Giulliano to have them disposed of. Otherwise the criminals would make him pay for his crime, maybe with a busted jaw, a broken arm, or with his life, depending upon how many times he tried to act on his own. Giulliano had a reputation as a brutal *capobanda* ("ringleader"). Liggio learned that the gangster had earned it by killing a policeman and fright-ening witnesses so badly that they refused to testify against him. Liggio wanted such a reputation. He wanted to be the *capobanda*.

The next year, Liggio was caught by three policemen stealing grain reserves. Jailed, he was soon released to stand trial later. But Liggio disappeared and within weeks one of the three policemen who had arrested him was shot to death in front of his home. The rumor was that the gunman was Liggio. No one would testify against him.

Within months, the other two policemen in the case were shot to death. That left no witnesses to the only crime with which Liggio had been charged. Still, Liggio did not appear in public. He came to the attention of the Mafia boss in Corleone, Dr. Michele Navarra, a physician at a local hospital who had a reputation as a healer of men and fixer of problems. If a con-tractor did not want labor problems, he paid Navarra; if a merchant wanted to protect his inventory, he paid Navarra; if a wealthy landowner received a threatening letter, he paid Navarra, and the threat went away.

Navarra did not have many enemies, but those he did have met death. The director of the hospital in which Navarra worked was gunned down. Navarra succeeded to his position. A courageous union leader who would not accept payoffs for labor peace was shoved into a car on the street, shot three times, and his body dumped out. A young boy who saw the murderer was taken to Navarra's hospital, allegedly after suffering a nervous breakdown. He died after an injection.

Liggio became known as "The Armed Arm of the Mafia" and lawlessness around Corleone grew to the point that a national police captain was sent in as a special officer to suppress the crime wave. He found witnesses to link Liggio to two murders. When it came time for the trial, the witnesses refused to testify. Anyway, Liggio could not be found. Few could remember seeing him. Those who did found it was best for their health if they forgot they ever had.

Liggio instilled so much terror in the area that it began to be rumored that he was going to take over from Navarra. Soon after this, on June 23, 1958, a lone gunman attempted to deliver *Il Bacio della Lupara* to Liggio. He was only wounded in the attempt, which signed Navarra's death warrant.

Less than two months later, as Navarra and a colleague, Dr. Giovani Russo, who had no known connection with the Mafia, were on their way back to Corleone from seeing patients in the countryside, the pair were ambushed by two men with submachine guns. Police found more than 100 slugs in the doctors and the car.

The investigation led to Liggio and one of his relatives. But witnesses would not testify. Police learned in their search that so few people had seen Liggio over the past years—or would talk about it if they had—that they had no clear idea of what he looked like. The only picture that existed of Liggio was one taken when he was a shepherd tending his family's sheep. He became "The Faceless One."

Dope, death, destruction of property, and kidnapping became so rampant around Palermo that the national Parliament in Rome named a commission to investigate. The commission reported: the Mafia controls the meat, vegetable, and fish markets in Palermo as well as the employment bureaus and the government operation to license shops. To sell produce, meat, or fish at one of the markets, one has to pay off the Mafia. To get a job, one has to pay off the Mafia. Even to open a new shop, one has to pay off the Mafia. Liggio is responsible for the growing tentacles of the Mafia.

As Liggio climbed to the top of the underworld, Mangano climbed steadily but far less spectacularly up the ladder of police officialdom. He was a top detective in Genoa in November 1963, when he was summoned to Rome for a special assignment that would come directly from the National Police Chief, Angelo Vicaro. Vicaro had followed with keen interest the career of Mangano as a Mafia catcher and had on at least one occasion encouraged him in a private conversation. The police chief considered Mangano as sort of a protégé. Mangano did not know this, or for what purpose he was being summoned to Rome. Once he got to Vicaro's office he did not have to wait long to find out.

"Angelo," said Vicaro, "I have admired your work for some time. Now, I want to give you the toughest assignment we have. From your record, I am confident that you can accomplish what I ask. I want you to catch Liggio. I want you to go to Sicily and stay there until Liggio is a prisoner. Basically, you will be on your own, with what help you need to be supplied by the local police."

Mangano was momentarily speechless at the magnitude of the assignment. Yet he was sure he could bring it off. "I will find him," said Mangano, "and I will put him in prison. You can be assured of that, no matter how long it takes."

"I know you will, Angelo. Goodbye, good journey, and good hunting."

If Mangano had any doubts about being able to accomplish the assignment, he did not share them with acquaintances. He exuded confidence. However, he had his family stay in Genoa, for their own protection. It wouldn't be above the Mafia to use them as hostages to get Mangano out of Sicily once the mafiosi found out why he was there. It wouldn't take them long to do that.

"When one speaks in Sicily," Mangano knew, "the Mafia hears."

Sometimes, for whatever reason, the Mafia waits to do its

hunting. It was not long before Mangano was sent to Sicily that the Mafia evened the score with a veteran prosecutor, Pietro Scaglione, who had spent most of his sixty-five years prosecuting mafiosi. As he neared retirement, he was known to have been working on a dossier that would contain all the information he had compiled on the underworld organization. Scaglione never finished the dossier. He forgot one important thing. Those who hunt mafiosi should never become creatures of habit.

After his wife's death in 1961, Scaglione began following the old Sicilian custom of visiting his wife's grave every day. One day, as he was putting flowers on her grave, he was cut down by a submachine gun fired from nearby shrubbery. Police found Scaglione sprawled on the grave amid the flowers he had brought.

Mangano was aware of the danger he was in as he drove alone into the center of the mountain fortress town of Corleone, dominated by a huge castle built when the Saracens occupied the island centuries ago. The ancient stone buildings in the town looked just as impregnable as the castle. To an outsider like Mangano, even though he was Sicilian, the townspeople were just as cold as the stone walls.

"You cannot imagine that town," Mangano would recall later. "Fear was in the air. At 8:30 at night every door was bolted. There was not a soul in sight. The only moving things were pigs, going through garbage."

Mangano took a room in a hotel just off the main piazza. After dinner he walked around to a cafe in the piazza for a coffee and cognac. He hardly had time to drink it before other cafe patrons began scurrying to their homes and the cafe itself closed. Mangano spent the first of many long, lonely nights in his room.

The next morning, Mangano went around to the local police station to introduce himself to the chief and tell him of the mission. Mangano had not telephoned or wired of his coming because he had seen no need to give the Mafia advance notice.

"So you want to find Liggio," the police chief reflected. "Well, Mangano, I can tell you that Liggio is no longer in Corleone. He hasn't been seen for years. Some say he is dead. They say he died of the tubercular condition from which he suffered for many years."

"But you do not know if he is dead?"

"I cannot swear to it, no."

"Who runs the Mafia here?"

"Aahh, Mangano, who knows who runs the Mafia?"

"I am told that it is still Liggio."

"You know more on the mainland than we know here."

"Are there any followers of Navarra left?" asked Mangano.

"There are none left. Those that were not killed fled the island or joined the followers of Liggio."

"There are followers of Liggio but no Liggio?" asked Mangano. "Who knows their leader now?"

"Do you know some of these one-time followers of Liggio?"

"We do. We will identify them for you if you wish."

"I do," replied Mangano, who knew that there was little chance of learning anything from them but he had to start his search somewhere. There was always the chance that someone might let something slip.

The police chief provided Mangano with a list of names and addresses of men, and their occupations, who were thought to have been close to Liggio at one time. The men ranged from landowners to a part-time mechanic, and the latter, it was said, could frequently be found at the piazza cafe where Mangano had taken coffee and cognac the previous evening. He would start there.

"Goodbye and good luck," said the police chief as Mangano departed.

At the cafe, the waiter pointed out the man Mangano was seeking. He was young and very well dressed for a part-time mechanic.

"Good morning," said Mangano to the man. "I am detective Mangano of the Italian police and I am told that you are an acquaintance of the man known as Luciano Liggio."

The man appeared only slightly surprised. That was probably because Mangano was making no effort to hide the nature of his mission.

"Did you not know," the man replied, looking into Mangano's eyes, "that Liggio is dead?"

"Were you at the funeral?" asked Mangano.

"I was not there but I have a friend whose word I do not doubt tell me he saw Liggio buried."

"Where is your friend?"

"In America; where I do not know."

"Many thanks," said Mangano.

Over the next few days Mangano talked with each man on the list and learned nothing. "Liggio is dead," he heard. "Liggio is away," he was told. "Who is Liggio?" he was asked.

After a week Mangano felt that everyone in Corleone knew his mission and he knew no more about Liggio than when he had arrived. He began to feel that he was being watched, that eyes filled with hate were following him wherever he went. He took to sitting only at a table in the piazza which was against the wall, so that he had a full view of the square. He checked under his car hood and under the dashboard for a bomb before starting his car. At night, he lay in his bed and listened in the silence for footsteps coming toward his room. When he heard them, his hand went to the pistol beneath his pillow and he would grasp the handle tightly until the footsteps passed.

As his questioning of residents and canvassing of the countryside got him nowhere, Mangano began spending more time at the cafe in the piazza, talking with a group of retired men who spent many hours drinking coffee and warming themselves in the sun. Mangano knew from experience that older men would sometimes tell of what they knew about the Mafia, perhaps out of guilt for not having told it before, perhaps because they knew they did not have long to live and *Il Bacio della Lupara* could not take that much from them.

The men were friendly enough but they volunteered nothing. They talked of the weather, crops, and politics. Then one night, when he had been in Corleone almost four months and was about to despair of ever finding the trial of Luciano Liggio, Mangano received a telephone call in his room.

"If you want Toto Riina," said the caller, "check the lawyer who has an office on the piazza."

The phone went dead. But Mangano's hopes soared. Riina was Liggio's right-hand man. If he was this close, he thought, Liggio is probably nearby. Perhaps the caller even knew where

Liggio could be found and was teasing him with a smaller fish to see how he did. Mangano spent a sleepless night. As dawn broke he went to the police station to see if he could get a mug shot of Riina. He had seen pictures of him but wanted to refresh his memory before visiting the lawyer. He did not know from the call if Riina worked in the lawyer's office or the lawyer would for some unknown reason lead Mangano to the Mafia figure.

He did find a reasonably up-to-date picture of Riina in the police files. By the time he entered the lawyer's office, he had the features committed to memory. Mangano identified himself to a secretary and asked to see the lawyer. She ushered the detective into an interior room and he found himself face to face with Riina. It took Mangano a split second to realize the circumstances, during which Riina rose to shake hands. By the time Riina stood up he was facing Mangano's pistol.

Mangano was astounded at the circumstances. So were the police, or at least they seemed to be when the detective brought in the Liggio lieutenant. Here had been one of the best known Mafia figures of the region practicing law (which he was totally unqualified to do) within a few blocks of the police station and apparently conducting a lucrative business. His clients probably came out of fear, Mangano felt.

While Riina's open presence in Corleone confirmed Mangano's worst fears about the inefficiency of the local police, it raised his hopes for capturing Liggio. He was certain that one of the retired men with whom he had been talking had been his informer, but he did not know which one. He spent more time cultivating their favor. And he questioned Riina, who proclaimed he knew nothing of Liggio's whereabouts. But after their session, Mangano decided to extend his hunt to Palermo and to start checking the hospitals there. Mangano never revealed what Riina said that made him follow this trail to Liggio, but it had to be some inadvertent slip or some detective intuition from the things that Liggio's lieutenant said. Riina certainly never gave any information voluntarily.

The hunt that began in the fall had extended into the spring as Mangano began the tedious work of checking hospital records to see if any patient was being treated for the now relatively rare disease of bone tuberculosis, or Pott's disease (so named after the man who discovered it). After a few days, when Mangano saw how long his job would take, he began to despair again of ever finding the man. He did not trust the police to help him in his search. Then the break came, again in the form of an anonymous telephone call to his hotel room.

"Go to the E. Albanese Clinic," said the caller. "Ask for a patient named Gaspare Centineo."

Another sleepless night. Again, with the first daylight Mangano was off on his mission. Again, disappointment.

"Mr. Centineo checked out yesterday against my wishes," the doctor told Mangano.

"Why did he leave?" Mangano asked.

"He had a visitor shortly before he left," the doctor replied. "Mr. Centineo summoned me to his room and asked that I remove his cast. I protested but he insisted. Then he left with the friend."

"Why did he have the cast?"

"He had undergone an operation some days ago to improve his deteriorating condition," the doctor answered.

"What is the prognosis for the patient?"

"If he takes care of himself he will have many years left," the doctor replied.

Good and bad, thought Mangano. He will live long enough for me to catch him, but also long enough to commit an untold amount of crime.

"Why are you after Mr. Centineo?" asked the doctor.

"The man you treated," replied Mangano, "was the head of the Mafia in Sicily. He is Luciano Liggio."

The doctor was able to identify the man who left the hospital with Liggio from a number of police photographs he was shown. The visitor was a Mafia figure who was active in the area of Palermo known as Greco, a section that for the past year had been synonymous with death to policemen. Seven officers had been killed there when their car was blown up. The killers had not been found. They were thought to be mafiosi.

To canvas the area, Mangano knew, he needed all the help he could get. The police this time would be anxious to help in an effort to avenge the death of their fellow officers. Mangano and several policemen visited the last known residence of Liggio's friend. Cleaned out. Scores of policemen came in to help comb the area, going door-to-door to ask questions and to search. Someone told a local detective, "Try a villa in Greco called La Rosa."

"This time, we will be prepared," the police chief told Mangano.

On a hot, windy May morning some 1,000 policemen, along with Mangano, surrounded Villa La Rosa. Warnings to surrender brought no reply from the villa. Mangano led the charge through the gates. Still, nothing from the nearby house. They entered the structure. Deserted.

"I had thought this would be it," Mangano recalled. "You cannot imagine the disappointment I felt."

A thorough search of the house revealed that behind loose panels in a closet were stairs that spiraled downward. Mangano was called. With drawn pistols he crept down the stairs, followed by several policemen with submachine guns. At the bottom they came to a closed door.

"This is the police," shouted Mangano. "If anyone is behind that door, they should come out with their hands up." No answer. Mangano kicked the door open. The room was empty, except for a bed and some small pieces of furniture.

"The room was as empty as I felt," Mangano remembered. "I knew that Liggio had been in that very room only recently and that this was the closest I would ever get to him. I felt that fate had in store for me to always be a step behind 'The Faceless One.'"

Intuition took Mangano back to Corleone. After two narrow escapes, Mangano thought, it would be logical for Liggio to go where he felt safest.

Mangano at first began to question some of the same underworld figures he had seen before: he was greeted with the traditional Sicilian *omerta*.

Mangano felt more at ease in Corleone than he had on his first visit. People talked with him, at least as long as he did not bring up the Mafia, and he was convinced he was in no danger now from the Mafia. Liggio knew that he would have an even harder time remaining "The Faceless One" if he had his henchmen kill the detective who was sent to find him.

After a few fruitless days, Mangano decided to turn to the elderly man he was sure had given him the tip about Liggio's lieutenant. Mangano began spending his days having coffee with the aging patrons of the piazza, waiting his chance to be alone with the man. He did not want their meeting to be in secret, or conspicuous, either one of which could turn off the information Mangano felt he might get from a casual conversation over espresso.

At last, the two were alone in the late afternoon. Quickly, Mangano began to tell the man how much good he had done by revealing the whereabouts of Liggio's henchman and how much better off the Sicilians would be with Liggio himself in prison. The old man at first feigned ignorance at what Mangano was talking about, but as the detective continued to praise his unknown informer, the old man looked into the afternoon sun and said: "If Liggio was not at La Rosa he should be here, at the home of Sorisi."

Mangano knew of the family. He thanked the man and hurriedly left. He did not want to wait too long for fear of missing the elusive Liggio again, but he felt he must have agents of his own National Police rather than the local police, whom he did not trust. A quick call to Palermo and he was assured he would have a dozen agents with him by nightfall.

At 8:30 P.M., Mangano rang the doorbell of Sorisi's home. Two women responded. "Oh, commissioner," said one, "I was just coming over to see you. Liggio is here. Here are the keys to his room. Go and take him."

Mangano was stunned. "I couldn't believe it," he later recalled. "The man who had been so elusive was being turned over to me by a woman who was as casual as if I were calling for a friend."

Mangano himself was as taut as a wire walker, he said later, as he made his way to the upstairs room the woman had pointed out. Several agents were behind him. The door to the room was closed, but light shone from beneath it. Mangano's heart was pounding as he stood in front of the door. He didn't utter a sound, but threw it open and quickly moved inside. A man lying on the bed sat up at the opening of the door. The light was poor near the bed, but the man spoke. "Commissioner," he said, "I am here. It is I, Liggio."

Italy's most wanted man, whose name had struck terror into hundreds of people and kept thousands more silent, had to be helped from the bed like a baby and strapped into a corset that kept him upright. The faceless one was no longer faceless.

13

The Paper Bag Killer

IT WAS A CLEAR, SUNNY DAY in San Francisco. The early morning fog that tumbles in from the Pacific had burned off, as it usually does, and the air was brisk and clean. Lorenzo Carniglia was walking up Third Street, his left shoe scraping the pavement lightly with each stride. He was a man of seventy, in good health, but none the less seventy, and he limped slightly. Carniglia was south of Market Street, walking north toward the center of the city, a short, stocky man whose bald head crowned a ruddy, lined, round face. He was a native of Italy, a semi-retired painting contractor who liked to be called a "self-made man."

Market Street is a broad thoroughfare, two pairs of streetcar tracks down the center, that bisects the heart of downtown San

Francisco. North of it are the department stores and office towers, the cable cars and the crowds of tourists. South of Market is different territory. Walking along Third Street, Carniglia passed two- and three-story industrial buildings, gray stucco warehouses and hotels that offered single rooms for twenty-two dollars a week. Rolled up in his right hand, Carniglia was carrying the daily *Racing Form*; he often took a bus from the Greyhound depot three blocks away to Bay Meadows, the track south of the city near the Bayshore Freeway. But there was no racing at Bay Meadows that day, and no bus. No one ever knew where he was going that Tuesday morning.

At 11:30 A.M. on October 16, 1973, San Francisco police patrolmen Alexander Barron and Thomas Burns were dispatched by radio to 345 Third Street. They arrived just as the ambulance was leaving. Lorenzo Carniglia had been gunned down by a young man who ran up behind him on the sidewalk and shot him three times at close range. The pistol in the young man's right hand had been concealed in a small brown paper bag. A parking lot attendant had seen him flee. Blonde hair bouncing on his shoulders, wearing a yellow shirt, he had run north toward Market Street and cut into a parking lot at the end of the block. He was gone.

In the weeks and months to come, the blonde-haired young man was to become known to police and the citizens of San Francisco as the "Paper Bag Killer." It was a case both fascinating and terrifying. There was a psychotic killer who apparently struck at random, a businessman who might have prevented it, but was too busy, and a family whose personal tragedies seemed unbounded. There was also the paper bag, the most common of everyday items, something half the people in the city might be carrying on a given day, and one of them might be hiding a gun.

Before they finished their shift, the patrolmen who responded first to the shooting on Third Street filed Police Department Incident Report 73-38209. Carniglia was still alive and they reported it as an attempted homicide. Later that day, a top-sheet was filed on their report: "Homicide—Originally reported as 217 PC. This date at above time this detail notified by San

Francisco Hospital that the victim of a shooting earlier this date at 345 Third Street had expired." The top-sheet was signed off by Inspector Frank Falzon, star 507, homicide detail.

Frank Falzon is a new-breed cop. He is young, thirty-three years old, a college graduate who has been a police officer in

San Francisco Detective Frank Falzon (*left*), who was responsible for the pursuit of "The Paper Bag Killer," with Detective Jack Cleary, Falzon's partner. Falzon describes the case as "my first and only experience with a true split personality. A real psycho." (*Mark Kautz*)

San Francisco for eleven years. Born and raised in San Francisco, Falzon is a man with an easy manner who likes to be on a first-name basis with people. He is a shade under six feet tall, stocky, with muscular arms, and his curly black hair ends in neatly trimmed sideburns. He walks through the Hall of Justice wearing knit suits and talks baseball with people in the lobby.

During his first year in the department, Falzon walked a beat in the Fillmore district, a black neighborhood plagued with the violence of an inner city. He had asked for the assignment. After a tour in the Tenderloin, the city's downtown combat zone, he was assigned to the vice squad as a plain clothes detective. He moved in a world of prostitutes, pickup bars, people just out of prisons, and people on their way to get them, and he acquired a reputation. He was a man who would get out of the car to chase a suspect, a man who would go into a building if something looked wrong, a man who worked hard and used his head.

In 1969, Falzon was assigned to the Bureau of Inspectors. He got his inspector's shield about ten years before most men even think about it, and was assigned to the homicide detail a year later. "I would not trade jobs with anybody, and I mean that," says Falzon. "I know a lot of fellows who can tell you exactly what they will be doing at twelve noon tomorrow. Being a policeman is never like that. You can be sitting down having coffee one minute and be off on a hot call the next. That is the challenge. You get caught up in the chase, the hunt, the capture. You know you are doing something for society and, when you are an inspector, it is your case all the way. You are not going to make it unless you give 100 percent, and that is where it is at."

There are eight two-men teams on the homicide detail of the San Francisco Police Department. In addition to regular duties, they rotate a seven-day "on call" assignment. The team on duty starts at 8:00 A.M. Any homicides in the city during that week are the sole responsibility of the on-call team. Frank Falzon was shuffling contact cards and doing general paper work in the homicide detail at the Hall of Justice when the call came in reporting the shooting on Third Street, the first of the paper bag murders. He was on call.

The area immediately south of Market Street is a honky-tonk, slightly skid row district. In every block, some of the buildings have been flattened in order to make room for parking lots. Falzon and his partner sped to the scene. When they arrived at the 300 block of Third Street, the responding officers had already sketched a chalk outline of the body on the sidewalk and rounded up witnesses. The two detectives began the arduous work of piecing together what clues could be found. There was a blood stain, a small one, maybe twelve inches around, on the sidewalk. A newspaper lay nearby; the victim had evidently just purchased the newspaper. Beyond those bits of physical evidence, there was nothing more. Falzon's partner is Jack Cleary, ten years older with sandy hair that recedes slightly from his forehead. A heavy-set man with the professional detective's penetrating and observant eyes, Cleary smokes cigars but not in the style of a gangster-movie cop, and wears blazers and flannel slacks. Falzon and Cleary started with the witnesses.

From several interviews, Falzon put together a composite description of the killer: white male adult, eighteen to twenty-two years, five feet nine inches, one hundred thirty pounds; light complexion, light blonde hair, neck-length, combed straight; baby face, wearing faded jeans and a yellow shirt. According to witnesses, the killer had run up behind Carniglia with the pistol concealed in a sandwich-bag-size paper bag, fired three shots through the bottom of the bag and fled. They knew the old man by sight, but not by name. They knew he did not live around there, people had seen him up near Market Street buying tout sheets for the horses. No one had ever seen the killer before. There were no shell casings on the sidewalk so the murder weapon was apparently a revolver. The killer had run down the street, cut into the parking lot.

Anthony Miller had heard the shots, looked out his third-floor apartment window and seen the young, blonde-haired man run into the parking lot. With the pistol still in his hand, the killer stopped at the far end of the lot, took off the yellow shirt and threw it to the ground. He then put on a green short-sleeve shirt, cut back to Third Street and ran half-way up the next block to a white van parked at the curb. He got into the van and pulled quickly into the heavy traffic.

Miller had not been able to see the license plate on the van, but the inspectors found the shirt the killer had discarded in the parking lot. It was a worn T-shirt, tie-dyed yellow, with a bold chain pattern blocked out on the front. Although tie-dyed shirts were popular in San Francisco, this one was unusual.

"Initially, my partner and I always look for a motive. You try to find a reason behind a killing. Why did it happen? Lately, that has been one of the major difficulties in solving homicides. There is no motive, no apparent motive. So many of these cases now, it is racial or political or something like that. You just don't know." Frank Falzon was sitting at his desk in the homicide detail. His desk faces Cleary's, both under one of the large west-facing windows in the Hall of Justice. He was talking about murder, about murder cases, the Paper Bag Killer and others, and how to solve them. The San Francisco newspapers often preface references to the homicide detail with the adjective "elite." Falzon talks about his cases with professional ease, taking them apart, what went wrong, what went right, what was interesting. The Paper Bag Killer? "It was my first and only experience with a true split personality," said Falzon. "A real psycho. You just do not expect a killer in this type of case to kill again in the same fashion."

Lorenzo Carniglia died in the trauma center of Mission Emergency Hospital. An autopsy showed he had been hit in the head, neck, and shoulder by bullets fired from a small-calibre gun; the bullet that passed through his head killed him. One of the slugs that penetrated his body was trapped in his clothing and recovered. The crime lab said it came from a .22-calibre pistol, but could say nothing more about it. Falzon and Cleary had the description of a suspect and a white van, no license number, which is not much with which to look for a killer. They turned to the victim.

"There were different investigative leads we started looking into about Carniglia," said Falzon. "The victim was a hard-working man and did leave rather a nice estate to his family after the incident. He did like to gamble. He was a horse race fan and we thought of the possibility of someone killing that man in connection with that. That got us nowhere."

Carniglia had started a small painting and contracting business when he settled in San Francisco after immigrating to the United States. He was retired, but still did a job now and then. However, when Falzon began talking to people about Carniglia, he found a person slightly different than he might have expected. Carniglia had the reputation of being a man who knew how to hold on to money and what to do with it. By buying and selling real estate, he had, over the years, acquired enough property to qualify as a wealthy man. The painting business was more or less secondary, and always had been. When he died, Carniglia owned eight residential buildings in the Potrero, Bay View, and Hunters Point districts, all on the San Francisco Bay side of the city.

Carniglia lived alone in a house he owned at 525 Texas Street, a working-class, blue-collar neighborhood in the Potrero district. He was separated from his wife, but their relationship, if not cordial, was at least polite. He had a large family and was close to them. Several of his sons and daughters lived near him on Texas Street, where he also owned some buildings. On weekends, he spent his time in places where other people his age gathered to socialize. He liked to drink and dance and have a good time with the women. He had, in fact, for a man of seventy, a quite active romantic life, Falzon remembers. It was worth checking. Irate husband? Maybe he had been stepping on toes? Who knows? They looked into it, and there was nothing there.

Carniglia was a man most people respected, even if they did not like him. He had worked hard and done well in an old-country Italian community where that meant something to people. He was honest to the point of doing business on a handshake and meaning it. He was also tough in his business dealings. He expected to collect money when it was due, and he always collected. He was a hard man with a dollar, and his family was convinced this had something to do with his death. The inspectors looked into it. "The man had a tremendous amount of real estate property in San Francisco and a lot of it was in so-called low rent areas," said Falzon. "So we looked for maybe a tenant he might have been pressuring on the rent, and things started looking good."

Most of the buildings Carniglia owned were in tough, racially mixed neighborhoods. There was a tenant in a building in Hunters Point, a black man, with whom Carniglia had been feuding. Carniglia handled the renting of his buildings himself. He also knocked on the door himself each month to collect the rent. There had been hard words many times between Carniglia and the man in the Hunters Point building.

Falzon and Cleary drove south from the center of the city one evening down to Hunters Point. The man they were looking for waited in the doorway for a moment after they identified themselves, then walked out, closing the door behind him. He did not want the kids to hear, he explained. Yes, he knew the old man was dead; he had heard it on the television. And no, he was not sorry; the old man had it coming. The tenant made no attempt to disguise his bitterness; he hated Carniglia and made no bones about it. Did he know anything about who had killed him? No, the tenant replied, if he had had anything to do with it he would have done it right there at the house where he could have enjoyed it. There was something in the way the man said it, something that made the inspectors believe him.

A man had been shot dead in broad daylight in the middle of a sidewalk in downtown San Francisco. After two weeks of work, record checks, phone checks and interviews, the investigation was getting nowhere. They did have one thing left: the yellow, tie-dyed T-shirt found in the parking lot. The crime lab had gone over it, run their tests, and returned it to the property section without coming up with anything that might lead to the killer.

Falzon and Cleary contacted the San Francisco newspapers. The pattern on the front of the T-shirt was distinctive enough to mean that someone had probably made it by hand. It was also striking enough that someone who had seen it might remember who was wearing it. The newspapers ran a picture of the shirt and a description of the killer. The morning paper, the *Chronicle*, boxed the picture for prominent display. Anyone knowing anything about the shirt or the person seen wearing it was asked to contact the homicide detail. Running a picture in the newspapers is the type of thing that always gets at least a few calls. They may just be cranks, they may be worth checking out, but there is invariably someone who feels they know something. The picture ran in the newspapers and also was shown on local television news programs. Falzon and Cleary never received a single call.

Two months and four days after Carniglia was shot, on a street corner three blocks away, a man in a raggedy overcoat picked a newspaper from a trash can that stood on the sidewalk near the Life Line Mission. There is a free breakfast at the mission and he was waiting for it to open. The man in the overcoat was heavy, but not particularly big; his face was rough red, his head bald and uncovered, and his hands were not just calloused, but cracked. He walked back and forth a bit in the bite of the December wind, his legs stiff and draggy, like an old man with arthritis, but he was not that old. He was a regular at the mission, or had been for the last few weeks, which was long enough to make anyone a regular south of Market Street.

It was December 20, five days before Christmas, ten minutes to nine on a Thursday morning. There was a bustle on the street as people headed up toward Market Street on their way to jobs in the stores and business offices. There were a few other men standing on the sidewalk, saying nothing, waiting for the mission to open. The Rev. Ralph Eichenbaum, who ran the Life Line Mission, was sitting in his car at the curb, thinking about what he was going to say that day. He preached a sermon —a message—which came with the free breakfast.

The man in the overcoat was standing near the southwest corner of Fifth and Folsom streets. There is a gas station on the corner and, from the back of it, someone was walking swiftly toward him. The person approaching was a young man, slender, wearing a hooded blue jacket and a knit cap that was pulled down to his ears. Stuck under his arm was something half concealed in a large brown supermarket shopping bag. He held it with both hands. The man in the overcoat looked up once as the younger man came straight toward him and stopped three feet away.

An instant later there was a shot, not the crack of a pistol, but a boom. There were at least a dozen persons near enough to turn and look. They saw the man in the overcoat fall forward, his face shredded and bloody even before it smashed to the pavement. The paper bag fluttered to the sidewalk. The young man stood there a moment, then turned and walked quickly back past the gas pumps to the rear of the service station, making no attempt to conceal the pump-action shotgun he was still holding with both hands. At the rear of the station, in an alley that serves as a narrow street, he got into a white Econoline van. The motor was running and he sped down the alley.

By nine o'clock in the morning, people at the homicide detail have finished a second cup of coffee. The on-call team may be anywhere, a few people will be at desks, maybe someone on the phone. Being "on call" is part of the job, says Falzon, it comes with the territory. "My partner and me, we're called the unlucky duo. It seems that every time we're on call, it's a bad week. It is murder week. There was one week, I started at eight o'clock in the morning and by eight o'clock Monday evening I had a homicide. It seems that every night that week I had another homicide and I ended up that week with eight different homicide victims. The last one received a lot of attention—the 'Popeye' Jackson case, the prison reformer that got shot. That was probably one of my worst weeks."

Falzon and Cleary were not on call the morning the man in the old overcoat was shot on Fifth Street, but the case was immediately turned over to them. There were too many similarities: the youthful killer, the white van and, of course, the paper bag. "I guess we more or less coined the name ourselves," said Falzon. "You get so many cases, especially when you are on call, that sometimes you cannot distinguish one from the other. Every case is important, but sometimes names just don't stay with you because you are interviewing so many people. So when we talk back and forth across the desks, my partner will start referring to a case and I'll say, 'What case are you talking about? The arson case? The paper bag killer?' In this case, we started referring to the Paper Bag Killer and the news media picked up on it when they were around asking questions."

There were other similarities in the two murders, Falzon pointed out. Both had occurred on weekday mornings a few blocks apart south of Market Street. Both of the victims were old, or looked old, and both were relatively short, heavy-set men. Both of the victims also limped, which, it turned out, probably had as much as anything to do with why they were killed.

The man in the overcoat proved to be something of an enigma. The regulars at the mission had seen him around for a few weeks, but no one knew his name. He had some kind of accent, did not say much to anyone, and seemed just as happy if no one said anything to him. In his pockets, police found a razor blade and scissors, each carefully wrapped in newspaper, glasses, a comb, a ball-point pen and eleven cents. There was a wallet in the torn pocket of a jacket he was wearing under the overcoat, but it contained neither money nor identification. The dead man was a John Doe on the original homicide report.

The staff at the mission had an idea the dead man had lived somewhere nearby; he had been showing up too regularly to have come any great distance. A check of the grimy hotels and rooming houses in the south-of-Market area was begun. The man in the old overcoat had stayed at several of them in recent weeks, moving frequently and for no apparent reason. The room clerk at a hotel at Sixth and Howard streets, two blocks from the murder scene, recognized the description; the man was currently staying there. He had signed the register as Ara Kuznezow, listing no permanent address. His room was bare and empty, but the inspectors found a New York City welfare card.

A check with authorities in New York provided little additional information. Records in the welfare office indicated that Ara Kuznezow was fifty-four years old, an Armenian by birth who had lived in Russia. When and how he came to the United States was not known. He was an architect by training and had a degree in architectural design, at least that is what he told the welfare office, but his credentials had not been recognized in this country and he had been unable to find work. No one knew when he had left New York or what had prompted him to cross the country to San Francisco.

Kuznezow had been in San Francisco for about six weeks. If he had had any contact with anyone other than the down-and-outers south of Market Street, Falzon and Cleary were unable to uncover it. They tried to establish some link, any link, between the two victims, Carniglia and Kuznezow. There was none, they concluded, and they were right. Both men were immigrants and there were certain physical characteristics in common, but the two victims lived worlds apart and had never met. Kuznezow was a cipher. Why anyone would have wanted to kill him was a total mystery.

By this time, the evening news reports were carrying the story of the Paper Bag Killer. He walked up to people on the street, apparently total strangers, and shot them dead with a gun hidden in a paper bag. It was something the city did not need; it already had the Zebra killings.

On October 20, four days after Lorenzo Carniglia was shot, a young couple was kidnaped from a quiet street in San Francisco. The man was severely beaten and his wife was hacked to death. The victims were white and their assailants were black, a fact which, of itself, would not have panicked the city. But other killings followed, fourteen of them, whites killed by black men who approached and killed without saying a word. Police assigned a special radio channel—code-named "Zebra"—to the hunt for the killers. There were obvious differences between the Zebra killings and the paper bag murders; no one ever thought they were related. The city, however, was becoming jittery and it increased the pressure on Falzon and Cleary.

Ara Kuznezow had been killed by a single blast from a shotgun fired directly into his face from very close range. He was dead on the sidewalk before the ambulance arrived and the autopsy report added nothing that was useful to the inspectors. A dozen witnesses were interviewed, but the information they provided was vague and contradictory. About the only thing they added to the description of the killer was that he had a light moustache on his upper lip.

The paper bag that had concealed the shotgun was recovered at the scene. It was a Safeway supermarket bag, one of maybe 10,000 distributed each day in dozens of Safeway stores throughout the area, which did not seem to offer much help. But the bag was made of hard, glossy paper, and technicians at the crime lab were able to lift several good prints from it. The prints were categorized and compared with each and every card in the fingerprint file, and the report that came back to the inspectors said there was no match. That was a mistake; there was a match, and the technicians had missed it. It was not until later, after a confession in the homicide room that Falzon describes as frightening and unreal, that the whole story of the Paper Bag Killer was known.

Falzon and Cleary turned to the white van, the vehicle the killer had escaped in after both murders. They came up with a witness who had been stopped at a traffic light on Fifth Street and saw the second killing. The witness tried to follow in his car as the killer raced away in the white van down the alley behind the gas station, but had lost the van a block away when it turned into heavy traffic on Sixth Street. He had not seen the license plate, but had noticed that there were windows in the rear of the van and also on the right side. It narrowed the search, but not by much.

The area south of Market Street stretches off into San Francisco's major industrial and commercial district. A few run-down blocks, inhabited by people like Ara Kuznezow, quickly give way to several square miles of small businesses, wholesale outlets, delivery services, and manufacturing plants. There was no shortage of white vans in such an area. Before they were finished, Falzon and Cleary had run checks on between 300 and 400 vans and interviewed more than 100 drivers.

There were certain facts they had to work with in searching for the van, said Falzon. Both of the paper bag murders had occurred on weekday mornings south of Market Street. The killer, they concluded, was probably a delivery man of some sort who worked in the area and whose hours put him on the street at that time of day. Two plainclothes officers from the Southern District, the sprawling police precinct that covers the entire city south of Market Street, were assigned to work with them. They went at it systematically, block by block, literally knocking at the door of each and every business.

The van they were seeking had been described as white, but witnesses have been known to make mistakes. They asked if the business used any light-colored vans. If the answer was yes, they asked about drivers. They had a description of the killer as blonde-haired and wearing a moustache, but hair can be dyed and moustaches can be shaved. If a business used a light-colored van, they asked to interview any driver who met the simple requirement of being young and slender. They checked out vans by the dozens, by the scores and, finally, by the hundreds. It is part of police work, such a canvass, and about as exciting as putting two fender bolts on automobile bodies moving down an assembly line. It is, however, the type of work that catches killers. Four months later, investigating a murder so savage it dumbfounded the city, it was precisely this type of work that enabled Frank Falzon to catch a raging murderer.

About three o'clock on the morning of April 17, 1974, on a quiet residential block in the city's Potrero Hill district, neighbors heard screams and saw flames flashing on the ground floor and in the upstairs bedroom of a neat yellow Victorian house at 1301 Kansas Street. The house had been painstakingly restored by the young couple that lived there, Frank and Annette Carlson. The neighbors were the first to reach Mrs. Carlson, who was lying on a porch roof outside the flaming bedroom. She was nude, barely conscious, and bleeding from stab wounds and a blow that had practically stripped her scalp from her head. When firemen broke through the front door a few minutes later, they found the body of Frank Carlson, the twenty-five-year-old assistant manager of a supermarket. His face and head had been battered to the point that they were no longer recognizable as human. Falzon was on the scene before the flames were put out.

Mrs. Carlson, a twenty-four-year-old artist, was taken to San Francisco General Hospital. She was in critical condition, so close to death that Falzon draped himself in a surgical gown and put on a mask to interview her in the operating room. An intruder had broken into the house, killed her husband, and raped her repeatedly, but it was the details of the methodical, almost sadistic violence that stuck in Falzon's mind. "It was the worst killing I have ever seen," he said. "It was so bad it was unreal."

Her husband was refinishing a table in the dining room that night and Annette Carlson had decided to go to bed early. It was about midnight when she awakened to find a man with a knife at the side of her bed. Her shouts brought her husband, but the knife deterred him. The intruder, a black man in his late twenties with a fleecy Afro, said he wanted money, that was all, so they did not resist when he ordered them downstairs and forced Mrs. Carlson to tie her husband into one of the dining room chairs. The man with the knife was ranting about drugs and needing money for drugs. They had only six dollars in cash in the house.

The intruder began to smash Carlson over the head with a heavy, steel-headed hammer. When the hammer head broke off, he picked up a two-inch-thick chopping board and cracked it over Carlson's skull. "Die, you bastard, die," he screamed as he searched the room looking for another weapon with which to continue the assault. Mrs. Carlson was forced to watch as the intruder shattered a large jar filled with pennies and finally a large vase over Carlson's skull, breaking every bone in his head as he killed him.

Mrs. Carlson, already in shock, was forced upstairs by the blood-splattered murderer of her husband and was raped repeatedly for two to three hours. The killer strangled her with a telephone cord, bludgeoned her with a paperweight, slashed her with the knife, and finally picked up a chair and shattered it over her head. She was unconscious on the floor as the killer pocketed four of her rings, splashed paint thinner over the bedroom and dining room, and set the house afire. Mrs. Carlson recovered consciousness as the flames licked around her body and crawled out onto the porch roof where she was found when the neighbors arrived.

During twenty-nine days in the hospital, Mrs. Carlson was interviewed several times by Falzon. At his request she drew sketches of the stolen rings. The killer had said he needed drugs and wanted money; Falzon expected that he would try to sell the jewelry. The sketches were released to the newspapers, and jewelry shops and pawnshops throughout the city were canvassed with the drawings. A jeweler in a downtown shop immediately recognized one of the sketches, a dinner ring brought to him three days earlier by a warehouseman who wanted it reset.

The warehouseman did not in any way resemble the killer described by Mrs. Carlson. He said he had bought the ring, worth

$1,800, for $300 from a man he did not know by name but could describe: he wore a postal uniform and lived in the Potrero Hill district. Falzon went to postal authorities and checked their personnel records until he located Angelo Pavageau, a twenty-five-year-old Vietnam veteran who lived a block from the Carlson house on Kansas Street and matched the description of the killer point by point. In Pavageau's house they found a boot that matched a bloody footprint in Mrs. Carlson's bedroom. Pavageau was convicted three months later of willful, deliberate, and premeditated murder and was ordered transported to San Quentin Prison, where he is held on Death Row.

The search for the white van, however, did not go as well as the jewelry store canvass in the Carlson case. Falzon and Cleary found plenty of white vans, but after three weeks they had come up with nobody who looked like a good suspect in the paper bag murders. They still had more territory to cover, and they went at it, day after day, knocking on doors, asking the questions, interviewing drivers, chasing anything that looked good. They made no secret of the fact that they were checking vans and word spread that they were looking for a driver. Ultimately it paid off. It was the canvass for the van, finally, that led them to the Paper Bag Killer.

On January 25, while the search for the white van continued, a call came into the homicide detail that was routed to Falzon and Cleary. The man on the other end, nervous and hesitant, said that he had heard they were checking on vans and he knew something that maybe they ought to be aware of. The man was reluctant to say much, but a friend of his, who drove a van, had told him something. No, it was too important to talk about over the phone. He would meet them, but only if they would keep his name completely out of it. Only after repeated assurances did he finally agree to meet the inspectors.

Falzon, Cleary and Lieut. Charles Ellis of the homicide detail left the Hall of Justice. The man they met was young and very nervous, as much frightened, perhaps, as anything else. This friend of his, the one who drove the van, was a young man whom we shall call "Bill." One day, when he was in Bill's room, the youth said, Bill had shown him a couple of guns and told him he was trying to kill a man because this man was going around raping young girls. In fact, Bill said he had killed the man several times but the man kept coming back. Bill now wanted his friend to help kill the man once and for all. The young informant told the inspectors he knew Bill well and had always thought of him as a "real good guy, straight and level." He could not believe what Bill had told him, but he had heard they were checking vans all over and thought he better say something to someone.

With a possible suspect at last in hand, Falzon and Cleary did not charge out to make an arrest. When the time comes for questioning, said Falzon, the more you know about a suspect, the better prepared you are, the more likely you are to find out what you need to know. Bill, they quickly learned, worked for a delivery service on Tehama Street. It was on the far fringe of the Southern District, where their canvass for the white van had not yet reached. They interviewed Bill's boss and learned his full name and that he was twenty-four years old. He was a steady, dependable worker who had never caused any difficulties. He had long blond hair, wore a little moustache, and worked weekdays from 8:00 A.M. to 4:00 P.M.

Bill's name was run through the records bureau. It was at this point that one of the ironic, sad twists in the case of the Paper Bag Killer came to light. In December 1972, almost a year before Lorenzo Carniglia was shot, a man had been stabbed in the men's room of the Greyhound bus depot near Market Street. The victim was a businessman, fifty-four, round-faced, bald and heavy set, who walked with a limp. His assailant had come at him from behind, reached over his shoulder and stabbed him in the chest. The businessman was hospitalized, but recovered. The attacker, whom neither the businessman nor anyone else had seen, escaped without a trace.

Six weeks after the first attack, late in February 1973, this same businessman was walking along Powell Street a couple of blocks north of Market street in the busy, downtown heart of San Francisco when a young man came pounding toward him, blonde hair streaming, knife in hand. They struggled and the young man with the knife fled up the street, where two uniformed officers apprehended and arrested him.

"The victim survived this second attack never thinking it was one and the same man who attacked him at the bus station weeks before," said Falzon. "When the case came to trial, the businessman was in Phoenix. He was not present to testify and the charges against Bill were dropped. He was put back on the street and that is when we had our two murders."

Bill's prints were compared with those taken from the paper bag recovered after the murder of Ara Kuznezow. They matched. At this point, the district attorney's office was notified. The following day Falzon, Cleary, and Assistant District Attorney James Lassar appeared before Judge Frank Hart in San Francisco Superior Court. Judge Hart issued a warrant for Bill's arrest that charged him with the murder of Ara Kuznezow. He also issued a search warrant for Bill's residence.

It was five o'clock on a Saturday afternoon, January 26, 1974, when Falzon and Cleary knocked on the door of Bill's home. It was in a neighborhood of elegant town houses and $150,000 homes with small, neatly manicured lawns. Bill lived there with his mother and father. As is the case with so many real-life dramas, the truth seemed stranger than fiction. Here was the trail in a tragic murder investigation leading to a milieu which, on the surface, appeared to be an archtype of stability. Bill's father was deferential when he opened the door and showed the inspectors in, but he was frankly unbelieving when they explained the purpose of their visit.

Falzon and Cleary were shown to an upstairs bedroom. They entered cautiously and found Bill stretched out on top of his bed. He made no attempt to resist and seemed, in his own way, glad to see them. At Bill's direction, they looked in a closet on the far side of the bedroom and found the shotgun that had killed Ara Kuznezow. It was loaded and ready for use. Bill had thrown the pistol used to kill Lorenzo Carniglia into San Franciso Bay from the bridge that stretches from San Francisco to Oakland, but under his pillow they found another pistol which he had subsequently purchased. It, too, was loaded. Clothing which tied Bill to both of the paper bag murders was found in the closet. Bill was told he had the right to remain silent, that any statement he made could be used against him, that he had the right to have an attorney present, and that he had the right to a public defender if he was unable to afford a lawyer. He was then arrested and taken to the Hall of Justice.

To the people who knew Bill, his arrest as the Paper Bag Killer was difficult to believe. He had graduated from high school in San Francisco and attended college there, transferring later to its suburban campus south of the city. He had worked for the delivery service for two years and his boss had nothing but good words to say for him. He had been offered several chances to move up in the company, opportunities Bill had always turned down, but he did his work faithfully and well. "I don't want to say anything against him," said his boss. "He did well by me." When news of Bill's arrest spread through the community, the reaction of Bill's family's neighbors was outright disbelief. He had been a good kid, they said, and like everyone else, they added that he never had given anyone even the least trouble. "It's totally inconceivable to think of him as a killer," said one man who lived nearby. "Quite frankly, it is a shock."

It was more than a shock to Bill's parents; it was another in a string of personal tragedies that had wracked the family.

Bill's father, at first unbelieving, listened to what the inspectors told him. He had no idea his son had weapons in his room, no conception that his son was capable of seeking out and killing total strangers on the street, but he eventually accepted the reality presented to him. "It's a terrible thing, two innocent men destroyed because of my son's mental illness," said his father.

Bill said nothing during the ride to the Hall of Justice. He was not aggressive or hostile, but he sat silently, withdrawn into his own thoughts. When they got to the homicide detail, Falzon explained the case against him. "I told him that the evidence against him was overwhelming and I went on to explain that we found the paper bag at the scene of the Kuznezow killing and that it had his prints on it. I told him he had been described in detail by witnesses and explained that once a lineup was held he was, without doubt, going to be identified. That is when he broke down. He started crying and said he would like to tell us everything."

Falzon took notes and a tape recorder was turned on for backup. There were a few questions, but, for the most part, Bill told his story without interruption. There was a man, he said, a man whose image was fixed in his mind, who was going around raping young women. He knew what this man looked like: his face, his height, his weight, and his limping walk. This man was raping girls, young girls who had never done anything, and that was why he had to kill him.

"In his mind, he would be in his delivery van, driving his route south of Market Street, when he would see these girls walking the street," said Falzon. "They would be wearing rouge, lipstick, and makeup, but he would see in their eyes a tear, and the tear would show him that this man had attacked them. He knew that he had to kill and kill again until he finally put this man away. But this man would come back and would·always come back. No matter how many times he tried to kill him, this man would always be there again on the street. It actually sent chills up my spine listening to him talk. He said the man tried to disguise himself by wearing different-size ears or a different nose or having sometimes thin fingers and sometimes fat fingers, but he could always tell because he could never change his height, his weight, the shape of his face and, in particular, his peculiar walk."

Frank Falzon had investigated several hundred homicides and mysterious deaths in the city of San Francisco. He had never heard a confession like this before. "Bill mentioned how he had tried to kill this man before, this man who he imagined was going around raping young girls. He said, 'I know at least four times I've tried to kill him,' and he went on to describe how he stabbed him in the men's room at the bus station and how he attacked him once on Powell Street and how he had shot him down on Third Street and how he had shot him again with a shotgun on Fifth Street. He said the man always kept coming back. He just could not kill him, but he had to because this man was hurting just too many young girls."

It was only at the point in Bill's confession where he related stabbing a man twice that the two attacks on the businessman fell into place. Neither the man himself, nor the police, had ever connected the two incidents. Bill had stabbed his fantasy rapist in the bus station and thought he had killed him. But several weeks later, while driving his van through the busy downtown streets, there he was again. The sidewalks were crowded with shoppers, but he seized instantly on this one man, the same man he had stabbed before, and was certain in his own mind that the man had come back again to rape young girls. He parked his van and, filled with emotions he described as fear and anger, went after the man a second time with a knife, determined to be rid of him once and for all.

Falzon later contacted the businessman. He was dumbfounded to learn that it was one and the same man who had attacked him on both occasions; the possibility had never crossed his mind. There had been a good, solid case against Bill when he was arrested after the second stabbing and Falzon said the two subsequent killings could probably have been avoided. "The investigation was very thorough and they had a good case," he said. "But the victim, who was in Phoenix, told the district attorney's office he would not be able to come back because his business there was more important. It was a preliminary hearing, but you cannot hold a person even at that stage if the victim will not testify. The way the laws are now, that is a problem for our district attorney's office and I think it is just as true elsewhere in the country. The district attorney's office had no alternative but to let Bill loose."

Bill was booked the night of his arrest at the city jail on the warrant issued by Judge Hart charging him with murder in the slaying of Ara Kuznezow. He was also booked, without warrant, on a murder charge in the death of Lorenzo Carniglia. The San Francisco grand jury later returned murder indictments against him in both cases and he was transferred to the county prison and held without bond.

Bill's family hired an attorney, Patrick Hallinan, the well-known and well-connected senior member of a father-son team that had handled many difficult criminal cases in the San Francisco courts over the years. According to Hallinan, Bill had a girl friend, a woman he had loved for many years, and she had been raped late in 1972. For reasons only he could understand, Bill concluded that he was somehow responsible for the rape and subsequently killed in the distorted belief that he was killing her rapist. From the description the girl had provided, Bill pieced together in his mind a picture of the rapist: an older man, round-faced, heavy-set, who limped or dragged his foot slightly when he walked. "His imagination created a fantasy world in which he was a Don Quixote trying to rectify the wrongs that were done to a girl he loved," Hallinan explained.

For his own part, Bill sat in the county prison quiet and subdued and waited for the court proceedings with detached interest. "I feel very strange about the whole thing," he said during an interview in his cell. "I just want to find out how it is going to turn out. I just want everything cleared up."

And, for what it is worth, the name of the young man who called the homicide detail when he heard they were checking vans is not to be found in the police records. "We left it out of the report just because we promised him we would not reveal his name unless we had to," said Falzon. "I don't even think I have it myself."

On Thrusday, May 16, in Department Twenty-three of San Francisco Superior Court, a hearing was held before Judge Morton Convin. Bill, charged with the murder of Lorenzo Carniglia and Ara Kuznezow, was found not guilty by reason of insanity. Incident Report 73-100684 is the last item in the files of the San Francisco Police Department on the Paper Bag Killer. Its brief final paragraph is typed in boldface: "_____, WMA, DOB 03/7/49, sentenced to Atascadero State Hospital for the Criminally Insane."

There is postscript to the paper bag murders—and so many other crimes—which does not appear in the official record.

The accomplishments of a working detective can be measured in arrest tallies and conviction reports; the rewards are more elusive. The money is good, better than walking a beat, but hardly worth undertaking a life in which the risk of death is real and constant. There is a sense of accomplishment, of contributing something toward making society better for people who want to live their lives honestly, pursuing whatever goals they might choose. But, as Detective Falzon expresses it, there are other rewards that often mean as much or more to him and his colleagues as these more tangible ones. Falzon recalls that Bill's father, after the arrest of his son, visited the Hall of Justice and walked into the homicide detail.

"The father was quite a man," the detective reflects. "He couldn't believe at first that his son was capable of doing what he did, but once he understood the facts he came down to see Jack Cleary and me.

"There were tears in his eyes. He shook my partner's hand and mine and thanked us for the way we handled the case . . . and for treating his son the way we did."